For Mum

Acknowledgements

Thanks to Richard Kerridge and Shelagh Weeks who both read this and gave such good advice; and to Mary Nichols, G. Q. Williams and Marcia Jennings for explaining things I needed to know. The Welsh Arts Council gave me a generous bursary that made possible a semester's relief from teaching, and Bath Spa University College have always been supportive and encouraging. Thanks for everything to Dan Franklin, Caroline Dawnay, Jennifer Barth and Joy Harris.

Everything Will Be All Right

Beginning

Pearl contemplates herself. She is seventeen.

She has lifted down the full-length mirror from its nail on the wall and propped it longways beside her on the bed, so that she is lying alongside her reflection. She is naked save for a metal stud in her nose and a leather choker embroidered with beads around her neck. Her toenails and fingernails are painted green. What she sees she does not find entirely satisfactory. Her skin is chalky white with a tracery of blue veins, a disconcertingly intimate inner layer, not like the honey-coloured surface of the girls' bodies in the magazines. Her breasts are too rounded and womanly, tipped heavily sideways because she is lying flat; one breast (she cannot see this from here, but she knows it and hates it) sags lower than the other. She would like small breasts, with brown bud nipples, not blunt pink snouty ones. Her stomach is too wide and pale, though she can feel her hip bones satisfactorily if she presses across them (in a habitual checking gesture) with her forearm. She is not fat, but stocky and compact; she would have liked to be gaunt and long. Yet even as she frowns at the detail of her body in critical scrutiny, she is also fascinatedly aware of this matrix of herself – breasts, belly, the little modest triangle of her pubic hair (she hates the way her mother's hair grows high up her stomach) – as a configuration that generates desire. She is not thinking at this moment of the desire of anyone in particular, but something undifferentiated, anonymous, vast. In the light of this effect, she contemplates her own body with awed surprise; it is a mystery beyond her control, a gift of power.

She is waiting for her friends to arrive. They'll spend a couple of hours dressing up together before they go out into town. Often this couple of hours and the intoxication of anticipation are the best part of the night (Pearl's learned this already). There's music (Erykah Badu) playing on her system. There's a bottle of Martini. Pearl has poured herself a glass and to go in it she has hacked off with a penknife a slice of lemon from the fruit bowl downstairs. The Martini has to be kept out of sight of Pearl's mother, not because she minds them drinking but because she might wonder where the money came from that paid for it. (It came out of the fifteen pounds she gave Pearl that morning to pay for her clarinet lesson.)

The floor of the room is deep in a muddle of Pearl's possessions and her discarded leavings: crumpled skirts and tops and balls of dirty socks and knickers, apple cores and a half-eaten slice of pizza, eye pencils and mascaras and a spilled bottle of silver nail polish, pages of notes for the history homework she's supposed to have handed in a week ago, magazines, an overflowing ashtray, beer cans, a scatter of bright Indian bangles, CDs, coffee cups growing fur. Under the bed just out of sight (where she nudged it earlier with her foot) there's even a used sanitary towel with a single brown smear of crusted blood. The slightly stale smell that rises from all this mess, mixed up with the musky perfumes that she wears, makes her comfortable like an animal in the smell of its own den.

She turns on to her side on the pillow and stares at herself with seriousness. She neither hates nor gloats over what she sees, she's not a dieter and vomiter like one of her friends, nor serenely in love with herself like another one. Fingertips seek out a blemish on her cheek and press it. Her nose is wide across the nostrils, her mouth is small but full and red in the pale face. Her hair in a new shoulder-length shaggy cut is hennaed dark red, with pink tips. Once she had hair of an extraordinary pale ginger colour, like pale sand (her mother says this regretfully, fingering the new cut); in any individual strand there were white hairs and ginger hairs and blonde hairs and strawberry-coloured hairs all mingled together, shifting, dazzling. Pearl doesn't regret dyeing her gingery hair. She presumes that underneath the dyed colour the real one is still there for her, a secret she will be able to go back to any time she chooses.

She hasn't put on her make-up yet today (she only got up a couple of hours ago, and mostly since then

3

she's watched telly) although last night's mascara is still smeared under her lashes. So she sees herself as if dangerously, cruelly exposed; unflinchingly she stares in her own eyes. She's trying to decide what she looks like, what she would see if she could really see herself, from outside. She's weighed down by the fixed terms of this identity, this unchangeable solid body, these familiar big eyes good at glowering in the perhaps too characterful perhaps rather pasty face. At the same time she fascinates herself. Why should she be her, in particular? What is it going to be like, being her, what will it bring? She and her reflection exchange a look of cool interested acknowledgement.

She isn't alone in the house. If she was, she would have her music up twice as loud, and she would already have expanded along the landing into her mother's bedroom to see what clothes she could borrow. Thinking of this, she swivels round and sits up on the bed, resumes a cigarette which has been burning away by itself in an ashtray, then lifts the mirror and props it back up against the wall. She opens her bedroom door a crack, turning down the volume on her system at the same time. All is quiet, all is still. Noiselessly, still naked, she pads along the landing into her mother's room, which is immaculately tidy as always, the navy duvet on the single bed straightened, the pairs of shoes lined up against the wall, the books bristling with paper markers piled tidily on the bedside table with the alarm clock and the paracetamol.

Pearl doesn't really like her mother's clothes. They're

much too sober and sensible, and they still have the stamp of the style that must have stood for political radicalism in her youth and which makes Pearl wince: flat childlike sandals, stripy knits, denim pinafores. But sometimes Pearl manages to persuade her into buying something more extravagant; there's a satiny pink top heavy with beads and sequins, a pair of loose green silk crêpe trousers. Pearl also sometimes borrows her plain black lambswool sweater and her amber drop earrings, her underwear, her T-shirts: mixed with her own things they're all right, and her mother's clothes have the advantage that they're clean and ironed (she will wash Pearl's too, but only if Pearl puts them in the laundry basket). Pearl is trying to catch sight of herself again. She checks the little swing mirror on the chest of drawers and the mirror on the inside of the wardrobe door. Against her mother's neat background her nudity seems out of place. In the wardrobe mirror, its silvering eaten away with tarnish, she is improbable, like a picture of someone lost: poignant, mythic. The young girl.

Zoe doesn't wear make-up but she does wear perfume, and Pearl helps herself liberally to Chanel Allure before she returns to her own room with the green trousers, leaving behind her a trail of scent and cigarette smoke as thick as paint. She also leaves ash on Zoe's carpet, and biscuit crumbs trodden in on her bare feet from a packet torn open and forgotten.

Zoe is reading downstairs.

She's reading an important new book about the

interdependencies of war, development, environment and peace. Even though it's a very new book it's been overtaken by events in the past few weeks: the escalation of the conflict in Israel, the stand-off over the spy plane between the US and China. She works hard at deducing from the arguments in the book what the author would offer as the significance of these new situations. (She knows him slightly, she's met him at academic conferences, so she can picture him speaking the words as she reads them.) She experiences a familiar kind of pleasurable tension at reading and responding to something good: a breathlessness, a clench of concentration in her chest. When she's really absorbed in her reading she's never relaxed, she changes her position often and urgently in her chair; at this moment she's hunched hawkishly over the page with her knees up under her chin. Frowning, she lifts her head from time to time, not to look around her but to screw up her eyes at the near distance, rehearsing what she's understood, testing it against possible counter arguments.

This isn't because she's unaware, entirely, of her actual surroundings. The blue walls which everyone told her would be too dark do collect a pool of shadows at the centre of the room, but Zoe doesn't mind. She has the lamp switched on even though it's still light outside, and the gas fire is puttering away. The room is tidy and the supper things washed up. The big clock on the mantelpiece that Aunt Vera (really great-aunt Vera) gave her when she moved into the retirement home, a real clock with works that need winding with a key and which has had to have a succession of expensive repairs, ticks out the minutes with calm meditative steadiness, although it tells entirely the wrong time as usual. It's the end of a grey day in a spell of unusually cold temperatures for April (a reflex now, to wonder whether that's part of natural climatic fluctuation or a result of global warming).

Zoe is aware of Pearl upstairs, too; she suppresses from time to time a twinge of irritation at the music that seeps distractingly into her concentration, and keeps a suspicious ear alert to Pearl's moving around. It's not just clothes she takes, but money, jewellery, Tampax, grass if Zoe ever buys it, expensive bath oils, shoes. (Zoe's taller and thinner than her daughter – in fact she's very much the shape Pearl would like to be – but unfortunately they have the same shoe size.) A precious bracelet which had belonged to Zoe's dead grandmother was borrowed without asking then heedlessly lost in a club somewhere; Pearl denied ever having set eyes on it. Zoe has thought of having a lock put on her own bedroom door, but decided against it on an issue of principle: you don't learn respect for other people's values through being forcibly shut out from them. She sometimes has the sensation of taking part in a painful and potentially disillusioning experiment in conflict resolution.

Zoe doesn't know yet about the clarinet lesson or the Martini, and won't notice the green trousers until it's too late and Pearl is exiting to a waiting taxi, insolently making a joke out of trying to conceal herself and the trousers amongst her friends. They will descend the stairs and surge along the narrow hall like a flock of bright-plumaged screeching birds. Unlike Pearl the friends are always polite with Zoe, but they will collaborate to deceive her nonetheless, crowding in front of Pearl and making charming considerate remarks to distract Zoe's attention from the trousers. Zoe will not be distracted, probably isn't even meant to be, it's only funny for them to pretend to care what she thinks. The trousers will be rolled up round Pearl's waist because they are too long; even so they will trail down over her shoes, Zoe will see that they are going to be dragged in the dirt and ruined. She will handle it badly, hear her voice fall into the familiar ugly wail of the worn-down and hard done by, instead of giving her blessing with graceful superiority to the fait accompli. Pearl, who quite apart from the trousers isn't even adequately dressed to keep out the cold – bare midriff, plunging neckline, transparent blouse, no coat – will hustle the others through the hall, hissing at them to keep going and trampling their heels and falling over them in her mock haste. (Is she drunk? Already? On what?) And then as the taxi drives off Zoe will only think, with a subsidence of resentment like a plunge of thrashing wings to stillness, how lovely Pearl looked in the trousers anyway.

Then she will go back to her book.

Zoe is used to this sensation of consciousness stretched between two opposed poles, the intensity of immediate personal life on the one hand and the intensity of impersonal intellectual thought on the other. The tension between them seems to her to be the very material of awareness. The only time she lost her gift for balancing the two possibilities was in the first months of motherhood, when she foundered under the sheer weight of material necessities: feeding, washing, cleaning, shopping, walking up and down at night with that baby when she might have been reading a book.

She used to think that women were better at managing the reconciliation between these kinds of awareness because of cultural conditioning: they'd simply never been allowed the privilege of the untrammelled pursuit of thought behind closed study doors. Now she thinks it probably has something to do with evolutionary biology too; it's probably hardwired. And anyway she doesn't envy the solitudes of the study any more. She's got too used to the unsettling stimulating astringency of the interactions of life and thought. When she sits back down to read about American foreign policy after her fight with Pearl, her heart will be pounding and her pulse racing with her sense of the precariousness of things, and her own imperfect capacity in the face of them.

Zoe's mother Joyce has spent the day with her Aunt Vera. Now they are sitting together drinking tea in Vera's room in the retirement home, watching *Who Wants to Be a Millionaire* on the television. Vera was a teacher at a girls' grammar school for most of her working life, and watches the programme regularly, but in a kind of torment. She disapproves of everything about it: the ignorance of most of the contestants, the fact it's on ITV, the fact that the contestants compete for money, the tackily dramatic music, the questions about soap operas and film stars. Really, Joyce supposes, Vera would like the format to be more like a school examination, severe and unsmiling and impersonal, conducted in a kind of religious hush, without commentary. This was the context in which Vera shone, all her life. Among all the pale scribbling girls in an examination room, she would be the one who knew with subdued nervous excitement that she was earning As. So now she can't resist being tested. Which South American country has both a Pacific and an Atlantic coast? Tomas Masaryk was president of which Central European country before the Second World War: Hungary, Poland, Romania or Czecho-slovakia? She very often knows the answers to these kinds of questions, even though she is ninety-four and has trouble remembering the names of the girls who look after her every day in the home, or news Joyce has told her about the children and grandchildren.

Vera is tall and craggy with age-spotted hanging jowls and iron-grey hair that in its heaviness escapes in discon-certingly wild-looking strands from where she sticks it up with hairpins behind a sort of velvet Alice band. In honour of their day out a defiant silver and diamond brooch is pinned on to the bosom which has so lost shape over the years that now it is simply a fat cushion held in place by her belt. The trip was probably a mistake, Joyce thinks ruefully. They haven't enjoyed themselves. They went to look for the house they had lived in together more than fifty years ago when Joyce was a child, Vera with her two children and Joyce's mother Lil with her three. The old grey square house was only a few miles outside the city, on the flat lands of the estuary near the bridge (fifty years ago there was no bridge, only a pair of ferries that chugged backwards and forwards across the water, or a long detour by road, for those who were travelling on westwards). At Vera's ninety-fourth birthday party, after a couple of glasses of fizzy wine, pressing her aunt's hand with its old cold skin loosened from the bones and improbable arthritis-knobbled knuckles, Joyce had decided it would be wonderful to take her out and go and see whether the old house was still standing.

She would never learn.

Her husband refused to take part in the quixotic expedition. —Didn't we try and find it once before, years ago? he said. —And there was just some big sprawling kind of industrial plant?

—I don't think so, Joyce said. —I don't think we were ever sure we'd found the right place. The roads had all changed.

—You can be sure, he said, —that whatever goes wrong will be held against you. You know what she's like.

—Why should anything go wrong? she protested.

And they did find the house: although it was true that Joyce cut her hand folding up Vera's recalcitrant wheelchair into the back of the car, and that about fifteen minutes into the journey while she was still sucking the blood off her knuckles, rain began to spit out of the slate-grey sky. Vera stared forward through the windscreen

11

with the fixed expression of stoically suppressed anxiety she always wore when Joyce was driving her anywhere, and which always managed to make her drive badly: she shot one amber light with uncalled-for recklessness and then stopped pointlessly at a green one.

There was no sign of the carbon-black factory they had found the last time they looked for the house (Joyce remembers this trip better than she let on to her husband). She felt at least a little lift of triumph at that: the plant with its blight of pipes and machine innards had been so desolatingly and conclusively ugly that she had stifled the idea of it in her thoughts, and now it seemed to have been wiped off the landscape as if it had never existed. But the pattern of roads still didn't seem to correspond with the pattern in her memory, and after a succession of fairly random turns she had just made up her mind she was lost when Vera saw something and Joyce pulled in to the side of the road.

—Isn't that it? said Vera.

Joyce didn't see how she could know. They stared through the rain at some piles of stone across a field. Joyce's vision was blurry: she really needed glasses now but was too vain to wear them. There was a fuzz of bright green everywhere in her blur, signifying that spring had come; but this was a messy kind of country-side, too flat and too near the city and the motorway and the power station to be anything but scruffy and disconsolate these days, criss-crossed with pylons, the field overgrown with some kind of low scrubby bushes, a solitary cow – no, shaggy pony – lifting its head to

look at them. In front of the piles of stone lay something on its side in zigzag folds like the pleats of a
concertina.

—We're looking at it from the back, said Vera. —It
was on a little hill like that. It's reclaimed land all around.
One of the drainage ditches ran east-west across behind;
do you see that line of trees?

Nothing she could see suggested any connection to
the past to Joyce. —Do you want to get out and have
a look? she suggested doubtfully. —Perhaps if I drive
round to the front of it there'll be a track.

—What would I want to do that for? Vera was irritated. She had been excited for a moment, identifying
the place, but really as it was such a ruin there wasn't
much for them to do except stare at it glumly from the
car. Joyce admitted to herself that she had hoped there
might at least be the shell of a house that they could get
close up to; or even that it might still be whole, and
inhabited, and that nice people might be living there,
and might invite them inside to walk around the rooms.
She had imagined finding herself in the little stone apple-
room above the kitchen, and all her childhood flooding
back. She wouldn't have admitted this hope of hers to
her husband.

—The orchard's gone, Vera said. —And that's the
staircase, lying on its side.

Joyce could see then with a lurch of her heart that
the zigzag thing must be a staircase. It was disconcerting,
if this really was the place, to think of them climbing
up and down it for all those years: it was so pointless

13

now, lying along the ground. And she felt a surge of anger against her aunt, not just for the usual things, the melodramatic intakes of breath when she moved and the dampening remarks and the looming problems of lunch and toilets (they ended up having lunch at the dismal service station just off the motorway before the bridge, where it was easy to manage the wheelchair), but also for ever having spotted the place. If Joyce had come by herself she could have driven round and round and never been certain she hadn't just missed it, or just remembered the roads wrongly.

After lunch she drove Vera across the bridge, sightseeing, and then took her back to her own house for supper. Now, in the relief of having Vera safely back in her room in the home and of her own imminent departure, she is saying nice things about their expedition, turning the story of it into a funny and perky one (no doubt the same story she'll tell her husband later).

—I'd never have seen the house without you, you know. How ever did you pick it out? I'm so envious of your sharp eyes. I don't think your sight's deteriorated one bit from what it's always been. And then your memory's so good. But it was so strange, to actually see the place. We were so happy there.

—Speak for yourself, Vera says. —I wasn't happy.

Joyce knows she overdoes this determined cheerfulness sometimes. Vera can't help responding to the flattery, but they are both rather ashamed of it, knowing it's not the whole truth, knowing it's compensation. In that room Joyce wants to heap encouragements and admiration on Vera's head, to make up for leaving her here. There's nothing wrong with the room as such, although it is small. It has a bathroom en suite. The tea that the girls bring is all right; it is made with tea-bags, but at least they bring milk in a jug. There are wall-to-wall raspberry-pink carpets everywhere in the home, and a great emphasis on a hotel-type kind of luxury, with reproduction antique furniture and big vases of silk flowers on tables in the hall. Vera was adamant she didn't want a council-run home; and the furniture is the kind of thing she aspired to herself in her middle age, when she had a bit of money to spend. But no amount of pretence that this is just another hotel can quite smother Joyce's horrible impression of how the ones who live here wait among the remnant of their possessions as if already in transit from their real lives.

When Joyce says she is leaving, Vera has one of her momentary funny turns and reaches round in a panic for her handbag, thinking she's coming home too; Joyce has to explain. Making her way out she is swift and free without the wheelchair. She notices that there are no mirrors where you might expect them – in the turns of the corridors, above the little pseudo-Regency occasional tables with their vases piled high with alstroemeria and peonies and lilies – and although she supposes this is not a kindness for the visitors she is quite glad not to come upon herself, in here. Two girls are laughing, squealing, making up a bed in a room she passes, the sheets flying and crackling, their voices rising and hushing with that pressured importance which means

15

they are talking about sex. With a rush of the desperate longing that most of the time she's so good at keeping at bay, Joyce yearns to be identified with them, and with all the sap and throbbing promise of the spring evening pouring in through the window beyond them thrown open high. She's so glad to leave the home behind and reach the street with ordinary people walking past and get into her car alone and put on a tape, something she scrabbles out of the glove box, a Taj Mahal album Zoe bought her for Christmas.

She leans across the passenger seat to pull out Vera's crocheted cushion from where it's slipped down the side of the seat and throw it out of sight into the back: in passing she throws a fugitive, perfunctory glance at herself in the rear-view mirror. Like most of the glimpses she has of herself nowadays, it's not conclusively satisfactory either way. She at least doesn't catch herself looking like one of those old collapsed ones who have given up. But she isn't confident either that what she sees – white hair cut in a short bob, tanned crinkled heart-shaped face, distinctive deep-lidded blue eyes, neat late middle-aged prettiness – isn't a mere hopeful habit of perception superimposed upon a reality that is in truth slipping away farther and faster than she knows.

The doorbell rings and Pearl's friends arrive. The girls are nice to Zoe, they ask her polite interested questions about her work. Pearl appears at the top of the stairs, wrapped in Zoe's bathrobe with her hair wet; laughing as if things have already started being funny, she calls to them to come on up. They aren't dressed to go out yet, they've brought carrier bags full of clothes, and they will spend the next couple of hours trying on and borrowing and pluming in front of each other.

Zoe is going out too, to see a late film at the Arts Centre with a friend, but she doesn't want Pearl to know this. If Pearl realises the house is empty she will invite a whole gang of people back to her room and then Zoe will either have to row with them to get them out or lie awake all night listening to their music and laughter and stoned noisy visits to the toilet to pee all over the floor (the boys) or throw up (one of the girls is bulimic).

As they pile upstairs chattering and Zoe is about to close the front door behind them, she sees that the clouds have broken up. The drab working-class terrace (built for the working class, that is, a century ago, and now shared by a whole mix of types and races in these socially more complicated times) is full of a rich thick yellow light. Above the roofs baroque dramas are being acted out in the sky: dark clouds part and effulgent pink and orange beams break through like revelations. Window-panes blaze. A blackbird is singing improbably in the street's one tree, a little skimpy one planted at a corner and almost defeated by the successive brutal scalpings of local gangs of kids. The blackbird is rather absurdly disproportionate to the amount of tree there is to sit in, like a bird in a child's picture book. There's a perfume of garlic and ginger in the air from the Bengali restaurant on the corner.

Zoe is infected by the girls' Friday-night mood, or the change in the light, or the heedlessness of the kids careering along the pavements on their bikes.

She thinks excitedly that anything could happen.

One

Just after the end of the war, when she was eleven, Joyce Stevenson won a scholarship to Gateshead Grammar: she was one of the top forty children in her year. Two years later, when they moved down south to live with her Aunt Vera, her Uncle Dick arranged to have her scholarship transferred to Amery-James High School for Girls, which was in an elegant eighteenth-century house in the city. New classrooms and laboratories and a gym had been added to the old building. The girls and the life there were subtly, complicatedly different from the children and the life Joyce and her sister Ann had known before: this had to do, they quickly understood, with a whole deep mystery of difference between the South and the North, in which their family was peculiarly entangled.

The Amery-James girls had a kind of sheen to them, their hair seemed glossier and their skin had a fresher bloom, their movements were slower and more measured. Joyce and Ann missed the boys, and the men teachers. You had to watch your tongue, to hold back on some of the quick smart joking things you might have said in the North, because here what counted for glamour and importance was rather a kind of restraint, and a collective know-how, knowing when it was the right season for French skipping and cat's cradle, knowing when these things were suddenly childish, knowing how to wear your purse-belt so that it didn't bunch up your skirt around the waist, knowing when to speak and when not to, and how to speak. There were a few girls there who had the city accent, comical and yokelish. You did not want, not even by default, to be counted among them. So Joyce and Ann determinedly set about losing the accents they had grown up with, never actually commenting to one another or to anyone on what they were doing, losing them until no trace was left and they no longer sounded like their mother or their aunt and uncle or their left-behind grandparents in the North.

The big old grey house they rented from the Port Authority was eight or so miles outside the city. At first their Uncle Dick drove them every morning in his car into Farmouth, the residential area behind the Docks where he worked, and they caught a bus from there into town. Then their Aunt Vera got a job teaching history at Amery-James. The girls had known, vaguely, that she had been a teacher before she married and had children, but had not imagined this was something you would ever pick up again, afterwards. It seemed incongruous (most of the teachers at the school were Miss not Mrs) and potentially an embarrassing pitfall, some mistake Aunt Vera had made in reading the signals of what was acceptable and appropriate.

Now Aunt Vera drove them in to school every morning, in the old Austin Seven Uncle Dick bought her, which usually had to be started with a starting handle (Lil, their mother, sometimes came out and did it for Vera so that she wouldn't get oil on her teaching clothes). They asked to be let out some little distance from the school so that they could walk the rest of the way without her. At least because their surnames were different most of the girls never even connected Mrs Trower to the Stevensons; and Aunt Vera never spoke to them any differently than to any of the others, or gave any sign of their relationship inside school time. In fact Joyce and Ann found that they could make for themselves a fairly effective separation between Mrs Trower who taught them history and Aunt Vera at home, closing off the knowledge of the one when they were dealing with the other. It was a relief that she turned out to be one of those teachers who elicited fear and respect rather than contempt. She was passionate about her subject, but that was tolerated as a kind of occupational hazard, with the same ambivalent tolerance that was extended to the brainy ones among the pupils. What was more important was that she was exacting and strict and could be scathingly sarcastic: Joyce more than once, and not without a certain private familial triumph then, saw her aunt reduce a girl to tears.

In the end of year revue they made fun of how,

although she knew all the clauses of the Treaty of Vienna, the 'Trower-pot' never remembered where she'd put down her chalk. Some girl would be chosen to impersonate her who could look tall and imposing and oblivious as she did, and whose hair could be arranged to imitate how hers was always escaping in thick untidy strands from where it was pinned up behind. Joyce would assiduously shut out a picture of Aunt Vera in her dressing gown in the mornings, her worn-out grey-pink corset and brassiere strewn on the bed behind her in a tangle of bedclothes, wailing to Lil at her bedroom door through a mouthful of hairpins that her stocking had a run.

—Hell's bells, Lil would complain, and come puffing upstairs with the soap, kneeling to paste it on to the run before it galloped. —You only bought them stockings last week.

Her aunt's impatience with ordinary everyday things was in reality much more complicating and painful than the innocently merry version in the revue. But the idea of the merry version was soothing; for her aunt, Joyce guessed, that journey of transition in the Austin Seven was in itself every morning a liberating shedding of complications, and an opportunity to become something more exciting and more charming than was possible at home.

—I'm really so very lucky, teaching at a school like this, she said to them one morning. They had stopped as usual in the suburban street of brutally pollarded lime trees ten minutes from Amery-James. Fringed blinds

22

blanked out the windows in the big dumb houses. —They think that because you're female you won't need any further intellectual stimulation after you're married. But take it from me, once you've been awakened to the life of the mind, you can't just smother that life and put it to sleep, however inconvenient it might be for some.

This sounded like something she had been preparing to say to them: a message for Joyce, probably, rather than for Ann, who didn't bother to work hard enough to get top marks. And perhaps partly because they were already in the territory in which she was the Trower-pot and must be taken notice of by the clever girls, Joyce did obediently think about her aunt's good luck that made it possible to step out of the mess of everyday life. Her own mother Lil, who'd never been to grammar school, certainly hadn't had that luck, and Joyce didn't want to be powerless like her.

After the car with all its important fuss had turned the corner and the girls began walking down the leafy cut-through, Ann launched into an imitation of her aunt which was much more cruel than the one in the end-of-year revue. Ann was almost as tall as Joyce although she was two years younger, and she had dark curling hair which made perfect ringlets when Lil put it in rags at night. Joyce was small; her hair was straight and a pale sandy red she hated. Ann wore her green coat swaggeringly with its collar up; her school hat had a permanent ridge from front to back where she shoved it out of sight into her satchel at any opportunity.

She pretended to be Uncle Dick in his courting days.

—'Go on, gi'us a kiss, hin.' 'Oh, no, I couldna do that. I'm awakening the life of the mind, you unappreciative man. I won't be needing any further stimulation.'

—You're a horrible little beast, said Joyce, scalded with her usual feeling of impotent indignation at her cocky little sister.

Ann crossed her eyes. —The life of the mind, she said, in broad Tyneside. —You mustn't let it go too far.

Uncle Dick was handsome. He was tall, with black hair slicked back with scented dressing and high cheekbones and remote-seeming eyes, like a Red Indian in a film. He was kinder, Joyce noticed, to her and Ann and Martin, than he was to his own children: he was disappointed with his son Peter for being such a crybaby. But mostly he was so distracted and so unaware of all the children that in the mornings when he used to give them a lift into Farmouth, they had shyly (even Ann was shy of him) to remind him to drop them off at the bus stop. If they missed the bus, though, he would suddenly seem to wake up to where he was, and race to overtake it, sounding his horn and leaning out of his window. But you had to wait for him to start off those kind of excitements; if you tried to be funny when he wasn't thinking about it he'd snap out at you.

They understood that he must have his thoughts on his job as Chief of the Docks Police, which gave him authority over the huge vessels unloading their cargoes, and the trains *Hallen* and *Portbury* in the sidings, and the ships' officers and the rough frightening men, the sailors and the dockers. There were new electric cranes to lift off the bales of tobacco and barrels of sherry and the imported cars (and once – he took the boys down especially to see it – four helicopters from the USA); but you still saw the dockers running down the gang-planks of the ships with long pieces of timber on their shoulders. If the children came home from school on the bus they were supposed to wait for their uncle in the Seaman's Mission just outside the big locked dock gates. This was run by a mad old woman called Mrs Mellor who told Joyce and Ann that you could catch a baby from using a public toilet: 'something could jump up inside you'. If it wasn't raining they preferred to wait outside the Mission on the pavement, even at the risk of having incomprehensible sinister things said to them by the men going by. The Dutch sailors were the worst. The children learned to smile politely and avoid meeting anyone's eyes.

Joyce's own father had been killed at Dunkirk when she was five and Ann was three and Martin just a baby. Their mother had a bottle filled with stones from the beach where he'd died: she'd gone to visit it with his parents after the war was over. Joyce could remember her father existing, and some things about what he looked like (he had pale ginger hair like hers), but she couldn't actually remember anything he did or how the days were different when he was in them. They had come down to live with her Aunt Vera partly thinking that their Uncle Dick might take up a father's place in their lives. Lil had said it would be good for them all to have a man around. To the children's relief, he didn't seem to be around all that much. He did a lot of driving backwards and forwards along the two miles between their house and the Docks, and he was sometimes at the house for supper; but he almost always had to go back into the office in the evenings. Joyce knew that when she saw into Aunt Vera's room in the mornings he hadn't slept there, although his suits still hung in the wardrobe and there were things of his – a hairbrush and cufflinks and collar studs – on the dressing table that stood with its back against the window. A series of coloured prints cut out from a *Lilliput* magazine hung around the bedroom walls: slim girls dressed only in diaphanous veils swinging round Greek pillars or gazing at their reflections in a lake. When Uncle Dick was in there once, getting a pair of shoes out from the wardrobe to take back to the Docks, he told Joyce they were all his old girlfriends. She thought it was funny, but she didn't repeat the joke to Vera.

So what happened instead of them getting a new father was that Aunt Vera got her job and went out to work every morning as if she was the man of the house and their mother Lil stayed at home like the wife and looked after Kay, Vera's daughter, who didn't go to school yet. Lil cleaned the house, washed the clothes, looked after the hens and geese, grew vegetables in the garden, and bought food from the delivery vans. Supper was ready when they all came home; the good table (they had to use the good table, it was the only one big enough for them all) would be laid with a blanket under the oilcloth to protect it; the kitchen would be dense with steam from the pans bubbling on the temperamental old paraffin stove which sometimes went wrong and gave out clouds of black smoke as well.

Lil didn't look anything like her sister: she was short and soft and plump with short dark hair that was always dropping out of its home perm. She knitted whenever her hands weren't busy with something else, one long needle tucked steady under her arm, the other one flickering in and out of the stitches; when the work dragged on the needles, she rubbed them in her hair to make them slip. She smoked, although Vera said it was common: when she hugged the children the tang of cigarettes and the hard outline of the packet of Woodbines in her apron pocket were part of her safe consoling flavour. Day after day, 'out in the back of beyond' as she put it, she didn't bother to change her shapeless print dress. Sometimes Joyce couldn't help seeing her mother through Aunt Vera's eyes. Lil didn't read books, she wasn't interested in the news or talk programmes on the wireless; she liked the dance bands and sang 'O for the Wings of a Dove' while she did the housework. She was quite incapable of that effort of self-transformation by which Vera and the girls pulled themselves up every morning to be smart and knowing and braced for Amery-James.

Sometimes Vera and Lil quarrelled. The worst quarrel was something to do with Ivor, Joyce's father. Lil had had a letter from one of his senior officers describing

27

how he'd died bravely, fired on by a strafing aeroplane while he was trying to help a wounded comrade in the water. This version of events had become a kind of family piety for the Stevensons, a poignant high truth. Vera was scornful of Lil for believing in that 'nonsense'.

—Don't you think they write the same stuff for every gullible widow? It's the final insult, sending out these sugarplum stories nobody in their right mind believes in.

—You always have to know better, don't you? said Lil passionately. —Why can't you just take someone else's word for it for once?

—Oh Lillie! Vera seemed puzzled by the vehemence of her sister's reaction. —I'm not insulting Ivor. I'm honouring his memory. But I won't swallow that old rubbish about honour and glory.

—Old rubbish! said Lil. —You think you can get away with saying anything to me. But there are people you wouldn't dare say that in front of.

—Do you want a third world war? said Vera. —Do you want our sons to die in the next war, because we've all swallowed up what we've been told like good little children?

Joyce couldn't stop herself wondering what it had been like for her father to die, if it hadn't been high-toned and beautifully sad. When she tested out the two possibilities in her mind she knew intuitively that what was hard and ugly was more likely to be true. And although Aunt Vera could be hateful with her loud superior voice and her bruising definiteness, Joyce thought that in such a contest it would be safer to be bruising than bruised. She wished she was tall and statuesque like her aunt; she began to adopt some of her mannerisms, her lofty absent-mindedness, her tone of superior scepticism towards everyday housework, her passionate responsiveness to the idea of philosophy, or classical music. There wasn't actually all that much room for philosophy or classical music in Aunt Vera's life, but their names were woven into her conversation like a wafted promise of a superior way of being. Joyce worked hard, poring over her schoolbooks, hoping that if she could somehow master these mountains of facts and processes then she might penetrate through at last to being adult and powerful.

She did very well at school. Her aunt was proud of her. Her uncle brought her home a four-volume set of American encyclopedias called *Worldwide Knowledge*. Lil was overcome and admiring.

—You ought to be grateful to your uncle, she said. —Imagine him taking the trouble to find these for you.

—Something somebody's given him off one of the ships, her aunt said sceptically.

The other serious quarrel the sisters had was not unconnected to the one about the war. One of the few times Lil ever took the trouble to dress up was when she went out to seances with a woman in Farmouth who was a medium. Then she put on her navy suit smelling of mothballs and her navy hat with the duck wing and her white gloves and sat looking unfamiliar and important in the car next to Uncle Dick, who gave her a lift to the house where the medium lived. Joyce and Ann begged to be allowed to go too – they were mad at that time on Ouija-boards and levitation at Amery-James – but Lil was dignified and immovable in her refusal.

—It's not a game, she said. —It's not for children.

Vera's outrage was out of all proportion to the occasion, as Uncle Dick pointed out.

—It's a bit of harmless excitement, he said. —Poor old Lillie, she doesn't get out much.

—There are so many other, worthwhile things that she could get involved in. I don't want her to be stultifying out here. There are gardening clubs, she's supposed to care about that, there's the choir, the Women's Co-operative Guild. But to lay yourself open to these charlatans, preying upon the weaknesses of the foolish, pulling muslin out from their stomachs and squeezing jellies in people's hands and pretending to make contact with people who no longer exist, who have turned back into molecules of carbon!

Vera never failed to mention that during the war Lil had been vaguely involved with something called the Magic Battle of Britain: they put up 'Cross of Light' posters in the London Underground and threw 'go-away powder' into the sea, where it was supposed to mix with the salt to stop the forces of darkness from invading.

—I don't know what we even bothered with soldiers for, Vera said. —Or artillery or aeroplanes. All we needed was that old go-away powder. It was that simple.

Just like the Queen of the Zulus believing she could make her people proof against the white man's bullets.

In fact what Lil reported back from her seances never seemed to involve the kind of dramas with ectoplasm and babies' hands that Vera feared and the children rather hoped for. Her stories were decorous and poignant; it was possible that she censored them for Vera's benefit. In the lamplight in the kitchen, once she had eased her feet out of her shoes and unhooked her corset, she told them about the sailor husband who had given his blessing to a second marriage, and the woman who had gone into a trance and imagined her dead father taking her into a lovely garden full of the scent of flowers in the darkness. When the woman said how she wished she could see it in the light, her father replied that if she saw it in the light she'd never want to go back.

Lil never seemed to make any very satisfactory contact with Ivor. Sometimes he came near, the medium said, he was trying to reach through, but he was naturally shy, he gave way to the others, he didn't like to push himself forward.

—I said: that's him! Lil told them. —That's Ivor. That's him all over. Trust him.

And so that was how Joyce came to imagine him losing his life on the beach at Dunkirk: holding back shyly, giving way to others.

Joyce was the eldest of the children. Peter, her cousin, clever and awkward, had a choral scholarship at the Cathedral School; he was the same age as Ann. Martin

31

her brother was younger and went to the local Juniors in Farmouth. Martin was brown and wiry, gallant and handsome: Lil said he caused her more trouble than all the rest put together. He came home with his school cap pulled hard down to hide a deep gash in his forehead from when he'd been playing about with the tools in a car mechanic's workshop near school; Lil had to soak the cap where it had stuck to the wound as the blood dried. He didn't cry. He burned a pair of trousers in the bedroom grate and told his mother he'd lost them so that she wouldn't see how badly they were ripped; she found the telltale scorched buttons. He made a parachute from his bedsheet and jumped with it out of an upstairs window and somehow only sprained his ankle. His teachers warned that he wouldn't get a place at a good school. Kay was the baby, who was just growing out of being everyone's little pet into a silent stubborn and stolid child, tall like her mother, with Vera's large long face, and startling white blonde hair which Lil cut in a short bob.

Dick and Vera were waiting for one of the new houses that were being built in Farmouth: in the meantime they were given the old grey house because the Port Authority had bought it up and wasn't using it. It had long stone-mullioned windows with leaded panes; inside the rooms were higgledy-piggledy and unexpected, with low doorways and crooked passages. A narrow spiral staircase behind the kitchen led up to a mysterious tiny room with stone shelves all round where they stored apples: in summer Joyce used to read there. There was a walled kitchen garden and outside the back door of the house a walnut tree and a huge William pear tree: fat pears smashed on to the path and in the autumn mornings when they first opened the back door, Winnie their brindled bulldog would push past them and dash out to gobble them up. They found a bat in the living room, its ears as long as its body (Ann put on gloves and carried it outdoors); once a solemn-staring owl was on the sill by an open window in one of the bedrooms. The bathroom was on the ground floor, and the bath had to be filled with buckets of hot water from the stove: outside the window the weeds grew tall and green and were all they needed for a curtain, until Joyce began to imagine she could hear rustlings, and made Lil pin up an old blanket when it was her turn.

The house stood on reclaimed estuary land, and wide rhines, drainage ditches covered with bright green algae, criss-crossed the fields all round. Ducks and moorhen swam on them, and the geese who were Ann's special friends: she stroked their fat creamy necks and kissed them on their beaks. One particularly severe winter they were cut off by snow from Farmouth for a whole week (Uncle Dick eventually got through to them with food and paraffin). Then in the spring when the snow melted, the rhines flooded and the house stood in a shallow lake of water. The children made a boat out of an old tin bath, the one Lil used to wash Kay in front of the kitchen stove.

Kay wouldn't go in the 'boat'; all the others became bent upon coaxing her into it, as if she was missing something transforming and essential.

—Cowardy custard! said Peter.

—You'll love it! Martin pleaded. —It isn't dangerous, see how shallow it is. It's so easy: look! It's jolly good fun. You can come in with me.

And he executed some nifty turns and splashed up and down, paddling with the spade. Martin was good at all these sorts of things: paddling a boat, climbing trees, clambering (unbeknownst to his mother) along the rafters in the hayloft at their neighbour's farm, or steering the old pram which they used as a go-cart on the causeway which ran down to the shore. Kay pressed her mouth shut and shook her head and clung to the little scrap of grubby blanket which was her 'sucky' to get her to sleep and which she took everywhere with her. (—One of these mornings I'm going to drop that in the stove! Lil said whenever she saw it. So Kay had learned to keep it out of sight, in her pocket or balled up in her hand.)

Peter was – inevitably – the one who tipped out of the tin bath into the filthy water. He lost his nerve when he drifted away from the house which stood on a slight rise: they knew they must be careful not to paddle near the rhines where the water was deep. He raised himself awkwardly in the bath to look behind him and then went in with a big splash and a funny truncated scream, and had to wade ignominiously back to the others, pulling the bath behind him. He was a strange mixture of genuine ineptness and deliberate clowning. He and Martin had vicious fights: when Peter lost his temper he would pummel Martin blindly and frantically, rolling his eyes up and crying loudly through clenched teeth. Martin said the sight of Peter made him laugh so much he was too weak to fight back.

Joyce was fifteen that spring: too old really to play at boats. It was only because she was small that she could fit in the bath, with her knees up to her chin. When she was quite a way from the others and their voices were remote, she stopped paddling and leaned cautiously back with the spade resting across the middle of the bath. She had been working all morning (it was a Saturday), learning the dates of the American Revolution, learning lists of French words for birds and trees, getting Peter to test her. She had her School Certificate exams in a few months. Her head was full of the sound of herself, reciting, repeating.

The sky when she leaned back and looked up was mostly a steady grey, like dull wool soaking up the light; over towards the estuary the grey had begun to break up and there was an opened gash of surprising brilliant blue with scraps of milky cloud floating in it. She imagined copying those clouds in paint, noticing how they had a bright hard edge of light against the blue. Then she thought about the art room at Amery-James, which was up a flight of stairs over the dining hall, and always seemed restfully separate from the rest of school. Instead of maps and blackboards and piles of sombre textbooks, the art room was filled with a clutter of interesting things to look at, vases of dried grasses and seedheads, printed silks and embroideries, a carved wooden mask, a bright coloured kite, a sheep's skull, huge pottery dishes with coarse bold colours and patterns unlike anything Joyce had ever eaten off in anyone's home. The room was high and light and airy and the walls were hung with pictures, some beautiful and some queer and incomprehensible. There were a couple of drawings of naked women, too, which Joyce studied with furtive curiosity, and which made some of the girls say there was something funny about Miss Leonard, the art teacher.

Joyce heard the others shouting to her, and realised that she was drifting towards where the rhine ran along the edge of the invisible field, marked out by a line of shrubs poking out of the floodwater. She let herself drift for a few more moments, wondering what would happen if she didn't act, if she let herself go, drifting on into the faster current in her ridiculous frail boat, perhaps being tipped out into deep water by a surge of turbulence, or perhaps being picked up and carried onwards, faster and faster until there was no return, towards the estuary and then the sea. There was no real danger, of course. If she'd wanted to she could have stepped out of the bath and walked back. When she did pick up the spade she paddled with studied insouciance, making strong elegant strokes and not deigning to look behind over her shoulder. She was coming to know that she could summon up this power to do things elegantly: not infallibly, but often. It was important to know how to carry things off, under the eyes of the others, the family, or the girls at school. She wanted never to make a fool of herself like her cousin Peter, who had reappeared buttoned up to the neck in his school blazer and was hovering outside the kitchen for a chance to dry his clothes over the stove without his Auntie Lil noticing.

That summer Aunt Vera often stayed late at school: she was rehearsing the historical pageant she was putting on to mark the Festival of Britain. Ann had to stay too: she had landed the much-coveted part of Mary Queen of Scots. (There was a craze for Mary, and a poem about her all the girls knew by heart and chanted in the lunch break with real tears in their eyes: 'So she lived and so she died,/Scotland's pawn and Scotland's pride./England's bane and England's heir,/Mary, fairest of the fair.') The School Cert girls weren't supposed to be involved in the pageant, they had too much else on their minds. Quite often Joyce had to wait at the Mission by herself in the afternoons, hoping Uncle Dick would remember she needed a lift. She would try to absorb herself deeply in her homework behind the windows of the little office, never lifting her head when she sensed the sailors coming and going on the other side of the glass, scaldingly aware of herself bent over her books in her prissy neat school uniform, and of the incitement to resentment or violence the sight of her must represent to these strong thwarted shameless men. When at long last it was Uncle Dick's tall shape in his dark coat and hat that loomed beyond the window, her heart spilled over with relief. The world readjusted itself back inside the shelter of his importance, his air of always being in a hurry, his loud lofty authority with crazy Mrs Mellor and with the men. 'Men', when he said it, shrank to mean only something about how they were employed, and set Joyce safely above them, condescending to them and beyond their reach.

One afternoon as they set off in the car Uncle Dick remembered something he wanted to bring back for Vera.

—Just making a little detour, he said to Joyce. —We won't be ten minutes.

He turned the car around and they drove through the streets to where the Authority were building several new houses, including the one for his family. The designs for the houses had been taken from the Ideal Home Show in London: some of them were already finished and lived in, two or three were still under construction. It had not been discussed, not properly, whether there would be room for Lil and her children when Vera got her new house. Joyce thought that perhaps her uncle had some news for his wife about it – perhaps it was ready and he had been keeping it for a surprise? But he pulled up to a red-brick house which already had curtains up and a striped awning over the door, although the garden was still a mess of clay on either side of the path.

—You wait here, he said. —Good girl.

He walked up the path, feeling in his pocket for a key; then he unlocked the front door and disappeared inside, closing it behind him. He was gone longer than ten minutes. Joyce tried to shrink in her seat so as not to be conspicuous to the children playing in the street. She took off her blazer. She pulled out her history book from her satchel and looked at it sightlessly.

Uncle Dick came back out of the house with a bundle wrapped in brown paper under his arm. When he was halfway down the garden path, walking rather quickly, the front door flew open again behind him, and a young woman ran out after him on high heels, blonde and slim. She was wearing lipstick and earrings and a pretty dress that seemed inappropriate for staying at home on an ordinary afternoon: beige, with a low-cut square neck and deep diagonal pleats across the skirt. She took Uncle Dick by the arms and remonstrated with him, seeming to want the parcel, but she wasn't looking at him: her eyes from the very moment she flew through the door had sought out Joyce in the car, staring at her greedily and challengingly as if this contact between them was momentous. Helplessly Joyce stared back.

Uncle Dick said something, not loudly (Joyce couldn't hear it) but fiercely, so that the woman jerked back from him as if he had hit her. Afterwards she always pictured the scene as if he had smacked her lightly and sharply across the side of the face, just as he sometimes smacked Peter when Peter was acting up, even though she knew he hadn't actually struck this grown-up woman, not in front of her. He strode to the car and threw the parcel into the back seat. He turned the car round; the woman had stepped back into her doorway, stroking down her skirt and tidying her hair. Joyce saw that she was defiantly aware, as she hadn't been in the heat of the argument, of people watching: the children who'd stopped playing in the street, and invisible others from behind the curtained windows of the inhabited houses. Joyce felt a pang of sympathy for how she was exposed.

—Oh dear, said Uncle Dick in a wryly amused voice as they left her behind. —Someone's upset.

This tone of light comedy in relation to what had just happened was so unexpected that Joyce forgot to be afraid of him.

—Who was that? she asked.

Uncle Dick even turned his attention from the road and smiled at her enquiring eyes. —Never you mind, he said. —Someone who'd better be our little secret.

—Is it her parcel?

—Oh no. It's just something she thinks she ought to have.

It was almost as though he was pleased that Joyce had been there to see. Perhaps he had taken her deliberately. On the way home he was expansive and genial with her as he'd never been before. When they had driven past the smelting works and left Farmouth and the Docks behind, she was able to notice that it was a lovely evening: the grass was long and a tender green in the fields, the hedges were laden with pink and white May blossom.

—You've no idea what it's like, Uncle Dick said. —All the responsibilities of a wife and family to support. Especially after the war, which gave a man a taste for independence.

Uncle Dick had been in the Royal Naval Volunteer Reserves (the 'wavy navy', because they had wavy white lines around their cuffs). He was Lieutenant-Commander of an aircraft-carrier, an American lease-lend.

40

—You get tangled up with a family, he said, before you know what opportunities are out there. Take my advice, and don't be in any hurry to be tied down with kids.

—I'm staying on at school, Joyce said, wondering if that was what he meant.

—Well, there's nothing wrong with that. Although I should think you'd want some fun, too. That's the trouble with your aunt. She takes everything too seriously.

While his ship was in New York for repairs, he had had apartments in the Barbizon Plaza Hotel; this name was always uttered with reverence in the family, as if it was the epitome of luxury. He had met Mrs Rothschild, who organised 'Bundles for Britain' for the sailors; and he had been given membership of the New York Athletic Club. Perhaps it was there he'd got his taste for independence.

—I've seen some things. Uncle Dick looked assessingly sideways at Joyce for a moment. —Some I couldn't tell you about, not yet.

Joyce had never heard him say as much as this at home; she guessed it was the way he talked with his men friends. She could imagine why he'd rather sit in a bar with these friends than be at home amidst all the steam of cooking and the smoke from the stove and the noisy children and wet washing draped everywhere (although she'd never seen inside a bar except in films). She felt shyly privileged that he shared his thoughts with her as they sped through the fields in the summer's evening.

—What was her name? Joyce asked him at the last

41

minute, as he turned down into the lane that led to the old grey house.

—Whose name?

—The lady you visited, in the beige dress.

—Betty Grable, he said.

Joyce protested: she wasn't a child, to be fooled. —If you don't want to tell me, I don't mind.

Uncle Dick laughed at her hurt face. —No, it really is Betty. Not Betty Grable, just Betty. On my honour. But don't tell. On yours?

She nodded.

Then, managing the bucking car with one hand down the rutted stony lane, he laid his other hand on her bare arm and said something strange. —I told her you were my daughter. Just so she wouldn't start imagining anything. You know what these women are like.

Joyce was sometimes allowed to hover on the edge of conversations Lil and Vera had in the kitchen when the other children weren't around. This was presumably because she was the oldest and a girl: they thought it was time she began to pick up on such things, just as a year or so ago it had been time for the sanitary pads and belt that Lil had slipped without explanation into her drawer. After the dishes were washed up the sisters sat at the table and drank milky coffee made with essence; when the light faded one of them would light the paraffin lamp and pump it up until the mantle glowed. The children would still be calling back and forth outside, their voices resonant and remote in the near-dark. Joyce squeezed herself inconspicuously with her book on to a little stool by the wall, picking at the black rubber flooring Uncle Dick had laid over the cold flagstones (it was made out of machine belts from some factory in the Docks that had closed down).

—It happened with Peter, and then again down here when I was expecting Kay, said Vera. —Not that you want them near you when you're off-colour. But you expect some consideration: not having the blame for it thrown up in your face.

—Men don't like it, said Lil. —Ivor didn't want anything to do with it. 'Let me know what we've had when you're all tidied up,' he said when things got started. Though he was always as good as gold afterwards, he loved the children.

—Dick hated the sight of me. If I ever came out of the bath in my dressing gown when I was in that way he'd make a face as if I'd shown him something nasty. I knew he didn't like to touch me, those times, even accidentally. He doesn't even like to be near me when I'm coming unwell.

—I suppose it's natural. We get used to it, don't we? It must seem strange to the men.

—I'm sure he used to talk with her about what would happen if I died, having Kay, said Vera. —There was something he said once, he didn't mean it to come out, something like 'if there are any complications'. And when I looked at him I just knew. And he knew I knew.

—You showed them, then.

—Oh, I wasn't going to remove myself for anybody's

convenience. I'm not now. Whatever she may think.

It was always difficult for Joyce to take in that only four years before Aunt Vera must have been pregnant. She tried to imagine her wearing the sort of coyly pretty maternity frocks over discreet bumps that you saw in the magazines; or smiling over tiny garments for her layette. But Aunt Vera didn't seem to have the necessary feminine attributes; she was too tall, too decided, too old, her body had entered into the phase of those lumpy stolidities that didn't suggest the things that had to do with making babies. The pregnancy had happened after the Trowers first moved down from the North. Joyce had heard Lil and the other sisters talk about this baby as Dick's 'little peace offering'.

Joyce noticed that when Lil and Vera talked about men, even Ivor, they often used this language of mock conflict, as if there had to be a war between men and women. Listening, soaking it up, Joyce thought how differently she would do things. She thought how much better she would handle Uncle Dick, if she was them. 'If he was mine,' she thought to herself, her face heating up at the illicit form of words. If she had been Aunt Vera she would have made an effort to make the place nice when he came home, instead of complaining to him about the children or the smoking stove or the stinking earth closet the moment he walked through the door. She would have talked about things he might be interested in, rather than going on about 'your beloved Churchill' or making sarcastic remarks about the Masons if she knew he was going to a Lodge meeting.

Even Lil somehow managed better than Vera. You could see she was in awe of Dick's authority in the wide world, granting him absolute superiority in all the mysteries she was defeated by. She was furious if ever her children were disrespectful to him: she reminded them how they were dependent on their uncle for a roof over their heads. But she also called him 'his Lordship' and commented tartly at tea if he'd 'deigned to honour them with his presence'. He meekly brought her his buttons to be sewn on and stood tamed and obedient while she tugged and stitched away at his collar or the waist of his trousers, scolding him because Peter needed new vests and socks and they hadn't enough money, biting off her thread with a fierce twist of her head. Once Joyce overheard her speak sharply of his 'carryings-on'.

He didn't mind Lil, he laughed and tolerated her remarks and sometimes forked out money from his wallet for something she said they needed. Or there might be a companionable moment when they sat out on the wall in the sunshine in the garden after tea and smoked together, Dick bending with disarming gallantry to light Lil's cigarette. But Joyce could also see how he discounted her because she was shapeless under her print dresses, and wouldn't even go to the girls' prize-givings because 'she wouldn't know what to say to anyone'.

—Present for you, Vera, Uncle Dick said, dropping the brown paper parcel down on the table which was laid for tea. Knives and forks clattered on to the floor.

Aunt Vera had only just come in from school, she still had her jacket on and she was taking off her gloves. She stopped short and stared at the parcel with suspicion.

—Oh well, if you don't want it, he said genially, —I'll take it back.

—What is it? She frowned as if this might be a trick at her expense.

—Open it and see.

Warily she tore the paper open. Lil came from the stove with a spoon in her hand to look, the children gathered round. Sometimes Uncle Dick brought thrilling things from the Docks: sweets, a wireless, pineapples, picture books, and once three hand-sewn American quilts, part of American support for the war effort which had sat forgotten in a shed somewhere.

Inside the paper were two bolts of cloth: a deep chestnut velvet and a slightly lighter brown satin. Lil reached out a finger to stroke.

—Real velvet. Don't any of you touch, she said in a half whisper.

—D'you reckon you can turn her out in something halfway decent, Lillie?

—Me? Oh, I'd be afraid to cut into that. It's too good.

—What's this all about? said Vera. —Do you want something?

—Only for you to get out and have a good time for once.

—You could use the velvet to make a matching jacket, Lil said. —A bolero.

—My idea of a good time is rather different to yours.

—Ladies' Night in July. I thought you might like a night out, something new to wear.

—Oh I *see*, said Vera. —Trouble at the Lodge. You need to present the respectable husband and father all of a sudden.

—Something like that.

—Suddenly I'm wanted.

—Too much to expect, I suppose, that my lady wife might make the effort for once?

—And suddenly no one else will do.

—Not for the moment, no.

Vera flashed out in extravagant triumph. —Oh, they won't have you there if you *divorce*. You can forget about ever being elected to Warden's Office once you embark upon that little scheme of yours.

Lil clapped her hands and flapped her apron at the children. —Go and do your homework, she said. —Tea in ten minutes.

Uncle Dick shrugged. —That's up to them. I've got my letter of resignation written out in my pocket, if anyone makes difficulties. And I'll take the cloth back with me if you don't want it.

—I've done faggots and roly-poly, Lil said. —Aren't you staying for tea?

Uncle Dick's refusals were always more like rebuffs than apologies: impatient indications of the more important business he had elsewhere. —I've got to be back at the Docks.

Lil picked up the knives and forks from the floor when he had left and wiped them on her apron, then she carried the fabrics out of the way of tea into the front room.

—You ought to go to this Ladies'-Night affair, she said.

Vera's face was closed.

—Why shouldn't you go? Why shouldn't you have something nice to wear? You're his rightful wife.

—I don't want to spend my evening listening to that mumbo-jumbo.

Lil swept her sewing table clear from all the bits left over from Ann's Mary Queen of Scots costume. Then she shook the satin and velvet out from their folds until they were heaped up in sumptuous excess in the dim light. The curtains in this room were always half drawn across – they didn't use it much.

Vera stood passively while Lil draped the brown satin over her grey pleated skirt and cream blouse, her usual things for school.

—It suits you! said Lil. —It goes with your dark hair. See how it hangs. It's such good quality, so heavy. Look how it takes the light. The dress wants a classic line, very fitting; then a velvet bolero with a three-quarter-length sleeve. You could bind the edge of the bolero with the satin. Wear it with those earrings Mam gave you. You could wear it for the pageant too.

Vera looked down at herself, hesitating. She leaned forward on to one hip to make the fabric swing and swirl.

—I certainly don't want anyone else flaunting about in it, she said.

Lil tucked an end of the velvet around Vera's shoulders and under her arms, then she and Joyce stood squinting their eyes at her, trying to blur the draped fabrics into looking like the finished outfit. She submitted to their attention with unaccustomed meekness.

—It could look very elegant, said Lil.

Lil and Joyce both set about persuading her, as if they knew something she didn't know about what this dress could do for her, something she was incapable of managing for herself. Now that Joyce had seen the blonde woman, she was afraid that her aunt didn't know what she was up against.

—I might go to art school, Joyce said to her art teacher.

Miss Leonard was tiny, ancient-looking, with a face as lined and vivid as a monkey's; she walked with an odd sliding motion, lifting her knees and carrying her head very high and far back as if she was keeping her face above the dull muddy water of the rest of school. Girls who wanted to get on with some drawing or painting were allowed to be up in the art room at lunchtime. Joyce was making fussy tiny changes to a drawing of an extravagant tropical shell gorgeously lined with pink, although she was sure that her fussing wasn't going to make the timorous drawing any better. She didn't know what art school was, really; any more than she had any clear idea of university, although she knew her aunt wanted her to go to one. She hadn't thought about going to art school until the very moment she said it.

Miss Leonard was working in pastels on a still life

49

she had arranged on a table for one of her classes: two jugs glazed in thick yellow against a scrap of oriental rug with a couple of lemons. She gave her a rapid unimpressed bird-glance.

—I thought you were one of the brainy ones?

Joyce blushed. —Oh no, not really.

—So why on earth do you want to go to art school, apart from being too stupid to do anything else?

—Well, I love art, of course.

One sceptical eyebrow went up: the eyes flickered rapidly, assessingly, between the lemons and her paper. —Oh, don't love art. That sounds frightfully high-minded. You'll never make a living at it, you know.

Joyce was shocked. —I never dreamed I could make a living!

—You have to teach, or else you do illustrating, if you can get it. Unless of course you're one of the lucky few. The ones who've really got it. Whatever *it* is. Talent, genius, originality, the right friends in the right places.

—What it is, really, said Joyce, —is that I love these things. I've never seen things like all these before.

Miss Leonard looked at her blankly. Then as if she had forgotten it existed she cast a surprised glance round the room full of the treasures that had pleased her eye.

—Oh. I see.

She put down her crayon and went over to shelves piled with a miscellany of crockery, topped with pieces of driftwood and a couple of ostrich feathers.

—Come and feel these, she said.

Anxiously Joyce took one of the big flat dishes from

her. Miss Leonard brushed off the dust with the side of her hand.

—Do you like them?

The dish was heavy, the clay half an inch thick, the uneven green glaze was decorated with swirls of brown so freely drawn that you could see the marks of the brush hairs. Joyce could hardly understand a way of making things that was so opposite to the one she had been brought up to admire; her mother's best tea set for example, where precision and delicate finish were everything and the making process was tidied secretively out of sight.

—I love them, she said.

—They come from Portugal. In Portugal the sun is hot, the people live out of doors so much more, they drink wine and eat fish cooked with olive oil and tomatoes and spices and garlic, off dishes like these. Their houses are often crumbling and untidy but inside and even outside they are covered with locally made tiles.

She took away the dish and gave Joyce a handful of tiles, each one different. They were in glowing colours, blues and reds and yellows: mostly patterns but some pictures, a fish and a bird, drawn as crudely and casually as a child might draw them. They didn't even seem quite perfectly square.

—You should go there, Miss Leonard said. —Or Italy. You should go to Italy too. You should eat *pasta asciutta* and drink Chianti. Children suffer under a blight of ugliness in this country. What's for dinner today, for example? Can you smell it? You usually can up here.

51

Boiled liver and cabbage? Boiled cod and white sauce? No wonder their paintings are ugly.

Miss Leonard was suddenly impatient with Joyce. She picked up the drawing of the shell as if it exasperated her and scribbled on it with a piece of charcoal, crudely, exaggerating the horns of the shell with bold black Vs.

—Don't be meek, she said. —That's what I can't bear. Boiled cod and white sauce.

The making of Aunt Vera's outfit for Ladies' Night was fraught with problems. Both the fabrics were difficult to cut and sew. Lil needed pinking shears and didn't have any. She cut the three-quarter-length sleeves of the jacket in one with the bodice and then let in gussets under the arms, but the gussets were difficult and puckered on the corners. Nonetheless there was a certain gathering excitement in the week or so while the dressmaking was advancing. It was full summer now. There were rust-coloured weeds and shaggy old man's beard among the tall mauve grasses; the full-grown leaves on the trees lolled in the heat and showed their grey undersides, the rhines were rank and shallow.

Aunt Vera stood on the kitchen table for Lil to do the hem. The floor was strewn with scraps of cloth and ends of thread and pins. They were still not sure how the outfit finally looked. Too many bits were provisional, pinned or unfinished; and then Vera inside it was too obviously her ordinary self, her hair untidy, her face long and tired with bruise-coloured pouches under the

eyes. She was scowling and fretting at being kept prisoner while Lil fussed. Joyce hoped something different
would happen when she did up her hair and powdered
her skin and put on her lipstick and scent, put in her
garnet earrings.

Meanwhile she was testing Joyce on her English
history. She told an anecdote about Palmerston which
Joyce had heard from her before, in school. Palmerston
said, 'There are only three people in the world who have
understood the Schleswig-Holstein question. One's
dead, one's mad, and I've forgotten.' There were other
stories about Palmerston: how he cheered when he heard
that the London dockers put a Hungarian general in a
barrel and rolled him down a hill, and how he was fit
enough to vault over a gate the day before he died. Vera
had favourites among the men in history. When she
talked about them her voice was coy as if she was sharing
some kind of flirtatious joke.

Into the indoor quiet erupted Peter and Kay with
news that they had caught an eel, Martin following
importantly with an enamel bucket which he set down
on the floor for everyone to admire. The eel stirring in
its dark coils in the bit of muddy water was like a sight
of something urgent and shameful that was best kept
hidden. Ann, who had been sitting on the low stool
learning her lines for the pageant, was fearless with
animals and wanted to reach into the bucket and touch
the eel, but Lil said she'd get an electric shock.

—It's the wrong kind of eel, said Peter impatiently;
but he held himself well back and peered into the bucket

with excited loathing, from a respectful distance.

—Take it away, children, said Lil, removing a mouthful of pins. —I do not want that dirty creature anywhere near this precious sewing.

—We could eat it, said Martin, trying to sound at his most reasonable and practical.

—We could not, said Lil. —If you think for one moment I'm going to grapple with that blinking thing and kill it and gut it, not even knowing whether it's habitable or not . . .

—You don't mean habitable, said Peter: but there was relief in his voice.

There came the sounds of Uncle Dick's car negotiating the tormenting ruts of the lane. Lil and Vera looked at one another.

—Can we keep it as a pet? said Martin. —Please? He didn't seriously expect an answer.

—D'you want him to see? said Lil to Vera.

—Heavens, Lillie, what do I care what he sees? Anyone'd think I was a bride in a wedding dress!

Obediently Lil went on pinning, while Vera on the table moved stiffly round for her as if she was on an old slow turntable. The children took the eel outside, Ann following them, chirruping coaxingly into the bucket. She was wearing her Mary Queen of Scots headdress, her heart-shaped face with its sly dark eyes uncharacteristically demure under its little Gothic vault. There was a pause while in the yard Uncle Dick duly admired the eel. He sounded as if he was in a good humour. He blocked the light, standing in the doorway, with Kay in his arms;

Lil lifted her head up from her concentration on the hem.

—What d'you think, Dick?

He was blinking in the shadows after the glare outdoors. Kay, who with no prompting or encouragement adored her father, had her head laid on his shoulder and was fingering his lapel while she sucked her thumb.

—Smells like a real old witches' kitchen in here, Dick said.

—That's them children bringing their creatures in.

—Well, let's see what kind of a mess you've managed to concoct. Turn round, turn round.

Lil stood back and Aunt Vera turned on her turntable again, looking tense and exposed.

—Lift up your arms. Turn round.

Obediently Vera lifted her arms like a ballet dancer. Lil pressed a hand to her heart. —Is it all right?

—Isn't it a bit tight? he said cheerfully. —It makes her look like the back end of an upholstered sofa.

—She does not! said Lil stoutly, but her voice was full of doubt. —D'you think it's tight?

—Should have cut it with a bit more room in it, he said, and they could see immediately that he was right. —And isn't there something funny with those sleeves?

—I *like* the sleeves, said Joyce, in a great effort of optimism.

—I could undo them, said Lil, —and try to get a better seam.

—Oh, it'll do, he said. —Don't bother.

—It's not worth the bother, said Aunt Vera calmly, lowering her arms. —It'll do as it is. I've got better things to do than stand up here every evening like a dress-maker's dummy.

And she looked around for her way down from the table; someone had moved the chair she'd climbed up by. The brown satin dress seemed suddenly exposed as an awful failure: the lovely luxuriant deeply glowing cloth had been spoiled, cut in clumsy lines that made Aunt Vera's belly a huge coconut perched comically on top of her long legs, and her bosom a pair of slanting torpedoes. When Lil moved the stool for her to step on to, Vera hesitated; and Joyce knew she was paralysed by her humiliating sense that the skirt might rip or she might topple.

—Allow me, said Uncle Dick. Smiling he offered her his free arm, and she let him help her down on to the stool and then half swing and half jump her from there to the floor. She stood flushed and stoical.

—There's room in these seams for me to let it out. Lil was contritely seeking remedies.

—Don't *fuss*, said Vera sharply. —Help me get the wretched thing off.

—Never mind, Lil, said Uncle Dick. —Your sister isn't interested in clothes, she's got her mind on more important things. She doesn't care what she puts on.

Joyce was suddenly hotly aware of her own frock that she'd changed into when she got home from school, a friendly old cotton thing with faded sprigs of blue flowers. She'd had it for years: Lil had made it for her when she was a flat-chested child and it was so familiar that she wore it as unthinkingly as her own skin. For the first time now she saw it as if she was looking at it with disgust from outside: how tight it was across her developing bust, how high the waistline came across on her chest, and how compromisingly short the skirt was, even though Lil had let the hem down twice. A kind of rage flared up in her at her mother and her aunt, that they were so unknowing, so helpless themselves, allowing her to go on wearing this and never seeing how it exposed her. She wanted to run upstairs to hide, only she couldn't move for fear they all saw how ridiculous she looked.

—In case any of you are interested, by the way, she proclaimed loudly, —I'm going to go to art school.

Of course they had all forgotten she was even sitting there; they turned on her slow glances steeped in adult preoccupations, wondering whatever she was talking about.

—You'll do no such thing, said her aunt. —Not with your brains.

But Vera's power was gone, standing there full of pins and in her stockinged feet, suffering so abjectly because her husband didn't like her in her dress.

Joyce didn't want brains. She thought instead of lemons: yellow, astringent, Mediterranean, against a dark and sensual background.

Joyce and a girlfriend took swimming things to the beach one day when the exams were over. This wasn't a friend from Amery-James, it was an old friend from the North, Helena Knapp, who was staying for a fortnight, and with whom Joyce had temporarily recovered an old, easy, satirical way of being. On the causeway leading down to the beach they passed a parked car, and giggling Joyce pointed out the naval peaked cap left on the back seat. Sometimes Martin and Peter came down here to spy on courting couples. There were shallow hideaways for lovers in the dunes that undulated rather unspectacularly back behind the shore, grown over with little dark green shrubby bushes and bleached long grasses. That afternoon the tide was out. It wasn't like real seaside: to reach the water they had to wade out for a quarter of a mile through mud which was soft and warm and sucking, melting away ticklingly under the soles of their feet. Mud clung like tan socks halfway up their calves. The coastline on the faraway other side receded in infinitely promising blue and purple layers of hills; further up the estuary, where the crossing was narrower, they could see the two ferries plying to and fro.

The skies were the only spectacular feature of the estuary scenery. Changeable and full of drama, they loomed domineeringly over the flat land and altered the colour of the water hour by hour: this afternoon it was pale brown like milky coffee. The girls, up to their mid-thighs in tepid water, watched a sudden jostling company of small angry clouds overhead; fat warm raindrops plopped down all around them. It seemed very funny, to be in their swimming costumes in the rain. Their costumes were new, they had chosen them yesterday in a department store in town: Helena's was a blue-and-white striped halter neck, Joyce's was a strapless bloomer suit, with a pattern of black-and-white birds against a dark pink background. Lil had given Joyce four pounds to spend out of the old tobacco jar where she kept her savings. The girls were in love with their new costumes, and couldn't stop looking down at themselves and at each other. They didn't really want to submerge in the muddy water and spoil them.

Someone was calling them from the beach. They both looked round: it was Uncle Dick. His car was parked up behind the other one, he stood on the shingle in his work uniform with his jacket over his arm and his sleeves rolled up. They couldn't hear what he was saying.

—What? they shouted back, knowing it was futile and he wouldn't be able to hear them either. They savoured a few moments' delicious remoteness, lingering there inaccessible in the spatter of hot rain, feeling the impotence of the figure on the shore to reach them.

—What in hell's name does he want? Joyce languorously wondered.

—The legendary uncle, said Helena. —Won't there be outbreaks of lawlessness if he's not at his post?

When he persisted and signalled furiously for them to return, they began reluctantly to wade back.

—Does your mother know you two are down here cavorting around half naked? he shouted as soon as they were in hearing distance.

—We told her, Joyce shouted back.

—She said we could cavort, said Helena placidly, covered by the noise of their rather exaggerated splashing through the shallows. —In our new costumes.

—You're asking for trouble. You know what kind of spot this is.

—What kind of spot is it? Joyce did a perfect imitation of nonplussed and wide-eyed.

—Get yourselves dried off, he said angrily, pointing to their towels. —I'll take you back in the car. Your mother and your aunt have no idea, letting you run around the place like hoydens. Anyway, it's coming on to rain.

—Hoydens? murmured Helena in delight. They rubbed their legs down, streaking the towels with mud.

—What do you think hoydens do? wondered Joyce.

—Whatever it is, I think we should try it. To begin with, they cavort.

—I love to cavort.

—So do I.

They sat in the back seat of the car: Uncle Dick had spread out a towel, so that they wouldn't make wet marks on his upholstery. He lectured them about looking after themselves and having some self-respect: because he couldn't turn round to speak to them the words seemed to emanate from his dark, stiff back. At some level they were genuinely impressed by his concern. As a matter of fact, a few days before, a couple of lorry drivers had given them a lift to the beach and when they got out one of them had grabbed Helena's hand and tried to put it on his trousers, until his friend swore at them and drove on.

But Joyce was also exhilarated by Uncle Dick's very exasperation and his fear for them. If there was danger, then that meant you counted for something. You had at least the power – the power that Vera and Lil didn't have – to disconcert him, to make him mutter to himself and drive with impatient thwarted accelerations and brakings. Behind the sternness of his back in its dark hot serge the girls sat basking in the miracle of their new costumes, which were hardly wet, and which they somehow knew he both wanted and didn't want to look at.

Two

One Friday in November Kay was hot and whining and clung to Lil. In the evening she was worse, and when they telephoned the doctor and described her symptoms he told them to take her straight to the hospital. Uncle Dick drove: Vera sat in the front seat, and the other children saw Lil put Kay into her arms, wrapped in one of the American quilts. They felt the drama of the occasion, but it did not occur to them that Kay would not come back. Just after the car had driven off they found her bit of old sucky blanket lying on the kitchen floor and Martin ran with it along the lane after the car; but they'd turned on to the road before he could catch up with them. Peter even clowned around after they'd gone, pretending he was ill too, looking up his sleeves and inside his shorts and claiming that each tiny freckle was a rash, squealing and insisting Lil came to look at it, until she rounded on him, asking him if he didn't have any heart. He then undid his shirt and pretended to look anxiously for this.

Lil got undressed and went to bed eventually, after sitting by the telephone for a couple of hours: this was a kind of endurance in itself, as she feared the thing and hated using it, never knowing which bit she was supposed to speak into (even though Uncle Dick had had it put in for her, so that she could place her orders for the delivery vans). It was Joyce who heard the telephone ringing in the deep middle of the night and who stumbled downstairs in the dark then stood with the receiver to her ear in the front room, standing on one leg and then changing to the other because the cold flowing into her bare feet from the stone flags was unendurable.

—We've lost her, her aunt said, muffled and different at the other end of the line; and confusedly Joyce thought for a moment she meant it literally, that somehow in the confusion and immensity of the hospital, where Joyce had never been, it might be easy to mislay a little girl, particularly one as stubbornly silent and inconspicuous as Kay.

Lil had heard the telephone too, and had followed Joyce down the dark stairs more cautiously. Now she was scratching matches, trying to light a candle.

—Tell your mother we lost her, Aunt Vera was saying angrily.

A match flared up and illuminated Lil's face just as she heard. Mutely Joyce proffered her the telephone, but Lil waved it off.

—I can't, I can't talk to her, she hissed, shaking her head. The match went out.

They stood in a cold dark silence, the sulphur smell livid on the air between them. Joyce understood that this was not just her mother's usual fear of the phone. Lil was thinking that if she'd been there with Kay, she'd have prevented this, she'd have held it off somehow. It was the way Vera was, so full of opinions, so determined to be different, that brought on catastrophe.

—Is she there? demanded Vera.

—I'll go and tell her.

—It was meningitis. The doctors gave her antipyretic drugs and antispasmodics. There was nothing they could do to save her. They keep them in the dark, because the light hurts them. I was holding ice to the back of her neck, to help the pain, and then she slipped away. They were bringing the serum from the infirmary to inject her with and the nurse had to tell them she'd gone. About an hour ago. We've been sitting with her, your uncle and I.

—All right, I'll tell her.

Joyce couldn't begin to find anything appropriate to say to her aunt: she felt herself a strangely neutral quantity, as if she didn't count, in relation to this disaster. After she hung the receiver back on the telephone she and Lil went on standing in the dark. Lil gave off an intense heat – she was always opening windows, and she often had to improvise a paper fan to cool herself – and also a special, encouraging smell, like sharp dried fruit (this was probably something to do with the cigarettes). Joyce knew both these things intimately, from all the childhood nights she'd slept with her mother, when she was ill or had bad dreams. She would have liked to cling to her now, to be consoled.

—I should have gone with her, Lil wailed softly. —I should have been there. They don't know her like I do. There was nothing wrong with her yesterday. It can't be right.

Joyce stood awkwardly, not knowing how to help.

Her strongest feeling in the days that followed was embarrassment, and a suspicious jealousy of this grief, dropped down like an extravagant unwanted drama in their lives, spoiling everything. She didn't even tell anyone about Kay at the College of Art, which she had begun attending that October. When she had to take a day off to go to the funeral, she simply said it was 'a relative', so that they all assumed it was someone old and unimportant; and the next morning she was back drinking coffee in a noisy, smoking, joking crowd in the Gardenia Café as if nothing had happened. Pictures of the scene rose in her mind: the small coffin, the stricken adults, Uncle Dick cupping his hand around his eyes to hide his weeping, the dismal Farmouth cemetery tucked at the end of a raw road that wound from behind the customs offices, past the bonded warehouses. She forced them back down again. These two possibilities must be held apart if she was to hang on to this new joyous life where she at last belonged.

For a week after Kay's funeral Vera stayed in her bed. The house was in disarray, the washing wasn't done, there were no proper meals, the children when they got home from school didn't change out of their uniforms but sat bickering or pretending to work or play battle-ships at the table while they listened to the noisy grieving of the two women, or the quarrelling between Aunt Vera and Uncle Dick. All the doors were left open, nobody tried to hide anything from them; this in itself was frightening. When a confused winter bird got in the house and flew around crashing into the windows it only seemed like a part of the craziness that had broken in. Guiltily Joyce tried to organise a few things. She brought home potatoes and meat from town and tried to cook stew, only she didn't know that it took hours for the meat to be tender, so they all sat round the table chewing and then leaving little parcels of pale chewed-up meat around the edge of their plates.

The other children were humbled to discover that Kay, who had been such an ordinary part of their lives and hadn't ever been much fussed over, could produce such extravagant adult effects. When Vera was crying Peter slammed the door and sat with his fists in his ears (it was a dreadful crying, in a voice of hers they didn't know, deep and cowlike). One evening Vera came down into the kitchen in her dressing gown with her hair wild and told Lil that she had seen a blue light hovering in her room, and how she had seemed to feel the weight of a child laid in the bed beside her.

—You know about this stuff. I suppose you'll say it was some sort of sign.

—I wish she would come to me, said Lil dully. —I can't feel anything.

—Is that the next thing? asked Vera. —Am I going to go mad? Am I going to start seeing visions and believing in spirits?

Then on the morning she was supposed to return to Amery-James she got up early and washed and dressed in her grey suit absolutely as usual, and pinned up her hair without a word, her brown complexion bleached, her lips pale, her eyes looking swimming and full not because she was weeping but because of how the flesh had fallen away from her face. Ann reported that at school the girls were frightened to do the least thing in lessons to cross her; a lugubrious cult grew up around her bereavement. Joyce was disgusted when she discovered that Ann had taken a photograph of Kay into school to pass around. Some girls had actually shed tears over it.

When Joyce was rummaging in Lil's drawer one morning, wanting to borrow her pair of black kid gloves, she found Kay's scrap of sucky blanket.

—Shouldn't you give this to Auntie Vera? she said.

—She's never asked me for it, she's never thought about it.

It hadn't been washed, and still had its grubby salty smell.

—Don't tell her I've got it, Lil said. —I don't see why I shouldn't keep something. It's nothing anybody else could want. But no doubt she'd find some way of putting me in the wrong over it.

She was sitting at her dressing table but not combing her hair or patting Nivea into her cheeks. Joyce put the bit of blanket away where she had found it, under the pretty, perfectly pressed blouses, satin, or with lace collars or embroidery, that were never worn. She wondered what her mother did all day at home without Kay to look after. When they all drove off to the city in the Austin in the mornings (Martin had after all got his place at the Cathedral School, and was already stealing chemicals from the science labs to make explosives at home) there was a bend in the lane where they used to look back and wave to Lil and Kay. Now Lil didn't even come out to see them off.

To Joyce's dismay, when she talked about the possibility of renting a flat in the city for her second year at college, Lil said she thought it was a good idea, and that she would bring Ann and Martin and come and live with her.

—I could get a little job to help us all out: with that and the pension we could manage fine.

—Is Aunt Vera's new house ready for her then?

—I hope she isn't building any hopes on that. Vera'll never see the inside of that house. It's time that she faced up to certain things.

It was true that they hadn't seen much of Uncle Dick since Kay died, after the first few days. When Vera was in her worst state, staying in bed all day and refusing to eat, he came once and went into the bedroom and brought out all his suits and ties. He didn't speak to any of them. Peter hated him. Joyce had witnessed a queer sort of fight between them: Peter planting himself with his arms and legs straddled across the kitchen doorway to stop his father getting out, saying he wanted to know 'what was going on'. He had a long bony face that had somehow never looked right on a child's body; it was better now he was growing taller and bigger to fit it, but he still couldn't stop himself weeping with vexation whenever he was angry. One of the hens scuttled past him into the room, and he kicked at it, missing and raising a flurry of squawks. Uncle Dick tried to push him out of the way and Peter clung to him with his arms and legs, sobbing that he wouldn't let him go until he told him where he was going.

Uncle Dick had looked at him dully and with disgust. —Think of your little sister, he said. —You should be ashamed of yourself, making a scene like a girl.

It seemed as though once the doors were opened in that house, any kind of crazy desperate thing could fly inside. In the spring after Kay died Vera was hatching a plan.

—Your aunt's got some daft idea, said Lil.

—It's not an idea, said Vera. —It's my duty.

Joyce stood blinking in the lamplight, in her taffeta striped skirt and her wellingtons: she was carrying her coat over her arm and her high-heeled brown suede sling-back shoes hooked by their straps over one finger. She had stayed for a party in town and caught the last bus home, which took her as far as Hallam: there she had fished out her wellingtons from under the hedge where she had hidden them in the morning and walked the last two miles in the moonlight. An owl had swooped over her head and her heart turned over; a car passed and she hid from it in the bushes. And all the time her thoughts had been so entirely absorbed in replaying the confused and intricately significant exchanges of the party she had left behind that now as the two of them turned on her as she came through the door she hardly knew where she was. She was afraid they would notice on her breath what she had been drinking: a fruit cup made deadly with pure alcohol stolen from the hospital by someone's boyfriend who was a medic. Luckily she had walked off the worst of her intoxication; only as she adjusted to the paraffin-smelling warmth she swayed with a twinge of nausea.

Lil had put a beer set on her hair and it was pinned to her head in flat curls tied around with an old scarf.

—Vera wants to bring our Gilbert to live here.

—Who's Gilbert?

—Our brother Gilbert.

—I thought he went away?

—He's been ill. He needs a home to go to.

—You don't know what he's like, said Lil. —For all you know, he may have had operations, he may be worse.

—Why did he go away in the first place?

—There was trouble. He fought with your grandfather.

—Your grandfather was a real Victorian, said Lil, even with pride. —He didn't have the modern ideas about encouraging children. After Ernest went off to the war he came down very hard on Gilbert, because he was the only one he'd got left, the only son.

When they lived in the North Joyce had often visited the tiny terraced house where her mother and aunt and

71

their five brothers and sisters grew up, with its curtains pulled almost across at the parlour window even in daylight, and a hairy sofa that prickled the backs of bare legs tormentingly. A short walk away from the house down a side street, through a door locked with a key, was her grandfather's garden full of brilliant flowers: once he had cut a big red one to put behind her ear, and then later at tea an earwig had crawled out of it and fallen on to her frock. Vera and Lil told fearsome stories of their father, of how he was so strict that when they were children they had to stand up to eat at table, and how once he snatched a book Vera was reading and threw it on the fire. Joyce found it hard to connect these stories with the gentle old man she remembered, scrupulous to protect her frock and shoes from dirt, laying out a bit of clean sack on top of a bucket for her to sit on. His huge hard hands and flat fingers were covered with old seams and scars that were blue like ink from the coal dust that got in (he worked in a mine). Dextrously he twisted off dead flower heads, pulled out weeds, and fastened leaning stems to lengths of cane with raffia; but when he put the flower in her hair his fingers trembled with the effort, as though she was something he was afraid to touch.

He was dead now, and her grandmother lived with one of her other daughters in Hebburn, and couldn't remember things.

—They were uneducated people, said Vera. —That could be forgiven them. But they had a hatred of learning. I used to creep down at night and rake up the coals to read by. Of course I pulled that book back out of the fire, but it was scorched and dirty. It was a library book: Mrs Craik's *John Halifax, Gentleman*. I thought I would never be able to visit the library again, I thought that was an end of everything I cared about. But then I met the librarian in the street, and she was so kind, and I told her all of it, and she came round and talked to Mam and Dad. 'You don't know what a precious thing you've got here,' she said. Not that they listened.

Several of Aunt Vera's stories featured women like this, enlightened and resilient and independent, intervening on her behalf with the forces of ignorance and superstition: as well as the librarian there was the teacher at grammar school who'd helped her to get into college, and an older friend at the Girl Guides who'd started her off on her botany and her interest in old churches.

—Uncle Gilbert won't want to come here, will he? Joyce asked. —Hasn't he got a home of his own?

Lil looked a heavy warning at her sister.

—I've changed, Joyce, said Vera dramatically. —I can't just sit back and watch all the iniquity of the world and not do anything about it.

Joyce shrugged. —Just so long as it doesn't mean I have to share my room with Ann.

—Vera should learn to let well alone, said Lil with foreboding.

It occurred to Joyce that Gilbert might have been in prison. The idea alarmed her; but she didn't want to ask them about it directly. There was something which made Joyce queasy in the conspiratorial way the two sisters sat brooding over things together at the kitchen table, even when they were quarrelling. Their talk was dark and thick and sticky as the malt and cod-liver oil the children were dosed with to keep off colds. She didn't want to give them the opportunity to hush up and exchange scalding glances and shut her out. She concentrated on her plans to get away and live a new young person's life with her friends in town.

Mysterious letters arrived at the house. Aunt Vera snatched them up and read them when she came in after school, not even waiting to take off her hat and gloves. Lil wrung her tea towel into a wet knot, in anxious resistance. Then in the Easter holidays Vera drove off in the Austin Seven and was gone three days without any explanation. Joyce was drawing in the apple-room when she heard the car whining in the lane and looked out of the window to see it nose on to the cobbles in front of the house, Aunt Vera sitting upright and tense in the passenger seat and at the wheel a boy with a long pale face and a tall shock of hair which looked fair through the windscreen glass. In fact when he stepped out of the car she saw that he was a man, not a boy, and that his hair was silvery like straw left to leach its colour out in the rain. Aunt Vera climbed out shakily from her side, and Joyce knew from the stoop of her shoulders and her brave lopsided smile as she threw her hand in a gesture of welcome around at the house and the outbuildings, that she was already full of doubt at what she had done, bringing her brother home.

Joyce could not think why Gilbert had come. He was tall and thin and although he didn't have a young face he seemed awkward like a teenager, with extravagantly long limbs, and ears and nose reddened as if they had stuck out too far into a raw wind. He stood lost in the slight drizzle in the yard and showed no sign of feeling rescued. Vera had to take him by an elbow and coax him inside. The sleeves of his suit were too short above his bony wrists.

—Lillie's here, Lil's here, she said. —Come in and see Lillie.

He submitted to it.

They were all introduced to him in the crowded kitchen (Peter came from his violin practice, Martin from where he was building a rocket in an outhouse). Gilbert's shirt collar was yellowed and tight over his adam's apple; his big shoes were cracked and hard and mottled with white as if they had been put away too long in a cupboard; his deep-set blue eyes were glancing and evasive. He put his arms around Lil, who turned to him with a blank reluctant face from where she had lifted a panful of her special doughnuts out of the stove; she patted his bent back as if she was soothing a child.

—Hallo Gil, she said warily. —After all this time.

At the kitchen table he ate the doughnuts one after another, while they were still too hot for the others to touch them.

—Did you fight in the war? Martin asked him.

—I did not, he said, licking sugar from his fingers intently. —I wanted to, but they wouldn't allow it.

75

The children couldn't always understand him; he mumbled to himself, and his Tyneside accent was broad.

—Gilbert was in hospital, Vera busily explained. —He's been ill a long time, but he's better now. And a good thing too, that he wasn't sent to the slaughter. This family gave enough of their young men.

—Our brother Ernest was killed, said Gilbert. —And Ivor, your father.

—He remembers! said Lil, as if he'd accomplished something.

—Well of course he remembers.

They gave him Kay's room for his own. Lil had dismantled the cot while Vera was away.

—Shouldn't there be another child? asked Gilbert. —A little girl?

For an uncomfortable moment they all thought he meant Kay.

—Oh, Ann's at a friend's house! Joyce suddenly understood. —She'll be back for tea.

He nodded. —I was sure there was two of you.

—Did they cut him? Has he had any operation? Joyce overheard Lil hiss to Vera under cover of a clatter of pans.

—He has not. The doctor said he had an insulin treatment. I can't speak highly enough of Dr Gurton. He's a very dedicated and very humane man. He spoke of great changes to come, with new pharmaceutical developments in the field.

—Gilbert doesn't seem too bad, said Lil cautiously.

* * *

He wasn't a nuisance around the place. He mostly sat in his room at first, or at the kitchen table, spelling stubbornly through an old newspaper; or he threw sticks for Winnie the bulldog in the field beyond the house. They were all obscurely weighed down with anxiety for him, however, and relieved if ever he showed signs of being happy with them. A one-sided grin slipped on his face occasionally like the quick flare of an unexpected light. Something in his movements was not quite right for a man of thirty: he was too quick and loose and absorbed in himself, he hadn't put on the containment and responsive gravity of a grown-up. Martin imitated his slow shuffling walk and his accent; Gilbert didn't seem to mind. He listened respectfully while Martin explained his latest science project. (This had to do with the parable about the man who was paid in grains of rice on a chessboard, doubling for each square. Martin and his friend were calculating how many grains there would actually be by the sixty-fourth square, and how many it took to make up a square inch, and whether the rice would really cover India a foot deep.)

In his suitcase Gilbert had brought a little case of bits of stuff for making flies for fishing, and for a while he and Martin drew close together, fiddling with pliers and cobbler's wax, tying fantastically intricate creations out of brightly dyed feathers and bits of tinsel and squirrel hair. He showed Martin how to wet his fingers and run them down the feathers so that the fibres separated and stood out at right angles to the quill. But Gilbert didn't have the patience for the fishing itself; much to Martin's indignation he wandered off and came home after an hour or so, leaving Martin to pack away the rods. 'He's got no sticking power,' Martin complained. Neither of them really knew how to fly-fish anyway, it seemed Gilbert had only been taught how to make the flies, not use them. The other thing Gilbert could do impressed Martin more. When he found that Martin had a welding torch and a clamp (they had been Ivor's), he asked for everyone's spare pennies and halfpennies, and in one of the outhouses he began welding together a model aeroplane out of the coins, a Hurricane. He had a picture to work from, torn out of a magazine. The model was a complex and beautiful thing: quite large, about eighteen inches from end to end of the fuselage. The coins were welded together like miniature riveted plates, then burnished coppery pink. Martin learned how to heat the coins and shape them, but he could never make them curve with Gilbert's precision. Gilbert even made a little pilot, with a tiny helmet, and tiny hands on the controls, and a tiny coppery face with a moustache. He said he had learned to do this in hospital. His life seemed to be made up of hobbies, and not of real man's work, as if he was stuck in boyhood.

He didn't like Peter playing the violin. Sometimes when he played Gilbert would take Winnie out walking in the fields, or he would sit shaking his head as if he had an insect in his ears; he suggested that Peter should learn 'something with a bit more life in it'. Peter, who was touchy about his playing, pretended he couldn't understand anything Gilbert said. In the evenings Gilbert twiddled the knobs on the wireless to find swing and dance-band music: sometimes he couldn't tune it properly and sat with his ear close to the wire mesh, frowning with ferocious absorption as he followed after the trailing ends of happy party music that came and went.

From time to time letters still came for Vera. One afternoon Joyce saw one of them lying opened on her aunt's dressing table. She took it out of its envelope and read across the top of the sheet of letter paper inside that it was from Appleton Mental Hospital. The Dr Gurton that Vera took every opportunity to mention was deputy superintendent there. His letter was very short, thanking her for sending him the latest news of Gilbert's progress, praising her for her enlightened views on the treatment of mental illness in the 'therapeutic community'. Scrawled across the bottom of the sheet he had added, 'I am sorry but I do not know the novel by A. P. Herbert on divorce-law reform which you recommend.' Perhaps Dr Gurton was trying to discourage Vera from sending him letters. Joyce had seen her aunt writing to him, covering sheet after sheet in her handsome spiky italic hand.

She didn't tell the others. She thought that the mental hospital was worse than prison; she felt incensed against Vera for inflicting Gilbert on them. She began to keep out of his way as if whatever he had might be contaminating. It wasn't Gilbert himself who disgusted her. He had shown her card tricks and blushed with pleasure when she couldn't guess how they were done. But the idea of his connection to such an unimaginable place, full of an assembly of all the horrors she had ever had a glimpse of in the street, in tow after shamed mothers, or hobbling and gibbering by themselves: that was unbearable, she had to shut it out. Uncle Dick on one of his rare visits to the house said that Vera must be out of her mind, bringing Gilbert to stay where there were growing girls. Vera retorted that it was Dick who shouldn't be allowed near growing girls. Joyce asked for a bolt to be fixed on the inside of the bathroom door.

She thought that Gilbert began to avoid contact with her, too. This might be because she was going off to college every day; perhaps he thought she was too full of her superior self. Perhaps he was offended by the careful rituals of preparation she went through in the evenings, as if she required more complex maintenance than the rest of them: rinsing her delicates in the sink, mending her stockings, altering clothes, spreading the blanket on the kitchen table to press with a flat-iron heated on the stove her outfit for the next day.

Ann and Gilbert hung about together, following after the geese and, as Lil called it, 'bothering them'. Lil had raised the geese from little grey chicks; she used their eggs for baking and omelettes, and they were supposed to be eaten at Christmas, although this year because of Kay no one had been able to contemplate asking Farmer Brookes to take them away and kill them. Joyce quailed at their loud gabblings and honkings and snapping beaks, but Ann was fearless with them, she loved them. They attacked any visitors with their wings open and their necks outstretched, hissing; the delivery men wouldn't get out from their vans until Lil had driven the geese off, flapping at them with her apron. Gus, Ann's favourite, was the ringleader and the most vicious. She crooned to him, smoothing down his creamy fat neck, burying her hands under his wings, kissing his beak: he loved nothing better than to stand pressed dazedly up against her while she tickled him. Gilbert, in a kind of symmetry, made up to Flo. Gus and Flo slept together in the grass in the orchard, a plump heap the colour of yellow cream, feathers as satisfactorily intricate as neat knitting. They always slept with one eye open; if two of them slept together, one watched right, one left.

Ann played with Gilbert as if he was another pet. He submitted patiently while she stroked the lines of his face with her fingers, pinched the lobes of his ears, nibbled his hands. They competed in 'scissors, paper, stone', and she always won because she saw his fist first and changed hers in a fraction of a second. He traipsed round after her in obedience to commands she snapped out in her bossy voice. She didn't call him Uncle Gilbert as Vera said they should, just Gilly. Once she dressed him up in one of Lil's dresses over his trousers, and tied a bow of ribbon in his hair and put lipstick and clip earrings on him. When Lil gave her a talking to, Gilbert said she didn't mean any harm by it.

—You don't know her, Lil said. —She means it all right.

Ann teased Gus and Flo, offering bits of grass and snatching them out of reach, ruffling their neck feathers the wrong way, picking up their patient pink feet. Flo

81

didn't mind, but Gus would lose his temper and then Gilbert laughed at him, and held his beak closed if he tried to snap at them. Their wings were clipped, but they could fly high enough to then come skidding down along the surface of the rhines with their feet out, sending up a crest of water to either side: they seemed to do it for the sheer pleasure of it. That made Gilbert laugh; he sat watching them for half an hour at a time, crouched down on his haunches with his elbows on his knees. Joyce remembered that in the North she had seen men sitting out in the street like this, the miners outside their houses and on the street corners, smoking and talking with their friends. Another thing that reminded her of those men was the way he smoked Lil's Woodbines, nursing them down to the last nub between thumb and forefinger, behind the palm of his hand. Vera got exasperated with how he mashed up his potatoes into his gravy and drank his tea out of a saucer, and how he liked to wash stripped down to his trousers at the kitchen sink, lathering and puffing and blowing. Joyce couldn't see how he was going to last in the South, where none of these ways fitted in with how people did things.

Lil had packed his bag to go into that place. Her mam had sent the neighbours for her when Gilbert started on his rampage in the afternoon. Not that any of them had thought he was going in for more than a few days. She hadn't thought at the time that he was sick, just angry. Gilbert had always had a temper: when he was a baby scarcely toddling he used to beat his head deliberately against the floor when he was crossed, he'd even crawl off the rug to where he could beat it against the bare tiles because it hurt more. And when he and Ernest fought as boys, Gilbert often came out best even though Ernest was bigger, because Ernest was slow and gentle where Gilbert was wild, he clung on like a vicious dog, she'd seen his big boot stamping down on Ernest's head where he had him pinned on the floor, cursing him from between his clenched teeth. This fighting used to break Mam's heart; Gilbert was her favourite, her late last baby, beautiful with his yellow curls. She'd dressed him up when he was small in a plaid tam-o'-shanter set sideways at a jaunty angle, there was a photograph of that somewhere. Not that Gilbert was angry all the time, of course. He could be a charmer, with his quick grin. Girls loved him, all the better it seemed because he was so moody, he was always going with one of them, then the girl would call round asking where he was and Mam had to lie for him, although she'd never tell a lie for anyone but Gilbert. Ivor couldn't get on with Gilbert. He'd said he was so sharp he'd cut himself.

Something had had to be done, that afternoon. He had thrown furniture down the stairs, and fired his airgun out of the window, although the window had been open and he hadn't hit anything. They couldn't even remember afterwards what the quarrel had been about. It would have been about nothing. It would have been their dad pulling Gilbert up as usual for some little thing, for picking up a comb that wasn't his and putting it in his pocket, or making some disrespectful joke about their grandmother, or even just pushing past Dad in a hurry on the stairs. You could see what it was that made Dad pick on Gilbert. Gilbert went about life in those days with an air as if he knew better than his elders. He didn't want to work in the mine like his dad and brother (not that Ernest could get work anyway, before the war). Gilbert was training as an electrician. He said, 'Dad, I'll be earning in a week what you earn in a month.'

Lil remembered packing up his shirts and washcloth and a razor (which of course they'd taken off him), laying it all out with his pen and some writing paper in the little suitcase like you would for a trip to the seaside. She did not see how he would ever be able to forgive her for this. She hadn't been in her right mind, that winter after Ivor was killed, although she knew she had seemed all right, she hadn't made a fuss, she'd got on with everyday life. But it should have been her they locked up and gave insulin treatment to, for being mad enough to calmly lay out her brother's things for him to go to that place. Now she couldn't look him in the eye.

It distressed Vera that Gilbert spent so much time asleep. He didn't get up until late, then often during the day when they looked for him they'd find he'd slipped back into his room and into bed again. She tried to get him to take an interest in things. She got down poetry books from her shelves and read to him, and in the evenings read from her complete set of Dickens ('my beloved Dickens' she called him). She suggested that they should go out walking and she could teach him to identify the flora and fauna of the area. She brought up topical subjects to discuss with him, collectivisation in the Soviet Union, vegetarianism, the atom bomb. Gilbert wrote a beautiful painstaking round copperplate hand (they knew this from the crosswords he did, or when he kept the score at cards), but he didn't show any interest in the diary Vera encouraged him to keep. She worried about what she called to Lil his 'physical needs'. Sometimes unselfconsciously he scratched or rubbed his groin and she quickly knocked his hand away.

—He needs to be doing some hard physical work, she said to Lil. —To tire himself out. Perhaps I'll ask at the farm if they need anyone.

Gilbert began to do some work for Farmer Brookes. It was a muddy old farm with a dozen cows and small fields growing mangolds and hay and millet. The farmer ran it with his wife; their son worked on the docks. Gilbert helped with the milking – which was still done by hand – and put the churns out on their platform to be picked up by the lorry from the Milk Marketing Board; he fetched the cows home from the fields in the afternoons and in June he helped with the hay harvest.

—It's what he needs, said Vera. —Outdoors physical work, wholesome and timeless, close to nature, not intellectually demanding.

Gilbert wasn't terribly reliable. Sometimes he got up late, or wandered home early, or forgot to finish some dirty job. Luckily the farm was run on haphazard lines, and the easy-going old farmer seemed to adapt to

Gilbert's arbitrary comings and goings. Anyway, he was only paying him a few shillings.

—Don't you think he's happy here? Vera wondered in the kitchen, bent over the dirty saucepan she was scrubbing at, burdened with worry, shedding hairpins into the dishwater. —Don't you think we did right?

—Search me, said Lil, with a closed face, cleaning eggs at the table with a wet rag.

—With his family round him instead of strangers, Vera went on. —Free to come and go as he wants, working out in the fresh air, taking a new interest in life. Dr Gurton thinks it must be doing him a world of good.

Lil had only been to visit Gilbert in the hospital once. The idea of this scalded her now, in his presence. How must he account for this, what must he think of her? She had pretended to herself that because he was ill he would not notice whether she went or not; but she was sure now that she had always known this was not true. When Gilbert was born she had just started in service; she came home on her days off and lavished all her love on him, imagining he was a baby of her own, dressing him up in his pretty white dresses and wheeling him proudly round the streets in the old pram. For her wedding he had been a pageboy in a velvet jacket, and he had sung out all by himself with 'There Is a Green Hill Far Away' at the moment she and Ivor were exchanging their vows (she was delighted, but Ivor was put off and muddled his responses).

She had not gone to visit Gilbert in that place again

because the one time she saw him there it had been a horror; she had been visited in her dreams afterwards by the little twisted man with a brown wizened face and cleft palate who had come into the room while they were waiting for Gilbert to be brought out; he had asked her for cigarettes and sworn at her when she didn't respond to him because she didn't understand. Everything she was afraid of in those days she had simply shut out from her thoughts. She had known that they were giving Gilbert something to keep him in a stupor, because she could smell it everywhere (Mam thought that the stupor was his illness). He hadn't said much: he told them that he had asked to work in the hospital laundry because you could give yourself a decent shave there at your own pace, and he complained that the pillows were stuffed with straw, and that they were put to bed at seven thirty. His voice was slurred as if his tongue was thick, and he had a bruise on his temple. When they got up to go he asked when he could come home with them, and Mam had said soon, as soon as he was better.

—I don't want to miss everything, he said. —I know I've got some catching up to do.

Mam went up there every week. Even Vera had gone more often than Lil had, even though she had never been much interested in Gilbert when he was born. It was Vera who told Lil that the patients weren't allowed knives, so they had to eat everything with a spoon. But Vera had been off in her own dreams, at that time when Gilbert was put away: with Dick gone in the Navy and Peter at school, she had volunteered to work at a book

87

collection point in a church hall where people brought their old books to be pulped and made into paper for the war effort. She said she was sorting and bundling up the books, but she was mostly feverishly reading them. She went home with armfuls more to read before she brought them back again the following week. She sometimes hardly knew who she was when you spoke to her.

Lil had said to her mother that there was nothing wrong with Gilbert. But her mother lived in fear of the doctors, and wouldn't argue with them or make any trouble when they asked her to sign papers. They said he had delusions, and that he was a danger to himself and others. And Lil allowed herself, so long as she didn't actually have to see him, to pretend to believe all this. She was kept busy anyway thinking about other things, the children and the house and trying to take in a bit of sewing to eke out her war widow's pension. But she knew all the time he must be wondering why his favourite sister didn't come.

Gilbert got lovesick over a girl: Daphne, a niece of Farmer Brookes's wife. She had a job in the smelting works, but she used to cycle up from where she lived in Farmouth and visit her aunt on the summer evenings.

Joyce knew Daphne. She had never spoken to her, but she had seen her, before she even knew she was Mrs Brookes's niece. One hot summer's afternoon a couple of years before, she and Ann had decided not to wait at the Seaman's Mission for their uncle but to walk the two miles home instead. The road ran past the smelting works; the workers must have been on a break, and because it was so hot they were out in the yard, the men in their vests, the girls bare-legged, smoking and bantering. Joyce and Ann had put their school hats in their satchels and carried their blazers over their arms, but nonetheless they must have looked unmistakably like the nicely brought-up schoolgirls they were: they toiled past in an agony of conspicuousness, their faces set in masks of indifference to the remarks and jokes that flew after them hard as stones, about French lessons, and hot stockings, and getting their uniforms dirty in the grass. Daphne was the loudest of the girls in the yard, and the one who broke into the Carmen Miranda impression ('I-I-I-I-I-I-I-I like you ve-ry much'), at the top of her voice, swinging her hips and waving her arms over her head, showing the sprouting thick dark hair under her arms, making everyone laugh at her. She was only about Joyce's age, but she was tall and big-busted, with a curved red-lipsticked mouth and luxuriant black perm. Her eyes were small and darting; black, with a slight cast in one of them.

After that, although she avoided walking past the smelting works ever again, Joyce seemed to see Daphne often, around in Farmouth and sometimes on the road up to the farm. And always Daphne seemed to look at her with dangerous, intimate mockery, although they never spoke. The whole gist of the teasing and the danger was that it was exposing and humiliating to be still at school, and superior to be adult and free and working.

Yet complicatedly what Joyce felt with a plunge of guilt whenever she saw Daphne was that there was no good reason why she should be still at school, and then at college, and why Daphne should have to be exposed to what Joyce imagined was the horror of the smelting works.

Gilbert borrowed an old bike from the farm and every evening that Daphne didn't appear he rode down to Farmouth to be near her. Sometimes she visited the house with some message for Gilbert from her uncle. It wasn't clear whether she encouraged him or not. If ever anyone saw them together, Daphne would be in the lead, swaying her hips to some dance tune inside her head, and Gilbert would be traipsing after, neck bent, eyes down. She called him Geordie and laughed at the way he spoke. Vera followed the affair with great anxiety, and warned Gilbert to 'be careful'; he shook his head as if her words were a distracting buzzing.

Martin and Peter hated Daphne and were terrified of her. She called them 'little boys', and told them how the farmers had to cut off the lambs' 'little winkies' to make them behave. They reacted to her violently, frenziedly: if she touched them they scrubbed the place with soap, and they said she smelled. She did wear a lot of scent – Chypre de Coty, which Gilbert replaced for her out of his wages from Farmer Brookes – and it was true too that if she'd cycled up from Farmouth she would be sweating, with big wet patches showing on her blouse under her arms, her face red, drops of sweat trickling down the sides of her nose. Joyce would have been humiliated and appalled at herself in that condition, but Daphne seemed to relish it, wiping her face with the back of her hand, blowing and gasping comically while she got her breath.

—Hot ride? Joyce said.

—Bloody hot, said Daphne. —Want to feel?

And she pulled her sopping shirt away from her wet back as if Joyce seriously might.

Daphne didn't exactly make conversation; she kept up a stream of jokes and sayings and teasings. When she made a burping noise she said, 'Pardon me for being rude, it was not me it was my food'; she told Peter to stop gawping or the wind would change and he'd be stuck like that; she said, 'Every little helps, said the lady as she piddled in the sea' and, when she leaned across someone, 'Scuse me reaching, I've just got off the boat'.

When Martin and Peter disappeared sometimes in the evenings, Joyce suspected they were haunting the dunes behind the beach in hope and dread of finding Gilbert and Daphne there together.

—She's foul, Mum, said Peter. —You should tell Uncle Gilbert he's not allowed to bring her in the house.

—He's a perfect right to make friends with who he likes, Vera said sorrowfully.

Influenced by Mr Scofield, his violin teacher, Peter had started listening to classical music. They had a gramophone in the front room that Dick had bought second-hand for Vera in the North: a tall wooden cabinet with a lid that propped open at the top, doors at the front, a wind-up handle on the side. The needles were made of bone and had to be sharpened on a piece of emery paper; new ones were kept in a tiny tin with the 'His Master's Voice' dog on the front. Peter sorted through the records in their brown card sleeves, mastering the names of the composers, sampling and replacing them, quickly expert in the rituals of placing the record, checking it for dust, lowering the arm. Vera found him adjusting the speed because the turntable was too slow and played everything slightly out of tune. She would never have noticed. She gave way to her son with a new respect and sat mutely while he explained to her.

—Listen to this, Ma. This is a jolly bit. Then it gets all tragic and moody. Especially listen to the horns. Only they ought to be brighter: the Philharmonic do it better, you should hear the recording old Scoffer's got, it's splendid.

The front room smelled of damp: the flags were laid directly on the earth, and they hardly ever lit a fire in there except at Christmas. It was overcrowded with big pieces of furniture, chairs and sideboards and occasional tables which no one had tried to properly arrange. Vera's things were heavy carved oak, she and Dick had bought them along with their first house in Gateshead. Lil's were cheap utility. They were doubled up in readiness for when their lives might separate again.

Peter was as tall as Vera was now. He started to advise her on her dress, as well as on her reading and her opinions. Her blue scarf was a ghastly clash with her green blouse; and if she didn't replace her horrible old handbag, he wouldn't be seen out with her. She ought to read Dylan Thomas and George Barker, not stuffy old Masefield and de la Mare. Vera was surprisingly compliant; almost girlish in her willingness to relinquish her command to this authoritative son. She looked at him in quizzical pleased surprise, as though she did not quite know where he had sprung from.

Gilbert said he was going to marry Daphne. No one knew whether he had really asked her. Ann pestered him over it, whether it was going to be in church, what Daphne would wear, had he bought her a ring, would there be bridesmaids.

—And if you have children, what are you going to call them?

—Now that's enough, said Lil sternly. —Stop that teasing.

—It's not teasing, Ann said, opening her eyes wide. —Isn't it real? Why can't I ask him?

One summer afternoon Joyce was packing in her bedroom: she was going to spend a week in Paris with friends from the Art College. Dresses and blouses and underclothes, carefully mended and pressed, were laid out on the bed beside the open suitcase. She had sewed herself a new grey Liberty print dress with a full skirt and a white patent-leather belt: to earn the money for this and for the trip she had been working since the college term ended for a friend of Uncle Dick's in a marine insurance office in the city. Swallows were swooping dizzily in the big empty blue bowl of sky outside, the wood pigeons were heating up their end-of-tether crooning, the weather was languid and dreamy. Then Gilbert was suddenly in the yard, home from the Brookeses' before he should have been, in a flurry of noise and banging.

Joyce looked out from her window; Lil and Ann ran out from the kitchen to see what the matter was. Gilbert picked up the tin bucket from where it stood outside the back door and sent it hurtling across the yard. Lil had washed the kitchen floor and the bucket was full of dirty water which sluiced out in an interesting arc, sending the hens squawking and flattening themselves close to the ground in panic. The bucket bounced off a wall and along the cobbles with a jubilant clanging. Lil and Ann screamed. Gilbert kicked at the hens and then he picked up the outhouse shovel and hurled that after the bucket.

—Gilly, don't! cried Ann.

—Stop it, stop that, said Lil, running after him and trying to hold on to him as he reached around for something else to throw, found the bike he'd just ridden back on and picked it up in his hands as if it was a toy. —Whatever's the matter? Put that down and stop misbehaving. You'll hurt somebody.

Gilbert didn't say a word. He lifted the heavy old bike right up above his head and flung it down flat so that it jarred and leaped and skidded on its side across to where Ann dodged quickly back inside the kitchen. The bike lamp crunched and sprinkled glass like sugar, the front wheel buckled. Gilbert shook off Lil and picked up a

94

rusted old rake which he thrust deliberately through a window with an explosive tinkling: it was only a small filthy old cobwebbed pane in the outhouse where they kept the chicken feed and paraffin. Then, with the rake, Gilbert strode off down the side of the house.

Lil burst into tears and held her apron over her face.

Vera had been making notes from a new book on Victorian social reform at a table in the front room. Now she came out blinking into the aftershock of the scene.

—Goodness me, she said. —Whatever was all that about?

—You see, said Lil, shaking her head behind her apron. —He isn't all right.

—What did he say?

—He didn't say anything. He's gone down to the rhine.

Vera took in the damage: it didn't look much with Gilbert gone, just the bike sprawled down and the yard untidy. —Well, this is too silly, she said. —I suppose I'd better go after him and ask him what's going on, if nobody else will.

She pushed her hair behind her ears and set off down the path with an impatient schoolmistress's forbearing frown and authoritative step.

—He's got the rake, shouted Lil.

—Oh has he indeed, Vera retorted, undeterred.

Joyce joined the others downstairs and they waited in the yard for Vera to come back.

—Will he try to drown himself? Lil thought suddenly.

Ann and Joyce looked at her in dismay; although, the

rhines were so dry in the summer months that drowning would have taken some ingenuity.

There was a sudden fracas of agitated honking from the geese down at the rhine. Then they saw Vera: running and leaping up the path in her stockinged feet, her shoes kicked off somewhere, her hair flying and her mouth open, yelling to them to get inside. They bundled in and she flew into the house after them, gasping for breath, and slammed and bolted the door, leaning back against it with her chest heaving and her hair all drooping out of its pins. She and Lil stared wide-eyed at one another.

—Did he say anything?

Vera shook her head.

—Did he go for you?

She nodded.

—Hell's bells.

For the rest of the afternoon they stayed bolted in the house in a state of siege, with someone on lookout in the upstairs window for when the boys came back from fishing. Lil thought they should phone Dick but Vera said to wait and see how Gilbert was when he calmed down. They waited for him to turn up at the house, with or without his rake. By night-time he still hadn't come: they went to bed with the back door bolted, but left the outhouses open so he would have somewhere warm to sleep.

In the morning Ann said that Gus was acting funny. Vera went out to see if Gilbert was anywhere around: she even went down to the rhine, treading carefully in her slippers in the dew, looking for her shoes beside the path.

—Gone, she said. —He's gone.

The sisters looked at one another in consternation.

—What will he do? said Lil.

—What shall I tell Dr Gurton? Vera wailed.

They stuffed her shoes with newspaper and put them to dry, while they used the telephone to call the hospital, long distance.

—Look at Gus, said Ann. —There's something wrong with him.

The geese were in the yard, wanting to be fed. Gus stood apart from the others, his wings half open and dragging, his eyes filmed over. He wouldn't let any of them come near him, he flapped and struggled if they tried, but they could see his neck was twisted with an ugly lump in it, and that he couldn't hold up his head. Vera sent Martin to call Farmer Brookes, who came round to have a look.

—How's he gone and done that? the farmer said.

—We don't know, said Vera and Lil together.

Lil said, —We just found him like that, when we got up this morning.

The farmer persuaded Gus that he meant well, and Gus let him probe gently with his fingers into the creamy neck.

—Looks like it's broken, I'm afraid, poor old chappie. Got caught, maybe, in a bit of wire or something: although he's not cut himself. Got any apples left to make sauce? Might as well put him out of his misery, Mrs Stevenson. Want me to see to it?

Farmer Brookes carried Gus off through the orchard in the morning sunshine, holding him around the middle; Gus opened his wings so that it looked as though the farmer as he walked was wrestling with an angel. Ann wouldn't watch him go; she sank down on the doorstep with her head buried in her arms in grief. They told the Brookes to eat the goose themselves.

When Joyce came back from Paris she caught the last bus out of the city to the Docks: she had arranged to telephone from the Docks police station for Vera to come and pick her up in the car. The bus was crowded: a horrible old sailor with grey stubbly cheeks and breath that reeked of drink fell asleep beside her, and his head rolled on to her shoulder so many times that she gave up trying to push him off. She concentrated all her efforts on keeping Paris intact inside her – coffee and bread and Dior and wine and a little restaurant with red-checked tablecloths on the Boul' Mich – so as not to lose one precious drop in collision with the ugly things of home. She had felt instantly, intimately, that she belonged to Paris; miraculously she had seemed to understand what the Parisians said to her, far beyond the reach of her schoolgirl French. When the bus stopped and all the passengers shuffled up to get off, she realised with a shock that Daphne had been sitting all the time only a couple of seats behind her. Joyce had to pull down her heavy suitcase from the rack; she was hotly aware of the other girl watching her struggle, but they didn't smile or even look at one another.

As Joyce carried her suitcase the fifty yards in the dark to the dock gates, Daphne came up swiftly behind her on her bike, which she must have left locked up somewhere near the bus stop. Joyce heard the whirring of her wheels and smelled Chypre de Coty.

—*Bong-jooer*. Had a nice time in old gay Paree?

—Yes thank you, said Joyce.

Daphne was wobbling on the bike, weaving the handlebars to keep pace with Joyce's walking.

—Where's Gilbert? she asked.

—I don't know. He went away, I think.

Daphne described a wide arc then came alongside Joyce again. —One sandwich short of a picnic, if you ask me. Something funny about him.

Joyce changed hands on her suitcase.

—Don't you think?

—I'm afraid I have to go in here, said Joyce. —To use the telephone.

Daphne grinned incredulously through the gates at the police station; possibly she thought Joyce was so frightened of her that she was going to take refuge with the law.

—Oh well, she said. —If you see him, tell him *au revoyer* from me. Tell him he's a naughty boy, leaving my uncle in the lurch.

She cycled off under the streetlamps, making the bike dance in wide curves from one side of the road to the other, sitting back on the saddle with her hands in the pockets of her short jacket.

* * *

They found out that Gilbert had hitched his way up north to see his mother; their sister Selina, whose husband played the clarinet at the Theatre Royal in Newcastle, gave him some money. After that there was no news from him for years. He left the model Hurricane with half a fuselage and one wing; Martin tried to finish it but in the end had to resign himself to building a crash scene around it, using artificial grass from the greengrocer's and making ruined buildings out of papier mâché, decorating them with German shop signs and a Nazi flag.

Someone explained to Joyce much later – at a time when all the old methods of treating psychiatric patients were coming into disrepute and everybody was reading R. D. Laing – what the insulin treatment actually consisted of. Patients fasted for fourteen hours and then were put into a rubber-sided bed, as a protection against the convulsions produced by the drug; an insulin coma was deliberately induced, and then the patient had to be revived by counteractive injections into the vein. These didn't always work: sometimes there was an unseemly struggle round the bed, bringing the patient back to consciousness. Joyce told admiringly then the story of her aunt's rescue; she didn't confess how fervently at the time she had wished Gilbert back where he came from, and how sometimes even now she looked and didn't look for him with guilty dread in the faces of the beggars and winos who passed her in the street.

Lil became convinced Gilbert had joined up and fought in Korea and died there. She said she'd seen him once at a seance; she spoke about it in the special voice she used for the transcendent: stubborn and emotionally uplifted.

—He was in uniform. He was all bloody. But he was very calm; and smiling. He came to tell us that he was finally at peace.

This voice particularly irritated Vera.

—It's enough to make anyone despair, said Vera. —How can you be comforted by something that didn't happen? You don't seem able to distinguish between dreams and real things.

Vera at that time was clearing out cupboards in the old house, throwing away the accumulated rubbish of their life there with ruthlessness and zeal. She and Peter were going to move into a flat near Amery-James, she was going to take out divorce proceedings against Uncle Dick.

—Peace! she exclaimed. —What kind of travesty is that? Peace, through war. Is that the best solution you can come up with?

Three

Ray and Iris Deare were one of the couples everyone wanted to know. They were both painters. As soon as Ray finished studying Fine Art at the college he had been invited to join the teaching staff; he taught drawing to Joyce in her second year. She was terrified of him, always imagining how impatient he must feel at having to be bothered with her flawed work. There were others in the class, talented and confident, with whom Ray carried on a dialogue she greedily listened in on and soaked up: Cézanne's *petite sensation*, the difference between Picasso's and Braque's Cubist experiments, the importance of the spaces between the shapes, the need for a pencil no harder than HB and no softer than B, Degas's lithographs of prostitutes. The first time she heard her teacher use the word 'prostitute' casually, as if it was just another fact in the world, Joyce felt something crumble in the pit of her stomach, choking and intoxicating her.

Ray hardly ever spoke to her directly, even when

sometimes he reached across her shoulder to change something in her drawing, so that his tweedy rough sleeve was against her cheek for a few moments and she could smell his cold pipe in his pocket. He was untidy, shortish, with a crumpled lyrical face and brown curly hair; his wet brown eyes might have been doglike, pleading and needy, except that they were always veiled with irony and jokes.

—Miss Stevenson, he said to her once. —You're not looking. You're only drawing what you think is there. Don't think. You have to learn to be stupid in order to draw.

Joyce didn't mind. She knew what he meant. She liked the invitation to be stupid. She practised losing herself in the quiet of the life room, where the intent soft patter of pencils and charcoal was as necessary and soothing as breathing. If anyone spoke it woke her as if from a dream.

Iris Deare was training to be a primary-school teacher. In the beginning it was Iris that Joyce was in love with, at least as much as Ray. It was Iris who invited her round to visit them at their flat perched high on the first floor of one of the old steep Georgian terraces that overhung the river in Hilltop. In the sitting room – the lounge, Joyce learned to call it – there were three floor-length sash windows. Joyce had never seen anything like this room before: it was an inspiration. The floorboards were painted black, the walls were grey and hung with paintings and drawings and prints wherever there was space; nothing in the room was there because it was useful, but only if it was interesting, or beautiful. A huge old antique chaise longue stood along the back wall, its leather ripped and its horsehair stuffing leaking out; it was heaped with cushions, embroidered oriental ones and home-made ones covered in Liberty fabrics or batik prints Iris had done herself. In one corner of the room stood an old rocking horse with its paint washed off and its mane and tail worn down to stubble: Iris had found it put out with the rubbish in the street.

—Poor old love, she said crooningly, rubbing the horse's stubble with her cheek, kissing his flaring nostrils that had once been brilliant red. —But *we* think he's a magnificent charger still, don't we?

One end of the long room, beyond a sagging screen of carved oriental wood, was given over to be Ray's studio. The flat always smelled of paint and turps. There were no curtains at any of the windows: Joyce couldn't imagine how that felt, never being able to close yourself off from being seen.

—Why would you want to shut that out? Iris reasonably asked, gesturing to the view of pale tiered wedding-cake terraces, steeply dropping woods, the twisting ribbon of the river, the cranes of the city docks (neglected because most of the traffic had gone to the port at the river's mouth where Joyce's uncle worked). Beyond the river, spreading to the hills in the distance, the flat plain was built up with Victorian terraces, warehouses, the tobacco factories. It was scarred with ruined churches and waste plots where the bombs had fallen.

Iris made coffee in a little metal pot that sat on the

gas ring, real coffee, which Joyce had only ever tasted in France. It was bitter and thick, not like she remembered it, but she swallowed it down as best she could, eagerly, like an initiation.

—Look, Ray, said Iris. —Isn't she just one of those Epstein bronze heads?

Ray was stretched out on the chaise longue reading the newspaper with his shoes off, bright yellow socks showing a hole. Iris swept Joyce's hair up and held it in a twisted knot on top of her head; she took Joyce's chin in her fingers and pushed her face round to present her profile. Iris's hands were very fine boned, like all of her: she was dark and tiny with a miniature perfection Joyce yearned for, creamy pale skin, high cheekbones, slanting interrogative eyebrows, a tense high ribcage, a long swinging rope of dark hair down her back. She smelled of the unusual French soap she used, made with honey and almonds; her nails were perfectly shaped and painted a dark crimson like her lipstick. Her slender fingers were weighted down with huge exotic rings she'd found for next to nothing in junk shops. Joyce knew she would have passed over these rings if she'd been looking, thinking they were brash and cheap, not seeing how clever and striking they could be if you knew how to carry them off.

Ray bestowed a cursory glance on Joyce, Iris holding her still for him to see; he grunted something that might have been an indifferent assent. She was embarrassed: she didn't want him to think she was pushing herself on his attention.

106

—It's your wonderful chunky squareness, said Iris. —You should wear your hair like this. And some huge primitive earrings, like an Easter Island statue.

Gently, not wanting to offend her friend, Joyce pulled away her head and shook out her hair, blushing. —I couldn't get away with it, she said. —I'm not beautiful like you.

Ray grunted again.

Joyce did begin to grow her hair, though, so that she could wear it in a swinging rope.

Because Ray had so recently been a student himself (he was only five or six years older than Joyce), he mixed with the students as much as with the other teaching staff. The crowd around him and Iris gathered at the Gardenia Café, or at the jazz club held in a disused floor of one of the old tobacco warehouses on Fridays, or at each other's flats and houses for parties. In fine weather, in their breaks, they draped themselves around the statuary of the Empire fountain opposite the entrance to the Art College: there were photographs of them disporting among the sea folk, someone astride a mermaid's tail, a face with puffed cheeks pretending to blow a triton's trumpet, hands squeezing a pair of verdigris-green bronze breasts. The men in the crowd were noisy, argumentative, the girls mostly deferred to them: they were louder, older, many of them had already done their two years' national service. And there were more of them, of course. Passionate discussions raged, always through a thick cloud of cigarette and pipe smoke: over art, over jazz, over privilege and class. At that time, in the mid-fifties, all the men wanted to be working class; they argued over whose parents were most authentically proletarian. Ray Deare's father was a travelling representative for the Co-op; Dud Mason's worked in a local print shop; Pete Smith's had been a milkman but now worked in an office for the GEC. Stefan Jeremy kept quiet; everyone knew his father was a partner in a London firm of architects.

The men leaped up shouting in the Gardenia sometimes when the argument got too heated, and threw back their chairs, and were asked to leave by the waitresses. Some of these waitresses, the attractive ones, would even be invited into the arguments to adjudicate. Dud Mason, big and bear-shaped, untidy curls pushed behind surprising tiny ears, would call them over to decide whether there was any point in figurative art any longer. Or Yoyo Myers, who was short and springy with a face as pretty as a girl's, and played the tea-chest bass in a skiffle band, would ask them whether they liked, really honestly liked, the sound of modern jazz. Some of the waitresses were students at the Art College or the University; some reappeared later in the crowd as the girlfriends of the very men they had had to ask to leave.

Joyce could have told everybody that her father had worked as a lowly porter on the railways; but the girls didn't seem quite as keen to own up to their working-class roots. Everyone had their idea of a rough-hewn male hero with cap and muffler and coat collar turned up (men at the Art College turned their collars up), but there didn't seem to be any glamorous aura attached to his female equivalent. The right match for the rough-hewn male was a *soignée* and worldly-wise female (who would perhaps tactfully temper his passions and smooth his rough edges). Lenny Barnes, for instance, made no efforts to cover up the fact that she'd been to finishing school in Switzerland. It was all a scream and ridiculously silly: she told stories about how they walked around with books on their heads and practised getting out of cars. There was actually a false car seat and a false door for them to practise with.

—I mean, as if people who haven't been to finishing school are always knocking themselves out when they do it, or falling in the gutter or something. Or perhaps they can never get out of cars at all and just have to drive round and round in them for ever.

Lenny would add casually, though, that of course you did learn a few things at a place like that; and she supposed it gave you a certain confidence.

The girls didn't argue as heatedly as the men. Sometimes they were funny and made everybody laugh, or sometimes they lapsed out of the arguments into their own talk, the sort of talk that the men disapproved of: who had fallen for who, who was going with who, scandal about someone pregnant, or poignant envious gossip about some couple getting married. The men didn't mind hearing that, say, Pete Smith had gone to bed with Sonia Kirschbaum; there was a whole code of response to that, a teasing acclaim for the man next time

109

he was spotted, a smoky look of new appraisal at the girl. But they didn't want to discuss it, to explore its implications. Certain less good-looking girls who went to bed with too many of the men got a reputation, and were spoken of with mock horror, the men pretending to be on the run from their predatory and smothering attentions. The other girls laughed at this.

Iris didn't gossip; she would sit cross-legged, even on the tall stools in the Gardenia, her chin in her hands, absorbed in listening to what Ray was saying.

—He's a genius, she told people flatly.

If Ray heard her he looked uncomfortable. Some of the others thought Iris was affected, and took against the proprietary way she talked about Ray, as if she was the priestess at his shrine. They all had high hopes of him, however: his inventiveness, his forceful different opinions, his charm. He was part of the promise they all held on to, that what was going on at the college would count for something, later.

Pete Smith told Iris that genius was an invention of bourgeois individualism, and that art could only become meaningful again when the artist was restored to his position as the anonymous chronicler of the collective. Iris smiled her slow enigmatic smile, lowering her eyelids painted with thick black lines, tapping one of her Sobranie Black cigarettes out of the pack.

—Pete, she said, —you make such a nice picture, all the happy workers making their art together, each one putting in his little bit. But I'm afraid Nature isn't so fair as you, she doesn't make everybody just the same.

How can you explain that the mark one man makes upon the paper is vivid with life, while another man can only make something second-hand?

Pete, who was lean and intense with a swept-back mane of hair and horn-rimmed glasses, shrugged coldly, taking this as a comment on his own work. —I'm not interested in the man, he said. —I want to feel history forcing its way into the art, destroying individuality, imposing itself ruthlessly.

Iris shook her head sorrowfully at him. —You know you have to love things in order to paint them.

—That sort of idea makes me sick, said Pete.

Joyce came to the college knowing next to nothing about painting. Her place had been awarded on the basis of the folder of work she had done at school. She had never been to an art exhibition. She knew the paintings in the city museum: although the Holman Hunts and the Ford Madox Browns and the Frederick Leightons melted her and set her dreaming, she understood quickly that she was not supposed to like them. The prints and pages torn out of magazines pinned up on the walls in Miss Leonard's art room at school had given her little inexplicable blasts and blazes of Van Gogh and Matisse and Utrillo before she knew who these were. Even now she was at college she couldn't afford to buy art books; none of them could afford that. When she got the chance – Ray and Iris had some books, and there was a college library – she pored over the reproductions, trying to make sense of what they taught in the Art History classes. She felt at sea amidst such acres and centuries of work. There were whole centuries of religious paintings and fat nudes that she couldn't make herself sympathetic to; they seemed to her stuffy and affected. It was so much easier to get excited about the modern things. Then Iris made her look at Piero della Francesca and Giotto and love them; she came to think of the trecento as a sort of Eden of innocence in art before the long fall into falsity.

Everything Ray Deare did made Joyce sure he was a genius. She listened to him in order to learn about life as well as painting. She had never heard anyone say the things he said. He said that art was play and that play was the truth of life, more real than work, duty, learning. He said he was ashamed of the dullness of obedient easel art, schooled and tamed. He said that sex was the true revolutionary act of play and sex had to be put back into painting. Painting and sculpture were the only forms capable of keeping faith with the truth of the body. (Joyce surreptitiously glanced at Iris when Ray talked about sex, wondering whether she would give away any sign of their intimate life; Iris's wide gaze at her husband never faltered, she didn't even smile.) He said that an artist had to be an outsider in his own society in order to be any good; that art had to welcome every intimation that came out of the dark. He said that the 1946 exhibition of Picasso at the V&A had changed his idea of art as violently and immediately as a collision with a charging bull, and that anyone who thought that Picasso had wasted his talent was an idiot without eyes. Or balls.

He didn't use quite these words in class, of course, but afterwards, in the Gardenia or the jazz club.

He was often the noisiest and most extravagant in the crowd, and even when he was putting forward his serious view of things he waved his hands around and jumped out of his chair in such a way that you knew he was aware that there was something comical and exaggerated in his performance. He didn't always say sensible or serious things. Sometimes you could tell that he took up a position merely for the sake of arguing it: that illustrations in women's magazines should be forbidden by law, or that the art market should be nationalised. When she first visited him and Iris in the flat, Joyce was disappointed. Ray seemed gloomy, and was mostly silent, or spoke with Iris about ordinary things Joyce had hardly expected him to know about: sandwich pickle they'd run out of, or a shirt that needed ironing, or some fuse wire he wanted her to buy. (Joyce thought it might be for artistic purposes, but no, he just needed to repair a fuse.) She soon came to feel the thrill, though, in touching up against this tender material underside to his mysterious artist's life. Anyway, it was a good job that Ray ignored her and left her and Iris alone to chatter. The idea of his asking her directly what she thought about anything made her hands clammy.

Ray's paintings frightened her too. They were mostly paintings of people; this was what the college was known for, anyone who wanted to paint abstracts went to the Slade or St Martin's. They were nudes, or portraits of friends; occasionally they were practice studies of fruit or flowers, or a bit of broken wall on a bombsite with weeds growing out of it. The subjects were elongated, squeezed, their faces hollowed, the eyes dark pits; his palette was muddy, browns and olive greens and creams, with a red which he seemed to use to show energy (Iris explained this). Often there was red on the nipples of the nudes, or between their legs. In the paintings of men friends a red light often hovered around the head like the tension of thought. There were a number of paintings of Iris, unmistakable for all the distortion because of the slanting lines of her face like a bird, and the long ponytail: some nudes, some heads, one of her reading a book, one that seemed to be of her painting, splodges of jewel-like colour squeezed on her opened hand as if it was a palette.

Whenever she found herself alone with one of his nudes Joyce stared greedily at his treatment of the breasts, the belly, the mound of pubic hair: the swirling thick brushstrokes made the flesh into a rich bitter pudding, pawed and stretched the female shape into an exposing, arousing ugliness, with breasts slopped liquidly sideways or hanging loosely. She could see that they were beautiful. The heaped-on thick pinks and creams and greens were a representation of how these bodies were pleasuring and powerful. Yet she felt a frisson of fear, as well as exhilaration, at the idea that her flesh might ever be stripped and seen like this. This picture of femaleness fought hard, in her idea of herself, with a different picture she clung to: the one derived from magazines and films, of flesh safely contained inside its flawless powdered skin, suggested by shadows under clinging clothes, contoured and lyrical and hidden.

The hours Joyce spent drawing in the long life room made her very happy. The room was austere and dilapidated, lit by tall windows on its north-west side, with off-white walls and bare floorboards sanded smooth by the caretaker Mr Bassett with his sawdust and broom. You could draw from the plaster casts of Greek and Renaissance sculptures and bronzes that stood around, or from the skeleton who hung in her little sentry box at one end of the room, or you could draw from the live models, usually Mrs Carey or Miss Alfred, who undressed in their 'cupboard' and were kept warm with electric panel heaters in winter. Nothing must be allowed to move or change while you drew, even when everyone took a break: chalk marks were made for where the model's chair and her feet and elbows went; you made marks for your own position too, and for the 'donkey', the trestle where you rested your drawing board.

In the breaks the students smoked and leaned out of the windows overlooking the busy shopping street; or they warmed themselves against the fat old radiators. The models wrapped themselves in their kimonos. Some of them were thin and destitute-looking, brought in 'off the streets', as Pete Smith said: he called them casualties of the post-war austerity. Others were confident and extraordinary. Jean Alfred, who figured in so many drawings and paintings by the students and teachers at the college, was said to have gypsy blood in her: she was tall with a big square mouth and slanting cheekbones. She dated some of the best students, and was rumoured to be carrying on an affair with one of the older lecturers, as well as having a gypsy boyfriend of her own. Her mother worked as a cleaner at the college in the evenings: they lived together in Churchtown, which was seedy and glamorously rough.

Joyce's drawing improved. She learned to spend two and a half hours on an ear and a bit of neck, connecting them with the background, getting them right. She entered into a sort of trance as she worked, absorbed in seeing and translating, shocked if the teacher interrupted to show her something, or if anyone new came pushing into the room past the thick black burlap curtain that hung inside the door to shut out sound and light and curious passers-by. She did understand, though, that drawing was supposed to be a preparation for something else. It seemed a great problem that she didn't really have any subject she urgently needed to paint. Some of the others were so sure, already: Stefan Jeremy with his sooty cityscapes, Yoyo Myers with his weird bug-eyed portraits, Mary Anderson with her studies of theatres and circuses.

It felt as if this problem of her lack of a subject was all tangled up with something incomplete as yet in Joyce's life with the crowd. She wasn't clear what role she was supposed to play with them. They partly adopted her as a little pet, small and tidy and obliging and good fun, always ready with her admiration for other people's work. They called her Ginger although her hair wasn't really ginger, it was a pale golden red. Yoyo took a handful of it and sifted through, sighing, despairing of ever being able to paint it because it was made up of so many different colours, white and gold and auburn and strawberry. In fact his painting of her head, with his characteristic staring bug eyes, won him the student prize that year, and was the first painting that he ever sold.

Joyce had been to bed with Yoyo, and with a couple of the others too. ('Shagged' the men called it, but the girls never said that. The word was hopelessly mixed up in Joyce's mind with dirty old tobacco and the sailors who had muttered things down at the Docks.) As soon as she started college she had set about ridding herself of her inexperience: the night she came home after her first time (they were still living in the old house then), she searched her face in her dressing-table mirror for signs of a new womanly allure. Her deflowering had not been in the least the bloody and momentous thing she had expected from her novel-reading. So this was what people really wanted of one another; this act of playful childlike gratification was the grown-up secret hidden under so much stuffy dullness! Everyone at college was going to bed with everyone else. At the beginning of the second year when they were queuing to re-register, Lenny Barnes pretended to start up an extra line and stood at the head of it calling out, 'Anyone who's still a virgin queue here!'

Men liked Joyce. She could easily have had a steady

boyfriend and got serious; but she held herself back, as if she needed to find out more before she could know what she wanted.

One afternoon the class went to draw outdoors in Hilltop and were defeated by the rain. They crowded for refuge into Ray Deare's flat which was nearby; Joyce made them coffee on the gas ring. Iris was at college. It was strange to be there without her; the flat looked dingier, with dirty dishes left around and a glimpse through a door on the landing of an unmade bed with its blankets hanging down on to the floor. The rain blotted out the view in the long windows in the lounge. Ray looked round for some fruit for them to draw but could only ruefully offer them a couple of sprouting potatoes and a spotty banana.

—Come on girls, someone suggested. —One of you get your things off.

There was a haughty-faced student called Gillian Corbin; she was the one you thought of when you heard the rumour that they let rich girls without talent into the college in the hope that they would marry and support the poor male artists. Joyce guessed Gillian was going to offer to undress. She knew that the others wouldn't want to draw her. Yoyo complained that Gillian always came out looking more like a statue than a statue did.

—Come on Ginger, said Yoyo. —What about you?

—All right, she said. —I'll do it. She looked at Ray. —Shall I undress in your bedroom? Perhaps Iris has a robe or something I could borrow. D'you think she'd mind?

Ray was always scrupulously courteous to the models.

—This one is really such a mess, he said in perplexity, looking into the room with the unmade bed. He opened the door into another bedroom across the landing. —This is better. This is where I'm banished to when I'm in the doghouse.

These were almost the first words he had ever addressed to her personally. They were suddenly as intimate as old friends. —I'll get you something to slip on, he said. —I'm afraid you might be cold. I'll light the heater.

She stood and looked around: another double bed, this one just a mattress on the floor. It looked as though only one person had slept in it, the blankets were curved into a little body-shaped cell. On the floor beside the bed was a glass with an end of something in it that looked like whisky, a bottle of aspirin, an ashtray full of dottle from Ray's pipe, and several books opened and left face down: D. H. Lawrence and Herbert Read and a copy of *Encounter*. It felt like a very male space, there were none of Iris's little touches of colour and ornament. She wondered what Ray meant by being in the doghouse and why he was ever banished here.

Then she started to undress. She had never modelled for a nude before. She wished there was a mirror in the room, just to confirm to herself that she looked how she believed she did: slim and tidy, with pale clear skin;

119

a neat muff of pubic hair darker than the hair on her head; round firm breasts (Yoyo had called them plums); curvaceous hips and bottom which she knew appealed to men, although she would have liked to be narrower and less firmly planted on the earth. Ray knocked at the door and held a silky dressing gown into the room without looking.

—I'll only be a moment, she said. —Almost ready.

She crossed to the bed, sat naked on his pillow and from there slipped herself down inside the space his body had made in the sheets; right down into it, so that she was quenched in its dark and immersed in its not unpleasant male bed smell, of pipe smoke and sweat and unwashed hair. For a few long moments she breathed in and out. She wondered if he would be able to smell traces of her when he slept in this room next: her Mitsouko left behind on the sheets, or some scent more secret and terrible. She didn't care if he did.

Then she wriggled out and put on Iris's dressing gown and without pausing to think about it walked out in front of the others and took the dressing gown off and let Ray arrange her on the chaise longue. At first the assault of everyone's persistent unapologetic attention prickled on her skin. It was disconcerting how they dropped their heads to their drawings and then lifted them to check against her: she kept expecting them to meet her eyes. As she got used to it, she felt herself float restfully free. It was enough to be seen. She wasn't responsible for herself, she didn't have to decide anything, or to act. It seemed a kind of triumph that even Ray Deare, whose knowledge and understanding stretched so far beyond what she could begin to imagine, should be labouring so absorbedly at representing her, while she sat dreaming.

—He'll find out for me, who I am, she thought.

She was pleased to be looked at: hadn't she given herself, in mirrors, just such an intense scrutiny, and been satisfied? And she felt full of cheerful contempt for anyone, her mother and her aunt for instance, who would have thought there was any shame in this.

Later she happened to mention it to her sister Ann. They were living at this time with their mother and Martin in a flat in Benteaston; she and Ann had to share a bedroom and Lil slept on the sofa in the living room. Ann was going to start at the University in September, studying literature.

—You're joking, said Ann, incredulous, admiring. —You mean to say you sat there naked while they all had their clothes still on and looked at you? You really mean everything off, not just your top?

—So what? Joyce said airily. —We all do it. They just needed somebody to draw.

—You all do it? You mean the men as well?

—Well no. She was patient, explaining the natural order of things. —It might be more awkward if the men posed, if they were your friends. The women don't mind. And anyway everyone likes to draw women's bodies best. They're more aesthetic.

She hadn't quite recognised herself when she looked at the drawings the others made of her. But that person mostly looked all right: looked like the kind of girl who commands art, full of personality and power. In Ray Deare's she was a concentration of white flesh, compacted under the force of thick wedge-shaped black lines, big knees drawn up in the foreground, black eyes staring over them with intensity out of a stark small face. She only saw it once, before he put it away: in truth her heart jolted, because he had not made her beautiful.

In the middle of her second year at the college, Joyce had to choose which course to continue with. She knew she wasn't good enough to take Fine Art. She had thought at first that she might take Illustration. She imagined herself in a light clean room full of plants and cushions, making fine subtle pictures of cats or children in Indian ink. Aunt Vera approved: Illustration seemed at once cultured and safe. Unfortunately, the other students who chose to take it – a middle-aged plump man and some plain dowdy girls – were not part of the crowd. Joyce was afraid their dowdiness might rub off on her, and she might miss some of the fun. So she opted for Dress Design. She knew she would be good at that; she loved clothes, she had an instinct for them. Anyway, as Lil said, with dressmaking she could always be sure of earning a living.

The Dress Design studio was in Kingsmile, a fifteen-minute walk from the main college building, upstairs above a Co-op shop; it smelled of cheese and margarine. The girls found rats in their lockers and the men from the Co-op had to come up to kill them. They studied tailoring, millinery, pattern cutting; there were screens dividing up the rough board floor between the various years and classes. Miss Allinson who taught was a sharp-tongued spinster with melancholy hooded eyes, exquisitely dressed (the best girls sewed things for her).

Iris made a great point of celebrating Joyce's decision.

—The men look down on it, she said. —But they don't understand: clothes are an art form in themselves. Just because they're stuck with wearing their boring frowsty trousers and jackets and things, they don't appreciate just how much real creative work we women have to put into what we wear.

—You seem to manage to do that and to be a painter too.

Iris made a rueful face, waggling her cigarette in the corner of her mouth while she talked, squinting her eyes against the smoke, cleverly folding a tiny paper ruff with her tapering hands. —Oh, my poor old painting. At the moment, that seems to be getting precisely nowhere. I'm so busy preparing classes for my children, learning horrid arithmetic to torture them with, trying to write my essay on Piaget.

She and Joyce were sitting cross-legged on the floor of the Hilltop flat, making hand puppets for a play Iris was putting on at the teacher training college. The heads were made of papier mâché, the hands and feet of chamois leather; there was a king with a fierce red face and a pretty pink queen. Joyce was helping to cut out the clothes. Ray was in college. They were drinking black coffee as usual. Joyce wondered about Iris's housekeeping: there never seemed to be proper food in the flat. She never saw Iris eat anything, although sometimes there were strange things in the kitchen cupboard, bought from the expensive delicatessen round the corner: French meat pastes and Scandinavian salted fish and pots of sour yogurt. Joyce didn't like to mention that she was hungry; in Iris's company such an admission seemed demeaning.

—Can you imagine, said Iris, suddenly putting the king puppet down in her lap, —what it's like trying to think of yourself as a painter when you're married to someone like Ray?

Joyce looked at her with earnest sympathy. —I do see what you mean, she said. —Although I love your beautiful still lifes.

Iris shrugged. —I worked so hard, she said. —All the years I was at the Art College I devoted myself to them, thinking that if I just persisted, then they must eventually come right.

Joyce wondered carefully. —Just because Ray's work is so special, it doesn't mean there isn't a place for yours. It's just a different kind of thing.

—It's worse than that. His paintings make me feel that my paintings are a lie. I thought they were authentic, but they weren't the real thing. I was always looking through somebody else's eyes. Perhaps I've never seen anything, really. Not like when Ray sees something.

Joyce looked at Iris in dismay. She could see this was a discovery it would be difficult to endure. She was thankful that she had not chosen Fine Art.

—I'm not even sure how much I want to carry on with my own work. I think actually it's more fulfilling, more truthful for me to put myself in service of what Ray's doing. That's why I'm training as a teacher, really. I needed to have something practical to get on with; and then it means I can support us both, if he doesn't sell enough work, or if he gets tired of working at the college and just wants to paint.

Joyce did not question Iris's estimate of the value of her own work. When she looked at one of her small still lifes again – red cherries heaped up on a plate, painted in fine careful brushstrokes against a dark background, one she had particularly loved – she thought perhaps she could see what Iris meant. Compared to one of Ray's paintings, it seemed, yes, closed and bounded by convention. This corresponded, too, to some limitation she intuited in Iris. Although she so admired Iris's distinctive stylishness, there was also something stolid and unvarying in her. Joyce thought this stolidity irritated Ray, and that Iris didn't know it. Things he casually and spontaneously said, Iris took over and translated into fixed superior positions. She thought he winced, sometimes, when his exaggerations came back to him as earnest doctrine.

Iris's problem was that she wasn't funny. In the crowd this was the one unforgivable lapse. Everything was funny, if only you were brave enough to see it. Their best times were when they were disorderly together, helpless with laughter, causing trouble and drawing disapproving looks, the girls complaining they were going to wet themselves. They told stories about the everyday things that happened to them which changed the ordinary greyness into a crazed colourful circus. An old man wearing all his war medals and no shirt saluted Dud Mason in the street every morning. While they were drawing once, Yoyo put on a lady's hat and brought some steps and looked down at them from one of the high screens placed behind the model, as though he was nine foot tall. An organist broke wind in church in time to the music he was playing and a choirboy fainted from suppressed laughter. A balloon bursting at Christmas blew off the paper hat of a dignified relative. Their parents' hard-fought-for respectability – all that lifetime's weight of effort over curtains and sideboards and putting milk in a jug and having a little stand to hold the cake plates and cleaning out your ears – exploded in a conflagration of mockery.

Joyce began to tell stories – tentatively at first, in case these things weren't actually funny but humiliating – about her mother and her aunt, and her uncle with his other woman. She told them about Gilbert, and how Vera tried to enlighten him through poetry. Ray laughed. He told them about the time when he had to run the gauntlet of catcalling women when his father took him into the garment-making rooms at a Co-op manufactory to be fitted for his school shorts. She was glad he didn't mind being funny at his own expense. This was another rule amongst the crowd: you were unforgivable if you took yourself too seriously (apart from your art, of course, which you couldn't take seriously enough).

Joyce didn't think Iris had irony. She had a suspicion that Iris never let up on the high seriousness with which she took things.

The whole crowd of them went to a fancy-dress ball at the teacher training college. As art students they had to outdo the staid and much more conforming student teachers. Joyce made herself a tight-fitting black catsuit with a long tail which she carried draped over her arm; she drew whiskers on her cheeks and blacked the end of her nose and sewed pink satin pads on to black gloves for paws. She pinned up her hair under a black cap on to which she had stitched pointed ears. Yoyo came as Harpo Marx, Lenny Barnes was a playing card. Ray and Iris came as an Indian raja and ranee; they had their faces stained brown and he wore a silky paisley turban and a moustache.

—Meow, Miss Stevenson, he said when they met up outside the training college.

—Meow, Your Worshipfulness, she replied (she couldn't quite think how one ought to address a raja). In her cat costume she felt licensed to be different from her usual circumspect self. She rubbed his nose with her black one, leaving a smudge, then did the same to Iris. Iris was poised and lovely in a full-length sari, a red Hindu wedding-spot painted between her eyes, her long plait hanging down her back with a flower braided into the end. She tickled Joyce behind her cat-ears.

The hall at the training college was new, all lined in blond wood with a pale parquet floor (the girls wearing stilettos had to take them off and dance in their stockings). They drank beer out of paper cups and danced to the trad band and then because it was Lenny's birthday someone opened champagne and they drank some of that too. One wall was glass from floor to ceiling; there were long bright African print curtains but these had been left open and outside as it got dark there came a huge brooding yellow moon, hanging close to the earth, glowing through the silhouettes of trees.

—The moon! The moon! called Joyce, caterwauling at the window.

—My cold friend, said Iris, pressing her face and hands against the glass. —Come to watch but won't come in. Hello, old friend! Are you lonely tonight?

Ray got out his pipe and smoked it, in spite of his turban. He even kept it in his mouth while he danced. Someone said he looked like Sherlock Holmes in disguise as a Lascar.

—A Lascar! said Lenny. —Oh, I want to be a Lascar. What's a Lascar?

Ray danced strenuously, hopping about and jerking his head from side to side, not perfectly in rhythm. He didn't like trad jazz, he preferred contemporary. Joyce was shocked at his jogging about so willingly, in his turban, with his eyes shining weirdly against the dark skin. She might have been disappointed that he hadn't remained loftily apart, but instead she felt a secret exhilaration, like an inward disrespectful joke, at being unbound from some of her awe at him. Even when he and Pete Smith were ranting about Munnings and the

Royal Academy, she had to swallow an exultant laughter at his mouth saying such serious things under his ridiculously waggling false moustache.

At the end of the evening the Deares invited everyone back to their flat for coffee. Iris had already said that Joyce could stay in the spare room. When they got outside – the moon was higher in the sky and farther off by this time, silvery cool – Joyce knew that she was drunk, with the wonderful kind of drunkenness where you progress along like a dodgem car by bumping into things and people and spinning forwards, but there is never any chance of hurting anybody or falling over. She took to tickling the others on their necks with the end of her tail. This seemed a perfect satisfying expression of her tenderness for them all; eventually Dud Mason caught hold of her by the tail and pulled it off and wouldn't give it back to her although she meowed piteously for it. (Dud was in a toga.) It was fun to be awake and alive and noisy in wet warm Hilltop, in all the rich green exhalations of the gardens, while behind the windows of the tall houses all the stuffy people lay sleeping. There had been a shower of rain while they were at the ball, the roads and garden walls shone wet in the streetlights.

When they got into the flat Dud said he was so hungry he could eat the rocking horse – he began, indeed, to gnaw on it – and then suddenly everyone was starving, and Iris and Joyce were making toast and frying eggs in the kitchen: extraordinary eggs which no sooner broke and were in the pan than they were cooked, so that even while they were dishing them up and handing them out (Joyce still with her cat-gloves on), the girls were calling everyone to come and look at the extraordinary miraculous eggs which cooked in an instant. The eggs, taken into the lounge and eaten with salt and dry toast, seemed delicious.

—Your friend's out there again, said Joyce. She meant the moon: it was pressed on to the night outside the long lounge window like a bright sixpence.

Iris was startled, and stared fearfully as if she expected to see someone standing brooding on the balcony in the dark. After that she subsided into herself and sat wrapped tightly in her sari on the floor, the skin of her face marked purple with tiredness under the eyes and around the fine nostrils. Ray brought out a bottle of whisky. Joyce drank some out of the bathroom toothmug that was the best he could do for a whisky glass (the others had eggcups and plastic picnic beakers). She had rubbed off her black nose and whiskers with Iris's cold cream, then washed her face in the bleak bathroom down half a flight of stairs, which the Deares shared with other tenants. Now she sat with her knees tucked under her among the cushions on the chaise longue, and felt the men in the room orbit deliciously around her. Dud Mason, who was a third year and older and so melancholy-funny, had coiled her cat-tail up as a pillow under his cheek. He needed consoling for his poor foot run over by a tank on D-Day, that made him hobble crookedly, and for his toga that made him look so foolish. Yoyo was plucking an imaginary bass for her benefit, to the Modern Jazz Quartet playing 'Skating in Central Park' on Ray's portable record player. Pete Smith, hunkered in a corner, was out of the reach of her charm, but then she didn't find him good-looking anyway. Gillian and Mary Anderson were eclipsed: Mary was asleep among the cushions (and anyway, although she was the best painter out of all the girls, she had buck teeth and thick pebble glasses); Gillian was waiting for a taxi to take her home.

Ray and Pete were arguing about Giacometti, and then about socialism, and then about primitive art. Ray still had his brown face but he had taken off his turban and his moustache. He was sitting cross-legged on the floor with his back to the rows of Penguin and Pelican paperbacks on bookshelves made of painted planks and bricks. Sometimes he waved his pipe dramatically in the air as if he was drawing things; sometimes he closed his eyes, sucking on it. Joyce remembered that he was only twenty-five or -six; when he was teaching she always thought of him as immeasurably older than her. His eyelids were deep and fine-skinned, crinkled; the flesh on his face was soft and thick, and his mouth was red with a lower lip so swollen it looked as if he had been stung. Someone had said that with his curls and that soft mouth he looked like a cross baby. He was always completely absorbed in whatever one thing he was doing: pouring whisky, constructing an argument, painting. If he tried, say, to pour coffee and talk at the same time, then Iris had apologetically to unpick the coffee pot from out of his hands before it got cold.

—What we have to do, he was shouting, —is to get right up close to Africa. You know, like getting up close to one of those totem figures, one of those really tall ones, with teeth and eyes and bits of hide and bone. We've got to frighten ourselves, that's the truth. All the old taboos, all the old forbidden things. You've got to cut through, all these layers of fuss, of baby clothes, and all this stuffing, all this stuffy upholstered old Europe with its taboos and its dead skin . . .

—And what about the Empire? Pete shouted back. —What about what's happening in Kenya? What kind of a civilisation is that?

—That's exactly it, that's exactly it, said Ray. —That's exactly what I'm trying to say.

—You're not making any sense at all, Joyce laughed at them.

—We are, Pete said indignantly. —You just don't properly understand what it is we're talking about.

When Gillian and Mary had left in their taxi, Iris stood up and said she was going to bed. Joyce thought that she had better go to bed too, although she didn't really want to; she felt her energy was inexhaustible and she was sure she would lie awake listening to the talk through the wall. The men were passing the whisky round and changing the record. (—You've got to hear this, Ray said. —This is raw jazz, really raw, really down to the bone, nothing pretty about this.) It would seem presumptuous to stay up without Iris and be the only girl.

The bed in the spare room was left as it must have

been when Ray last slept in there. Joyce reassured Iris that she didn't mind not having clean sheets; it had clearly not occurred to Iris that anyone might. Her face was dislocated by a yawn so deep that she hardly seemed to hear Joyce saying goodnight. Joyce undressed listening to the music and the rumbling of voices through the wall. She had brought her pyjamas and her tooth-brush in a bag; when she had taken off all her things (thinking that it was the second time she had been naked in this room) she realised that she had left the bag in the lounge, but it didn't matter. It wasn't cold. She climbed in between the sheets in her bare skin, and must have fallen asleep as soon as she put her head on the pillow.

When she woke up she had no idea how long she had been in there, or how many hours the others had gone on talking: the lounge was silent now and the flat was dark. What she knew was that someone was in bed with her: a naked man. She could feel him bulky and hot and soft beside her, she could smell him, a spicy mix of sweat and spirits and smoke and something personal, a green smell like cut grass. She was sure the man was asleep because he was breathing through his mouth, heavily, in a broken snorting pattern: he must be lying on his back. She too was on her back. She had no idea how long he might have been there. In her dreams, perhaps, she had been aware of an arrival, a stirring of accommodation to another presence. In her dreams she must have let him climb in, as if this was something understood

133

between them. It was his snorting breathing that had waked her.

It was so dark that she could not see anything, not her own hand in front of her eyes, let alone the face of the man whose heat was radiating against her where her thigh touched his. And yet, in spite of the dark, in truth she knew immediately who he was. (It was not only her thigh that touched him. She could feel under the toes of her left foot the hairy calf of his right leg, and his right arm was thrown heavily, carelessly, across her belly, palm up. Vividly, too, she was aware of them circulating the same air in their noisy breathing: she could taste the whisky in it.) It would have made perfect sense for it to be Yoyo: although it wasn't supposed to be common knowledge that they had slept together, he might have been tempted by such a lucky opportunity as this, might have pretended to settle down on the floor in the lounge and then crept into her room later. But Yoyo would surely have wakened her. And anyway, she never for one moment thought it was Yoyo, whose presence in a bed was light and neat as a boy's. She put her hand to where this man's head should be on the pillow, and felt curls, damp and short, and then with her fingers felt bits of a face, incomprehensible in its arrangements in the pitch dark, but known to her, known vividly.

She leaped up into a sitting position, pulling away from where she touched against him as if she was burned.

—Mr Deare! she hissed. —Mr Deare! Wake up! You've made a terrible mistake. You've come to the wrong bed. I'm in here.

For a long moment there was no response; only a whistling exhalation on a different, prolonged note. Then the snoring broke off and he also sat up abruptly in alarm; he grabbed her painfully tightly by the shoulders with his hands as if she needed protecting from something, or he did.

—Who are you? he whispered urgently into the dark.

—It's Joyce, she said. —Joyce Stevenson.

—And what am I doing in here?

—I think you made a mistake. You came to bed and you forgot that Iris said I could stay the night.

—Jesus Christ. I wasn't asleep?

—You were. You must have gone right off to sleep. Then I woke up.

—Jesus Christ.

It was so strange that they couldn't see one another although he held her tightly in his hands for these few minutes while they spoke. He groaned, a groan out of all proportion to what had happened: as if he confronted a wholesale indictment of his irresponsibility, his drunkenness, his insensitivity. —I'm such an idiot, he urgently whispered at her.

—No, not at all, it was an easy mistake to make, it doesn't matter.

—It does, it does, he hissed, insisting. —What should I do now?

—Just go back to your own bed. There's no need for us to mention anything to Iris. There's nothing to mention.

—All right, he said. —Are you sure?

—Of course I'm sure. Nothing's happened.

—All right. If you're quite sure.

As he let go of her and moved to feel his way out of the bed, his right hand fell from her shoulder – palm open, hot and damp from where he had gripped her – and brushed quickly across her breasts, so quickly that she couldn't be sure whether it was an accident or not.

—Goodnight then, she said into the dark. —Don't worry about it.

—You're very good to make no fuss. I hope I've got all my clothes.

—If there's anything here in the morning I'll put it out on the landing.

—I suppose this is all really very funny.

—It is, she whispered firmly. —It's terribly funny.

When he had gone she lay awake, parched and nauseous with hangover, feverish with consciousness of what had happened. She had done nothing to be ashamed of, and yet she felt that something precious had been spoiled: she wished she never had to see Ray Deare again. She also wished that she dared to slip into the lounge and fetch her pyjamas out of her bag, so she could cover herself up; her naked breasts felt hot and heavy and she ached from imagining, over and over, although she forbade herself, his hand across her front.

The next day, at about three o'clock in the afternoon, someone rang the doorbell of the Stevenson flat in Benteaston.

They were all at home: Lil and Joyce and Ann were

washing up Sunday dinner. Martin was excused washing up in return for polishing shoes: he had all these spread out on sheets of newspaper in the middle of the carpet in the front room, and put on a great appearance of rubbing and buffing every time one of them came through, although it was obvious he was mostly engaged in reading all the articles in the paper. He read things out to them from time to time.

—Listen to this. 'House painter hypnotises woman while her teeth are extracted.'

Lil, who had read the paper through already that morning, obliged by exclaiming in astonished sympathy.

—'Widow leaves six thousand pounds, car, house and wines to chauffeur.' 'Man digging in garden finds unexploded bomb.'

Ann and Joyce ignored him. They got through the mountain of dirty dishes and pans in a trance of uncommunicative efficiency, only scowling if they bumped up against one another in the cramped little kitchen while they were putting things away. It was Joyce who hung her soggy tea towel over her shoulder and went to see who was at the door: sometimes some of her college friends came over on Sunday afternoons to take her out for a walk on the Heath.

Ray Deare stood on the path, hangdog and miserable, with his shoulders hunched up and his hands thrust into the pockets of his tweed jacket. Joyce hadn't seen him again since she'd found him in her bed; she had slipped out of the Deares' flat early in the morning before anyone was up. There were traces of brown make-up in front of Ray's ears and in his eyebrows. It was a muffled grey day, cool for summer, very still. In the tiny paved front garden the blooms on the aged pink standard rose that Lil had tried to prune into shape sagged gloomily earthwards, turning brown before they'd opened.

—I couldn't believe that you'd just gone, he said. —You left this. I thought I'd better bring it.

He held out the little pink-painted basket she had forgotten, with her pyjamas and toothbrush inside. Joyce supposed that he was miserable because she had blundered into his sacred privacy, even though it was through no fault of her own. There were things about him that he must know she would not be able to forget: his yielding hot soft flesh; his smell close up, sweet and ripe like grass; his humiliating shy panic when he discovered his mistake. And now nothing that she did would ever be right for him again. She wondered how he'd found out where she lived.

The woman from the flat upstairs was hanging over the banisters with curiosity, her hair in curlers and a net. —Is it for you, dear? Joyce reassured her it was, but she made no move to retreat.

—I just had to come and apologise for yesterday, Ray said.

—There was really no need. Do you want to come in?

Even as Joyce offered this and he accepted it she realised what a mistake she was making. There was nowhere in the flat that she could take him. The tiny hall was windowless and half filled with the hallstand.

The whole place reeked: of cabbage, boiled bacon, the wet cloths off the steamed pudding, shoe polish. She led the way into the front room and then stood helplessly. Martin's polishing had spread right out across the floor, there was no way to walk round him, and anyway, she could hardly have taken Ray into the bedroom.

—How about this? Martin read with glee, partly for the benefit of the visitor. —'Woman who died: "Nothing wrong".'

Lil came out of the kitchen wiping her wet red hands on her apron. —Come on in, pet, she said. —You're too late for dinner. Would you like a bit of cold bacon?

—Oh no, said Joyce. —He wouldn't.

—I won't, thank you, said Ray with weary politeness. —I'm not hungry.

Since they moved into town, Lil had got a job working in a cake shop. The frilled caps and aprons she had to wear were draped across a clothes horse on the hearthrug along with the girls' stockings and brassieres: this normally stood in the kitchen sink, when it wasn't full of dishes.

—Excuse the mess, said Lil cheerfully. —Let me lift that bedding off the sofa so you can sit down, and I'll make us a nice cup of tea.

—This is Mr Deare, said Joyce. —He's one of my lecturers. This is my mother, and my brother and sister.

—I thought you were just one of Joyce's chums, said Lil in real dismay.

Joyce thought that Ray ought somehow to have explained himself, to have taken charge of the situation from his position of authority. Couldn't he at least have said that he'd come to talk to her about her work? Instead he stood cowed and desperate looking, as if he might make a dreadful mistake and accept the cup of tea.

—We could clear up in here, offered Lil, flustered. —If you need to talk to Joyce. We could all wait in the bedroom.

—I haven't really come to apologise, said Ray to Joyce, ignoring the others gawping at them. —I've come to finish what we started.

—Actually I shouldn't have brought you in, Joyce said then, recklessly. —We don't really have the space, as you can see. I'll get my coat. We could discuss things as we walk along.

—You've still got that tea towel round your neck, said Ann.

Joyce unwound it with superb indifference, then fumbled in the dark in the hallstand for her outdoor shoes.

—Will you be long? said Lil with foreboding.

—Might be.

It didn't matter that she knew she sounded falsely bright; she would have pretended any brazen thing, just to escape. Efficiently she steered Ray out into the street.

—Shall I put the kettle on? Lil called after them.

—Don't bother to wait for us.

They walked up towards the Heath. It was an ordinary Sunday. Family groups or couples or absorbed solitary walkers straggled desultorily on Clore Hill which was so bustling and purposeful on weekdays, now muted with its closed shops and its road empty of traffic. Joyce walked as though she was wearing giant boots, the kind that make you take huge mile-long strides with every step: she was leaving her old self behind for ever in no time, in a few minutes.

—I love you, Ray was saying. —I've fallen in love with you.

Of course this was ridiculous.

And yet Joyce was also ready for the possibility that it was true. Secretly, she had probably always believed that if only someone ever uncovered her real self it might command love like this, all at one blow: like a vindication from outside of all the innumerable tiny things that made her up and that otherwise only she would ever know.

This peremptory absolute need had seized Ray Deare once or twice before, since he had been married to Iris. He recognised the helplessness, and the astonishment at his own abjection. Every day he moved safely amongst women, enjoying the nearness of their bodies, their scent, their various blooming faces: students, models, women passing in the crowd. And then suddenly by some signal, some tiny-seeming word or touch or hint, one of them would separate herself from that background awareness and swell until she filled out all his thoughts, consumingly, swallowing up the point of everything else. It was impossible to work so long as he felt like this. Impossible to eat, to think, at least

141

until something was settled one way or the other.

Joyce laughed out loud at him, shaking her head.
—Don't be ridiculous, she said.

Her earrings and her ponytail swung excitedly. She had put on a suede jacket to come out with him, and knotted a scarf jauntily round her neck, a beige silk one decorated with a pattern of coins: her clothes were always easily stylish, she made no fuss. How unusual it was, to have that red hair with a skin so creamy pale and clear, even with a hint of blue vein at the temple. He grasped at the top of her arm as they walked, wishing they weren't hurrying, longing to be with her somewhere alone where he could convince her, not absurdly on the public street; he was furious with anger at everyone they passed who looked at them.

This wasn't exactly like those other times. With those other girls he had known, even while he was burning up for them, that he wasn't afraid, he could pull himself back if he wanted.

—Do you think I'm ridiculous? Do you really think that?

He searched her face, trying to read her expression. Probably she thought he was stuffy, and ancient. She might be disgusted because he had touched her last night; for all he knew she was a virgin and it had been her first contact with a naked man. Perhaps he had smelled, or snored, while he lay beside her.

—Well no, of course you're not a ridiculous person.

—I love you. Everything about you.

He had not undressed and lain beside her last night

because he had had too much to drink and had forgotten she was staying. It wasn't even because he had been swollen and agitated with desire for her, although he was now, hardly knowing where they were walking to or what he was saying. He had lain beside her because she was the one who matched him, the one he ought to be lying down with every night of his life. He'd only known that for a few hours, but it seemed quite certain. He tried to explain to her.

—I chose you, without knowing what I was doing.

—That wasn't what I thought, she said. —I thought you'd hate me!

—Hate you! If you only knew!

She covered her face with her fingers. He couldn't see if she was smiling, or distraught at him.

—Whatever will my family think?

She was only a child. He needed to remember that. He must treat her with absolute tenderness. The idea of how young she was pricked his eyes with tears.

—I don't care, he said. —I had to tell you. I don't care what they think.

They reached the top of the hill and set off across the Heath for the water tower with its ring of trees, then down into the lumpy secretive craters where the bombs were supposed to have fallen. It was a dull afternoon. He took her hand – warm, small, strong – and pulled to try and slow her down. She let her hand stay in his. In here it seemed possible for him to try to kiss her. If they emerged from the craters to the level grass again he'd have lost his chance.

—You don't know me well enough to be in love with me, she said.

—I don't need to know you. Not in the way you mean.

—But I'm not like you. I'm not brilliant or an important artist or anything.

—That's exactly it. I don't want you to be those things. You're real. It's so real. You're not trying to be something else.

The path became too narrow for them to walk side by side. She went first and he followed, frowning, tripping over the bramble roots that grew across the dirt, not daring to reach out for her. He stared at her body moving under her clothes. Surely she had modelled for him once or twice; he tried to remember the detail of how her buttocks curved generously from her narrow waist, how her wide thighs slanted down into her knees. He couldn't believe that he had not loved her then, when he was drawing her.

The idea of Iris was stuck in his mind all this time, of course, quivering and sore like a dark poisoned splinter. He and Iris had talked about having children. He had told her he wasn't in a hurry, and then she had said that the idea of feeding a baby disgusted her. Iris had strange moods; there were hours at a time she would sit staring at nothing, or with her face wet with tears. When she was like this everything he said was wrong; he crept around the flat guiltily, or escaped to meet his friends. Involuntarily he pictured her sitting like this now, numbly absorbed in the idea of his treachery, although she couldn't actually know about it yet.

—You have a lovely nature, he said, stumbling after Joyce. —Mine is so stupid and so ugly. You don't know me. If you knew me, you wouldn't want me.

—I know your paintings, she said.

—It's true. You know my paintings. That's all you need to know. You see? You understand everything, without even trying.

She stopped still on the path ahead of him.

—All right, she said, softly so that he wasn't sure at first if he had heard her properly. He couldn't see her face. —All right then.

He came up behind her and put his arms around her, reaching inside her jacket so that her breasts were in his hands, springy and jutting in the stiff brassiere she wore under her wool jumper; he kissed her neck on the nape and behind her ears, with the soft tail of her hair in his face. She smelled of bacon and syrup with traces of perfume from last night; wholesome and good. He stood kissing her for long minutes like that, pressing her breasts with his palms, before she turned round in his arms and kissed him back full on his mouth, with a boldness that must mean she had some experience in such things (which after all was probably a relief). Now he couldn't believe that last night they had lain side by side and he had let her send him back to sleep with Iris.

A man walking his dog had to step into the long grass to avoid them where they blocked the path, grumbling at them disapprovingly.

—We can't ever go to your flat, Joyce said matter-of-factly in his ear now. —And you've seen mine. We won't ever be able to be alone, you know.

He suggested something hesitantly, fearful she might be offended. —I've got keys to my parents' house. They're away at Torquay with my sister for a week's holiday. I'm looking after the cat.

She put up no fight at all. He felt her give way; she sagged heavily against him.

—When? she said. —When can we go there?

—I don't know. What about your mother?

—She'll be all right. Is it far?

—The other side of Benteaston, in St Peter's. About forty minutes' walk.

—Do you have the key on you?

—Yes, he said, feeling in his jacket pocket. —Oh God. And some scraps for the cat. He pulled out the greasy package done up in waxed bread wrappings that Iris had given him to take. —I'd forgotten all about these.

—You won't ever be able to talk again about my lovely nature, Joyce said with her face pressed against his shoulder. —Don't think I don't know what I'm doing, deceiving Iris. Don't think I don't know that it's wrong.

—We aren't going to deceive her, Ray said. —I'm going to tell her. In the next few days I'm going to tell her. You're the one. I'm going to marry you.

He hadn't known this was true until the words were out.

He was full of fear of Iris – the idea of her and of what was going to have to happen to her seemed

146

wrapped in thick and ugly shadows. He was also angry at her, because she made what he had to do so difficult.

—Don't be silly, Joyce said, without lifting her head from his shoulder to see his face, laughing muffledly, happily. —Don't be so silly. It can't be true.

Joyce hadn't thought at all about his parents' house while they were on their way there. It had been merely their destination, aimed at blindly as they hurried with their burning purpose along the quiet Sunday streets. (Really, she pictured them burning with it, the suburban pavements along which they passed scorched and flaming behind them.) She had imagined how they would turn to one another once they were alone at last, but she had not imagined any particular setting for this clinching encounter, no furniture or rooms. She knew things about his family which should have prepared her for just the kind of place it was: his father working for the Co-op, his mother with her whist drives, his sister at secretarial college. He had dropped her hand as they approached; of course the neighbours knew him and would know his wife. A tall tabby hailed him in a hoarse accusing meow from where it waited on the doorstep beyond a little green-painted gate, and he spoke back to it, apologising for being late. The house was on a corner in a quiet avenue of similar houses, fringed fawn blinds at its windows, a striped sun-awning rolled up above the front door, two apple trees and an Anderson shelter in the back garden. If it had been a slum, with cracks in the walls and damp running down and crusts of bread on the floor, Joyce

147

would have taken it in her stride. But she stopped short in the entrance hall when they had shut the front door behind them, disconcerted because it was so ordinary.

The hall was dim, the blinds were drawn; spilled drops of sapphire and ruby glowed on the tiled floor where light came through the stained glass in the porch. With Timmy the cat winding under his feet, Ray led her through a dining room with a tall wooden overmantel and a ticking clock and brass fire irons; pools of pale light were collected on the high-polished table and sideboard. There were dark squares and rectangles of paintings hung by chains from the picture rail but Joyce knew without looking that they weren't Ray's or anything remotely like Ray's: they were cows wading in brooks rusty with sunset light, or yearning shepherdesses on the moors. It wasn't quite like anywhere that Joyce herself had ever lived: more – much more – comfortably furnished and prosperous than anything Lil had ever been able to afford; not as eccentric and distinguished and ramshackle as the old house on the estuary; more old-fashioned than Aunt Vera's bright flat with its pale blue Formica kitchen. She watched Ray hunting in a cupboard in the breakfast room for a plate to put the cat's scraps on. He was still mysterious, the artist with the gift of knowledge. But he was also, after all, just the boy who had grown up in this house, and played with his sister under the shelter, and knew where the forks were kept and where the matches were and had been given, like her own brother, a printing set or a penknife for Christmas. (He showed her afterwards where he had in fact tried out his new penknife, years before, on the arm of his mother's leather-covered chair.) This vision of his familiarity, like a vision of their closeness to come, was more shocking to her, more absolutely a revolution in her apprehension of everything, than even the flame of excitement that licked her as she waited for him to take her upstairs and make love to her.

—I do know you, she said into his neck, wrapping herself about him from behind while he washed his hands at the kitchen sink. —I do know who you are.

—I know you do, said Ray. —That's why I've chosen you.

—Sometimes you'll wish I didn't. You'll wish I was someone more remote, and lofty minded.

—At this moment, he said, —I can't contemplate it. Not with you pressed up against me like that.

He brought sheets, and they lay down under a green silk eiderdown in his old room, which was papered with a pattern of green trellis hung with baskets of flowers. Joyce said she would launder the sheets and iron them before his mother came back. Probably it was strange for him, this bringing her here to his childhood bedroom: he was more shy and self-doubting than she had imagined, after all his talk. They didn't put on any lights or draw the curtains, in case the neighbours saw. Ray brought in a portable enamel paraffin stove; as the hours passed and it grew dark outside, an image of the pattern of diamonds cut in the top of the stove was cast tremblingly on to the slanting ceiling.

* * *

Joyce changed her mind, later, about Iris's paintings. Years later she bought one of Iris's small oils which she saw in an exhibition of local artists. This was when all the turmoil was behind them, all the shouting and weeping and shamed relatives and clumsy ugly self-justification; they had arrived by then at a point where she and Iris could even occasionally meet at the same parties, although they ignored one another. Iris was painting under her maiden name, Iris Neave, although she did remarry (she never had children). She must have recovered from the crisis of confidence in her work that she had once spoken of to Joyce.

The painting was of a little cream jug and a spoon on a white tray cloth edged with lace. It was curious how Iris who was no good with real food or hospitality (Joyce was the one who turned out to be good at these things) should choose so consistently to paint domestic objects: fruit and cakes and labelled jars of jam; teapots and sugar tongs and plates of nuts and cheese.

—Dainty, said Ray. —So dainty it makes me want to smash something. How can she still want to paint as if the world hasn't changed? Tray cloth indeed! Who uses a tray cloth these days? It's too pretty; don't you think it's saccharine and mendacious? (It was he who seemed to have clung on longer to the need to justify himself: he wasn't ever very nice about Iris.)

But Joyce didn't think so, although she didn't try to explain, and didn't really even examine for herself what it was she liked about the picture. If she happened to glance at it, it was a soothing still point in her busy days.

She liked the careful continence of the brushstrokes. She liked its irony (Iris surely knew the tray cloth was old-fashioned?) She liked the idea that the cream was held there inside the jug and never poured.

Four

It had been going to be such a lovely Saturday.

Full, and busy, but Joyce didn't mind that. In the morning, while Daniel had his nap and Zoe played, she made the chocolate cream pudding from a Len Deighton recipe cut out from the newspaper: cream, eggs, sugar, butter, brandy, chocolate. The family had been eating meanly for a week – beans on toast, tomatoes on toast, plates of cheese and lettuce for her – so that she could splash out on this dinner party. She stuck sponge finger biscuits like a palisade all around the cut-glass bowl Lil had given her, then poured the chocolate mixture into the middle and put it in the fridge to set. She impressed herself by resisting the temptation to taste any or scrape out the bowl, and as a consequence felt gratifyingly hollowly thin.

When she had washed up the cooking things she had time to sit down at the table and drink a black instant coffee while Zoe had squash and biscuits. Zoe – a steady, shy four-year-old, with light brown hair cut short like a boy's – was taking advantage of Daniel being out of the way to fill in her magic colouring book: you brushed the drawings with plain water and like a miracle colours sprang out from the page. She worked painstakingly and neatly, her tongue stuck out in concentration, on a panting dog with its head cocked winningly sideways, boys playing ball in a suburban garden, a little girl in a maid's apron and cap. Ray had groaned at the colouring book in real pain when Zoe first brought it home (his mother had bought it for her); he threatened to throw it out, but Joyce understood the appeal of these happy obedient pictures and had signalled frowningly to him not to make a fuss. Anyway Ray had soon forgotten about the book's existence.

Yesterday Joyce had dusted and vacuumed and washed floors until she was sweating and gritty with dirt. Today, for the first time in weeks, the sun shone into their basement flat: a weak sweet early spring sunshine which fingered its exposure into some forgotten corners and found out cobwebs, so that she had to get her duster out again. She didn't mind the excuse for gazing critically around her. The rooms awaited company like a stage set: centred on the distinction and seriousness of Ray's paintings, glowing with the careful thought and tending she had put into all that surrounded the paintings, the tasteful and original furniture and ornaments. She was full (it had turned out) of ingenuity and practical resourcefulness: she knew how to make their flat look modern and stylish even on Ray's meagre income (he was only working part-time at the college and hadn't sold much work this past couple of years). She rescued some dainty kitchen chairs someone had put out for a Guy Fawkes Night bonfire and painted them with black enamel. She had flat squares of foam cut and covered them in thick coloured cottons, orange and olive green and mustard yellow, then piled them up in a block. She spread tall grasses and flower heads out to dry on newspapers above the immersion heater in the airing cupboard, and arranged them in two old earthenware tobacco jars she had bought in a junk shop for a shilling. The look she went for was contemporary Scandinavian design, earth colours and clean shapes: a black wrought-iron candelabrum, stainless-steel cutlery, coarse-woven linen place mats.

The plan was that when Daniel woke up she would take him and Zoe round to her mother's. Lil still lived at the same flat in Benteaston, along with Martin who was studying for his doctorate in chemistry and working as a labourer building the new bypass. There Aunt Vera would look after them until Lil finished work at the cake shop. Aunt Vera did have grandchildren of her own, but they were in America, and so she yearned for a share in Joyce's. She was not exactly a natural with small children. Daniel and Zoe preferred Grandma Lil, who would greet them with bags of leftover cakes and arms open wide, shouting: 'Who's my bestest bestest girl (or boy) in all the world, then?' But they tolerated Vera and her shy stiff efforts to be strict with them, and to encourage Zoe's reading and get Daniel to talk. (She reproached Lil for using baby language with him, insisting that this would 'hold him up'; Lil took no notice.)

When she had left the children, Joyce had an appointment at the hairdresser's; after that she would come back to the flat by herself and get on with cooking the fiddly beef olives that she was doing for the main course. The little packages of thinly sliced beef spread with mushroom stuffing had to be tied with threads individually before they were sautéed. She had made the chicken-liver terrine for the first course the night before. Ray would pick the children up on his way back from the college, and there would be plenty of time to get them into bed and asleep before the guests arrived. Joyce already knew what she was going to wear: she had made herself a new low-cut dress from a piece of grey slubbed silk left over from the days of the dressmaking business she had before the children came along. It had a difficult deep cowl neckline, three-quarter-length sleeves, and a peg skirt: she had bought a narrow black patent belt to wear with it. It was hanging now against the wardrobe in the bedroom, with a piece of tissue paper round the neck to protect it from dust, ready to put on after her quick last-minute bath. She could already imagine herself, moving suavely in the sexy, top-heavy way forced by the shape of the skirt, wafting perfume, welcoming the guests into the rooms subduedly, enticingly lit by well-placed lamps and rich with the smells of the food cooking. Miles Davis would be weaving his spell from the record player.

Of course it would be up to Ray in fact what record

he put on. Sometimes he didn't choose the kind of thing that Joyce wanted: if he was in a certain mood he might put on very far-out noisy fast jazz, that nobody else really liked. But it was no good worrying now about what his mood would be, at a point when there was nothing she could do about it.

The first thing that went wrong was that when she had got together a bag with all the things the children might need in the afternoon, and was just about to put their coats on and fasten Daniel in the pushchair, the front doorbell rang, and Ann was standing there with a girl-friend.

Ann hadn't really settled to anything since she finished at the University (she hadn't done well in her exams, she had had a wild time instead, and been the first person in town – by her own account – to wear black slacks so tight-fitting that they had to be zipped up the inside leg). At twenty-six she had been engaged twice and twice broken it off: one had been unsuitably too nice and one unthinkably too nasty (not that that would have stopped her in itself, but it turned out that he had been living, all the time they were engaged, with some woman who even had a child by him). She had worked in a shoe shop, and as a nanny for some 'ghastly' children, and currently had a job as a waitress at the cafeteria in the zoo. Her latest boyfriend had made Joyce's heart stop cold in her chest when he was first introduced: he was a grey-faced ratty little man who wore a Teddy-boy drape suit and worked at a bookie's.

Luckily he didn't seem to be as keen as Ann, and she made all the running, lurking about waiting to catch him as he came out of work, traipsing round the pubs to find where he might be drinking.

Joyce would have liked to have turned her and her friend away there and then, telling them frankly that she had no time to spare; but she didn't have quite that kind of relationship with her sister, and she knew Ann would take offence if she was blunt. Although Ann's style at the moment was to appear defiantly and extravagantly ordinary, full of contempt at any pretension to superiority, this did not mean that she was indifferent to criticism. In fact she was particularly touchy and quick to imagine she was being condescended to.

—What a shame, Joyce said, frowning and shaking her head as if with real regret. —I'm just on my way out. I've got an appointment at the hairdresser's. (She didn't want to mention the dinner party in case Ann took it into her head to turn up uninvited: she was quite capable of this.)

—Just let us in for a quick coffee, Ann wheedled. —We're absolutely gasping. We've been working like blacks.

Under their drooping macs, worn undone with the belts hanging down, they were in their waitress uniforms, striped like nurses' dresses. The zoo was only ten minutes' walk away from Joyce's flat, but Ann hadn't ever come round in her breaks before, so no doubt this was supposed to be something of an honour.

Joyce looked at her watch. —I've got to take the

children round to Mum's. Auntie's looking after them. But I suppose I could stop, if it's just for ten minutes.

—You're a brick, sis, said Ann, who never called her that. They piled past her in the narrow entrance passage: both of them had their hair back-combed into bouffant mounds and their faces elaborately made up with black eyebrow pencil, thick mascara, pink lipstick. The friend, who was tall and skinny with a poor complexion, gave a startled hostile look around at the flat glowing with good taste.

Ann hugged the bemused children. —You poor little things, she said. —Mummy's going to leave you with old Auntie Vera. I'll bet she makes you do lots of horrible jobs for her. That's what she used to do with me, when she was my teacher.

Daniel began to cry, not because he understood but because he had only just woken up.

—Mummy, we don't want to stay with Vera, Zoe whined.

While Joyce put the kettle on to boil, Ann took her friend into the lounge.

—Come and look. D'you want to see some paintings by the great artist?

They were smoking: Joyce was sure they were dropping ash on the clean carpet. She overheard them whispering together and then exploding into giggles. In her extreme irritation she forgot her diet and ate two biscuits.

—We reek of elephants, said Ann. —We took a ride. Lesley likes the keeper who does the rides.

—I do *not*, protested Lesley.

The girls bantered private jokes and opinions of the zoo staff over their coffee as if Joyce wasn't there: or perhaps she was required as witness to their devil-may-care fun. It was hard to believe that Ann with her studied flat hardness was the same girl who had once carried a volume of John Donne poems ostentatiously round with her everywhere and insisted on reading aloud from it in the street. By the time they finally left, Joyce was half an hour late: she would have to ask to use the phone in the cake shop to persuade the hairdresser's to hang on for her.

As Ann and Lesley skittered their way down the drive to the gate in their high heels, lighting up more cigarettes (only in order to shock, Joyce was sure), their voices squealing and screeching unnecessarily loudly, Joyce glanced involuntarily up at the windows of the ground-floor flat where the Reverend and Mrs Underwood lived. It was a huge Victorian house: there were two more flats above the Underwoods, let to old ladies. You didn't often see the Underwoods themselves at their windows, but set into the glass panes in their front room were those kind of ventilators that looked like empty reels of recording tape: these turned and rattled in the slightest breeze, and to Joyce they always seemed to be taking note on behalf of the Reverend of any inappropriate behaviour from herself or her family or visitors. He was an old square bear of a man with ragged grey hair, not feminised in the least by his black cassock whose skirts flew out ahead of him in pace with his long stride; his wife was grey and fragile and oozed a compensatory sweetness. The Reverend growled and barked whenever he met Joyce, often incomprehensibly, always with imperturbable and disapproving authority. Ray and he had had one or two blazing rows, over music in the evenings or the children playing on the front lawn, but Joyce was sure it was for her that the Reverend reserved his most disgusted disapproval. No matter how abjectly friendly and conciliatory she tried to be, she was sure he could see through this to her essential light worldliness.

She finally got the children settled down with Vera. Vera seemed to have girded herself up in an overall for the occasion, as if looking after them might involve particularly dirty work; there was uncharacteristic trepidation in her face. The children were also subduedly ill at ease. Daniel got out his Dinky cars; Zoe tipped her jigsaw out on the dining table and stolidly began to sort out the edge pieces.

—She's so like Kay, said Vera, as she always did. —It's the same face.

Joyce wouldn't hear of it. —Not in the least. She's like Nana Deare, she's nothing like my family.

And she touched Zoe lightly with the back of her fingers against her cheek, as if to ward off even the remote chance of harm through analogy. She slipped out while Vera was offering the children squash, and hardened herself when she heard Daniel wail by thinking ahead to the hairdresser's and the beef olives and the need to brush the lounge carpet again. In the cake shop her mother in her frilled apron and cap was picking out iced fancies in the tongs for a customer and arranging them in a box. Joyce squeezed round the counter into the little cubbyhole at the back where the phone was fixed on the wall in the midst of a flurry of pinned-up orders and invoices.

—Madam may be delayed now, said the receptionist at Hair Boutique. —We always give priority to the clients who arrive in time for their appointments.

—Blast, blast, breathed Joyce to herself, clenching the receiver with her fist in its tan glove that matched her shoes and bag. She hadn't wanted to arrive there on that footing, flustered and in the wrong. She knew how important it was to assert in these situations one's serene sense of superiority, from which, firmly established, one could then condescend as nicely as anything if one wished.

She left a threepenny bit for the call beside the phone. Lil looked up from tying the box of cakes with paper string.

—Mrs H says I can go at three, she said muffledly out of the side of her mouth. Mr and Mrs Harper were good employers – they let the staff use the shop phone, for instance, as long as it wasn't too often – but of course you were not supposed to carry on conversations about your private life in front of the customers. Lil was happy in this job; she enjoyed the camaraderie with the other 'girls' and all the minute variations in the same safe daily routine. (Sometimes if Joyce thought back to the days out on the estuary, when her mother had been left alone all day so far from anywhere and with no transport, she wondered how she had ever endured it.)

—I should think Vera'll be glad of you by then, she whispered back.

—Don't you worry about her, pet. You go on and enjoy yourself.

Joyce had never been to this hairdresser's before; she had hardly ever needed to have her hair done, since she had been wearing it for years in a long plait down her back, or pinned up behind. But now she had made up her mind to have it all cut off. She had been nursing for several weeks now a vision of herself, different: freed of the plait and its vaguely East European peasant overtones, too sincere and poignant and wholesome. Her new look would be more urbane, teasing; more grown-up and modern and knowing. She was ready for something new, although her thoughts on this as yet didn't go beyond the hair, and the grey dress.

Hair Boutique was on Green Street, the steep elegant street with the best shops that led down from Benteaston into the centre of town: the name was scrawled diagonally in pink cursive script across the plate-glass window thickly draped inside with white nylon. It was expensive – Joyce was going to pay 10s 6d for her cut and set when she could have got it for five shillings where Lil went – but she dreaded having her idea for her hair misinterpreted, and it had seemed safest to go for the most fashionable place.

The hairdresser – Jacqueline – gazed sceptically at

Joyce's face in the mirror in the little cubicle, playing with her hair which she had let down from its pins, scrunching it up and then scraping it back. Jacqueline herself was pretty: blonde and fine-boned and thin as a wraith, steely with repressed impatience.

—Madam's face is quite square in shape. Are you sure you don't want to go for something softer? If you want it short, then how about a bubble cut? That suits an extrovert personality. It's got more bounce to it than the elfin look.

Joyce stuck to her idea but felt nonetheless exposed and foolish. She imagined that Jacqueline picked up her hair with more disdain and brusqueness, once she knew she was not to be persuaded.

—I suppose we could put a few stand-up pin curls in on the crown, she said, making the best of a bad job. —That might give it a bit of body.

One of the juniors brought a portable washbasin into the cubicle: it fastened into some kind of plumbing arrangement in the floor. Joyce needed to spend a penny (another thing she had not had time to think of, in her rush), and asked to be directed to the Ladies. As she crossed to the stairs behind the receptionist, dressed in her pink cape with her hair spread out on her shoulders, she happened to glance outside the window: you could see out through the drapes although you couldn't see in.

Ray was walking down the street right in front of the salon.

Her first reaction was irritation, if anything at all,

164

because this was not a part of the day when she had planned on having to be thinking about him. But there was no reason why he should not be walking down Green Street, which was only five minutes from the Art College where he was working in his studio.

Then he paused, as if waiting for someone to catch up with him, and the someone who rejoined him and walked on with him – as if she might have stopped to look in a shop window for a moment, say – was Minkie, Minkie Gray, who was not only a girl who sometimes modelled for Ray and his students, but was also one of their dinner-party guests for tonight.

Again, for a moment, nothing; and then the beginning of things.

Joyce carried on past the receptionist and up the stairs to the lavatory, which although it was perfectly clean was not in the same luxurious style as downstairs. She balanced just above the seat to pee as she always did (she knew Mrs Mellor in the Docks was wrong about catching babies from toilets, but doubtless there were others things you could catch), and was smitten there with the first real shock of astonished disbelief, so that her legs trembled violently. She quickly pulled up her knickers and straightened her skirt and sat down hard on the closed lid.

Minkie had probably just been sitting for him and they were having a break and going to buy a cup of tea. Or he had been out on his own, perhaps getting that adapter plug he had promised to buy and kept forgetting, and had just bumped into Minkie. Or perhaps it could even be that Minkie had wanted to buy something for her, Joyce, to give her at the dinner party tonight, and had asked Ray to help her choose it. Strangely, though this last was the least likely explanation – apart from the improbability of anyone bringing anything more than flowers or maybe chocolates to a dinner party, Minkie never had any money anyway – it was the one that stuck in Joyce's mind and soothed her the most. She could imagine as if it had already happened the flood of relief and gratitude she would feel when Minkie gave her whatever it was (a scarf? soap? sugared almonds?) and said in that arch little-girl way she had, something about how she 'almost had to drag old Mr Grumpy Guts out with her to help her choose it, he was so cross at being disturbed'. Ray would frown irritatedly and complain to Joyce about her later. These were supposed to be the categories of emotion he felt about Minkie, if he thought about her at all: irritation and a kind of alarmed surprise at her silliness. Joyce could imagine him incandescent at her thinking fit to break in upon his precious work with such a trivial, and typically female, distraction. (A present indeed! What did Joyce need a present for?)

However, something in the way that they had moved together, paused and then moved on down Green Street, made it seem to Joyce that Ray's reactions to Minkie might need rethinking. Strangest of all was how they hadn't spoken; she was sure (although as she played and replayed the scene over in her mind she became less sure) that as Minkie swung into step by his side and they resumed their journey down the hill, they had not done what you would expect acquaintances to do, and bolstered their being together with interested mutually accommodating talk. Even if Ray hadn't been eager to talk then Minkie should have been. But they had simply swung into step together and moved off at one accord, quietly adjusted to one another without words.

Minkie was an odd-looking creature, but certainly attractive. She had a cheeky freckled face with a turned-up nose, and a head of short dark loose curls; she dressed in eccentric art-student clothes and played up the fact that she looked as if she ought to be buttoned into a red jacket as a pantomime boy. Joyce thought she had been wearing something like that on her way past the window just now, some kind of short military jacket with brass buttons from a jumble sale, although she couldn't have sworn to it. Minkie was thin and flat-chested: Ray had said her breasts were 'pancakes with cherries', and that had stupidly made Joyce feel safe. It had been Joyce who suggested inviting Minkie to dinner tonight; she was always short of single women, and she had had some vague idea of pairing her up with the single man who was coming, John Lenier, one of Ray's jazz friends. Ray had neither encouraged nor discouraged her over Minkie – he hadn't seemed at all interested in the party – although he said something about thinking she was barking up the wrong tree with John Lenier. But then Joyce had only thought that men didn't see these things the way women did.

Joyce pulled the chain and washed her hands and dried them on the pink roller towel. She checked her reflection in the mirror to reassure herself that no shock showed on her face: no, if anything she looked more remote and less flustered than she had been when she arrived. She waited until her legs had stopped the worst of the trembling, then went back downstairs to her cubicle, where Jacqueline plaited her hair, laid the cold steel of her scissors against the nape of her neck, and took the plait off in a couple of wide-jawed crunching bites. It lay in Joyce's hands still warm: known intimately to her and yet suddenly strange, in its mix of pink and pale gold and ginger.

—It's a lovely colour, Jacqueline conceded. —Although it's a difficult colour to match with.

Joyce's head felt light and free. All the time while the junior shampooed her, while Jacqueline chopped away at her hair with a blade set in something that looked like a Stanley knife, and then while she sat with her pin curls in a net under the dryer with cotton wool in her ears, reading a magazine, she felt this curious lightness. The two things seemed to her only equally important: important that her hair should turn out well, important that Ray should have some explanation for why he was on Green Street with Minkie. She didn't speculate any further; she felt herself poised, for the moment, upon the brink of speculation. She wondered, almost, who the competent elegant-looking woman was who sat in the mirror opposite her, legs carelessly crossed, absorbed in her magazine. She looked as though she had a rich life, full of drama and fun and interesting friends.

—It does suit you, said Jacqueline, when she was combing out the curls, pushing them up with her fingers. Joyce thought Jacqueline saw her too, the suave cool-eyed woman with the easy elfin hairdo and the interesting life. Ever since she came down from the Ladies, indifferent to what was going on around her, Jacqueline had treated her with more respect.

Joyce in her new hairdo looked experienced.

Not with the kind of experience her mother's generation had, pressed down like a dark burden upon your shoulders. This new generation wore it lightly and playfully, like a boy, simplified: free of all the old creaking corset-boned apparatus of women's troubles.

She left to catch the bus home with the plait wrapped up in tissue, nestled in the dark at the bottom of her bag, weighing it down, even while her new head floated weightlessly on her new bare neck.

Minkie was late. Dud Mason and his wife Penny and John Lenier were already there when she rang the bell, and they had opened the first bottle of Mateus Rosé wine.

The front door to the flat was down some steps off the drive; it opened on to a long passage floored with linoleum where they kept all their coats and wellingtons and Ray's bicycle and the pushchair. The lavatory was at the far end of the passage, although everyone was supposed to keep the door shut so you couldn't see straight in there from the entrance. Joyce had done her best with it but the passage always made you feel draughty and rather dismal until you went through the glass door to one side and into the carpeted hall. When Joyce opened the front door there really was a moment's pause while she expected Minkie to hand her something: that present, soap or sweets or something, that she ought to have been buying when she was out with Ray. Ray hadn't said anything yet about having seen Minkie earlier, although Joyce had made several opportunities for him to do so. It was dark outside, but the electric lantern above the door was switched on so she could see Minkie peering out palely from where she was swathed in some sort of man's greatcoat several sizes too big for her. It had begun to rain; from the garden above there came an intimate pattering, drops burying themselves in the thick shrubs.

—I'm so sorry, pleaded Minkie in her baby voice. —I'm late and I haven't brought anything. I'm unforgivable. I really don't deserve to be let in.

Joyce laughed. She had a suddenly illuminated vision of how dreadful it must have been for Minkie to be asked to dinner tonight, under the circumstances. She could imagine how she must have struggled, trying to make up her mind whether to come or to cry off, pretending she had a cold or something. She could imagine, too, how little help Ray had been. 'What am I supposed to do about it?' he would have said tetchily. 'Just tell her you're busy or something.' Joyce really couldn't have done any better if she had contrived the whole thing devilishly.

—Come on in, she said gaily. —We don't care how unforgivable you are. We're already tipsy.

This was true. She was borne up by the wine swimming in her head, she wasn't taking her usual care not to drink too much in case of spoiling the cooking. In the warm hall she helped Minkie out of the heavy wet coat; the dark curls were wet all over with tiny droplets of rain. Under the greatcoat she was wearing a sort of green embroidered sarong thing, wrapped tight and flat round her breasts, leaving her shoulders bare. It didn't really work. Joyce could guess how at home in front of the mirror it had looked like a posture that Minkie could strike: extravagant and original and defiant. But actually it depended on that still posture in the mirror; once she had to move around in it she clearly felt self-conscious and foolish, as if she had dressed up for a part in the wrong play. Joyce in her understated grey dress had the advantage of her.

—I love your hair! cried Minkie. —It really suits you.

—Do you? Yes, it was high time. I'd had enough of that silly old look. Come and get a drink.

The guests looked up hopefully towards them as they came into the lounge. Ray was holding forth to Dud about the Summerson Council, which had been set up the year before to report on and validate all the art education courses in the country. This was a subject which touched a painful nerve, Joyce knew. He overreacted ferociously to the modernisation the council was encouraging precisely because it galled him to be caught out on the other side, suddenly seeming to stand for

171

traditional values in the face of the new art. He still thought of himself as the new art.

—So what do you think the latest is? he declaimed dramatically, stabbing with his pipe, standing with his legs apart and his back to the oil fire, keeping the warmth off everybody else. —I go into the life room at the beginning of the new term, after the Christmas break, and all those beautiful old casts, all those exquisite Greek and Roman and Renaissance forms, are gone. Just gone. All at once after three thousand years they're not in fashion any more. We've got nothing to learn from them any more. I try to find out where they are, what's happened to them. Nobody seems to know. It's like a murder. I feel as if a murder's taken place and everyone's ashamed and nobody will talk about it. The bodies have been got rid of somehow. Did they break them up? I mean, did they actually stand there and hack them to pieces with a hammer? Or did they get poor old Bassett to do it? It would have broken his heart, that's for sure.

—Minkie hasn't brought any wine! Joyce announced. —Shall we let her have a drink?

She thought she saw him falter for one instant, when he saw Minkie. He screwed up his face in an even more terrible frown. —I'd like to say we're in the hands of the barbarians, he shouted. —But it's worse than that. The barbarians at least have a beauty of their own. These people – these idiots – these absolute cretins – they don't know what beauty is, even to hate it. They don't know the difference between art and advertising.

—Shh, said Joyce. —Remember the Underwoods.

(The Reverend sometimes banged on the floor with his stick if there was jazz, or shouting.)

—It's the beginning of the end of drawing, said Dud, who was easily made gloomy.

As if overcome, Ray went to change the music on the gramophone, making a show of the delicate care with which he handled the records in and out of their paper sleeves. Predictably, he put on something that Joyce didn't like, something squeaky and fast and frantic, Mingus probably. This was obviously the part he was going to play tonight: the tormented artist unable because of the scale and purity of his feelings to put on a social show as other people could. There had been a time when Joyce was in awe of him in that vein. He had the same focused glow as when he was working; it gave an edge of concentration to his shambling looks, untidy soft hair he wouldn't get cut often enough and fleshy pouchy face, like an angel gone to seed. (He was thickening around the waist, too, he would have to watch that: with his short legs it wouldn't suit him.)

She thought that their guests already sensed something was wrong. Penny, who was very pregnant, sat guiltily at the edge of her seat as if she felt herself accused of breaking up plaster casts. John Lenier looked as if he was hoping for an opportunity to come in with something funny, to make them all laugh and defuse the gloomily denunciatory mood. He'd probably never even heard of the Summerson Council, and couldn't care less.

—Of course Minkie can have a drink. John leapt to his feet. —I'll pour it for her. What would she like?

Joyce decided that John would be her ally for the night. She liked him anyway. He was tall and lean and took life lightly. With his silky grey hair (prematurely grey, he was only in his twenties, like her) he made Joyce think of a graceful poplar turning up its leaves in the breeze. His cream-coloured polo neck was just the sort of thing she wished that Ray would wear. He told her what a lovely room this was, what subtle colours she had chosen, and admired her dress and her hair. When he handed Minkie her glass of Mateus he said that she looked in her green sarong as if she might dance for them later. Minkie was grateful, but Joyce was pleased that he had felt the need to be kind and rescue the silly sarong and give it a reason for existence.

Joyce burnt the toast that was supposed to go with the terrine. Also, the creamed potatoes had lumps because she couldn't be bothered to mash them vigorously enough, and the beef olives were overcooked and some of the sauce had burned on the bottom of the frying pan. She was completely indifferent to the food, slopping it out carelessly on the plates, eating it without tasting it. She had promised herself for days, in return for starving herself, a portion of chocolate cream pudding, but when it came out of the fridge she didn't even want any. Only Dud and Minkie ate it.

They had all got riotously drunk somehow. They weren't used to drinking much these days, and John Lenier had brought a bottle of vodka as well as two bottles of Black Tower. Penny slipped away from the table quite early on and fell asleep on the sofa in the lounge. It wasn't quite clear whether they were having a fantastic time or whether it was a dreadful disaster. At certain points they were all screaming with laughter as if everything anyone said was exceptionally miraculously funny, although Joyce could never remember afterwards any of their jokes that night, only Dud coming back from the lavatory wearing one of the children's balaclavas which he had picked up from the coat hooks in the passage. After that everyone who went came back wearing something until the kitchen floor was cluttered with sou'westers and gloves and umbrellas and Zoe's scooter (the children were mystified and delighted to find these things in the morning).

At other points, on the contrary, Joyce was suddenly given a vision of their party as a hellhole, a Bosch-like slithering charnel nastiness, where she and Ray exchanged in naked moments a look like a rictus of loathing, seeing down to the very bottom of each other's obscenely motivated souls. Then it seemed as if what was happening was something so awful and so utterly unlike anything that had ever happened before that in the morning when they were sober they would no longer be able to live together, ever again.

Dud told Joyce in low tones (once he was sure Penny was asleep) how he had loved her at art school.

—You remember those little folded cards we had with our timetables on? Every time I knew you were going to be in a lesson, I wrote JS in tiny letters in the corner, on that square.

This was gratifying but familiar territory, and Joyce knew where it led: Dud with his arm around her, or pressing his bear-bulk against her under the table, mumbling mournfully about how she was a very special person. Then he would be blushing and full of mawkish contrition when he met her next, hoping she wouldn't say anything to Penny. She fended him off, it was John she was intent upon. They seemed to be getting on very well, whispering satirically about the others, exchanging ironic looks, confiding together over his hopes for a career in photography (the words came into her head: 'she took a charming interest'). He was full of praise for the beautiful food, although she noticed he left one of his beef olives and stubbed a cigarette out on the plate. He kissed her hand once and held on to it for a few moments, pretending to guess her perfume; she was shocked by the thudding excitement with which her whole body responded to the little game. When she pulled her hand out of his cool silvery grip he slid his thumb suggestively along her palm; involuntarily she imagined them kissing lips, playing with tongues.

Ray was explaining to Minkie in belligerently insistent detail how if you were drawing the docks you had to begin drawing at the bottom of the steps when the tide was out and then you could move your drawing further up as the tide came in.

—I don't understand it, said Minkie miserably. —But it doesn't matter.

—But why don't you understand it? It's very simple.

An idiot could understand it. You begin at the bottom, when the tide is out . . .

Then there was a time when Minkie was lying sobbing on the bed in Ray and Joyce's bedroom, although it wasn't ostensibly about the docks, it was because Dud had been describing to her the diseased eyes that he was paid to draw for the medical records at the hospital, and although she had told him this was making her feel sick, he wouldn't stop. Joyce said she was going to check on the children (presumably the children were asleep? perhaps she really did open their door and look in on them, although she had no memory of that), and then she walked into the bedroom and up to Minkie on the bed, singing a song of her mother's that used to make her cry when she was a little girl. The bedroom light was off but she could see in the light from the hall behind.

> *All in the merry month of May*
> *When green buds were a-swellin',*
> *Young Jimmy Groves on his deathbed lay,*
> *For love of Barbara Allen.*
>
> *All slowly slowly there she came,*
> *And slowly she came nigh him.*
> *And all she said when there she came:*
> *Young lad I think you're dyin'.*

She had a poor singing voice; she had no idea where the plan came from, with its cardboard-theatrical threat and mystical resonance so unlike her usual brisk daytime self. Minkie stopped sobbing and gazed at her with eyes that were swimming in tears and fearful. She lay with one arm flung out across the bedcover: on her wrist was a thick bangle of polished wood. Joyce was convinced all at once that this had been a present to Minkie from Ray, worn tonight for good luck, or in defiance.

—I'll take that, I think, she said, and slipped it off the girl's limp unresisting hand. —D'you mind?

Minkie dumbly shook her head.

(Did she put the bangle on and wear it back to where the others were still shouting and laughing? The next day she found it among the dirty dishes in the kitchen; she took it with her when she went out with Daniel for a walk on the Heath and dropped it into a litter bin among the sweet wrappers and lolly sticks, although it was a lovely thing, a shame to lose it.)

At some other point that evening they were all talking about Mary Anderson. When she was at college with Dud and Joyce she was an odd-looking girl with elderly parents and thick pebble glasses under which her eyelashes grew long and luxuriant as if in a greenhouse. Now she was making a name for herself as a painter.

—I remember I told her to go to the Dubuffet exhibition in '59, said Ray. —That's what you can see in these latest paintings, that sort of inspired graffiti. The Dubuffet set free something in her imagination. That's what they don't understand, these ideas men: that you can be free, and yet paint in a tradition.

—Because she can draw, said Dud. —Even though they

178

aren't naturalistic forms, it's there, the truth in the pencil.

Joyce envied Mary, for those minutes, desolatingly.

—But would you want to go to bed with her? she laughed.

She couldn't believe, the moment she'd said it, that she was capable of anything so stupid. She and Ray stared at one another; she imagined that their pupils were dilated like cats', gaping blackness.

—I would, said Ray. —She's mysterious.

—Mysterious? What's mysterious? You didn't use to think that. That just means ugly. You're just impressed because she's somebody now.

—Yes, I suppose I am. It's something, that she's somebody.

—You men! she exclaimed, flinging her arm in a grand gesture of disgust, knocking over a glass. Although after all it was she who had said the stupid thing, who had lowered everything to the personal, sexual question.

Eventually Reverend Underwood came thundering at the front doorknocker in his pyjamas and dressing gown. He and Ray engaged in a shouted argument while the guests, half relieved at being shaken out of the evening's dark tangle, hurriedly got their things together and made subdued farewells.

—Thanks for a lovely time, whispered Penny, snugly rounded, blinking from her innocent sleep. —I'm sorry I've missed all the fun. Dudley loves coming here.

Usually after their dinner parties Joyce and Ray cleared up in fatigued companionable silence, moving coordinatedly around one another under her command, piling up plates and emptying ashtrays. Tonight Joyce gave one shuddering look at the mess; her bones ached and her head swam and she was nauseous. She was incapable of restoring order. She didn't even want to. While the front door was still open and Ray was saying goodbye to John and Minkie, she clambered out of her clothes in the half-dark bedroom, leaving them in a heap on the floor, and lay down on her back in the bed in her baby-doll short nightdress, keeping still as a statue, staring at the ceiling, listening to Ray padding round the rooms, turning the lights off, checking at the children's door.

She knew that when he came to bed he would want to make love to her: his heart would be pounding from his furious quarrel with the Reverend Underwood and he would want calming down. She waited for him like a stone, promising herself to endure it as unforgivingly as if she was having an examination at the doctor's. It seemed to her that if she could just keep her mouth closed on this silence she would be punishing him, holding on to what he didn't know she knew, even though it lay huge and heavy in her head. She was quite sure that he hadn't an idea that she had guessed. He would have to wait for Minkie to tell him (women were so much better at these things); and she imagined that even then, even when he came to her with big dog-eyes full of contrition, wanting to explain, she would refuse to speak about it to him.

—Should I put the leftovers in the fridge? he asked, standing in the doorway, aggrieved at having to do her chores; he thought she'd flaked out on him because she was half-cut.

—Put them wherever you want.

For another few minutes she heard him banging things ill-temperedly around in the kitchen; then he came and climbed into bed, and after a bit, reached out and touched her breast, which was their sign. Obediently she got up and put in her cap in the bathroom.

—Only if you'd like to, he said.

—I don't mind.

She lay as if she was an effigy on a tomb. He laboured on top of her and she pressed her nails into her palm because it was disgusting, and thought the words 'his hairy rump', although that wasn't fair, he wasn't particularly hairy. Towards the end she pretended, and stirred about a bit, just to get it over. She thought she only wanted him to fall asleep and leave her alone to think. At the same time she felt so sad, and even ashamed, that the thing that had been so transforming and incandescent between them could have become as diminished and miserable as this.

His climax, though, groaning and collapsing on top of her, affected her as unpredictably as if he'd released a spring: not of sexuality but of rage. As he rolled off her she pushed away from him and leaped out of the bed.

—I'm off, she said. —I'm going.

He propped himself up on his elbows, startled out of post-coital relaxation. —What do you mean? What's the matter?

—I'm going. How could you?

181

—How could I what? You said you didn't mind.

She went into the bathroom and washed herself in cold water, and then dressed, though not in the grey dress: she felt herself trampling that under her feet as she moved backwards and forwards in the room, choosing slacks and a striped cotton top from her drawers, pulling a comb through her hair, picking up to take with her in her handbag a change of knickers and her toothbrush and make-up bag and perfume.

Ray by this time was standing uselessly beside the bed; he had put on his pyjama bottoms for decorum's sake.

—What's going on here; what's all this about?

—I'm going, she said. —Where does John Lenier live?

—Jesus Christ, Joyce, what are you talking about? You're making a terrible mistake.

—I'm talking about M-i-n-k-i-e. Someone who was here tonight. Some nice little cream pancake with cherries on the top. But two can play at that game. Don't bother to tell me where he lives. I'll take the address book.

She didn't know how much it was really about John Lenier.

There was no doubt that as she left the house and hurried through the dark windy night to the telephone box (John's address wasn't in the book but his telephone number was) she was full of a sexual excitement focused on him. She wasn't imagining that she would take much time telling him how she felt about Ray and Minkie; all that was needed was a bare explanation of the need to make up for everything that had been spoiled in her bed

182

just now. Her rage was a licence: her mind feverishly threw up fragments of scenes with John, his grateful astonishment, his hesitating and at first elaborately courteous advances, that languorous delicate alertness of his applied to her, bent over her, minutely responsive to her pleasures, taking his own with an exquisiteness she intuited in him. More, too: other things flashed on her mind's eye, an accelerating daring, initiations into new things (she wasn't specific as to quite what new things), an open-eyed consent to some definitive crossing into adult territory. It was high time, she thought, that she grew up.

If John had been another man, the night might have had a very different outcome, the things dreamed up in fantasy might have taken on solid form, everything from then on might have turned out differently.

On the other hand, as soon as she knew he wasn't going to play the part she had imagined for him, his importance fell away as if it had never existed, releasing her into a kind of calm and disclosing her real situation in a new perspective. Perhaps she knew she had made a mistake as soon as she spoke to him in the phone box, her whole body shaking so profoundly in time to her heart's thumping that it even distorted her voice; the box meanwhile was being buffeted from outside, gusts of wind rattling twigs against the glass.

—It's Joyce, she said. —Something's happened. I need to talk to you. Can I come round?

At least he didn't sound as if she'd woken him from sleep; he was sober and careful. —Joyce? Oh dear. Well, of course you can. Where's Ray? Wouldn't you rather that I came to you? I could easily pop my things on.

—Oh, no. It's easy now, I'm already out, I don't want to go back. Just tell me how to get to where you live.

She thought he'd offer to come out and find her; instead after a moment's thought he gave her precise directions to his address. (It wasn't far, a ten-minute walk, a few streets away.) The real man, of course, was never going to be as obediently pliant to her desires as his simulacrum in her fantasy; it was understandable that he responded guardedly to this casual party flirtation returned upon him, rawly exacting. No wonder, even, that he wanted to know about Ray: husbands began to count when things got serious. Nonetheless something in his voice cooled her and warned her off, so that by the time he opened his door to her ten minutes later in the red silk paisley dressing gown that somehow suddenly made everything come clear – he might almost have put it on to help explain – she was all ready for her disillusion. The dressing gown gave it away like a piece of crude stage machinery signalling a point; even to her, who had been so obtuse, so sure of her command of the way things were, so oblivious to essential missing pieces of information. This must have been what Ray was trying to tell her while she was busily planning: first, to have John for Minkie, then for herself.

It was simply never mentioned after that between her and John: the possibility that she had come to him in hope of something rather more than the clean handkerchief and cocoa he considerately provided, or that he might have ever had to deliver up to her the awkward explanation of why he would not be able to play his part in her revenge. Instead, awareness of all this hovered with the effect of high comedy between them and made them get on rather well, as if they had been together through some danger narrowly skirted. Even though she poured out her story to him, crying copiously into his handkerchief, and told him things she had never spoken of to anyone else about the difficulty of living with Ray, and even though John consoled her so tactfully with his calm estimate of the unimportance of what had happened, nothing that they said to one another seemed completely serious. At some point the conversation even turned to her admiration of the way he'd done his flat, which was all black and white with a spatter of bright colours in the cushions and rugs.

—He doesn't really like her much, said John, thinking back over his impressions from the evening. —I'd never have had any idea of anything between them, if you hadn't told me.

—No, he doesn't like her much. He thinks she's silly.

—Well, bless her, she is, rather.

—Don't bless her. I want to tear her hair and scratch her eyes out.

—No you don't. She's a daft little girl who thinks it's clever to pout and play baby. She isn't even worth wasting your anger on. She's a little shallow pond and you're a lake, a deep still lake, just a little bit ruffled on the surface for the moment.

—Oh, John, you're so nice to me. I only wish I believed that Ray thought that.

—He's not an idiot, is he? Don't you think he knows it? Look, what you need is to get some beauty sleep, go home, forget making any ugly scenes. He knows you know: you don't need to say anything more. Just be your gorgeous self, make yourself look like the sophisticated glamorous woman you are, cook him one of your wonderful meals, put on the lamps and the music, take the time to sit down and talk with him about painting or whatever, and don't you think he'll put some important questions to himself about why he's been playing around? D'you think he wants to sit down and talk about art with Minkie? Maybe it's been difficult for him, with the children. Maybe things haven't been everything they used to be between you. Buy yourself some gorgeous new underwear and some perfume and make him fall for you all over again.

—Oh, I know I could do that, she said, frowning.

—Well of course you could.

—I don't know whether it's what I want to do.

Eventually John brought a pillow and sheets and blankets and made up a bed for her on his sofa, where she fell almost instantly asleep, with no idea what time of day or night it was, except that it was still dark.

When she woke she could just make out the shapes of objects in the room in a grey dawn light. Her head felt clear, she was perfectly well, she must have worked right through the terrible hangover that surely had been in store for her in all the excitement of the night before, her escape into the dark, her tears and her pouring out of all her troubles. These had used up all of the poison in her.

She woke thinking about Ray: not about Minkie and all the stuff from last night, but about his work. His latest paintings, for the last eighteen months or so, had been something new. He was putting the paint on more smoothly, and if you drew your attention away from the surface details of the brushwork, you could suddenly see revealed a glimpse of likeness, verisimilitude, as if under the necessary play of the paint he had trapped a shadow of the real presence. Joyce knew that this mixture of an expressionistic style with some of the devices of illusionism was an eccentric, original technique; and knew what practised virtuoso handling of the paint was required to produce such a complex effect. The other thing he had changed was the way he arranged the bodies on the canvas, his new choice of a cramped picture space with body parts improbably crowded together. Some of the new nudes had startled and unsettled Joyce when she first saw them: he had asked the model to take a contorted position, legs apart, genitalia brutally exposed and foregrounded, the model perhaps looking out from the picture with her head almost upside down, twisted under her knee. The models could only hold these contortions while he made quick sketches. When he worked the sketches up into paintings he didn't square the drawings up as he had used to do, he copied freehand and exaggerated the distortions and the improbability.

These were beautiful pictures, Joyce was sure of that. She knew that she was able to make an objective estimate of his work because she also had an uncanny instinct for when his paintings failed, which came from knowing him so well, recognising when he was weak or false or trying to cover up something he couldn't do. These new ones frightened her, but they weren't ugly. They looked unflinchingly deep into the layered appearances of flesh, seeing things that were true. She trusted him, not personally, but objectively, that he was able to see the truth: this was not in their daily life, when he was often wrong, but beyond it. She could see it when it worked, the translation of the truth of life into pictures, but she couldn't do it for herself. My love for him rests on that, she thought. Everything rests on that.

It had been a while now since she had modelled for him; he had made some drawings of her pregnant with Daniel, and afterwards breastfeeding him, but because of the children there simply wasn't time these days for her to sit for long enough. She had even been glad that it had stopped; there had seemed to be something irreconcilable between her two roles, as the effective manager of his domestic life and as the still, mute object of his study, on whom he concentrated, but as if she wasn't there. Sessions with him weren't necessarily calm or good-tempered, either; if he was struggling, scraping off paint or screwing up drawings, she used to feel guiltily responsible, drained by the intensity of his effort but helpless to make it work, angry with his anger because it seemed self-indulgent, not directed at real things. Now she was sorry, she wanted that discomfort back; she thought that perhaps Minkie had modelled for one of those searing nudes, exposed and altered by his scrutiny.

How had she imagined that this man might be chastely domesticated, on her terms? She had hung his pictures in her home as if she could gloss over what was inside the frame and use it as a sign of taste merely, to hang among other signs, curtains and lamps and interesting objects from the junk shops.

Joyce cleaned her teeth and washed her face in John's bathroom (lucky that she had brought her toothbrush), surprised and pleased by her reflection in his mirror with its new short hair.

She should go back.

Perhaps if she went now she might even get there before the children woke up.

She let herself into the flat with her key. Probably the Underwoods heard her coming back just as they must have heard her leave last night (she always imagined them side by side in a vast mahogany bed, listening from under some sort of overhanging ecclesiastical ornamentation), but she didn't care. All was quiet. She thought that Ray would probably be asleep, and that she might embark on the clearing up, and then make breakfast for him and percolate real coffee when he woke. She slipped off her shoes and crossed quietly to their bedroom in her stockinged feet; the door was slightly open, as they always left it, so as to hear the children if they cried out in the night.

Ray was sitting in all his clothes at the window, where it was becoming light, and day outside: a tentative spring day under veiled blue skies, meek after the tantrums of last night, smelling of the soaked earth of gardens (she was exhilaratedly saturated in it as he couldn't yet be, from her walk home through the early streets where she met only the milkman). When he saw her in the doorway he jumped up off the wooden chair where she usually piled her clothes at night.

—Hello. You can't have been very comfortable, she said.

—I wasn't. He hesitated. —Did you mean the chair? Or about – things?

She laughed. (Both of them were using subdued undertones, so as not to wake Daniel. Zoe was a lie-abed, but Daniel was an early bird, usually first calling to them from his cot around six or half past.) —Both, probably.

—Well, no. No to both.

—What are you doing up? You'll be exhausted.

He looked at her suspiciously. —Have you been asleep, then?

—After my night of torrid passion.

—Was it? His voice cracked somewhat.

—What do you think?

He was exaggeratedly relieved, flinging his arms up as if he had kept them by his sides in a tension of suspense. —I was beginning to wonder. I did try to tell you.

—You didn't try all that hard.

—Is it funny?

She smothered her giggles in her hands. —Probably. When you come to think about it. My crazy fling. *A trip to the moon, on gossamer wings.* Have you been sitting there all night?

—Waiting for you. But not all night. I cleared up.

—Oh, you didn't. Not all on your own? How awful!

—It was awful. Not the clearing up. An awful night.

—I know. Listen.

But she didn't know at first what she had to say. She crossed the room to where he stood and stopped just a few inches in front of him, so that they could feel one another's body warmth rolling off them in the cold morning and taste one another's breath, hers minty, his stale and boozy. His clothes from the night before were crumpled and his hair was dishevelled and his face pasty and grey around the jowls with stubble. It seemed a comically appropriate atonement, that he had kept his dismal vigil while she slept those hours away at John's as easefully as an angel.

Ray put his hands up to take her shoulders, but she caught them in hers and held him off.

—I don't want any lying, she said.

He shook his head mutely.

—Not from either of us, I mean. Not from me either, about what I feel. It makes me want to kill you, when I know you've slept with her. It makes me feel desperate, and helpless. I don't know what to do.

—It didn't mean anything.

—No, it did, it did. That's just what I don't want you to say. It did mean something.

He shrugged. —OK, it meant something. But not what you think.

—I don't know what I think. What did it mean?

—I suppose it was just sex. How can I put it?

191

However I put it, I'm in the wrong, don't think I don't know that.

—Don't talk about wrong and right. I don't want us to be together because of the old rule book.

—I see.

—And that was a lie already. Coming from you. 'Just sex.' That word 'just' is a lie, to hide its importance from me.

He searched her face, to see how much he could say. —All right, that was a lie. I was obsessed with her, for a short while. Perhaps a month or so. The idea of her devoured me. Now I can't imagine why, it's so thoroughly over.

Joyce flinched, she was shocked, she felt a rich pulse of blood in her heart. —'Devoured' you.

—You asked me.

—I almost can't bear that, that the idea of her devoured you.

—It's men, he tried to explain. —This is how it takes us, sometimes. I'm so sorry. It seems such a cheap trick, now I'm having to put it into words. I can't even believe, myself, that it ever seemed important.

—How many times, exactly, precisely, did you make love to her? Don't lie, whatever you do.

He had to mentally count them, humbled and blushing, and she stared at his eyes as if she might catch in there some flicker of the pictures that he summoned up. —Six? Yes, I think, six.

—And was it good? Tell the truth.

—How am I supposed to answer that, to you?

—But answer it.

He sighed. —At first it was good. Then I got tired of her, she got on my nerves. Don't think I don't feel like a swine.

After a pause Joyce said, —I don't want to contain you. I don't want to be your lock and key.

—Sometimes it feels to a man, he said slowly and hesitantly, —as if women want to make the world sweet. Are you going to be angry if I say this? But it's not sweet. And it's sometimes a strain, standing on guard, pretending to the woman that everything's going to be all right, everything's nice.

—Is this sex we're talking about here?

—It's partly sex. Yes, I suppose it is. And freedom, not getting all tangled up in sweet things, being able to slip the rope sometimes.

—Well, I might want that too, she said.

He was startled. —Might you?

—I might. Didn't that occur to you?

His face was full of trepidation. —Are we talking about freedom? I don't know, it's not the same, freedom, for men and women. Just biologically, even. Say I'd been wrong, last night, about John. I don't know whether I could deal with that: you, with another man.

—You would just have to, she said. —Maybe. If that's how we're going to manage things.

—I see. I see what you're getting at.

She let him, then, hold her by the shoulders, gripping tightly.

There was so much more for them to say, and to sort out.

But at that moment, like a bird piping, the baby sang out from behind the bars of his cot.

Needless to say, there was plenty of clearing up left to do. Ray's idea of a tidy room was not the same as hers; he had done his best, but he had no idea where most things went, or how to deal with the dirty pans, or how to wrap up the things that needed to be stored in the fridge. And he hadn't been able to use the vacuum in the middle of the night. (Goodness knows what the Underwoods even made of his running the hot water.) She sent Ray back to bed to sleep ('Daddy's got a bit of a headache') and set about seeing to all this, as well as preparing the children's breakfast and getting them dressed and making the beds and rinsing Daniel's nappies and putting them on to boil; and all with an exultant lightness, nursing a secret and liberating excitement like a teenager who's been kissed and carries the feel of it around all day on her skin. Every time she had to pass the closed door of the bedroom she was aware of Ray in there as if he was an adventure that awaited her.

Then the tiredness hit her, like a cosh, at about eleven, when she put Daniel down for his nap and took the chocolate pudding out from the fridge and helped herself to a big bowlful (her diet seemed trivial, compared to what was happening in her marriage). When she had eaten it she felt sick, and thought that she might lie down on the sofa to snatch some sleep for half an hour before she began to prepare the Sunday dinner. Zoe would be all right, Nana Deare had taught her to knit and she was practising. It was true that she couldn't turn round at the end of a row, so that every ten minutes she had to come to Joyce to put the needles back into her hands facing the other way; but Joyce was sure she would be able to do that in her sleep.

As soon as she closed her eyes she remembered the plait of hair which had lain forgotten in its tissue paper in the bottom of her handbag ever since she came home from the hairdresser's. It seemed somehow disrespectful to leave it there unregarded any longer; even risky, although she didn't know exactly what was at risk, except that the hair left for too long washing around in the depths of the bag might pick up bits of lint, and dirt from the loose coins. So she stood up again, crossed the hall, opened the bedroom door, signing to Zoe to keep quiet, then tiptoed cautiously into the half-dark. The curtains were closed, the room smelled fustily of sleep, the hump of her husband snored from under the blankets pulled up over his head. Her handbag was still where she had put it down when she came in from her failed attempt at adultery early that morning. With an odd sense of enacting something like a ceremony, she pulled open her underwear drawer, lifted the plait from her bag, sinuous and suggestive in its crinkling paper, and buried it at the back of the drawer under all the layers of her things.

The thought came to her unbidden, that the plait would keep its colour through all the years while her own hair turned grey.

Five

In Zoe's memory, Fiona first came to their school the day they did air pressure. At junior school they only did science in an occasional, desultory way, when their excitable Welsh teacher was in the mood for it. Drawing autumn leaves or testing milk and vinegar with litmus paper was a glamorous respite from the routines of English comprehension and maths.

On this particular day (they were Junior Three, so Zoe was ten years old) he crowded the whole class into the staffroom, which was enough of an adventure in itself: this was normally a forbidden sanctum whose threshold they were not allowed to cross. Usually the only time a child was allowed in here was if they had fainted or been sick and were waiting, perhaps wrapped in the old blue cellular blanket, to be collected by their parents. It was always consoling to be reminded that this snug refuge was only a step away from the rough struggle of the echoing lofty classrooms with their gothic windows too high to look out from. The staffroom was homely with a gas fire and armchairs and crocheted cushion covers smelling of mothballs; there was a tray with a teapot and knitted cosy, jars of coffee and sugar, a biscuit barrel with a wicker handle. The teachers' coats were hung up on hooks in one corner, proving that they really did sometimes go home and have real lives elsewhere. Zoe was prone to a little rush of worship at the thought of her teachers' private lives. She was really very happy at that school.

Beside the fire was a gas ring where the teachers boiled their kettle. Mr Lloyd had brought in from home an empty metal paraffin can with a screw lid. He impressed upon them, first, that they were not to touch anything, anything, in the staffroom, and, second, that this experiment was much too dangerous for them ever to try for themselves, and, third, that it would have been even more dangerous if he hadn't scrupulously washed out every trace of paraffin before he started. Then he put the empty can with its lid unscrewed on to the gas ring and began to heat it.

It was of course the aura of danger that the children loved with this teacher. This was true even when they weren't doing science, even when they were writing out, say, five sentences with speech marks at the beginning, five sentences with speech marks at the end, and five with speech marks in the middle; or multiplying £19 17s 8½d by 7, 9 and 11. He was a short, springy, vital man with a lick of shining black hair that flopped forwards and had to be tossed back out of his eyes; a passionate Baptist, who explained to them as if it were a truth that brooked no argument the flawed logic of the Roman Catholic celebration of Christ's suffering. He cultivated a volatile and histrionic relationship with his classes, irresistible to certain of the girls and the cleverer boys. It did not occur to Zoe at the time to wonder how those other boys felt about him, the ones whose failures were the necessary grist to his teaching performances, and whose ears he twisted, or whose legs he slapped behind the knee.

—What's inside this can? he asked them, while it was heating.

Surely that was easy.

There was a whole ritual performance attached in Mr Lloyd's class to the answering of questions. If you knew the answer – or, riskily, if you didn't but thought he wouldn't pick on you – you thrust your arm up and called out, 'Sir! Sir!' urgently, eagerly. Mr Lloyd meanwhile would fasten on one of the children, usually one of the boys, who didn't know the answer, and persist in trying to elicit it from him. Those who knew, or were pretending they knew and had probably by now forgotten that they didn't, would carry on calling out, pumping their arms in the air, and – not in the staffroom obviously, but if they were in their normal classroom – actually climbing on to their chairs and jumping up and down on them, in a crescendo of desperate appeal. This wasn't an occasional performance, but repeated every day, usually over times tables or spellings. Mr Lloyd would eventually turn in disgust from the ignoramus he was persecuting and ask one of the panting, desperately certain ones; sometimes it would turn out that he or she had no idea of the answer either. Then the others who had subsided momentarily into a post-climactic lassitude would revive and start the chanting and pumping fists in the air again.

—Sir! Sir!

But today no one, not even Zoe, or Barbara Mole or Pamela Warren or Neil Ashley or David Tew or any of the others who were usually to be counted on, could give the right answer.

—What's inside this can? he said again, smiling round, enjoying their perplexity.

Nothing, they were sure. He had turned it upside down, he had passed it round, they were sure that it was empty.

—There's something inside this can, he said. —What is it?

The answer dawned slowly, you could see one or two hug the possibility to themselves, then look round cautiously to see if others were thinking the same thing, putting their hands tentatively halfway up.

Zoe saw where the new girl was sitting. She had been introduced to them that morning, and Zoe had felt the customary mixture of pity and initiated smugness at the thought of the tangled web of school codes and hierarchies that was bound to trip her up and expose her before she learned to fit in. Her name was Fiona Martin. That might be a point of vulnerability, to begin with: the boys might call her Martin, with its humiliating implications of uncertain gender and a taint of maleness.

She was also wearing a woolly home-made-looking top and skirt, very neat, in brown. Zoe had once worn a woolly skirt her Grandma Lil had knitted her, and Gary Lyons in words seared on to Zoe's memory had asked if it didn't 'itch her fat arse'. She had refused ever to wear that skirt to school again.

What was striking however about Fiona Martin while they were thinking about air in the staffroom, was that she was not looking round to see what the others thought, nor was she frowning in the required perplexity, nor did she look anxious or defiant like one of the naughty or dull ones. She was composed, and sat straight-backed with her legs crossed, watching Mr Lloyd steadily as if expectation of his explanation of the mystery was a quiet pleasure, but nothing to make a fuss about. She was very pretty: Zoe had not taken that in adequately, earlier. That would make a difference to how she was treated. She had smooth olive-coloured skin, features of a satisfying neatness that insults could not hang on, and fine straight black hair cut off in an unusual bob just above her shoulders (the fashionable way for girls to wear their hair that year was in two low-slung bunches, like Judith in the New Seekers). It ought to have been terrible, to be new: and yet Fiona Martin looked as if she wasn't afraid.

—If I took all the furniture out, would this room be empty? Mr Lloyd asked. He held out his cupped hands. —Are my hands empty? What's in my hands, now?

They began to understand. There was air, air was everywhere; they waved their hands about in it with

201

sudden consciousness. Paul Andrews, the clown, pretended to get a handful of it and drop it down someone's back.

—Air, sir. It's air.

—Lyons, what is it?

—It's air, sir.

—And air is made up of molecules, like everything else, bouncing against one another and against other molecules. That's called air pressure: the molecules of the air pressing on everything around them. We don't feel it because we take it for granted. But we would certainly notice it if it wasn't there. Watch this.

He explained to them about the molecules of air inside the can becoming farther and farther apart and moving faster and faster as they heated up. Then when the can was very hot he screwed on the lid, using the pot-holder the staff used for their kettle, and turned the gas off.

—As the air cools, it contracts. The air pressure on the inside of the can weakens, it's pressing less hard than ordinary air. The air outside the can is pressing with normal air pressure. The air outside is pressing in harder than the air inside is pressing out. Watch.

It worked very satisfactorily. Under pressure from something quite invisible and intangible, the solid-seeming metal container buckled and crumpled, giving out twanging, booming noises like protests. Zoe felt it as if it was happening in herself, that invasion and hollowness, that caving in, helpless and extravagant and pleasurable. Fiona Martin watched with a slight unperturbed curve of the lips, as if the exhibition only confirmed something she had long intuited. And the idea of the buckling container became a kind of shorthand sign for Zoe for years afterwards, signifying that moment of momentous first encounter with someone who is going to be important, and be loved.

A large proportion of Zoe's efforts at that junior school were devoted to making herself as acceptably inconspicuous as possible. This wasn't easy; she couldn't help herself being determinedly opinionated, any more than she could help her square pink face and thick light-brown bunches and her sturdy arms and legs (she wasn't really fat, she knew; Gary Lyons would call anyone fat who wasn't lean as a knife, as he was). She looked like the Dutch girl in clogs and cap who stood with the Eskimo and the barefoot coloured boy and the little Red Indian squaw in the picture that hung over the entrance to their classroom, gazing adoringly up at a blond Jesus bringing together the children of the world.

One of the things that Zoe had to keep out of sight at school was her disdain for the present. Once she had come, through books mostly, to believe that there had really been other times in the past when things were done differently, she felt sure that the past must have been a better place. This was first and foremost an aesthetic judgement. She flinched from the raw ugliness of modern things; bleak concrete shopping centres built up where the old streets of the city had been bombed, and plastic teenager dolls, and crimplene clothes. She bothered her mother for stories about the time when she lived with Grandma and Aunt Vera and her cousins in an old grey house on the estuary with no gas or electricity, where there was an orchard and a little stone room for storing the apples, sweet-tasting queer-shaped apples of a kind you couldn't buy anywhere any more. When they drove out once to look for the house, all they could find was a filthy carbon factory.

When she went on holiday to the Gower Peninsula with her parents and wound up the car windows going through Port Talbot, she stared straight ahead in shame; the naked innards of the steelworks stank and sprawled across the coastal plain. It was a horror to her, guiltily pushed away just out of reach of conscious thought, that anyone should have to live under those blighted hillsides where the trees were stunted and blackened; it made a shadow in the corner of all her pleasure in the sea and the beach and the cottage they rented, where she played out her games of past times, trailing about in long skirts, baking, washing herself in cold water, stitching elaborate layers of underclothes for her rag dolls (she wouldn't use nylon lace, or plastic buttons).

She couldn't quite believe that if you pushed hard enough you wouldn't be able to make the passage through to the past from the present. She read books where children managed this – *A Traveller in Time* and *Tom's Midnight Garden* – and they fuelled and sharpened her desire. Real people, astonishingly but unarguably, had once worn these clothes, handled these things; all that was now saturated with mystery had once been casually used. If you touched them yourself, possessed them, put them on, might you not take on something of the superior substance and depth that the past had, in contrast to the shallow present? This active nostalgia, and an elegiac sense that the best things were gone, were Zoe's first strong abstract emotions.

Her cult of the past translated itself into a quite passionate materialism. During this time, her last years at junior school and first years at secondary, there was a craze everywhere for Victoriana, for the old things that only a decade before everybody had been ripping out of their houses in disgust – the old dressers, the old brass fittings, the old fireplaces. Now when Zoe's parents bought their first house, a teetering, skinny, four-floor, eighteenth-century terrace house which they had to convert from grimy bedsits, her mother papered the lounge in imitation William Morris wallpaper and knocked out a 1930s tiled mantelpiece to expose the original deep recess behind. 'Original' became a word of powerful magic. Junk shops were treasure troves, and Zoe and her mother drew together in their deep interest in buying things. Zoe started a collection: a little leather-covered inkwell which clicked open to reveal a glass bottle; a wooden trunk with cast-iron fittings which Joyce had found thrown out on a skip and which they had stripped down together; a dove-grey Edwardian silk parasol with drawn-thread-work around its rim, given to her for Christmas by her Aunt Ann. Zoe tried to do drawn-thread-work herself; she made patchwork and tatted lace on a tiny old ivory shuttle.

She had a couple of friends at school who read the same books as her and were happy enough to dress up whenever they saw each other at weekends, to play Victorian governesses or ladies and maids. At first she dreamed, against all probability, that Fiona Martin might share her passion for the past. She looked for a sign, an exchange of glances when an extract from *The Young Brontës* was read out in class, an unnatural informedness with regard to dance programmes or gophering irons. But as she grew accustomed to Fiona's being at school and the sign didn't come, she realised that she was even glad of it. Fiona wasn't meant to yearn, as she did. It didn't matter that Fiona didn't dream about how things could be otherwise, because Zoe was the imaginer and Fiona was the thing itself: the still point, the Princess.

Zoe soon understood that one reason Fiona hadn't seemed afraid of coming to a new school was because she had had so many more terrible things to practise being brave on. Her cousin, Jackie Potter, was already in their same class, and so the word quickly got around – bred out of the little closed circles of murmuring girls with their arms hung around one another's necks in the playground, faces long with portent or indignation – that Fiona's parents were divorced. 'Divorced' in those days stood for something lurid, only half-comprehended, shaming. Zoe wished she hadn't heard, and refused to tell anyone else, although she was supposed to; she had been in trouble for this before, when messages came down the line with the tag to 'pass it on'. She feared and hated those closed circles of girls, and all the high dramas they generated out of their intimate heat: once-favoured ones excluded and weeping, once-excluded ones reinstated and brilliant with relief, lashing out in turn to prove themselves.

Because she was pretty and well liked, Fiona with her divorced parents could have queened it, ostentatiously afflicted, her protectors scowling about them to forestall any intrusion or insensitivity. Instead, when once the divorce was awkwardly produced in conversation, her smile was quite steady, and her perfectly light and polite tone deflected any further enquiry.

—Yes, they are, she said. —But it's all right. It was all for the best.

The girls' toilets were in a sort of shed at the end of the playground; it was customary for five or six girls to share one dank cramped cubicle, shuffling round to wee and wipe themselves on the hard paper in turn. Fiona sometimes stood in with Zoe and Barbara and Pam, and sometimes in Jackie Potter's cubicle across the way; only she could have moved effortlessly across the gulf dividing these two extremes of playground society without causing offence. Jackie had a memorable woman's face, black-rimmed big eyes, and mobile mouth. She claimed a knowledge of the body and its forbidden and savoury effects that the nice girls in other cubicles couldn't but respond to with fascination as well as disgust. Once, for example, she had a 'suppurating sore' on her belly, which girls queued up to see (Zoe, Pam and Barbara did not want to, nor were they invited, although the idea of the suppurating probably preoccupied them all the more for remaining non-specific).

Jackie was supposed to be having sexual intercourse with her boyfriend, who was fifteen (she was ten). In private with her friends, Zoe poured fierce scorn on this, claiming that it was physically impossible, although her sense of the mechanics of sex was vague. There was something in Jackie's stories she angrily resisted even while they worked powerfully on her imagination, conjuring an underworld of scuffles and shriekings and groping exchanges of intimacies, out on the streets as the light faded, slipped from the leash of parental scrutiny. The boyfriend's pronouncements on male need, passed relishingly on by Jackie, seemed even savage: apparently he liked girls 'with a bit of meat on them'. Zoe was horrified to think what for: she pictured him sinking his teeth into a leg or a neck as part of some sexual process.

And somehow, mysteriously, Fiona was part of all this, although she gave none of it away; her name was mixed up with boys' names in Jackie's account of the arcane negotiations that always sounded more like a kind of war than 'love'. 'Martin loves Diana.' 'Lester says he loves Fiona more than he loves Sandra.' Fiona didn't even blush. 'So he says,' she laughed lightly; or, 'I don't think so.' And yet she must have been there, she must have come out on the street with the others in order to be 'loved'. You could tell from the way Jackie pressed her, too, that she was not marginal to these transactions, that Jackie even gained status and negotiating power through being her cousin. Yet it was impossible for Zoe to imagine Fiona of her own volition choosing to go down on the street and be snatched at and fought over. She had a way of moving through arrangements as if they were always other people's, so that they seemed to leave no trace on her.

Already, other girls in Jackie's crowd looked marked and set apart from the good children. Their skin was sallow and bruised easily, their hair was lank; some had gold hoops in their ears and their clothes were skimpy hand-me-downs, stained and unironed. It wasn't entirely unattractive, this marked and used look; it was certainly to be preferred to looking like the children from the Homes, who were bottom of the playground hierarchy, neat always, but with giveaway chopped-off haircuts, clothes all tainted with the same sad charitable greyness, and smelling sometimes of wee (Jackie Potter only smelled of strong perfume). Fiona's appearance, however, gave nothing away. She could have been one of the girls who went riding and had ballet lessons, for all you could tell. She didn't speak with a broad local accent, but Gary Lyons couldn't tease her for sounding 'posh', either. What stood out was something quietly adult in her demeanour and in how she was dressed: clean white jumpers and tartan skirts, white lace tights and black patent shoes with straps across.

Fiona was very willing to be Zoe's friend; the only difficulty was that she was willing to be everybody's. Zoe was jealous, and persistent; she grabbed Fiona by the arm in a quick settling gesture of claim and possession whenever they had to make pairs for games or Music and Movement; she asked Mr Lloyd if she could move to Fiona's table, pretending she was sick of Paul Andrews banging down the desk lid on her head. She would have liked to help Fiona with her work; she had done this for other friends. But although Fiona didn't have the usual outward signs of cleverness – the clumsy mix of awkwardness and smugness – she turned out, to Zoe's surprise, to be as quick and clever at most things as she was herself (only she didn't get the stars that Zoe got for her stories; Mr Lloyd was a fan of Zoe's descriptive passages). She was invited to become part of 'grub days', when Zoe's gang took turns bringing in something to eat in the playground: sultanas, or salt, or stock cube, wrapped in a twist of paper tissue. Fiona brought in hundreds and thousands, they all wet their fingers and dipped in. At home Zoe pestered her mother until she bought hundreds and thousands at the supermarket which Zoe then licked up alone in ritual imitation of her favourite.

There was eventually some understanding in the class that she and Fiona belonged together, though it was never enough for Zoe, because Fiona wouldn't unbend from her even-handedness. She was a serious and sympathetic listener, but she didn't volunteer needs or prejudices of her own. She would gracefully detach from Zoe's group to join in some game of 'Please Jack May We Cross the Water' or 'I Wrote a Letter to My Love' which had swollen to fill the whole space of the concrete playground between its high walls. Zoe and her friends kept aloof from these. Fiona was quietly expert in all the variants, the forfeits, the different dipping-outs; she sang out confidently 'Jack says anyone with blue', or skipped round the outside of the ring giving no sign when she let fall the handkerchief behind some chosen person's back.

She came to Zoe's house to play. Zoe, who had longed to reveal her whole real life to her friend, was aware of herself in a rush of showing off, talking in a silly artificial voice to Daniel, rolling in the goatskin rug in the lounge which left her covered in hairs, rudely stealing biscuits Joyce would have given to her anyway, playing all her piano pieces over badly and much too fast. She was hardly able to take in that this was the real Fiona, transplanted disconcertingly into the too-familiar spaces. They adored the kitten; Fiona was politely interested in Zoe's treasures, her inkwell and her white china horses and the beaded pincushion with 'Baby' on it. Then they were at a loss for what to do. Zoe simply didn't know what Fiona liked.

Shyly she suggested the dressing-up box, offering Fiona the best thing which she usually took for herself: Nana Deare's wedding dress, full-length in cream silk with its dry stretchy stickiness under the fingers, sewn across all round the skirt with tiny tucks, buttoning with pearl buttons up the inside arm and down the back. She helped Fiona put it on; they fastened some of the surplus skirt up out of the way with an elastic Brownie belt round the waist. Zoe pinned up Fiona's hair behind a velvet Alice band, and fixed white clip-on earrings on

211

her ears; they went to look in the full-length mirror in Joyce's room. Even Fiona seemed moved: she stopped very still at the sight of herself, and allowed Zoe to powder her face from Joyce's compact.

—Pretend you're a pirate's moll, said Zoe. (She had watched a series about eighteenth-century criminals on television at Grandma Lil's, and found its glamorous lawlessness very exciting.) —The bunk beds are the ship, the top one is the deck and the underneath one is the cabin where we eat and sleep.

—What's a moll? agreed Fiona, willingly.

—You're his girlfriend, and all the respectable people disapprove of you, but really you're the one who truly loves him.

Absorbedly, they played this game for hours, and revived it sometimes afterwards when Fiona came again to tea. Although its narratives were somewhat repetitious – crisis and injury and nursing back to health, Fiona calm and capable and reassuring; Zoe, when she wasn't strutting on the upper deck, desperate and terminal with a lot of groaning and fainting and feverish tossing about – its satisfactions never seemed to pall.

Momentously, then, Zoe was asked to tea with Fiona. They walked subduedly to Fiona's home together after school, oppressed with awareness of the advance in their intimacy. Fiona turned in at the gate of one of the big shabby stuccoed houses fronting on to the Heath, a higgledy-piggledy clutch of bells beside the door signifying flats and bedsits. Fiona had her own door key, and

212

didn't seem sure whether her mother would be there or not (there had never been a day when Joyce wasn't waiting at home for Zoe, with milk and cake or biscuits). Inside, when the front door banged shut on its heavy hinge behind them, Zoe was for a few moments afraid of the strangeness of the cold echoing stairwell, its brown lino and bare bulb and brown-stained old wallpaper, smelling of stale dinners and alien sour toilets.

—We have to hurry, said Fiona. —The light switch goes off by itself.

Fiona's mother loomed above them over the banisters before they reached the second floor in their scramble; she pressed the light on again.

—Greetings, my darlings, she said. —I haff put ze kettle on for tea. (She often put on a foreign accent when she was in her playful mood.)

Zoe thought that Fiona looked disappointed to see her, although this might have only been because there wasn't much space in the tiny two-roomed flat; mother and daughter shared a poky bedroom whose window stared out at the blank side of the next-door house. The kitchenette was no more than an alcove behind a curtain printed gaily with wine bottles and bits of leafy trellis and lemons (Fiona's mother called the flat a maisonette, too, and Zoe a brunette: for ever afterwards Zoe associated these diminutives with her). The flat was clean, though, and optimistically prettified with plants and ornaments: a china bell in the shape of a lady in a crinoline, a painting of a kitten in a bamboo frame, nylon fluffy rugs in pastel colours. Zoe couldn't repress her furtive guilty judgement against these choices; she couldn't help feeling that Fiona must admire the superior good taste in her own home.

Fiona's mother looked like her, with a heart-shaped face, bright liquid eyes, and precise features like a neat appealing animal. She had the same black hair and olive skin, except that the hair was permed, not sleek, and her skin was powdered and puffy. Like Fiona she was daintily decisive in all her gestures, tying on a frilled pinny to get ready their beans on toast (the kind of pinny Joyce, who wore a striped butcher's apron, said was only good for playing at house); repairing her lipstick with a sceptical glance in the mirror; unclasping her handbag to fish out her cigarettes, which she kept in a metal holder with her name – Jean – engraved on it in flowery letters ('given me by an old boyfriend', she smiled, squinting through smoke). She reproached herself for smoking – 'Horrible habit! Bad girl!' – slapping the back of her own ringed hand.

—I'm glad, she said, —that Fiona's made a nice friend. Someone to get her into the right crowd at school.

When Jean squeezed Zoe she sank into sweetish softness spiked with jewellery and hard buttons and long nails, smelling of cigarettes, and flowery perfume, and something else fruity and rich and rotten, which Zoe later learned to recognise as drink: gin and Martini, or brandy and Babycham. A little bar was installed across one corner of the sitting room, with shelves and a counter made from coloured glass, paper cocktail umbrellas, a jar of maraschino cherries, and a chrome cocktail shaker. Jean talked to the girls about her various 'boyfriends' (Fiona said some of them were quite nice and some were horrors), and about the staff at Brights Hotel where she worked. 'That barman's a right little so-and-so. Quel charmer! Now Cook and me, Cook and me *don't* get along. She's a dirty you-know-what, and can't forgive anyone who's younger and gets out more than she does.' (For a long time Zoe imagined Jean at Brights dressed up smartly and acting in some kind of hostess-like role, receiving guests: she only had a very vague idea of what went on in hotels. But when once she and Fiona had to ask to speak to Jean at work because Fiona had lost her key, she was wearing a housecoat and rubber gloves and pushing a cleaning trolley between the bedrooms. This was only Zoe's mistake; there had been no pretence on Jean's part, nor was there any embarrassment at them finding her there.)

Fiona showed Zoe her satiny nightdress case, and her Tressie doll whose hair wound in and out of her head, and a miniature brass lampstand with a glass shade; when you pulled a chain like a lightswitch it brought down a tray with three tiny bottles of very dark brown scent.

—My daddy gave it me. They used to be nice. Only I didn't use them and they've got strong.

—It's really sweet, said Zoe (which was not a word she used under normal circumstances). In spite of herself she was entranced. —If you're divorced, she said warily, —do you see your daddy often?

Fiona shrugged. —It just depends. He has to travel about a lot, for his work.

215

—That's a shame for you. I suppose he's nice, is he?

—He is quite nice, said Fiona. —But I'm used to it.

—Why don't you girls go outside and run around before it's dark? said Jean, who was doing her nails in a cloud of nail-varnish remover.

—Shall we? asked Fiona. —We could go in the Dumps.

Zoe was surprised: it looked dark enough already, outside the window. She would not have been allowed to go out at home; she felt a flicker of fear, as if she shared for a moment in an adult's apprehension of herself not properly taken care of, tumbling about alone, falling into the so-much-warned-about gap left open by adult neglect.

—Let's, she said.

It wasn't as dark outside as it looked from indoors. The light was only just beginning to drain away out of a sky stacked up with golden clouds, against which the stubby thorn trees of the Heath stood in black fairy-tale outline. Opposite the house, only twenty yards back from the edge of the road, there was a long untidy hollow, said to be some kind of bomb crater, although Nana Deare thought she could remember it from before the war. The top surface of the Heath was kept mown all summer; when the classes from school came up here at playtime on fine days they built huge child-sized nests out of the heaps of cut grass. But the Dumps were impossibly crooked and steep-sided and so were allowed to grow wild, with long grasses and flowers and clumps of bushes. A crooked little dust-path wound through the length of them; about a quarter of a mile at most.

Zoe and Fiona wandered hand in hand, and Zoe showed Fiona that you could eat the 'bread and butter' berries off the hawthorns. They had hopping races up the path, elbowing each other off, holding their spare ankles up in their hands behind; they played at paralysing one another's fingers, stroking wrists with a special circular technique. They had the Dumps pretty much to themselves, only meeting a couple of dog-walkers and one of the usual old tramps who haunted the place. A slanting chilly late light glided on to the Heath from behind a cloud and smothered the Dumps in shadow. The girls knew it would be dark next. Then there was an eruption of noise some way off: calling, a snapping of branches, scuffling, yelps of laughter.

—Oh, hell, Fiona said, —it's probably that lot.

It was the first time Zoe had ever heard her use bad language. (Jean said 'sugar', and 'scuse my French'.)

—What lot?

—You know: Lester and Jackie and that.

Zoe started to worry; she could imagine how 'that lot' might be delighted to find one of the conforming and obedient children from school exposed out here where their power was unchecked. —Are they allowed to play out in the Dumps?

—What do you think? Fiona frowned. —No one bothers where they are.

—Let's go back to your house then.

—There's no time. But there's a den, we could hide. Probably it's so dark they won't see us.

There must have been nights, Zoe realised, when Fiona came out to play with these others in the Dumps voluntarily, and was part of the whooping and yelling and breaking of trees. For now, though, Fiona pulled Zoe after her into a thicket of bushes with a secret space inside, a dusty mud floor littered with a few dirty sweet wrappers. Perhaps she decided to hide partly because Zoe was a liability and it was inconvenient to be found with her. They crouched down on their haunches, holding on to one another for balance, smelling the day's heat baked into splintery wood, and pungent leaves, and dog dirt. They felt one another's breathing; Zoe was aware of Fiona's soft skin and her aura of talcum powder and clean washing, and found under her fingers the fine gold chain Fiona wore with a cross around her neck. They shook with silent giggling, half nervous, half real fun.

It wasn't Jackie and Lester and 'that lot' after all; the boys and girls who came racing, pounding, leaping through the Dumps in the long last shadows of the day were strangers. The thudding of their feet and the blare of their yelling hung there for moments after they'd passed through; one boy shouted out the word 'fuck', and something worse, and the terrible names used so flauntingly tore a vivid gash in the air. She and Fiona clung together, laughing into one another's shoulders. Zoe was completely happy. Instead of imagining life's possible intensity she was inside it, it filled her.

As the girls crossed the road on their way back to Fiona's house, Zoe's father drew up in his car. He looked surprised to see her out at that time; and in truth when she looked around her through his eyes she saw that it was effectively, by any adult standards, dark.

—We've been in the Dumps, she called out ringingly, to forestall any idea of her having been put upon or taken advantage of. —We've been having a super time.

Ray peered at them worriedly. —You should have crossed on the zebra, he said.

—Oh, it's all right, said Fiona. —My mum lets me.

—Well, I'm not so sure. The cars come round that corner very fast. And it's dark.

Zoe knew he wouldn't be able to sustain the burden of responsible parental anxiety for very long; her favourite tease of him was for his laziness. After all, nothing had happened, there had been no accident, the girls were safe. He might not even mention to her mother that they had been out on the Heath alone at night, because he got irritated with how she fussed and worried over her children. When he was a boy, he said, he came and went as he wanted, as long as he turned up with clean hands for meals. Fiona walked neatly backwards up the path away from them, opening and shutting her fingers in a little coded farewell.

—I don't need to go inside to thank the mother, do I? Ray asked Zoe.

She snuggled up against the sweet tobacco smell of the top pocket of his corduroy jacket. —I told Fiona to say thank you. And her mummy doesn't even have to come to the door. Fiona has her own key, on a string round her neck.

He was safety, and rescue, and she was very glad of him; but she didn't need him to know anything about the dazzle of the places she'd been without him.

Grandma Lil died. She had had for years a swollen mole on her temple which her daughters had urged her to show to the doctor; one afternoon it burst and released a blood clot into her brain. She came home from work at the cake shop with a severe headache; Martin asked the neighbours in the flat downstairs to telephone for an ambulance when she began vomiting and passing out. By the time Joyce and Ann arrived at the hospital she was in a coma and the nurses sent them home, telling them to call first thing in the morning.

Joyce went out early to the telephone box, which was about a hundred yards down the street, against the long high red-brick wall of a small factory which made brake linings. This was a street of handsome Georgian houses in Kingsmile, but at the time when such streets were only just beginning to be bought up and decorated and made fashionable. Most of the houses were still multi-occupancy, some of them with ancient layers of flaking paint and dirty windows hung with rags of lace curtain. When Joyce had made her call she came home and sat down at the breakfast table without taking off her mac or untying her scarf. Daniel noisily poured himself cereal. She told them how while she waited to be put through to the ward a fire had broken out in a house opposite the telephone box.

—There were real flames leaping up out of the

windows of the first floor, and billowing smoke. And there were people waving for help at the windows of the floor above. I thought that really I should use the telephone to call the fire brigade, but while I was thinking that I got through to the ward and the Sister told me that Mum died this morning. And then two fire engines rolled up and firemen got out and put ladders up to the windows and carried the people down over their shoulders.

She looked with puzzlement at Ray. —Did I really see that? Or was I just having a hallucination?

He shrugged helplessly. —Do you want me to go and look?

—No, not really. I don't really care.

All of them felt the painful strangeness of Joyce sitting motionless at the breakfast table in her outdoor things, with her basket on her lap, the familiar smart little basket shaped like a segment of orange, whose leather top fastened over with a clasp. Ordinarily she would be standing in her apron at the cooker or at the sink, busy supplying them with tea and toast and (in Ray's case) bacon and eggs. Grief came over Zoe in the form of a monstrous embarrassment, so inhibiting that her limbs felt wooden and her tongue wouldn't move properly. She had to hold in her mouth a little square of soggy toast that she couldn't swallow.

—Grandma's dead, Grandma's dead, hooray, sang Daniel just under his breath, shovelling in spoonfuls of crispies. (He was only eight.)

—Don't worry about him, said Joyce quickly before

Ray felt obliged to be stern. —He's just upset and doesn't know what to say.

This gave Ray his pretext for transferring his irritation to Joyce, angry with her because he was so sorry she was hurt. —He gets away with his sheer insensitivity and rudeness as usual.

Joyce looked at Ray as if she was seeing him from far off.

The children didn't go to school. They spent the rest of the day at Zoe's Aunt Ann's; she had married a man in import and export and lived in an expensive flat in Hilltop with baby cousins that Zoe loved to play mother to. Cliff looked after them all while Joyce and Ann went to the hospital to get Lil's things. Then they came back and sat at the kitchen table drinking coffee and crying and making arrangements, talking on the telephone to Aunt Vera who called from the school, worrying about Martin who had refused to get out of bed that morning. Joyce had brought him home from the hospital last night; she hadn't wanted him to go back to the flat on his own.

—There's nothing left for me to do then, is there? he had said when she woke him up to tell him the news. Since he had failed to finish his doctorate, he had been spending his days inventing things and building remote-controlled toys for the children instead.

Zoe fussed busily over baby Sophie, changing her bootees and matinee jacket, filling her dummy with rosehip syrup, piling cushions so she could sit tilted crazily but gamely to one side in her playpen heaped with educational toys. (Joyce and Ray made fun of all

the fashionable baby paraphernalia Ann had bought.)
She worked perhaps too hard (she felt it herself) playing
peep-bo and pat-a-cake, to get Sophie to crack into huge
toothless smiles for her: as if the smiles might consti-
tute some kind of proof against disaster. When Ann
took Sophie to the clinic to be weighed and to pick up
her orange juice, she went along. Somehow her aunt's
unhappiness seemed more approachable than her own
mother's, which she dared not even directly contemplate, because the fabric of the world required her
mother to be believing and hopeful.

—At least, she said to Ann, who wheeled the pram
rather fast into the wind, so that Zoe had to skip along
beside her to keep up, —at least you've got it over with
now. I mean, you won't have to dread its happening any
more. (Zoe had used this consolation to support herself
through visits to the dentist or the breakage of favourite
ornaments.)

Ann turned on her a bleak blank face. —But it's not
fair, she said in fury. —Just when she was coming up to
her retirement. It's so unfair.

Zoe skipped on beside the pram in silence, trying not
to come anywhere near the real thought of beloved
Grandma Lil lost to her, wrestled somehow obscenely
away out of existence. Underneath all the protective
wadding of kindness and reassurance that it was the business of adults to surround you with, there lurked this
lethal truth, dangerous as a naked wire that you might
at any time put your hand on by mistake.

*　*　*

223

After Grandma Lil's funeral the family went back to Ann's, where the children were waiting for them with Uncle Cliff. Zoe imagined that a cold wind from wherever they had been was clinging in the adults' sombre clothes. The women's faces were framed in wet headscarves, a jumble of umbrellas leaked across the black and white tiles of the entrance hall. Aunt Vera said loudly to several people that when it was her turn she didn't care if they buried her in a cardboard box. An Auntie Selina had come down from the North, shepherding an old man Zoe supposed must be her husband; Selina looked so like Lil – small and stout with rich brown eyes and hair and a tilting nose – that it was obvious every time Joyce caught sight of her she felt the shock of a hopeless hope. Selina wasn't quite like Lil, though; she stared more pointedly around her like a sharp brown bird, she didn't smoke, she didn't spill over with news, she didn't have Lil's way of subsiding comfortably into the corner of a chair, managing glass and fag together in one hand. The old man sat very upright and still on Ann's beige leather sofa, his feet in giant shoes placed tidily together on the shag-pile carpet, his brown creased skin stretched tight on his long bony head, his full head of white hair so fine and light that it wafted in the movements of air when anyone passed. Ann held his hand and called him Gilly and seemed extravagantly moved to see him; Zoe crept close to listen to his voice. She had thought this way of talking was special to her Grandma Lil (Vera sounded something like it); now she was discovering a whole tribe of relatives who made the same

224

warm kind sounds. Uncle Gilly didn't say much, mostly he was shyly refusing the food Ann pressed upon him.

—Go on, Gilbert, you may as well take something, it's all very nice, encouraged Selina, busy with her plate. —He's only put off if he thinks it's foreign food. You'd think he'd have got used to it in New Zealand.

Gilbert said softly that he didn't mind if he had a piece of ham.

—Gilbert was Lil's little favourite when he was a baby, Selina said. (So perhaps he was not her husband.) —Isn't that right, Vera? He used to call her Nolly. When she was in service and coming home on her day off, Mam would stand him on a chair at the window in the front room to look out for her, and he would start calling out Nolly, Nolly before she even turned the corner of the street. You could put the kettle on when you heard him. She sewed him a little pageboy outfit to wear at her wedding. D'you remember that, Gilbert? D'you remember being a pageboy?

—No, said Gilbert, smiling apologetically, shaking his head so that his white hair floated, starting work on cutting his ham into neat small pieces.

Zoe and Fiona went to different secondary schools. Zoe, along with Barbara and Pam and Neil Ashley and David Tew and a couple of others, sat the examination for free places to the direct-grant schools. This little gang of clever ones had been marked apart from the rest of the junior-school class almost since anyone could remember, given extra bits of work and spoken to differently. They carried the teachers' aspirations, fulfilled their longings for tests and triumphs. The other children – Gary Lyons or Paul Andrews or June Fitch – were threatened that they would 'end up at' Langham Road, which was the local comprehensive school, 'if they carried on the way they were' (and they did indeed end up there, probably regardless of whether they had carried on or not).

It was never seriously suggested that Fiona might sit the examination and get a free place too. Everyone knew, Joyce said at home, that even the free places could be expensive enough once you had paid for the uniform, and books, and hockey boots and tennis rackets. Children from poor 'backgrounds' would find it difficult to 'keep up' with the others ('background' was the euphemism then, conjuring an image of the tragic individual spotlit against murky indistinctly outlined tenements and slums). Fiona smiled and shrugged and said she didn't fancy it, as if she put rather a low value on anything the direct-grant schools could have to teach her, and saw alternative and more intriguing initiations ahead at Langham Road. Their separation seemed to Zoe a fitting and even a poetic thing; it kept her feelings for Fiona twisting poignantly in her heart. She thought of Amery-James School, the all-girls school where she duly got her free place, as somehow belonging in her world of the subtle past, and Langham Road as modern and brash and present. At this threshold she felt as if she were submitting to a sacrificial destiny. Zoe's mother and her Aunt Ann had also been to school at Amery-James, and her great-aunt Vera had taught there for half a lifetime (she retired the year before Zoe started). She was taking up a place sanctified by tradition. It helped that the school was in an old eighteenth-century house with an oak staircase and stone-flagged floors, and that they had to buy her uniform in an old-fashioned department store on Clore Hill, where bills and payment and change were whisked around a system of pneumatic pipes to and from a glassed-in counting office. (The store was so expensive that they couldn't get everything they had meant to, and Joyce had to buy some of it later from the second-hand cupboard at the school.)

Within a couple of weeks of beginning at Amery-James Zoe felt differently. The rituals which were soothing to read about in books were irksome and depressing to live inside. Days were beset with pitfalls and anxieties – had you remembered to hand in your maths homework on the right morning? had your mother remembered to sew your name-tape in your knickers in case there was a spot-check? had you returned your library books and brought in your science overall and your cakes for the cake sale for the form charity? Joyce found for Zoe a green mac that was not quite *the* green mac sanctioned by the uniform list. The teachers would pull her humiliatingly out of the crocodile of girls on their way to the sports field to lecture her on how it was unacceptable. She had to visit the second-hand cupboard again, and buy a mac of the right kind.

Certain teachers, especially the older ones – Miss Webb, Miss Anstruther, Miss Langley – cultivated a game it was dangerous to become involved with, in which a brutal unsheathed cruelty (personal insults, contempt, a lashing loss of temper, shouting) would alternate with rewards, flashes of comradely inclusiveness, a calculated letting down of guards. The game's brutality was sanctioned by the brutality of intellectual competition in the world outside, which was after all the *raison d'être* of the school. The physics teacher brought their marked homework into the classroom in three piles: good, acceptable, and unacceptable. The unacceptable pile wasn't only work done carelessly or incompletely; some of the girls had tried hard but simply not understood. The sheer burden of work seemed crushing. Under the school's discipline Zoe learned French and Latin effectively (which no one seemed to do at Langham Road), and struggled with the most advanced Nuffield science teaching. Even though she liked English and her English teacher, the books she read there (George Eliot, Kipling, Robert Frost, Hopkins) were contaminated for her by the place, she was not able to touch them again for years afterwards. Every evening after school there were two or three hours of homework. In the lunch break, faced with an afternoon of maths and double Latin, Zoe's heart would quail; it could not be endurable, surely something would give way. But of course it was endurable, it was only school and not real torture, and at last the clock would deliver up hometime and the walk to the bus, which waited in a somnolent lull for twenty minutes on the suburban corner before it turned around for its return journey into town. Here at last was repose, in the gap before the driver started up the engine and the conductor came selling tickets; she sank into herself, dreaming, alone, hugging her briefcase on her knees, turning her head away if girls in green uniform got on.

In assembly and at commemoration services the girls were addressed as if they were part of some ennobling crusade on behalf of enlightenment. Zoe was shocked to find herself implacably opposed to the very principle of the place. She wasn't much liked by the teachers or by many of the girls; she could see herself that there was something unattractive in how she cherished her apartness, unresponsive in class, refusing to be charmed when the teachers were funny and courted them, sceptical of the togetherness of the gangs of girls. One of the fiercest of the teachers, Miss Webb, with frozen pale blue eyes and white hair wound in a plait around her head, took passionately against her.

—I see Zoe Deare is wearing her usual charming scowl, she would say, enlisting the rest of the class on her side in a spatter of giggles and exchanged gleams of treacherous amusement. —Do you have a pain, Zoe?

Zoe was absent-minded, hopeless at remembering all those little details of preparation that could ensure an uneventful life at Amery-James. One day she had been supposed to bring a board and a polythene bag into Miss Webb's geography class, where they were going to make clay models of a shadoof, an ancient Egyptian irrigation system. Miss Webb boiled over into a torrent of righteous chastisement when Zoe turned out to be the only one who had forgotten. She actually took her by the shoulders and backed her across the classroom, shaking her so that her bunches flew and berating her in panting breathy bursts. The class drank up the spectacle in hot-faced silence.

—Little sour-faced miss – lazy – sloppy – sulky attitude – your sort of girls don't get anywhere in a school like this. Don't think I don't know your type!

—I don't even want to, shouted Zoe in bewilderment. —I don't even like this school.

—And this school doesn't like you very much, either!

After this episode, Ray and Joyce came to see the headmistress, and Zoe was taken out of Miss Webb's class.

Later, much later, Zoe was able to appreciate that the lives of some of these teachers must have been pioneering in their dedication to women's education. Some of them had no doubt sacrificed married life and family in order to keep their independence and pursue their careers; probably some of them, their names in gold up on the honours board in the hall, had been to university at a time when women were not even awarded degrees. Zoe's own great-aunt Vera when she was at Amery-James had been by all accounts (including her own) one of the fierce and arbitrary teachers, and yet Zoe liked her. She never quite found a way to explain to her great-aunt that she and Amery-James had found themselves incompatible. Vera had been so proud when she got her free place, and had bought her the black leather briefcase she had at first eagerly filled with her books. With twinges of guilt Zoe allowed her to think that she had become one of those girls who romped and cheered and belonged. It was a revelation, anyway, when her aunt talked, to hear the teachers referred to by their first names: Jennie Anstruther; Ruth Marsh (the English teacher Zoe liked); Beth Webb. Behind their school-shapes they sounded suddenly girlish and tentative and incomplete. She never told Aunt Vera about her quarrel with Miss Webb. At least she could safely report her marks, which were always rather surprisingly good, considering how her teachers despaired of her.

Zoe's family moved again at the end of her first year, this time to a tall Hilltop terraced house that had been a girl-students' residence, so that it had gas rings in every room and a rope fire escape wound on a red-painted reel in a bathroom with five sinks. (Joyce dedicated herself energetically, indefatigably, to her vision of its transformation: she made it beautiful.) From the new house it was only fifteen minutes' walk to Fiona's; she and Zoe made lingering transitions between their homes, looking together in all the shop windows on Clore Hill at things they planned to save for: felt pens, autograph books, sewing sets (Zoe), those electric lights filled with slowly moving blobs of different-coloured oils (Fiona). They bought licorice and Parma Violets in the sweet shop.

Fiona listened to Zoe's tales of Miss Webb.

—I don't know how she'd get on at our school, she said. —The boys are terrible for mucking about.

—Are they? asked Zoe with a voluptuous inner shudder. —What do they do? What do they do *exactly*?

She longed for mucking about. She even thought tenderly of Paul Andrews and his banging desk lids.

—Nicking pencil cases and chucking them around, said Fiona. —Or flicking stuff, chewed-up lumps of paper and things. The latest is trying to set fire to their haversacks. It's pretty boring.

To Zoe, whose lessons mostly passed in a subdued silence, this sounded as exciting as a carnival.

Zoe, who had been such an easy child, became moody and distant at home. Joyce found in her bedroom lugubrious messages she had written to herself for the first day of the holiday. 'Appreciate to the full this wonderful day of freedom. How lucky you are. Six whole weeks! Don't waste this precious time.' From Ray's vantage point in his new first-floor studio, spacious and full of good light, he could see his green-clad daughter plod into view at half past four every after-noon, weighed down with her briefcase, snuffed under her horrible hat. He mourned the bossy bouncing child she had been, full of schemes and passions. Joyce and he agreed that she didn't have to stay on at the ghastly place. He rather liked the idea of taking his daughter out of the school everyone else was trying to get their daughters into; after all, they were Labour voters and supposed to believe in a state education system.

—Daniel seems perfectly happy at Langham Road, said Joyce. (When he started there Zoe had been two years at Amery-James and showed no signs of coming round to it.) Every evening if it wasn't raining Daniel was out with his friends in the park, playing football or cricket according to the season.

—He certainly doesn't seem overburdened with homework.

—He's a late developer, Joyce reassured him. —You just wait. There are great depths in Daniel.

—I'll take your word for it. They certainly haven't been much plumbed so far. He hasn't spoken a word to me for weeks.

It was true that if Ray passed him on the stairs Daniel actually startled as if his father were something sinister whose existence he preferred to forget. If Ray addressed any remark to him directly, Daniel mumbled at his shoes. He never brought his friends into the house; Ray suspected this was because he didn't want them to catch sight of his paintings. In the park, Ray knew, he was a different creature: mouthy and caustic, popular, with his mass of fair curls and easy gift for sport. His offside drive was already better than Ray's had ever been.

Zoe brooded gloomily over the possibility of leaving Amery-James.

—But what if I don't fit in at the new school? she asked accusingly. —At Langham Road they all wear make-up and go out with boys.

—Wherever you go you will be your same self, Joyce consoled her. —Anyway, I don't expect they 'all' do.

—They go out dancing at the Locarno.

—That might be nice?

Zoe gave her a dark look. —What if I'm ruined for either school?

—It's up to you, darling. We don't mind one way or the other.

—How am I supposed to *know*? she wailed.

Ray suffered for his daughter; Joyce was brisk. —What more can we do? she shrugged. —She has to decide for herself.

Joyce was so brisk these days. She was so busy, to begin with. It was she who built the shelf units for the lounge, hair tied up in a scarf, working with a saw and a spirit-level, scribbling calculations, hinging the louvred doors. Or she was on her knees, scrubbing off the stripper from the floorboards in the kitchen; or she was tiling and grouting in the new bathroom. Ray was shut out from her confabulations with the builder Mike, their faces absorbed and rapt with costing and planning. It was awful that she had assigned to Ray the most splendid room of the house as his studio. He wanted to give it back, and to retreat in relief to the old inadequate space at the college he had complained about for so many years, but he didn't dare. The new studio was so tall and white and absurdly expectant of great things from him that he found himself in reaction painting tinier and tinier pictures, book-sized, postcard-sized (he forbade himself to go any smaller).

Joyce had become beautiful in a way Ray had not calculated for: flamboyant, perming her hair into thick waves, flaunting her backside in tight white trousers and her front in clinging T-shirts or low-cut filmy blouses in psychedelic colours. He prowled after the baffling, arousing woman she had become around a home that seemed to be always full of other people. He would find Joyce closeted clandestinely in the kitchen with her

Uncle Dick in his policeman's overcoat and greying film-star, war-hero good looks. (Their meetings were clandestine because Dick's new wife – not the women he'd left Aunt Vera for – wasn't all that much older than Joyce and didn't like him to have anything to do with his previous family.) Ray had no idea why Joyce gave Dick house-room, let alone ladling out her home-made flapjacks and perked coffee and all the sweetness of her engaged attention for him, as if she was hungry for his approval. When he left he stuffed a five-pound note into her apron or her pocket and she cried over it. Ray kept out of the way in case Dick tried to advise him on tongue-and-groove panelling or the purchase of taps (he didn't seem able to discuss such matters with a woman).

Joyce had to make elaborate arrangements so that Dick wouldn't run into Vera; since she retired from teaching she had also taken to popping round. ('We have to have her,' Joyce assured him. 'Why do you think Pete took himself off to the other side of the world?') Vera was engaged in self-improvement, taking Russian classes, cycling over the Heath for exercise. She enrolled at the university Extra-Mural Department for a course on 'The Nude in Art', and hovered in an agony of indecision between being proud of her relationship to a successful painter and appalled at what he painted. 'It's not that I'm a prude, Ray,' she said. 'It's just that you make it all look so ugly.' Or sometimes the kitchen would be overflowing with women unknown to Ray, frantic as an aviary with their high-pitched chattering. As if she didn't have enough else to do, Joyce had taken it upon herself to organise a craft co-operative, selling goods on a stall in the covered market. The kitchen table would be piled with pots, peg dolls, felt mice, prints, batik tea cosies, greetings cards made of pressed flowers, macramé hangings for plant pots. Joyce worked out the rotas and manned the stall two days a week. She sewed patchwork jackets and waistcoats in the evenings while she watched telly, and was voracious for scraps; she had her scissors into his old shirts and ties sometimes before he'd even worn them out.

From time to time in his flight around the house Ray stumbled in some quiet spot upon Fiona, Zoe's little friend, and they exchanged complicit glances as if neither of them had any very good reason to be there. Fiona had had her hair done in what Zoe impatiently informed him was a feather cut: short, with long ends trailing down the nape of her neck. With her head freed and her eyes with their deep steady gaze exposed she looked like a rough little waif from a Dutch genre painting. She wore blue eyeshadow and plucked her eyebrows into a quizzical arch; she had stayed small while Zoe grew taller and more awkwardly skinny.

—Fiona's such an attractive girl, said Joyce. —I'd love to dress her. It's a pity about the dreadful way she does her eyes.

—I like them, said Ray. —The eyes are exactly what I like.

—Do you really? You wouldn't let Zoe do it.

—Wouldn't I? Anyway, it wouldn't suit her. But Fiona's a sharp little kid, I like her, I'm glad that Zoe's got all sorts of friends. Some of those Amery-James types are pretty ghastly. I see them parading out when I pick her up. How come the private schools get more than their fair share of the ugly ones?

Ray persuaded Fiona to sit for him. She stepped warily the first time into the empty white space of the studio (she couldn't be any warier of it than he was); but she made an excellent model, keeping obediently still for longer than he had thought possible at her age, not self-conscious, not wanting to talk. Zoe visited them sus-piciously with coffees and biscuits, explaining to her friend that Ray always made things 'look funny', and she mustn't expect much. He did two paintings (small ones) of Fiona in the buttoned-up Crombie with a triangle of red handkerchief sticking out of its pocket which apparently was de rigueur for 'skinheads'. He made her face a funny crumpled shape like a little intel-ligent dog, staring knowingly out of the frame without smiling; in one of the paintings she held a cigarette tight between her fingers curled into a fist.

—You're not supposed to know I smoke, she said when she gave the picture her coolly appraising stare. He thought she liked it.

He took her hand (stubby, not beautiful) and unfurled her yellow fingers to show her how he guessed.

Something crumbled slowly in Zoe's fixed idea of things: the yearning which had been for a lost past swung into a different, present, plane; she began responding to the idea of 'ordinary people' with the same vibration of romance that had once thrilled at 'olden days'. She told girls at school that she was a communist, although she had only a rather vague idea of what that might involve. She knew it was defiant; she knew communism, which her father spoke about with a tender but wary excitement, envisaged an order of things which would do away with the game of advantage as played at Amery-James. Ray and Joyce used 'anti-communist' as a disparaging critique of certain kinds of things that were said on the news; there was a hopefulness, a moving optimism about human possibilities, in believing that the communist countries were probably much better than some people wanted you to think. When there was a general election in her third year, she was proud of being driven up to school in Ray's shabby old Cortina with Labour stickers in the back window.

Fiona wasn't getting on very well with her mother. Jean had left Brights and was working in a café making greasy breakfasts; she complained that she couldn't get the smell of frying out of her clothes or her hair. She was still pretty, although she was putting on weight around her waist and her complexion was muddier. She always asked Zoe how she was getting on at school. When Zoe said she was thinking of changing to Langham Road, Jean gave her a sharp look, almost as if she'd seen through with contempt to some effort of Zoe's to ingratiate herself.

—What would you want to go to that dump for? You should think yourself lucky, at the grammar school.

—She's a bleeding liability, said Fiona, upstairs in

Zoe's bedroom, tapping an Embassy Regal out of her packet with one hand in a deft habituated movement. Zoe didn't smoke, out of fear that she'd make a mess of it. Humbly she brought ashtrays. According to Fiona Jean's latest boyfriend was 'the strong and silent type'.

—So silent, he's only learned about twenty words, and most of them aren't very nice. She has to account to him for where she is every moment of the day, or he starts breaking the place up. I can't wait to get out of there and get somewhere of my own, I honestly can't.

Zoe registered this grown-up proposition with a lurch of awe: the time for her to leave behind her room in the family house seemed to belong in some era of the remote future. —What about your dad? she wondered shyly. —Have you ever thought about going to stay with him?

Fiona gave her a look. —Oh, *him*. No thank you: not unless I wanted to spend my life in a pub and live on fish and chips.

In many ways this was the most intimate period of their relationship. Fiona confided in Zoe as she never had before. —I want to stay on at school, she said. —I want to get good qualifications. I'd like to study languages and be one of those secretaries who work doing translations or stuff. I'm going to go to London, get myself a flat.

They spent some time then going into the details of how they would decorate their flats. Zoe had visited a friend of her mother's in a tiny mews apartment in central London, painted in white and turquoise, with a table that let down from the wall on a rope and a bath in the kitchen which covered with a board to make a work surface. Both of them were entranced by the idea of this. All Fiona's plans seemed possible to Zoe. She would know how to manage these things – dashing to work on the tube in the mornings, growing perfect nails with half-moon cuticles, shopping for tea for one – as Zoe never would. In elegant midi-skirts and black patent leather boots she would look like the models in the fashion magazines with their mournful faces full of initiated knowledge.

—And the one thing for certain I don't want is some cretinous boyfriend glooming around in the background, said Fiona with puritan zeal, and Zoe earnestly agreed.

The girls were paid to help out sometimes with Joyce's parties. Joyce would work herself into a frenzy of preparation, cleaning and cooking. The house had to look like a dream of its perfect self: the tall light rooms with their floor-length windows, the wrought-iron balcony laden with pots of flowers, big rice-paper lampshades, walls hung with paintings and drawings and huge tarnished old mirrors in crumbling gilt frames, rough North African blankets and Joyce's patchwork cushions heaped up together on the low white sofa. The production of the dream was grim sweating effort: Joyce with her hair wrapped in a scarf rapped out her orders according to a meticulously prepared plan of attack. When the dusting and polishing and vacuuming was done, the food (which she would have been getting ready for days) had to be arranged on the huge pine kitchen table: bowls of tomato and bean salads set out, parsley finely chopped, the home-baked ham sliced, the lemon fridge cake cut, paper napkins layered between all the plates.

Fiona had the right deft touch for all this; Joyce delegated to her and praised her 'good design sense'. Zoe was given the easier jobs, like mixing chives into the potato salad, where it didn't matter if things looked a mess. She asked whether Jean might be invited to the party. Whenever the two mothers met, Joyce was obliviously condescending, and Zoe, watching, saw that Jean kept a private reserve of sceptical dislike behind the awkward appreciative noises at 'the lovely house' and 'all your artistic things'. She longed to repair this breach.

—I'm not really sure that she would fit in, darling, said Joyce doubtfully.

Anyway, Fiona wouldn't hear of it.

'The party' loomed in anticipation, the capacious repository of hopes and imaginings: anything was possible. There was a joy in being part of the team behind the scenes, working in coordination, haunted by the idea of the crowd who were going to fill up the expectant spaces. They talked of the guests in tones at once slavishly subordinate and derisory. 'They're bound to put wine glasses down on the polished surfaces.' 'What sort of time d'you think we should make them coffee? Otherwise they'll just go on and on drinking.' 'Put ashtrays everywhere. Some of them will stub out their cigarettes on the furniture, if they can't see one.'

Until the last moments, Joyce was demonic, snapping,

frantic, possessed by the plan; Ray sulked, disclaiming any involvement in the contemptible female-ordered complexities of socialising with one's kind. They transformed into their laughing light-hearted social selves at the very stroke of the doorbell announcing the first guests. (Zoe and Daniel had for years done clowning imitations of this abrupt about-face). Joyce was suddenly radiant, relaxed, ready for fun, big crescent-shaped pewter and turquoise earrings (to match her turquoise halter-neck top) dangling under her thick red hair that had so many colours in it: pink, red, honey, straw. She glanced offhandedly around at the house glowing with her labours as if it had arrived in that condition accidentally and somewhat to her surprise. Around Ray's voice booming, holding forth as he opened bottles, and Joyce's peals of laughter at someone's funny story, the party took off.

The girls had to go around filling up glasses; in their giggling retreats to the kitchen for more wine Zoe explained who people were. Her Aunt Ann was wearing a white Ossie Clark dress with a red rose in her cleavage. Yoyo, an architect, was supposed to be one of Mum's old boyfriends. Alan Frisch (everybody called him just 'Frisch') was a painter, even weirder than Dad, with bits of straw and stuff stuck on to paint as thick as mud, and Dad was jealous of him. Dud Mason was there with his second wife, very pregnant. The two beautiful young doctors had an 'open marriage', and had adopted coloured babies. Uncle Martin, Mum's brother, had brought his latest girlfriend, a Swedish au pair. (Uncle

Martin had invented a synthetic fibre which soaked up oil, and was trying to sell it to the government to use on spillages from tankers at sea; Mum and Aunt Ann had small prototypes for taking the fat off the top of casseroles.) Dad's sister Fran had brought the cousins to stay the night, but they were little and had been put to bed.

Later, when everyone had had supper and all the poised perfection of the house had been sucked down into a vortex of wine and music and smoke and food debris littered everywhere, Zoe and Fiona were probably supposed to go to bed too; but by that time the adults in the house had abdicated all responsibility and no one cared, so they sat side by side on the stairs sharing a bowl of salted peanuts, squeezing apart to make a gap when anyone wanted to go up to the bathroom. They took turns making forays into the lounge where the party was thickest, pretending to be looking for plates to clear, then reporting back on who was loud, who was happy, who was drunk, who was flirting. Joyce was usually flirting, radiantly and decorously holding off some dedicated man. ('She's *awful*,' deplored Zoe.) Ray would be at the centre of whichever knot of debate and dissent was most intense. ('Jesus Christ,' they heard him shouting. 'This is the tragedy of art under the later stages of capitalism. Success is failure. Failure is success.') The guests had been putting on Jefferson Airplane and the Stones and Dory Previn; now Aunt Ann was dancing to 'The Age of Aquarius', absorbed and solitary, weaving her arms around snakily, unpinning one by one the strands of her thick dark hair from where her hairdresser had pinned them up, and letting them fall on to her bare tanned shoulders. Uncle Cliff (who had just done a deal selling luminous paint to slaughterhouses in Denmark) watched over her through his puffing of cigar smoke from the sofa. He was short and plump with a sprouting moustache and thick hair that looked like a wig although it wasn't, and he had driven her to the party in his Jaguar.

When Zoe finally left Amery-James and went to Langham Road, and was much happier there, she saw even in the first week that Fiona wouldn't be able to be her friend at school. After all, crossing the gap between the schools could not bring her inside Fiona's world. Even at Langham Road there were gradations and abysses of status and identity so that Zoe quickly found herself belonging in the set of quiet studious safe ones (though the studying was so easy now that she was usually fairly effortlessly top of the class). Fiona receded ahead of her among the unattainably different bad girls who were glamorous and dangerous, with heavily made-up faces and short skirts and shirts stretched tight to bursting over developed thighs and breasts. Platform heels click-clacking, they yelled and cat-called their way along the school corridors, congregating in the toilets to smoke and do their eyes and sometimes wreak a kind of mayhem of unrolled toilet paper and blocked sinks, or a mess of flour and eggs if it was someone's birthday (the eggs had to be ritually broken on their heads). Fiona of course wasn't one of the rudest or roughest of them; her appeal as ever was in how she held back with a reserve of watchful fastidious amusement from their excesses.

Some of this crowd Zoe knew from junior school: Jackie Potter and June Fitch and a few of the boys, although none of them ever acknowledged that they remembered her. (Gary Lyons had been killed with three friends, driving a stolen car.) Most of them were only waiting to leave school at sixteen and find work in shops or offices or garages or at the cigarette factory (whereas Zoe's new friends had ambitions: not to go to university perhaps, but to teacher training college, or into local government). At Langham Road the teachers often liked these bad ones, even though they were constantly in trouble. Their attention as teachers naturally had to be mostly on the obedient boys and girls who would take and pass examinations; but in truth they couldn't help themselves looking yearningly across at the wild children, especially those progressive teachers whose ideal was a kind of revolutionary rescue of the disregarded, and a redress through art or books or politics of the system which failed them. The men teachers were more flattered by the bad girls' teasing than by the adulation of the good girls; this contained flirtation was one of the strong dynamics in the school, smouldering and giving off its steady heat.

Fiona was not unfriendly to Zoe at school. She was even in some of her top-set classes, because she was good at languages, and so quick-thinking; but she sat slightly apart like an honoured visitor from another tribe,

245

greeting Zoe with a wink or a hand quickly touched on to her shoulder when she passed behind her chair. Zoe was grateful for that much. On one exceptional occasion they did spend an afternoon together: this was in the fifth year, and they had by this time stopped seeing one another out of school. They were supposed to be doing games, but at Langham Road you could easily avoid this if you wanted to; you could carry tennis rackets, for instance, over to where some group was practising athletics, and look perpetually as if you were on your way somewhere else. (Zoe rejoiced at her escape from the frozen drudgery of the hockey pitch and the vicious competition of the netball court at Amery-James.) It was one of those April days that seem exquisite through windows, with a perfect china-blue sky and bright puffs of white cloud; in fact a fierce wind had been blowing for hours and she and Fiona shuddered with cold in their thin games blouses and went to sit in shelter behind the groundsman's shed at the edge of the field. Scraps of brilliant green young growth from the trees and bushes growing on the boundary had been torn off by the wind, and were heaped up against the shed, an autumn harvest of spring leaves.

—I've got something to show you, said Fiona. She undid a button and felt around her neck inside her blouse, her olive skin smooth and clear apart from a couple of dark moles, the glimpsed shadowy swell of her breasts in their lace bra mysterious and adult. Zoe, who was tall and clumsy and flat-chested and had to wear an orthodontic brace, felt shamed beside her

246

perfection. Fiona pulled out a ring on a fine gold chain.

—Look. I'm engaged. Only it's a secret. You're not to tell anyone.

—Engaged? But who to?

—No one you know. No one at this school. He's much older. And he's not from round here.

The ring was warm from lying against Fiona's skin. Zoe examined it helplessly: gold, with a green stone, cheap-looking to her. Fiona leaned back against the slatted shed wall with her eyes closed, her arms hugged round her knees against the cold.

—He loves me, she said slowly and voluptuously. —He's crazy about me. He can't get enough of me. He wants me to leave school and have his babies and all this stuff.

—Oh my God, Fiona. You mustn't do that. Remember what you always said? You want to get a good job as a translator, remember, and a flat in London? And you're only sixteen.

—Oh yes. And I might still do all of that. I haven't decided anything. I haven't said when we will marry or anything.

But her face was suffused with thoughts that made her eyes open wide and heated her skin. The way her mouth slipped secretively round the word 'marry' made Zoe know that she was lost. This wasn't what Zoe had expected, and she felt cheated.

—You mustn't give it all up for a boy, she said. —There's all the rest of your life for that.

—He isn't a boy, said Fiona, dropping the ring on its

chain back down into her blouse where it was hidden.
—He's a man. That's what's different. You'll see.

And so they parted. Fiona did stay on for a few months
in the sixth form to do A levels with the hardworking
girls and boys, but she was fatally bored, she yawned
openly in class, all the liveliest of her friends had left.
Zoe was happy there, but she saw that it would not do
for Fiona. At about the same time that Fiona stopped
turning up for classes Jean left her job at the corner café
and moved from the flat opposite the Heath, and so Zoe
lost touch with them finally and totally. Perhaps it didn't
matter, because life filled up with other things; and so
quickly, changing during those years at such a rate that
it seemed as though almost every six months or so you
shed one self and stepped into a new one, leaving behind
a phase of your personality and your role and your
desires as mere discarded skin.

Once during the summer before she went up to read
history at Cambridge (it had turned out to be that easy
to do well at Langham Road), Zoe thought she might
have seen Fiona again. It was an odd, sour summer;
things were happening at home. Daniel was playing in
a band; he had moved out into a sordid flat with filthy
purple and orange wallpaper, and was taking a lot of
speed and dropping acid. He told Zoe in all seriousness
that he saw eels swimming around in the toilet. Ray was
mostly at work on a new series of pictures in his studio
at college (having a studio in the house hadn't worked
out); these were the studies of Moira, a sixty-year-old

schizophrenic who lived in hostels and on the streets, which many would rate afterwards as his best work. When he was home he always seemed to be on the phone to friends. Zoe lay on her bed and could hear his voice climbing up and down, booming and hectoring, taking up much more than his half share of the conversation; without being able to hear his words, she could guess that the gist of it was how he was always right, how he knew so much better than everybody else, how everybody else was an idiot or a sell-out, you couldn't expect anyone to understand. She could tell from this that he was unhappy.

That summer they all seemed to be listening out for signs of life and clues as if they hardly knew one another. In the middle of one night Zoe woke as instantly and completely as if a clear small bell had sounded through her dreams; her mother was speaking downstairs to someone in a voice of such quiet tenderness and sweetness that Zoe's heart twisted. She couldn't make out what they were saying, and she didn't recognise the male voice (it certainly wasn't Ray's, and anyway Ray was probably sleeping at the studio). A deep vibrating bass responded to Joyce's sweetness like counterpoint, like some essence of male and female interaction. They were speaking together so softly and discreetly, being so considerate of the sleeping house, it was only through some miracle of intuition that Zoe had woken up to hear it at all. Joyce after a while closed the front door very quietly; then Zoe knew from the intimate creakings of the old house that her mother was moving around downstairs, not bustling or tidying, just wandering between the rooms, barefoot on the thick carpets.

Zoe had got a job for the summer, working in a dry-cleaner's in St Peters. They had the contract for the New Theatre; there had been flooding in the theatre wardrobes. It was Zoe's special assignment to go through the plastic bags of sodden costumes, ticketing them and sorting them for treatment, growing emotional from handling the sad largesse of soggy flounces, brocades, beads, veils, velvets. She worked in a big airless back room and didn't often need to visit the front of the shop, but one afternoon she went in to ask the manageress something about her hours just as a customer was going out of the door: a young dark-haired woman, pregnant, struggling with a baby in a pushchair and a small child on reins. It was only after Zoe had asked Mrs Doyle her question that she was suddenly convinced that this customer had been Fiona Martin. Explaining hurriedly, knowing how foolish she must seem, she scrambled under the counter and ran after her into the street. There was quite a crowd of shoppers, and several women with pushchairs.

She called Fiona's name, and one of them turned round. She really looked very like Fiona, although her long hair was hennaed and tangled and she was dressed carelessly in an old T-shirt and slacks stretched over her pregnant stomach, as if she hadn't even looked in a mirror that morning. Her face (if she was Fiona) was still fresh and her eyebrows had grown back into their pure clear line. She did smile and look hard at Zoe, but only for a moment or two, before turning away as if after all she hadn't recognised her, and forging on with the pushchair, hitching the reins a half-turn tighter round her hand to keep the walking child close by her side.

Zoe checked the ticket on the garment she had deposited and it wasn't in any name she knew; but then, Fiona would probably have been married. She had hoped it might be something pretty for her imagination to work on, a party dress, something spring-like; but it was only a man's cheap suit, worn and with something spilled down the front of the jacket. Mrs Doyle promised her that if anyone came in to pick it up while Zoe was there she'd let her know (Zoe did check from time to time, and one day the suit was gone without anyone having mentioned it). For some reason this non-encounter was a strong blow; Mrs Doyle found Zoe half an hour later struggling in tears over a bronze-coloured satin petticoat thick with stinking mud too wet to brush off. She made her a hot sweet cup of tea and put an arm around her shoulders, blaming the dry-cleaning chemicals.

Zoe read all sorts of things into Fiona's long look at her (it grew longer in memory). Irony; condemnation; a knowledge of Zoe's life, all her superficial success, her self-important cleverness; an intimation of unreality in Zoe's very existence. Fiona hadn't even been willing to exchange a few words with her; as though she suspected that Zoe's very desire for her friendship was something fake, something to show off, some deal Zoe was trying to make to get absolution for her own privilege, for university, for 'Cambridge', for arty parents and a big house.

Probably, Zoe knew, she had made all this up. Probably the woman hadn't been Fiona in the first place, just some projection on to a stranger of her idea of how Fiona's life might have been: her body subdued to the discipline of that unimaginable mother's life, her expression one of weary scepticism, as if she was awakened to something Zoe hadn't even begun to be able to see.

Six

Usually, Zoe didn't stay the night with Simon. After they'd finished making love he would send her home: always much too soon for Zoe, who would be drifting into a sweet heaviness among the crumpled dragged sheets and the mounds of pillow and kicked-aside duvet. She would have given anything to sink down and down and find her sleep inside the heat of his nearness, inside the smell of him, peppery and astringent. But Simon would never lie stilled and satisfied for long. If she lay with her face pressed against his fine ribcage or his long honey-brown back she felt the change of his mood distinctly, like something chemical altering in his tissues: abandonment and languor transforming into alertness, then restlessness, and then, if she stayed too long, or resisted or protested, into impatience. So she would force herself awake, and find and pull on the clothes she had carelessly torn off, and fish around on the dark floor for her shoes. Her head would be swimming and her legs still trembling. Sometimes she even felt nauseous: this was shock at the sheer effort, she thought, of taking back into rational possession the flesh that had been so opened up and lost.

Simon would get up and put on his jeans and help her find her things. He would come with her to the back door, and check that her bike lamp worked. He didn't like her to kiss him goodbye; he said he 'preferred to keep things separate'. She cycled off, doing her best not to wobble for as long as he could see her, making her way confusedly until she woke up properly to the empty night streets: a narrow way between sleeping terraced cottages, then Mitchams Corner roundabout, where in the day the lanes of traffic thundered but now the traffic lights often changed colour only for her, although she still obediently waited, one foot on the road, when they were on red. Sometimes, although she never remembered this when she was with Simon, she was afraid as she pedalled home: that someone would leap from the bushes and drag her down as she crossed Jesus Green, or that when she had to get into college through the under- ground bike shed because the gates were locked, someone would be lurking there to rape her and smother her.

It was a cold winter. By the time she climbed the stair- case to her room her jaw would be in spasms of shud- dering and her hands even inside her gloves would be frozen into the shape of her grip on the handlebars. Because her room was one of the modern conversions in the attic, it didn't have a gas fire, only an inadequate electric heater; so when she undressed for the second time she kept her socks and pants and T-shirt on under

254

her nightdress, piled her coat and dressing gown on top of her duvet, and lay shivering in her bed, hugging her knees. She didn't mind all this. She imagined that somehow she was testing herself, hardening herself, making herself more like Simon. In her half sleep she dreamed that she was hugging cold steel to her breast, and that even the pain it caused her did her honour.

Simon told her he had been an insomniac since he was a child; the night had become the time when he read and wrote. A big old office desk, stained with ink and scarred with ancient jagged scratches as if someone had once raged against it, was pulled under the window of his room in the house he shared with student friends. The walls of the room were papered in a glowering green splodged with brown motifs that sometimes looked like grinning demon faces; he didn't care, he didn't notice it. When Zoe was gone, he worked. When she returned, the desk would be heaped with new piles of books bent open to some important page, new sheets of scribbled notes in his neat black writing, difficult to decipher because he formed so many of the letters with the same steep uphill curves. His reading often had nothing to do with the papers he was supposed to be preparing for, but his supervisors didn't seem to mind. One week it was American poets: Ashbery and Ed Dorn. (He didn't like Ginsberg.) The next week it was Arthur Golding's translations of Ovid, and then Brecht's *Little Organum for the Theatre* and then Villon; and then critical books and books of philosophy (new names to her: Saussure and Barthes). He would crawl into bed before dawn and sleep all through the morning; he never went to any lectures.

It was true that this wouldn't have fitted in with Zoe's rhythms at all. She was up before eight and always had a good breakfast of muesli and wholewheat toast, to set her up for lectures and work in the university library. Simon woke in the afternoon, and drank black coffee, and hardly remembered to eat unless she brought him something. He wouldn't sit down to a meal, but cut himself pieces of cheese or bread and ate them walking about, or looking out of the window. Sometimes one of the others in the house cooked a pan of chilli or spaghetti bolognese and they would all eat standing up in the kitchen which nobody ever cleaned, with its sink full of dishes, and its burned pans, and the patina of oily grime on all its surfaces. Zoe admired the kitchen as evidence of their minds on higher things.

She had known from the first time she saw him that Simon was brilliant. When she came to the college for her interview she had been put in the charge of a first-year historian with straw-dry fair hair and blotched pink, plump arms and circles of sweat on her shirt who was supposed to take her on a tour and talk about her experiences of university life. Her name was Amanda. (They had studiously avoided recognising one another ever since Zoe turned up the following October in her own right.) Zoe suspected that Amanda's experiences of university life thus far had not been altogether sweet, and that she was understandably reluctant to share them;

also, Amanda was having trouble that day with the leather thong that fastened one of her sandals. At Amanda's very worst moment – when her sandal had slipped right in the middle of crossing a busy road with fast cars, and she had had to save herself in a sort of undignified running stumble, hanging on to her heel – a boy had passed them going the other way, pausing to look up and down at the traffic just long enough for Zoe to take him in, not even seeming to see the two girls caught out in their weakness at his feet.

—Who was that? Zoe asked.

Amanda could hardly be expected to recognise every student they saw. However, something in her hot face and angry concentration bent over her sandal gave away how his passing caused a definitive sharpening of her pain. She didn't even bother to pretend to turn around to see who Zoe meant.

—Simon Macy, she spat out. —English scholarship. First-year. Very brilliant apparently. Destined for great things and all that. I've never spoken to him, so I've got no idea.

Neither of them chose to mention his narrow hips, the long wolfish lean lope, the skinny T-shirt under an Oxfam-shop suit jacket, the straight jeans and Chinese canvas sandals. Or the stormy marks on the fine clear face, purple shadows under his eyes and beside his nose, a tension where his jaw was hinged, the shadow of a moustache on his upper lip. Or the thick long brown-black hair pushed carelessly behind his ears, or the cigarette held dangling in his fingers. These were imprinted, though, on Zoe's imagination, even before she heard that he was also destined for greatness.

When she decided at Langham Road to take the Cambridge entrance examination, she hadn't had any idea which college to apply to. No one in her immediate family had been to Cambridge, and only one of her teachers. She browsed through the brochure and chose the place that looked nicest in the photograph. Only a few of the colleges were mixed. She wouldn't contemplate an all-girls college; she thought it would be like Amery-James all over again. What luck, she thought, when she saw Simon! What luck to have chosen his college. She only thought that if she got in she would see him from time to time. She never dreamed she would even speak to him.

The others who lived in Simon's house were fairly brilliant too, although they weren't so beautiful. Marty, with untidy shoulder-length curls and dark-rimmed glasses, was a gifted linguist doing Arch and Anth (Modern Languages too boring, just translation and the lower forms of criticism). Joshua, freckled and lisping, was supposed to be doing English, although he smoked too much and never finished any work and Peterhouse had threatened to kick him out; his dad was an Oxford economist and a friend of Michael Foot. Lennard had a strong Manchester accent and a proletarian rage, although his parents were teachers at a grammar school; he was tiny and vivid and spotted and did history, favouring the *annales* approach of Braudel and Bloch. Zoe was the only girlfriend. Lennard was intermittently in pursuit of a half-Polish nurse with a wide heart-shaped face, slanting eyes and shapely breasts; whenever Trina came round they all commented afterwards on how good it was to spend time with someone from the 'real world' and how refreshing her intuitive sound judgement was. She made them almost meek. She told them their kitchen was disgusting and refused to eat anything they cooked in it.

These friends were vociferous in their arguments with one another. They did not argue about personal things; they treated one another's private lives with elaborate tactful avoidance, almost squeamishness. Simon, for instance, did not know until Zoe told him that Marty had two younger sisters or that Joshua had been desperately ill when he was fifteen with hepatitis. But they reserved for one another's opinions a bluntness and cavalier contempt which made Zoe quake. Marty was a member of Cambridge Amnesty International group, and sat for hours in a cage outside Kings to raise awareness; Lennard hung around and shouted through the bars at him that human rights were a bourgeois conception and Amnesty a tool of American imperialist ideology. Simon argued that the future of literary analysis probably lay in computer-assisted readings of stylistics; Joshua groaned and said that was just more clever boys solving chess problems. Simon thought that English was a subject for dilettante belletrists anyway, and history dreary empiricism; he should have done sciences, only his maths wasn't good enough. Marty argued that Simon's beloved Brecht had betrayed the proletariat in the 1953 uprising in the GDR, and that his layman's enthusiasm for Levi-Strauss's structural anthropology ignored the problems there were in reconciling his closed systems with the results of fieldwork.

—Brecht's not my beloved anything, said Simon. —Although you're being pig-headedly naive about the options available to him in 1953. But I don't have beloved writers. Love doesn't come into it. If you want the smearing of disgusting empathy across the text, it's Josh who goes in for that kind of thing.

—Fuck you, said Josh. —Fuck fuck fuck you, you cunt.

—You see? said Simon. —For him it's all feeling.

They didn't argue with Zoe.

She was very tentative, anyway, in putting her opinions to them: these were all second-years, and living out in their own place free from the childishness of life in college. She had no idea how you attained their kind of bold certainty, which was almost a physical attribute like deep voices or broad shoulders; she felt her own inward contemplation so much less steady and more flickering than theirs. And so when she proffered something into the conversation, it tended to produce a blank effect like a missed beat in a complex pattern of exchange and response; or Marty would kindly pick up something close to what she'd dropped as if he was covering for her. Simon in particular never responded directly to anything she said, unless they were alone.

They were talking, for example, about the kidnappings (there had been a spate of them, Schleyer in the autumn, Empain and Moro in the New Year). The newspapers printed the photograph that the Red Brigade had sent to Moro's family: he was holding a copy of *La Repubblica* with the headline '*Moro assassinato?*' Lennard called it the symbolic enactment of profound class antagonisms; Marty feared the romance with terrorism was a dangerous distraction for left politics.

—They're no fools, said Simon. —Look at how cleverly the photograph exploits a classical aesthetic: the powerful man brought low; the end already known and named; the moral painted on the wall behind. It's pure spectacle.

—I wonder what he thinks, said Zoe. —I wonder what he was thinking while the picture was taken.

Simon got up abruptly and left the kitchen. He would do this in the middle of a conversation; afterwards she would find him reading in another room.

Lennard hunted with fierce rustlings through the rest of the newspaper. —Who knows the footie scores?

—Do you think he only hates them? Zoe persisted. —Or do you think it's possible he begins to see himself through their eyes?

—Did City win?

—It's a sweet idea, Zoe, said Marty.

—But who cares? said Lennard. —It isn't personal. He isn't a person: he's a representative of a system.

When Moro's body was found a few weeks later in the boot of a car, Zoe felt as if it was a response to her sentimentality: a brutal shutting up of hopefulness and personal interest.

She studied the things that Trina said, which every-body liked. This was because Trina was natural: she wasn't trying to impress anyone, she didn't think before she spoke. Zoe could perhaps have tried playing the role of this natural female, washing up their dishes and chiding them for their laziness and dirtiness, chattering about shopping and clothes. But then, this wouldn't in fact have been natural in her, only another complicating layer of falsity, in which Simon would surely have found her out.

Zoe was able to see the romance of the old university. She experienced an appropriate thud of aesthetic response whenever she walked up over the Backs, past the gardens and over the bridge and into the seventeenth-century college court. And yet she never felt it was really hers. She was only admiring those things as a passer-through. Also, she found herself fairly indifferent to the weight of tradition which squeezed some of the other students so painfully. She only once wore her gown and had formal dinner in Hall, with Latin grace. After that she used the cafeteria in the basement. The oldness of the university and its complex hierarchies and all the inhibiting burden of competition and thirst for accept-ance that it imposed didn't loom dreadfully and over-whelmingly over her; they didn't interest her much. People anxiously questioned where you had been to school. She told them proudly that she had come from a comprehensive (Amery-James was her secret). In the political climate of the late 1970s they were obliged to respect you for that, whatever they privately thought.

She was probably able to step around the workings of the place so casually because she was a girl. The traditions of belonging weren't designed around girls, it was easy not to be hooked in. Her mother had hinted that at Cambridge at last she would meet boys who'd appreciate her (no doubt doing some private calculations about the tiny numbers of women in relation to men). But in reality the effect of that outnumbering when she first got there, before she had Simon, was that it had made Zoe feel invisible, cancelled out. Of course there were a few beauties among the girls who attracted attention and were fêted and pursued. But she was never going to be one of those. She had dressed so as to make sure no one even thought she was trying to be one of those, in trousers and jumpers and a duffle coat.

She had worked hard from the beginning, but that hadn't been entirely satisfactory either. What she had expected when she came was passionate argument; instead for the first few months she had the sensation of swallowing down mouthfuls of ideas she wasn't able to share with anyone. You were supposed to pour out all your arguments in writing in your essay, and then your supervisor would make a few responses in the margin, or explain some controversy of interpretation of the facts, or recommend further reading. This wasn't the exchange that she had longed for. And she had got herself into a group of nice-enough friends who would only talk about their subject chaffingly, jokingly. They loved history, they often knew more than she did, they could confound her with their information, but the way they spoke about it kept it fenced in like an absorbing hobby. They teased Zoe for taking things too solemnly.

Simon embodied the intellectual passion she had dreamed of. He made no separation between his life and his work. He reacted to books with a fierce partisanship as if writing was a matter as serious as life and death. She knew he changed himself, in response to what he read. Perhaps Zoe still didn't get the arguments she had expected. But she didn't mind swallowing down her own ideas, as long as she could be sure she was submitting to the real, superior, thing.

Simon told Zoe things he never told anyone else. Under the hot dark tent of the duvet – their bodies tangled together in his single bed so that she couldn't see his face, his voice muffled in the pillow, vibrating in his chest where she pressed her head against him – he let slip fragments of information about himself. The broken pieces were often confusing and incomplete, as if he was giving them to her deliberately in a code she didn't yet know how to read; she put all her effort into patiently learning to interpret the least stirrings of his thought, his most opaque remarks. She hardly knew where this confidence of his came from, that she could be trusted to guard what she knew about him with instincts of concealment and protectiveness as fierce as his own. But he was right to trust her: she didn't tell anyone, not for years and years.

She told him plenty about her life, too, and readily,

when he seemed to want to know; he would listen with affectionate interest. When they were alone he called her his 'pony' because of her long mane of straight light-brown hair, and her fringe always falling over her eyes. He was surprised when she said she didn't think that she was pretty. ('You're nice,' he said. 'Zoe. Clear eyes, these straight eyebrows like brushstrokes, this wide sensual mouth she keeps so carefully closed. A shy pony, nervous with strangers but will take food at my hand. Why would I have wanted her, if I hadn't thought she was nice?') She told him that she had been an obstinate little girl and an awkward teenager, and he found for her a Goethe poem – one of the Roman Elegies – which said that the vine blossoms were unpromising but the ripe grapes 'yielded nectar for gods and men'. She felt blessed; she learned the poem by heart (in German, which she scarcely understood). But their confidences were not given in an arrangement of mutual exchange. Hers were daylight stories (at worst, maybe her mother was having an affair); she felt ashamed now that she had ever thought she suffered.

Simon had had an older brother who had killed himself at Oxford when Simon was thirteen. He hadn't left any note; it was even just possible that he had over-dosed accidentally (the inquest had been inconclusive). Before he died he had broken up with his girlfriend (but she wasn't important, Simon said); also, he had only got a 2.1 in his PPE finals, when he had been predicted a First. Simon's brother had told him what to read, and taught him what to laugh at, and to play cricket. He had written letters to Simon at boarding school every week, with funny drawings of himself falling asleep over his books, or dancing at a party, or waving placards in some political demonstration.

—I was bewildered. His death bewildered me. At that age.

—Of course, she whispered.

—Bewilder: 'to lose in pathless places'.

—Yes.

—A couple of years after that, I wanted to fuck his girlfriend. I mean before I even knew how. Ex-girlfriend. The one who, maybe. That grew to a fixation for a bit. I thought I knew how to find her. I had this idea, about if I did.

—Was she important after all, then?

—And since then I don't sleep. Not nightmares. Just: awakeness. This power to hold up everything in my mind: a bright light switched on. Sometimes I think I can see everything. It's like radar: when I look at a page, I can see right through it, how it's put together, and why.

—Yes.

—I burnt up all Ricky's letters. Couldn't bear the thought of my mother getting her hands on them. Anyway I got too old. Had to leave them behind.

—Why not your mother?

—Oh. You don't know what they're like. What they turned it all into.

He told her about the family house in St John's Wood, worth a quarter of a million; they also had a flat in Lewes and a house in Scotland. His father had been something big in ICI. There was a visitors' book in the guest room ('they don't have real friends, they wouldn't know how'), and over the grand piano in the sitting room hung a portrait of his brother painted in his Winchester scholar's gown.

—The piano isn't there because they like music. Why did I have viola lessons every week for twelve years? It's just 'done'. How would you know you had children if you weren't shelling out for the right school and all the appropriate cultural trimmings?

He told her how he'd fought with his father – physically, punching and kicking – when he was home from school one weekend aged seventeen; and how his mother had called the police and had him arrested and he had spent the night in a police cell.

—It was because I was going around the streets at that time in bare feet. He tried to make me put shoes on. That's why I kicked him first: he was trying to force these horrible brogues of his – you know, from some fucking Bond Street shoe shop – on to my feet. Without any socks or anything. But it was her fault. She started it. With some remark about her floors. I mean as if my feet were any dirtier than shoes. But of course they were too naked. The real, forbidden kind of naked. Not the bikini, décolletage, socially sanctioned kind.

After Christmas his parents sent him a letter and a cheque (he was on the minimum grant, because of their income). Cross-legged on the stained and greasy carpet in the glow of the gas fire, his hair falling forward across his frown, Simon rolled himself a joint in fingers that actually shook: 'to smoke them out of my mind'.

—It's a kind enough letter, Zoe said lamely.

—That's because you have no idea. Why couldn't my father have given me the cheque when I was home? Then we could have looked one another in the eye, for once. They're so angry with me because I won't feel guilty at taking their fucking money.

—There's no sign that they're angry with you. They seem very interested in what you're doing.

—Anaesthetised politeness alternating with bouts of inchoate violence. The bourgeois ethos precisely. The smothered horrors in its family life analogous precisely with its effects in the political world. How charming do you think Pinochet is at dinner parties? While at the very same moment – in the same, synchronised moment in real time, say, that the Nuits St Georges is being brought round by soundless-footed waiters – his special forces are dropping political prisoners out of helicopters over the sea. Under the same white moon.

—But your father isn't Pinochet.

He looked on her darkly. —You want to *know* what involvements ICI have in most of the places that figure pretty largely in Marty's Amnesty handbook? How much time do you have?

—No, no, I do sort of know. But it's not quite the same. I mean, there is a difference of scale: your father hasn't ordered anyone to be killed.

—That's exactly the mistake that sentimental revisionism makes: imagining you can draw the line somewhere, not understanding the totalising bourgeois world-view, how it contaminates everything it comes into contact with. It hollows out the truth and replaces it with shams that only look on the surface like real things. If you want to save yourself, you have to repudiate the whole lot, get it out from under your skin. It's respectable housewives shopping for Yves St Laurent in Selfridges who cause blood to be shed in Angola and Eritrea.

—So what should we do? asked Zoe, chastened. —To live differently?

—Not torchlit Broad Left marches or picketing at Grunwick or sending telegrams of solidarity to the Chilean people, that's for certain. Or the Nursery Action Group.

After a pause she said, —What, then?

He shook back his hair impatiently. —You have to change your mind. Actually change your mind.

Zoe bent over his mother's letter again. There was news of relatives Zoe hadn't heard of, of a dog who wasn't well. Simon wasn't to work too hard, or forget to enjoy himself. This was written hastily, and then underlined, with 'Please' and a question mark. —It sounds as if she's worried about you.

—And you can just imagine it. Is he taking drugs? Has he kept up the insurance on his viola? I hope if he's sleeping with this girl he's taking all the proper precautions. Is the mess produced by his grotty friends compromising the market value of the house we've invested in on his behalf?

—Perhaps she just wants you to be happy.

—Oh well, he said. —Happy. Well then. Jesus Christ.

He stood up abruptly and rummaged on top of his wardrobe among empty hi-fi boxes and cricket kit, squinting his eyes in the smoke from the roll-up drooping at the corner of his mouth. From underneath the mess he pulled out a brown viola case.

—Fuck the viola. Fuck that.

He put it on the floor between them. The instrument inside, when he pulled away a silk paisley scarf, was dark toffee-coloured, gleaming, richly complex. Zoe for a moment thought with joy that he was going to play it. Jumbled in the case were rosin and tuning pipes and a home-made stuffed-cloth chin-rest with an elastic loop.

—Here's what you have to do, he said. —Here's how to put an end to it.

And he raised his foot in its clumsy winter boot and brought it down on the viola with a crunch, and a tortured stifled jangling of the strings.

—Oh, no! cried Zoe. —No! No!

In the spring she caught a virus and was ill with a high temperature for a few days. Simon made a surprisingly tender nurse. He called her a 'sick little pony' and put her in his bed and brought her aspirins and made her drink glasses of lemon barley water; he wiped her face with a flannel rung out in cold water and brushed her hair out of her way; he rang to cancel the supervision she was supposed to be having on her essay on the taxation policies of Edward III. Then he sat at his desk and worked, and through the vertiginous swoopings and retreats of her delirium she was aware of something deeply consoling in the steadily turned pages and the patterings of his fountain pen. He read her a poem by Beckett and in her dreams, obedient to its instructions, she wandered backwards and forwards in a shadowy bare corridor between doors that slid shut at her approach; after a while, though, she added in some kind of brightly coloured darting bird that had never been in the original, and then the corridor was lined in red velvet and ran twisting underground and became her sore throat, and the poem drifted away altogether.

She almost didn't want to get better. There was something delicious in this enforced passivity, handing responsibility over to him, with no need to think or act for herself; although she also knew she ought to be ashamed of such weakness, and that he would think less of her if he ever found her faking. And then she was deeply touched by his gentleness: this must mean – mustn't it? – that he cared for her. She was not allowed to ask if he loved her; she'd learned that very early on.

—It's not a word I use, he'd said. —It's a kind of sentimental bondage: like the bourgeois exchange of rings. Once I've said it to you, you'll expect me to repeat it, and then sooner or later it will turn into a lie just by wearing out. The love words are dead words, they kill. You should hear it when my parents are arguing. 'Don't be ridiculous, dear.' 'How dare you say that, darling?'

When she was recovered from her virus they all went off for the day to Ely, in a car which Marty borrowed from a friend who kept it illicitly (undergraduates weren't supposed to have them). It was an effervescent spring day; the wide sky over the flat land looked washed clean as a pale sea, with a few lemon-glazed strips of cloud on the horizon and bright watery sunshine; birds put back their wings and made heart-shaped dives into the low-growing scrub. It was Zoe's first visit; they went to the cathedral and then to the Old Fire Engine House for tea. In the Lady Chapel she was overcome by the lofty cool stone vaulting and wavering greenish light like a pool of air.

—Not that it would have been like this, said Lennard sternly. —It would have all been painted in bright colours. Our sense of what's beautiful in it belongs to a purely contemporary aesthetic.

—Whatever Lennard says, said Zoe softly to Simon while the others made their way out of the chapel and down the deep fall of worn steps, hands in pockets, actively resisting awe —whatever he says, I love it here.

He smiled and put her hair out of her face which she knew was earnest and heated. Nervous that he might disapprove, she told him about her obsessive passion for the past when she was a child, and the longings she had had for there to be a way into it out of the present, which had seemed so ugly.

—Oh, me too, said Simon, to her surprise. —There was a door at school that was always kept locked – it was probably just a laundry room or something – and I built this whole fantasy world, that if I could only press through the door I'd find myself in another time and space. I was convinced it was only a failure of my imagination that prevented me. Of course if I got through I was always conveniently going to emerge as a member of the landed aristocracy.

—Oh yes, me too!

—Late sixteenth century, I favoured. Hawking and riding to hounds and probably getting caught up in Essex's doomed rebellion against the old queen.

—I liked the nineteenth century.

—God no. Who wants to come after the stinking Industrial Revolution? And all that lachrymose prudery?

—Well, I see that now.

Later in the same spell of good weather Simon took her punting; she brought a couple of her girlfriends who did history. He had spent the previous summer working for Scudamore's, hiring punts out to visitors, and so he was fast and flawlessly competent, as steady on his bare feet on the back of the punt as if he was on land. He stood braced with his jeans rolled up, dropping the pole through his hands until it hit the bottom, bending his knees to push against it when they were in deeper water, using it like a rudder to steer. Deftly and narrowly he skimmed the dithering punts full of beginners, not even acknowledging in his expression their separate existence. The girls lay back and watched; the low-slung punt enforced the postures of idling privilege even in these studious girls dressed in sober jeans and draggled Indian-print cheesecloth skirts. They would have liked to be teasing and ironic with Simon – this was their comfortable mode – but his silence and good looks made them shy, and they slipped along the lapping green-smelling river with its flotsam of twigs and duck feathers and fag packets mostly without talking. Possibly it was not for all of them the occasion of unalloyed pleasure it must have looked to anyone watching. Yet even while Zoe was full of worried consideration for her friends (who clambered on to dry land at Granchester as if they were made clumsier by Simon's hand held out to help), she couldn't help the sight of him dancing joyously on her eyelids closed against the bright sunshine.

And one night he played her an old 78 of Kathleen Ferrier singing the 'Abschied' from *Das Lied von der Erde*, in a recording made by a private collector at the Carnegie Hall, so crackling and distorted that it was difficult to listen to.

—There was a period when I was quite seriously deluded, he said. —I found this in a junk shop in the sixth form. I was convinced that I could hear Ricky speaking to me in the crackling. Pretty weird. But don't you think: if the dead could come back and speak to us, it might sound like this?

—*O Schönheit*, the voice sang, through a storm of interference. —*O ewigen Liebens, Lebens trunkne Welt!*

—What does it mean? Zoe asked. She didn't know much about classical music: this slightly sickened her, its suspenseful nervous expectancy and its fullness of longing.

—It's all about how the dead are in love with the world they have to leave behind.

She knew that Simon was thinking about death all the

time, in a way she could not imagine for herself. This was understandable – sacrosanct, and forbidden territory – because of his brother. She knew that she, with her shallower life, had no authority to try to speak to him of these dark things. She only hoped that when they were making love she could pass over some healing into him out of her own deep reservoir of hopefulness and belief.

There was a wedding in Zoe's family that summer. Zoe's Uncle Peter (who wasn't strictly her uncle, but her mother's cousin) came back from America to live and work in England. He was leaving behind the American wife he had been married to for seventeen years and bringing home a new bride (English, though she had been working with him in New York) closer in age to his oldest daughter than to himself. Everyone was scandalised over the youth of the new bride; on the other hand they couldn't help being delighted at the thought of having Peter back among them, with his New York cleverness and sophistication. The first wife, although she was very dynamic, had fought so bitterly with Peter. She had wanted to pursue her own career with a theatrical agency on Broadway, and had demanded he do his share of running their household. Joyce and Ann sighed over Peter's 'chauvinism'. But they couldn't help approving of someone who would look after him more appreciatively.

Joyce asked Zoe whether she would like to 'bring her boyfriend'. Zoe winced at that awful word 'boyfriend', and thought for a moment they wouldn't go. She had new standards of seriousness and a new sensitivity to what was right and wrong. Her parents hadn't met Simon yet; her mother's curiosity over the telephone ('we're dying to get to know him, darling') sounded almost predatory.

—He's not my 'boyfriend', she said. —It's not like that.

—What do you mean? asked Joyce. —Don't you sleep together?

Zoe put the phone down in her disgust.

They did go to the wedding, anyway. Simon said he didn't care, and secretly Zoe longed for everyone in her family to see him. Peter called them the celestial twins because they came dressed alike in white collarless shirts over jeans, and they were both tall and lean with long hair tucked behind their ears (only Simon didn't have a fringe). The joke went around the wedding and Zoe heard other people use it, asking 'where are the twins?', and 'what are the twins doing?' She felt a thrill at the idea of their connection visible to everyone, setting them apart. When Simon, as if it was not even an issue, said he was not going to sit down for the reception dinner but would wait outside, Zoe followed him into the garden without a qualm, wearing the same steady and remote smile as his (even though she'd seen where Joyce had written their names on little cards set out on a table with Daniel and their American cousins). They sat cross-legged in the sunshine beside an ornamental pond full of water-lilies, smoking and watching iridescent dragon-flies hovering above the lily pads. The reception was in a big eighteenth-century house in the Hilltop area of the city which could be hired out for functions. Inside the orangery the playing of a string quartet was half smothered by the noisy boisterousness of the wedding guests. Simon described to her a Berliner Ensemble production of *Mother Courage*.

Joyce came looking for them, carrying two full glasses.

—Time for champagne and toasts! Come on you two! Don't go and be so superior that you miss all the fun.

She was wearing a dress she'd made, green Liberty cotton printed with tiny bunches of cherries; her hair was cut in a new layered way that exposed too recklessly, Zoe thought, how the light red was fading underneath into colourlessness and grey. She was always vigilant for glimpses of haggardness and wear under her mother's petite prettiness. She dreaded that Joyce would try to engage Simon in conversation, imagining she was drawing him out about Cambridge or poetry or 'left-wing' politics as she called them.

—I suppose Simon will find us all awfully loud and boisterous, Joyce said, —if he isn't used to our sort of family occasion. We do tend to let our hair down. His family's probably much more respectable.

Simon smiled his fending-off smile. —We're so respectable I don't think we even do family occasions. So I won't be able to tell whether you're more loud and boisterous than the average.

—We're very rude. But I don't care. God knows what the bride's relatives are making of it all. They seem a bit squaresville and they're probably shocked.

—Mum, all right, we'll come inside.

They stood at the back of the orangery and Simon drank down his champagne before the toasts were made and squinted through his smoke at the guests on the top table who stood up to make speeches, smiling privately to himself but not laughing at the jokes. These jokes were mostly about sex, and produced loud shouting laughter and heckling from Peter's side of the family; the bride's relatives and the more elderly guests were more subdued. Zoe decided not to even smile.

Peter had put on weight in the last few years. His head which had been clumsily heavy when he was younger seemed in proportion now; his thick shoulder-length black hair was speckled with grey and he wore big tinted glasses and a patterned tie. The bride in her youthfulness was insubstantial beside him; pretty enough, blonde with blue eyes and an anxious pink rash on her throat and arms. In an accent tinged with Americanisms, Peter made an emotional speech, saying how happy he was at coming home at last to live close to his 'beloved mother' (there was a flashed exchange of glances between Joyce and Ann). Zoe had always liked Peter's extravagant openness, his clowning confessions (she and her family had spent two happy summers at his place in Vermont). Now she prickled uneasily as if he exposed too much. When the speeches were over and everyone was mingling he embarrassed her by reminiscing nostalgically to Simon about his days at Peterhouse.

The American children of Peter's first marriage sat gloomily apart: one leggy sixteen-year-old girl and two younger plump pasty sons in bow-ties ('they look,' said Joyce disapprovingly, 'as if they haven't been brought up on home-cooked food'). Vera tried to fuss over them, magisterial in a white blouse with a tie neck and a dark skirt whose waistband rode up on her round high stomach, but they looked at her as if she was an eccentric stranger. Although she had talked endlessly about her grandchildren across the Atlantic – how clever they were, what opportunities they had, what a lovely home – in truth she hardly knew them. She gave herself up instead to basking in the attentions of her son. She forgave any number of missed birthdays, scrawled postcards from exotic holidays, and expensive gifts sent as substitutes for visits, when he walked with her around his guests, his arm around her shoulder, almost as if she was his bride. (Meanwhile the actual bride took her uncomfortable turn with her recalcitrant stepchildren.) There had been some talk of inviting Dick to the wedding. His second wife had died of breast cancer and now he was married again to a nurse he had met at the hospital; they were both retired and lived in the country. Peter and his mother were adamant, though, that he was not to be forgiven, even though Joyce and Ann pointed out that the thing he was not to be forgiven for was more or less what Peter was doing to his first wife now.

Ann said she wanted to talk to Simon about John Donne.

—I knew his poems by heart once. I used to recite them in the street.

—Really?

—Sweetest love, I do not go, for weariness of thee . . . The lying toad. He is, of course, almost certainly weary of her. But then you're young so you don't know about that.

Her cream crêpe de Chine dress was made up to look like something Edwardian, with leg-of-mutton sleeves and rows of tiny buttons up to the elbow and up the side of the high neck. Although she had a round belly and a waddle when she walked, her dainty hands and feet and little sharp face were still pretty as a quick-eyed little creature, a marmoset. Her dark hair was permed into a mass of curls.

—Haven't you two got anything stronger than tobacco? My kids are driving me berserk. Sophie wanted to be a bridesmaid, can you believe, and is still sulking. I was hoping we could escape to the grotto for a secret smoke. Did you know there was a grotto? It's supposed to be divine. Now I'm forty the only chance I get to carry on with beautiful young men is likely to be stealing them from my niece.

Simon smiled warily. —A grotto sounds interesting, he said.

Zoe going in search of more drink bumped into Ray looking huntedly around him. —Is your mother anywhere in sight? D'you think I can get away with a quick cigar? Just one of these little ones?

—She's with the caterers. You're probably OK. Why don't you come and talk to me and Simon?

—Oh, he's much too stringently intellectual for me.

—Dad, I wish the two of you would get on. He hates

this kind of phoney occasion just like you do.

—Who says I hate it? I'm having a wonderful time. Our transatlantic cousin is one of my favourite people. Not only that but I'm hoping he's going to be one of my customers, now he's moving home. He buys contemporary art, you know. Of course this is hardly the New York market, but at least we're cheaper. He'll buy Frisch; he'll certainly buy Frisch, he'll love it. Anyway, what's your friend got to complain about? Free booze, free grub, good music? Why the hell isn't he enjoying himself?

—Don't call him that: 'my friend'. His name's Simon.

—It would be. How sure I was that he couldn't be a Wayne, or a Terry. You've let me down, Zo. I was counting on you to bring home someone vulgar and unsuitable, just to see the look on your mother's face. We'll have to see what Daniel can do. I'm quite hopeful, actually, in that respect. I think the purple hair is a promising sign.

By the time Zoe found a half-full bottle she had lost Simon, and then she spotted him making his way down between two tall hedges in search of the grotto. She had been drinking champagne on an empty stomach and she felt dizzy and desperate.

—Do you hate them all? she asked when she caught up with him.

—Don't be silly, he said. —Don't exaggerate.

—I know what you think. They all put on such an act. They make such a display of enjoying themselves. It's all so false, and so materialistic.

—You don't, actually, have any idea what I think.

—My dad's different. He's serious about what he does. You do like his paintings? (She had shown him that morning around the ones hung on the walls at home; he hadn't commented.)

He shrugged. —No, not much.

This was a hard blow; she had counted on his admiring them, taking them to stand for what was deep and true as everybody else always had. She struggled to smile and keep her composure, but her face was stinging and her eyes were watering as if he'd actually struck her. She was caught out in her own unexamined enthusiasm, exposed and curling up.

—Oh, don't you? she said, trying to sound blithe and mildly surprised. —I'm very fond of them. Perhaps you need to get to know them better.

—I doubt it. I can see exactly what they are. I just think figurative painting's bankrupt. A dead language. There's nothing left for it to say. The visual arts – whatever mess they're in – have left behind that kind of simplistic confidence in representing the real.

For one electrifying split second Zoe could imagine how it might be to hate Simon. It was like a white fizz, a surge of light from the back of her mind in which everything looked differently: his absorbed frown, deciding at a fork in the path which way to take; his slouching step in his sloppy espadrilles; his rudeness to her family; his immovable calm certainty that she was wrong. She pierced through, just for that second, into a deep dark reservoir of protest, agitated and incoherent.

Then she pulled herself back from the brink of it, remembering how she needed him for her happiness. She trotted penitently after him down the path, reminding herself of how much she wanted to be part of the purity and consistency in his way of looking at things. The changes that hurt her most were the ones that made her strong. If need be she would unlearn her taste for her father's paintings, too; she knew she could do that, do it easily.

But the moment's shock left a little tender place, a chill of hurt.

Peter and Rose were staying, and all the close family came back to the house for tea or more drinks except Vera, who had been dropped off at her flat to rest, and the stepchildren, who had escaped, to everyone's relief, to 'check the place out for a bit'. Zoe and Simon disappeared upstairs to her room, which was also a relief. Joyce felt tense under the reproach of Simon's coolly scrutinising look; as if there weren't enough things for her to be worrying over! (She hadn't even had time yet to think, how dare he disapprove? What does he know, about us?)

—He's very gorgeous, Zoe's chap, Ann said. —Very sexy. And terrifyingly intelligent. But not much sense of humour.

While Joyce organised tea, Peter brought the wedding presents in from the car and heaped them on the big pine kitchen table.

—Open, open, open up, chanted Ann. —We want to see what you got.

—Isn't this supposed to be a decorous occasion, when

Rose makes a list of who we need to thank for what?

—Spoilsport!

—OK then, I capitulate! Get ripping!

Rose did in fact make a list.

—Jesus God, what are we supposed to do with these? They look like instruments to procure an abortion.

—Oh, look, multicoloured tumblers in little wicker baskets! Aren't they just frightful?

—Frightful as fuck. Who were they from?

—Pasta maker, pasta maker. You've got two pasta makers.

—His and hers! So we can each make our own spaghetti.

—I'll bet on a minimum thirty-six crystal goblets. People always give crystal goblets. There were definitely some crystal goblet givers there today.

—But we hate crystal goblets.

—Well, you're going to have to find some way to learn to live with them. Lots and lots of them.

—I told you you should have had a wedding list.

—Oh but Joycey, wedding lists are so infra dig.

—Open ours, open ours, clamoured Ann. —If you don't appreciate it I'm going to have it back.

Ray and Joyce gave them a painting. Peter and Rose got genuinely very excited about this. It was a smallish dark painting of a man slumped in a chair with his back turned, leaning his head on his hand, his elbow propped on his knee.

—I did suggest, said Joyce, —that it wasn't exactly a weddingy subject.

—But it's just how Ray feels about weddings, isn't it! Say the word wedding to Ray and that's precisely the posture of his inner man.

—I don't know if I was thinking about weddings in particular, said Ray, giving the painting a careless wary glance. —It's just the usual kind of existential angst. I thought you might enjoy it.

— It's fantastic! Absolutely fantastic. I love it. I'm going to love to live with this guy.

—Me too, said Rose.

Joyce felt hollowed out with hospitality.

Peter insisted that she went to lie down. He put his arm round her to escort her to her bedroom and called her 'sweet coz' and thanked her for organising everything so wonderfully, whispering in her ear so that his hot breath tickled her. She couldn't forgive him, though, for refusing to invite his father. She knew how much Dick had wanted to come. Peter was obstinate; there was something self-preening in how he cultivated and clung to his childhood's hurt. Joyce put her dress on a hanger and lay down on the bed in her silk dressing gown embroidered with poppies. It was early evening; the thin white cheesecloth curtains drawn across the open windows swelled and lifted in the breeze, making squares of reflected light swim on the wall. Dick often came to see Joyce, she had visited him and Ruth in their cottage. Whenever he came he brought presents: his home-made wine (which Joyce had to save for parties because Ray wouldn't touch it), bundles of old silver teaspoons bought at a sale, newspaper parcels of runner beans or sweet peas from his garden. Joyce couldn't help herself basking in his rusty old charm. If he took her out for lunch he pulled out her chair and helped her off with her coat, so that she felt taken care of. No doubt there was a great deal of delusion in it. No doubt the women who had lived most intimately with him had reason to resent the lightness and sweetness he could make when he chose. Joyce knew for herself how the thirst for lightness and sweetness could lead you into twisted snarled-up ways.

She almost slept; at least, her thoughts floated some little way above the bed, although she couldn't let go of the busy responsibility that had stretched her thin all day, the worry over all the ones who needed to be placated and appeased and looked out for. Fran, Ray's sister, was a widow of six months and although she was a hearty sensible creature was bound to be stricken and sorry at a wedding. Martin and Ingrid still weren't pregnant. Frisch had come with a new girl and Joyce had had to judge delicately the degree of friendliness to show towards her, considering how very recently she had been friendly to the one displaced. A good friend of Joyce's from the days of the craft co-operative (her brother had been at school with Peter) told her over lunch that her breast cancer had come back; hard to believe when she looked so radiantly well. And even as Joyce dozed she couldn't help her high-strung nerves tuning in to any possibility of raised voices, in case it was Ray and Daniel picking another fight over nothing. It had been a mistake, Daniel's coming back to live with them after his band split up and his flat fell through, and Joyce had had to nurse him through a bad night with the magic mushrooms. Ray couldn't bear it that Daniel didn't know what he wanted to do next.

Joyce opened her eyes and came wide awake and thought with clarity while she followed the line of a crack across the ceiling how much she would have liked to talk about all this with Zoe. Wasn't that what mothers and daughters were supposed to do? Wouldn't she have loved more than anything to tell Lil? She had been so busy – today, yesterday, this month, last year – that she had probably let slip precious opportunities for making contact with her now-grown-up child. Zoe and Simon had missed out earlier on their tea. If she took up to Zoe's room a tray with three cups and slices of Ann's cake (full of brandy), perhaps they would let her in and she could tell them funny stories from the day, confide in them about her difficulties. Simon's silence might turn out to be only the insecurity of youth.

Joyce had made up the packaway bed for Simon yesterday although she had known he wasn't likely to sleep in it. It had seemed a strange thing even so, to prepare a bed for a man in the room full of Zoe's childish possessions, her teddy and favourite doll still on her white cotton bedspread, her story books muddled in with her A-level texts on the shelves in the alcove, her china animals on her treasure shelf. When Zoe first moved into the room years ago she and Joyce had decorated it in blue and white; Joyce made blue curtains and covered the bedside table in blue, with a white fringe glued around it. On the wall were pictures Zoe had made on holiday in Wales out of shells picked up on a beach and stuck into Polyfilla, and an appliqué snowman Joyce sewed for her when she was a baby, with snowflakes in cross-stitching.

She pictured herself taking up the tea and cake and hearing from behind the closed door a quality of silence – paused and creaking, taut with held breath – which would make it impossible to knock. Or she would knock and say that there was tea and Zoe would say muffledly OK she'd fetch it in a minute, and Joyce would have to carry the third cup downstairs with her again, so that they wouldn't even know she'd tactlessly tried.

Zoe had had sex twice before she went up to Cambridge, but those hadn't been very happy experiences, both at parties, both drunk, one of them outside up against a wall, the boy seeming exasperated with her for her incompetence at managing what had surely been a near impossible physical contortion, into which pleasure couldn't imaginably have entered. She had decided that she was not going to be very good at this kind of thing. Therefore she had gone to her first few university social occasions expecting to be a shy observer, unnoticed and wondering and perhaps, if she could rise to it, some-what ironic.

It was probably because she had thought herself more or less invisible that she had allowed herself to stare at Simon Macy. Josh, who was kind, had invited a first-year friend of Zoe's to a party at his house, and she had begged Zoe to go with her so that she would have someone to walk back to college with afterwards. Zoe hadn't even realised when she agreed that Simon lived there, although she certainly hadn't forgotten who he was; from time to time in those first weeks she had caught sight of him, each glimpse like a jolt of longing – unappeasable longing, she was quite clear about it – earthing itself through her. There was something in the particular combinations of his nervous fine-boned paleness with his dark hair, and his absorbed obliviousness with his confidence, which answered exactly to her idea of a desirable male, and set him apart in romance from all the other students. The romance thickened when the weather sharpened in November and she saw him in an old Oxfam-shop fur coat, the collar turned up around his lean face pinched and bruise-coloured with cold. She knew perfectly – crushingly – well that she wasn't alone in any of this. Loads of the girls liked Simon Macy.

At the party she sat inconspicuously on the edge of a group of people she didn't know, drinking mouthfuls of warm Rioja from a plastic cup. She hadn't dressed up; even that would have been presumptuous, as if anyone was likely to look at her. She was wearing her comfortable cords and her desert boots and an old navy V-neck jumper she used to wear to school, and her hair was tied back. She had, in honour of the party, fastened it with a blue ribbon. There were a couple of really beautiful girls there – one of them, she knew later, was Trina – with their eyes elaborately painted, wearing old

1930s dresses that showed off their silky curves. They were dancing and performing at the centre of things; literally, they seemed to be acting out scenes from some play they had been in together at school. Watching them and swallowing down the Rioja, Zoe felt sad, as if this was the youth that books and poetry celebrated, and she was shut out from it by something helplessly prosaic in her constitution. At the same time, she couldn't have wanted to be them; finally there seemed to her something foolish and exposing in how they presumed upon admiring male attention.

Zoe had known Simon was there as soon as she came in. He wasn't in the room constantly, he came in and out (this was his habit at parties, she learned afterwards). Once he came back eating an apple, once with his finger in a book, as if he had been distracted from reading in another room. The party, it was clear, was not quite enough for him. His only wholehearted participation was when he sat cross-legged to roll another joint, tearing papers and strewing tobacco on the back of an LP cover (Velvet Underground, Talking Heads, Josh's dub reggae).

At some point he was gone again and she didn't see him come back in; and then with a scalding stir of adjustment she was aware that he was standing right beside where she sat. She was intimately close to his long bony feet with the big toes turned crookedly outwards; she could have touched them with her hand. Then he dropped to squat beside her, offering her the joint. She would have accepted it, just so as not to seem like a stodgy little first-year, only she was afraid she'd choke and make a worse fool of herself.

—No, I don't take it, she said idiotically, shaking her head.

—Oh, don't you? he laughed. —What do you take?

—Nothing really, apart from this horrible wine.

—I meant, what subject do you take? If you are a student? Are you?

—I'm at your college, she said. —I do history.

—That's just what I would have guessed. You look calm, and factual.

—Oh dear. That's probably exactly what I am. I was actually – just then – thinking about the medieval Italian banking system.

—The medieval Italian banking system! He seemed pleased with that, settling back to sit with his arms around his knees. —You'll have to tell me all about it sometime. I'm fascinated.

She was dizzy at the idea that he imagined they might have further conversation in the future.

—But you haven't been thinking about medieval banking systems all evening. You were watching me.

—Oh no! Zoe flushed guiltily. —I've been watching everybody. I don't really know anyone here.

—Don't be embarrassed. I really thought you were. Every time I glanced up, you were looking at me.

Dumbly she shook her head. —Not really.

—I thought you'd like it if I came over to talk.

—Well, I do like it. If you don't mind.

—How did you know, anyway, which college I'm at?

—I've seen you around.

—You see! You have been watching!

This time she shook her head, not meeting his eyes, but smiling. —Everybody knows you.

—No they don't. Not as well as you do.

—I don't know you at all, she said sensibly.

—Well, would you like to?

She simply nodded.

And that was when he touched her for the first time: transferring the nearly smoked end of the joint to his left hand very deliberately, slipping his right hand under her thin wool jumper and running it lightly around her waist until he found the top of her hip bone, pressing in against the bone under the waistband of her trousers. It was the deliberateness that undid and dissolved her when she replayed this moment of his choosing her over and over afterwards: the idea of his consciously coolly initiating their crossing over from talk into sex, not waiting to fumble into it later in the dark, or through drink. His fingers were cool, though not cold; she could feel his long tapering fingertips and longish nails, and she was seized, just from this touch, by an excitement she certainly hadn't felt those times with the other boys, although she knew something like it from occasions alone and dreaming. Disoriented because her dreaming desires had impossibly erupted into actual life, she sat amongst the noise and chaos of the party in stillness and a kind of hallucinatory ease, as if like Alice in Wonderland she had grown larger than the room, looking around with eyes that saw everything and nothing.

She learned afterwards that Simon's touching her was always a preliminary to sex. In between times, he didn't like any physical contact, he didn't want her to kiss him or put her arms around him, he never held hands with her when they were walking together. Also, they were never to talk at other times about what they did in bed. Once Zoe had adjusted to all this, she didn't mind it; she too came to feel that all that pawing and clinging to one another that other couples went in for was cloying and infantile; their sentimentalities and spilled-over confidences were a kind of rubbish that might contaminate what was real, which must be kept clear, and utterly private.

When Simon took her to his bed that first time, while the party was still going on downstairs (her friend after all had to walk back to college on her own), she was so afraid that she shook while he undressed her, and hoped he didn't notice it. All longing had died down in her and she only hoped the thing would be quickly over with and she would acquit herself without disgrace. Judging from her previous experiences, she supposed her role in the business would be primarily to be accommodating and instrumental; so she was taken aback and dismayed when, kneeling beside her in the near dark (he had spread out his duvet on the floor in the light of the gas fire), he turned his attentions to touching her, with no sign of the urgency or male peremptory haste that she remembered. She had thought of these touchings as solitary secrets, or perhaps as teenage substitutions for the 'real thing': in the first moments she was so shy she tried to stop him, kept her legs together and twisted away from him on to her side, hugging her knees childishly. Then naturally as he persisted she forgot herself, and uncurled, and opened her legs, and lost herself, and even forgot, sooner or later, that this was him; and then she wasn't afraid – although she was astonished and wincing at it afterwards – of showing herself to him, greedy and inventive and exposed.

The next afternoon, even though she told herself brutally that he probably often did what he'd done to girls at parties, and that it did not mean he would want any further connection with her, she cycled over from college, rang the doorbell until Marty let her in, picked her way through a deep disorder of bottles and beer cans and stale overflowing ashtrays – in that house the mess from parties was never really cleared up, it was just allowed to wear away with time – and presented herself with a thudding heart in Simon's room. He was working. He made her wait while he finished; she sat on his bed in absolute silence for two hours while he typed, scribbled, opened up books and read absorbedly, sighed, wrapped his hand tightly in his hair in the intensity of his concentration, scribbled, typed again. She wondered sometimes afterwards whether this had been a test, which she had passed. Even when he wound the last sheet of paper out of the typewriter, she was afraid he might send her away. But he didn't. In a restless afternoon dusk – cars ploughing home on the wet road outside, lights sliding across the ceiling, the door locked, the others rousing out of their beds and shouting round the house and once knocking – they began again (only it was always each time different) what they had left off the night before.

It was this devoted attentiveness of his to sex that she thought of as her great good luck. Each time when they came to touching she felt a little beat of fear that he might frown and make his face of fastidious dismissal and deplore the importance that she placed upon it. But he had never let her down. Each time it was a blessed dispensation, that with a serious face and rapt attention he applied himself to making love to her with all his intelligence and grace.

Seven

Zoe could imagine having a child, but not a baby. The child when she imagined it was a tiny elflike thing, her spirit-companion, playful, looking laughing at her with dark eyes full of knowingness. But she realised there was an intermediate phase before knowingness was possible, and that was a kind of blank to her. She couldn't think what you would do with a baby all day.

That autumn when she was pregnant she was working three afternoons a week in a shop across the road from the entrance to the maternity hospital. She wasn't very busy. It was a shop that sold handbags and luggage, the customers were occasional and took a long time choosing. So she was often looking out of the windows across at the hospital when one of the new mothers came out and got into her husband's car to be driven home for the first time. The mother would be followed by a nurse ceremonially carrying the baby wrapped in a bundle of white shawls; the nurse would hand it to the mother when she was safely in the passenger seat. If Zoe tried to convince herself that she would one day soon have a bundle of white shawls of her own, then what she pictured wrapped up inside it was something like a mouse, or a kitten, something soft and mewling and tender, but remote.

Simon and Zoe didn't have a car. She supposed she would get a taxi home with her baby. This would be just another way in which she was unlike the other women she met at the antenatal classes; unlikenesses that made her feel lacking and yet at the same time aloof, privately cherishing the original way she and Simon had of doing things. She supposed she would get in the taxi on her own, with her baby. When she arrived back at the little house they rented in the Kite, she didn't know whether Simon would be waiting there for them. He might choose to go on one of his long walks that day, or to be working on his thesis in the university library. He hadn't wanted a baby. She had pretended that her pregnancy was an accident (the truth was, it was something between an accident and deliberate: she had left off her cap when she couldn't quickly find it on one occasion, not knowing whether she hoped she would get away with it, or hoped she wouldn't). Even so, he hadn't wanted it, he had said they should find a doctor to get rid of it. But she had left it too late for that before she told him.

The arrival of the baby still seemed far off. She swelled up and was in love with the extraordinary shape of herself in the bath, and then with the baby leaping and jumping inside her, but the days ticked by very dawdlingly towards the date they had given her at the hospital. They had fine weather that autumn: skies like old watercolours, powder blue with tall ragged white clouds; the massive city trees bronzing and crisping at the edges; the spires and turrets of the colleges sharp grey as pencil lines against the air. She cycled between her jobs (as well as at the handbag shop she worked one day a week on a greengrocer's stall on the market, and two evenings and Sunday mornings as a barmaid at the Portland Arms), standing up on her left pedal when she took off from the kerb, glancing behind her and scooting off with her right foot like a real Cambridge lady-habituée, proud that she was strong and capable and that her pregnancy made no difference to her. (She cycled into the hospital the very day before she had the baby.) She pitied and was privately sceptical of the ones who moaned about backache and tiredness.

Unlike the other women at the classes, she hadn't got everything ready. That was what they said to one another: 'Have you got everything ready?' as if having a baby was a household routine like preparing a room or packing to go away on holiday. Zoe knew from novels that a new baby could sleep in a pulled-out drawer at first, as long as it was lined with soft blankets. She held off contemptuously from those practicalities that turned the baby's arrival into another dreary opportunity for consumerism, for discussions of the purchase of prams or sterilisers or washing machines. (Her mother had washed all the nappies by hand, so she was sure she could do the same.) She changed nothing in the house, and she and Simon didn't talk about what was coming. They made love from behind because her huge stomach got in the way; but still they didn't actually ever mention the baby, after that first terrible week of his cold furious insistence, and her stubbornness, resisting him.

It was not quite true that she had made no preparations at all. At the back of the drawer where she kept her jumpers and shirts she had a little cache of baby clothes: some tiny white vests and socks her mother had sent, two little matinee jackets knitted by her grandmother, a couple of second-hand Babygro suits she had bought herself from a charity shop because they looked clean and pretty and hardly used. She had blushed when she was paying for them because in spite of her big annunciatory bump she didn't really feel she was one of the grown-up women who had the right to possess such items. Sometimes when Simon wasn't in the house she got these things out from the drawer and unfolded them, frowning as she tried to imagine what kind of tiny creature might be fitted inside them.

And then she was on a trolley being wheeled somewhere and she was looking into Pearl's eyes and Pearl was looking back into hers. This was not any baby she could ever have imagined herself having. It wasn't mouse-like or curled up or tender at all: it had huge strained-open eyes of dark night-blue, staring at Zoe with something like the same indignant awareness of outrage and violation with which Zoe must have been staring back at her.

'What was *that*?' The mutual accusation seemed to bounce backwards and forwards between them. 'What did *that* to me?'

The last few hours of history still seemed as loud around them as a battle, the blazing assaults of pain, the drama of doors slamming and feet running in the race to the delivery room, Zoe's noisy vomiting into a kidney bowl, her shouting out numbers at the top of her voice, counting through her contractions. She couldn't wait to tell any of her women friends never, never to be tempted to put themselves through this, that it was much more terrible than anyone could imagine in advance. (Needless to say she quickly forgot it, in her absorption in her new life with the baby.)

—You've been so good, the student midwife said, squeezing her round the shoulders.

But this baby didn't care for any of that.

Its hair was not nestling fur, but a tall gingery crest. Its nose was broad with flaring nostrils. Its mouth was fat with flat squashed lips, an angry purplish red, down-turned at the ends with dissatisfaction.

—Who are you? she whispered to it as they were hurried, staring at one another, down to the ward on the trolley. —Where did you come from?

She knew in those first moments that this baby was never going to grow into any elf-creature, or spirit-companion to her. Actually, she knew in the same moments that the spirit-companion had been a silly idea; as if your child could be just a broken-off piece of your-self. Real things were always more tremendous – more unhinging – than the things that grew out of your own thoughts. Perhaps the only thing left over from the dream-child was her name. Zoe clung to that, as if to attach to this new creature just a small something of her own, a memory of the wild child from Hawthorne's *The Scarlet Letter* which she had studied at A level: Pearl absorbed on the shore in her games with the weed and the shells, loving but free.

The week that Pearl was born, Simon was away giving a paper at a conference in Manchester. He hadn't left a telephone number. Zoe lied on the phone to her mother, and said that although he hadn't been able to get back in time for the birth, he had seen the baby since and picked her up out of her little cot of transparent plastic and held her. She also lied that it was Simon who had first pointed out what now was obvious, that the baby looked like her, like Joyce. Joyce wondered, but vaguely, if she should come up and see them. Zoe who so wanted her to come said firmly that it would be a better idea if she gave them a few weeks to settle into their new routine.

The lying to her mother was something new (Zoe usually scrupulously told the truth); it was something that had come about in the rush of change and bloodiness and her attention focused with the nurses on her bodily functions, as if she had lost track for a moment of her higher self. But the hard-edged gap between them, narrow but deep, which both dissimulated with bright capable voices, wasn't new. Zoe would have liked to talk with her mother about feeding the baby and about nappies, but Joyce's vagueness warned her off; she remembered their truce of sceptical disapproval, how each politely withheld their verdict on the other. Zoe thought she could guess what her mother thought of her life with Simon; she could imagine her making a funny story to her friends out of how they lived on black coffee and bread and cheese, without a washing machine or an electric kettle, and with a bath in the kitchen; how they spent their money on books and music instead of furniture; how when Joyce and Ray came to stay Zoe had forgotten that they would need spare sheets.

When Zoe had first told Joyce that she was pregnant, she had had a sentimental idea that this would lead to a moment of closeness between them; but Joyce at the other end of the phone had seemed shocked and even irritated.

—What about your PhD? she had asked, as if she was actually disappointed, although she hadn't ever shown much interest in it before. (Zoe, anyway, was convinced that the subject she had chosen to work on – the effects of pre-war government education policies on responses to conscription in the First World War – was the wrong one. She struggled on with it, and had folders full of notes and a card index of references, but she found it hard to imagine ever finishing writing it up. She persuaded herself it was more important for her to bring in money so that Simon could finish his.)

—Oh, I can pick that up later. At the moment,

anyway, it's not practical for both of us to be studying at the same time.

—But is Simon going to be able to bring in an income to support you, while you're at home looking after the baby?

Zoe had sighed deeply. —Mum, this isn't what I wanted to be talking about, not right now, not when I've just told you something important.

—I'm sorry, I can't quite take it in, that's all. All the implications.

—It's a girl, Joyce said to Ray after Zoe telephoned from the hospital. —She's going to call it Pearl.

She hesitated in the kitchen doorway as if she didn't know where to go with the news. It was just after breakfast; Ray was reading the paper and drinking coffee at the big pine table. He took off his reading glasses.

—Good God. Pearl Deare. Sounds like something out of music hall.

—But I suppose it will be Macy.

—So we're grandparents.

—I can't believe that, said Joyce. —I'm not ready for it. I don't feel like a grandmother.

—We could just go, said Ray. —I'll fill up the car, check the tyres, you throw some things in a bag. We'll drive, it won't take more than five or six hours on the motorway. We'll book into a hotel somewhere in Cambridge.

—I don't know how to contact her, said Joyce.

—We don't need to, we just turn up. We know which hospital it is.

—I was seeing Ingrid for lunch tomorrow.

—Cancel her. She'll understand.

—I'd need to have a bath and wash my hair.

—Run it while you start to pack. I'll ring Ingrid.

Joyce put the plug in the bath and turned on the hot tap. Slowly she moved about her bedroom listening to the bath fill up, pulling out the drawers, walking into the built-in wardrobe and running her hand along the hangers, some outfits still in their dry-cleaner's polythene. Nothing seemed right. She didn't like anything she had. What could one possibly choose to wear on such an occasion? She pulled out her good grey wool crêpe skirt and matching jacket with padded shoulders; but that might be too hot in a hospital, and it would crumple on the journey, and she remembered that last time she wore it the skirt was uncomfortably tight. There were some black silky trousers that were always comfortable, but the material had gone cheap and snagged if you looked up close, and anyway she had a sudden fear that her thighs looked fat in them, like a bar-room tart. She took down one thing after another and threw them on the bed.

Ray found her standing naked in the bathroom. She was staring in the mirror, which she had wiped clear of steam with a towel. The bathwater was almost at the top of the bath.

—What is all this about?

—Do I look like a grandmother?

—So that's what it is. You could have a been grandmother at thirty-six. Some women are. It doesn't mean anything.

305

—But I'm not. I'm not thirty-six.

—You have the most beautiful body. Look at you. As beautiful as ever. I can't resist the sight of you.

—You're not enough, she said.

—I see. He looked crestfallen, resigned.

—Don't be silly. I meant, you're married to me therefore it doesn't count. It only counts from strangers. Only strangers see whether you look like a grandmother or not. Whether you're someone they could want to make love to.

—So that's why you don't want to go and visit Zoe's baby.

—She doesn't want me anywhere near it, either. You know what they think of me. They think I'm a bourgeois housewife. They think all I care about is shopping and decorating.

—You're almost certainly making all this up, he said.

—Maybe.

—We won't go. It can wait. We'll go when you're ready.

He put his arms around her from behind; in the mirror the sleeves of his suede jacket were brutal against her soft nakedness.

—Manet, he said. —*Déjeuner dans la salle de bains.*

Other friends came to visit Zoe in the hospital and saw Pearl before Simon did. Probably some of the mothers on the ward thought that Joshua was her husband, because he came in to see her twice at that hour when the husbands came (some alone and devoted, with flowers and lots of gazing into the crib; some with older children, being jolly with the new baby while the mother made up to the others, laughing at the clothes they were dressed in, asking what their father had been feeding them on). Zoe was Mrs Macy on the nameplate above the bed, the midwife had warned her of untold complications if she used her unmarried surname, and so she had amusedly agreed to it. She didn't however lie about this: she told the women who had become her friends in the beds to either side of her that she wasn't married, that she and her boyfriend didn't believe in it, that he was away and she hadn't been able to contact him.

Joshua didn't really make for a very satisfactory husband substitute: he still wore his hair long and had a straggling beard and traipsed around in an old greatcoat, with a plastic carrier bag in which he kept his poems. He had only got low marks in his finals but seemed to find it impossible to leave Cambridge, so he took on small gardening or typing jobs and rented a dank basement room lit with a forty-watt bulb to save money. Zoe dreaded him visiting her at home because he stayed talking about books and music for hours, and if it was raining outside he took off his socks without asking and wrung them out and hung them to steam in front of the fire. Still, it was sweet of him to come to the hospital, and he got very excited about Pearl, holding her as if she was a particularly slippery kind of fish, adjusting his body position contortedly to her slightest stirrings. He asked if Zoe was planning to educate her at home, and suggested that if so he could teach her Latin as part of a balanced curriculum. She looked forward more to visits from her friend who was a post-graduate at Churchill, and from the manageress at the bag shop, who brought her some baby sleepsuits Zoe was very grateful for. (She was beginning to wonder anxiously what she was going to do at home about the limited supply of baby clothes; they seemed to get wet and dirtied so quickly.)

None of these visitors from outside really seemed part of Zoe's new life with the baby; she felt much closer to some of the other mothers. In the bed to her right was a good-looking blonde woman with a hairdressing business. She had tried for a baby for eight years and then given up and started her business instead; just when it was really taking off she had discovered she was pregnant. She said she had cried every day of her pregnancy. Now she lay gazing in worship through the side of the transparent cot at her tiny son, although she still had no idea how she was going to manage looking after him. In the bed to Zoe's left was a dumpy woman with a pudding-basin haircut who had three children already; they came in with her husband who worked in haulage and wore a shiny suit to the hospital. Zoe was deeply impressed with this woman's quiet competence at soothing and feeding her baby, and managing the older ones. She confided tearfully, however, after her family had gone, that she hadn't wanted more children, but her husband wouldn't let her use any contraceptives. Indignantly Zoe and the hairdresser took her part.

—It's your body, said the hairdresser. —It's you who has to go through that torture.

—Don't get me wrong, said the woman. —I will love the baby. But there's no room for another one, and I've got no washing machine. And I'd just started at a little job of my own, which I won't be able to manage now with her.

Zoe confessed to them about how she had accidentally on purpose lost her cap, and not mentioned it to Simon. She was very moved by her intimacy with these women, and by what seemed to her their quiet heroism (everything in those hormone-heady few days was heightened). She thought how glad she was to get away from everything associated with the university: she felt as though she was recovering in a grateful rush her conviction of how deep and complex and sustaining people's lives were outside the lit circle of intellectual thought.

On the last day of the week she spent in hospital Simon came. It wasn't even visiting hours; the sister pursued him down the ward and wanted to send him away, but relented when he shrugged and charmed her with what Zoe could tell was his mock-courteous, most exaggeratedly upper-class manner. People responded to this presumption of authority in him as part of his disconcerting physical appeal: he was tall and very thin, and his hair these days was cut so short that it was like moleskin against his scalp, flickering with the change of his facial expressions. Zoe was changing Pearl's nappy on the bed; Pearl was squirming and crying. Until she was aware of Simon coming down the ward towards her, Zoe had been dealing quite calmly with this, tucking under and pulling tight, with her fingers inside to safely guide the pin as she had been shown by the nurses, knowing she could calm her down afterwards with feeding. When she saw Simon her hands were suddenly hot and fumbling, and the nappy fell open, so that when he came up to the bed he saw the whole raw little body, quivering and flailing in its distress, with the long slit up between its legs and the big plastic clip on its cord, which was drying out (nicely, the nurses said) into a greenish stump. The huge night-blue eyes fixed balefully upon Simon and the baby's whole head suffused with blood as she redoubled the intensity of her squalling.

Zoe knew that he was thinking the baby was ugly.

—So it's a girl.

—It's Pearl.

—Pearl Deare? That's ridiculous. It sounds like a wartime cabaret singer.

—Not Deare. Pearl Macy. I thought she'd have your name. Officially.

—Officially? I see that officially you've taken my name too. (How had her nameplate caught his eye so quickly? She had been going to take it down if she knew he was coming in.) —Is there some conspiracy, to implicate me here?

He sounded as if he was joking, but she knew he wasn't.

—The midwife said it would make things easier.

—I'll bet she did.

—Anyway: how are you? she said brightly, trying to

carry on with the nappy as if it was something ordinary to her. —How did the paper go?

He shook his head in irritation at her transparent effort to distract him. He didn't want to talk about that here. Looking around at the scene of shapeless swollen women in their nightclothes, some reading magazines, some staring dotingly into their cots, some dozing (the sister pulled curtains around the ones who were nursing, because a man was present), a tiny spasm of distaste tightened a muscle in his cheek. Zoe imagined that the ward smelled offensively: of milk, of baby excrement, of women's blood, of disinfectant and hospital dinners.

She put Pearl to the breast to feed, to calm her down; but there was something preposterous in doing it in front of Simon, as if this was a show she was putting on for his benefit, an ill-judged attempt at a maternal display. It was not even a very well-prepared show. Pearl wouldn't latch on to her nipple, she gasped and blubbered and half sucked and then lost her hold in frantic breathlessness, throwing her head from side to side against the breast; she arched her back and shuddered with sobbing and got herself into a worse state than she had ever been in before. Zoe was desperate and sweating, with her distended breast exposed. The nurses had to come and help, swirling the curtains around her bed behind them to cover her shame.

In the middle of this scene, Simon turned around and left.

It was Carol from Churchill who arranged to come to the hospital at lunchtime the next day with a friend who had a car, to pick up Zoe and Pearl and drive them home.

Joyce and Ray sent a cheque for two hundred pounds towards things for the baby. Zoe bought a pram and a cot second-hand from the Spastics shop, a basket for her nappy-changing equipment, and a plastic changing mat; she spent the rest on an automatic washing machine, which she had plumbed into the little covered yard at the back of their terraced cottage.

The washing machine made life remarkably much easier. In fact, before she bought it, Zoe simply hadn't been coping with the amount of housework to do. Simon would take a bag of their clothes down to the launderette every week or so, as he always had, but he didn't offer to take anything of the baby's, so that in the evenings (Pearl's best time for sleeping) Zoe found herself at the kitchen sink looking out of the window into the dark yard – or at her own blurry reflection, hunched and desperate – rubbing through the little sleepsuits and Babygros and plastic pants and cardigans and muslin wiping cloths (also her own bloodied knickers for the first couple of weeks), while the nappies boiled in a pan on the gas stove, filling the house with a foul steam. Somehow nothing ever came quite clean with handwashing (she supposed it was her inexperience, she was beginning to take in the infinite amount of ordinary things she didn't properly know how to do); the babysuits were permanently yellowed with baby sick at the neckline, or stained on the legs from leaking nappies. She remembered from somewhere to soak her own knickers in salt for the stains before washing them, and that helped; but on the clothes horse in front of the gas fire everything looked dingy and dispiriting, particularly when the rest of the house was such a mess because she hadn't had time to tidy. Sometimes in the evening the baby bath from the morning with its water cold and scummed with soap and bits of cotton wool was still sitting on the table waiting for her to empty it.

So she was fervently thankful for the automatic washing machine.

When she had first gone to antenatal classes they had all been given a little booklet printed on poor-quality paper with information about pregnancy and childbirth and babycare. It was illustrated with old-fashioned line drawings of mother and father and baby in which mother wore a frilly tight-waisted apron and father a tie, and both wore screwball-comedy expressions of mock joy and mock despair as they juggled with their cute cartoon infant. Zoe had despised this booklet at the beginning, and almost thrown it away. She had looked at its descriptions of a day with baby, and wondered whatever you were supposed to do in the long gaps between the four-hourly feed and change routines. On the list of things to take into hospital with you for the birth had been included eau de Cologne, and dutifully, although with no idea what she might need it for, Zoe had acquired a huge cheap bottle of this from Boots. (Years later she still had it, almost full, and the smell of it would bring back overwhelming memories of the maternity ward, the vast baths with thundering hot water where she had soaked her soreness and afterwards splashed her neck and arms with the cologne she hadn't found any other use for, the smell of it mingling with the new strange smell her sweat had in those days after the birth.)

Now, although the booklet was stuffed in the drawer where she kept Pearl's clothes and where Simon wouldn't look, Zoe made constant and humbled reference to it, to try and find out what she should do to manage better this new life she found herself inside. Pearl wasn't what they called a 'good' baby. This was the first question all the new mothers asked when they met at the baby clinic, looking into one another's prams: 'Is yours good?' (Zoe never saw either the hairdresser or the wife of the man in haulage again.) She knew everything was wrong with this; she was repelled by the smug relish of the mothers of the 'good' ones, and she could imagine just what Simon would understand about their use of that word 'good', its repressive moralisation of any behaviour that didn't fit into a convenient pattern. And yet it was a relief to confess to someone else whose baby, like hers, didn't sleep in the day and woke up every two hours at night, who was moving like her in a fog of fatigue, falling asleep on her feet doing the washing-up, falling asleep whenever she picked up a book to read. She longed sometimes when things weren't going well to telephone Joyce and pour out her troubles. Instead, whenever they did speak, she was careful to present herself as coping competently. ('You were such an easy baby,' Joyce had told her. 'I never knew what any of the fuss was about.') They sometimes spoke of the possibility of a visit, but they never fixed a date.

—Whenever you're ready for us, Joyce said.

—Whenever you can make time, said Zoe.

The thought of other wakeful mothers was consoling when Zoe was walking up and down in Pearl's room trying to get her to sleep after a night feed (on bad nights she stayed in there on the studio couch because it was pointless to disturb Simon, getting in and out of bed every time Pearl cried). She would be holding her upright against her shoulder the way she liked best, jogging her slightly and rhythmically until her right arm ached, letting her suck on the first knuckle of her left hand. After a while she would feel the alert little body dropping into softness against her, yielding up its conscious awareness, the wet mouth falling away from where it sucked. Without stopping the jogging, Zoe would lower her with slow smooth movements on to the cot, face down, rocking her against the sheet with both hands, gradually lessening and slowing the rocking and taking away the hands, one at a time, hovering ready to pounce back and rock her into sleep again if she roused. Then – silence! – Zoe would creep off to her couch and lie down. The temptation was to lie strained awake listening to Pearl breathe, but Zoe knew she could not afford to waste these blessed spaces of peace; she trained herself to fall almost instantly into sleep by running over and over the dates and details of the Education Acts or the clauses of the Treaty of Vienna, not testing herself, only moving her mind round and round inside the loop of known things until it fell through and was swallowed up. On bad nights it might be only five or ten or twenty minutes later that she was shocked awake again by Pearl's hard little cry, vindictive-seeming, full of outrage.

In the old days before Pearl, Zoe had hardly been aware of housework. She and Simon had developed a pattern of dealing with minimal engagement with the material substratum of their lives. The vacuum cleaner stood in a corner of the living room and occasionally one of them would plug it in and run it over the floor. In the mornings whoever was last to leave rinsed through the few dishes in the sink. They cleaned out the ashes of the front-room coal fire when they made a new one. They bought little bits of shopping on their way home from work or the library; they never made a list. They lived on bread and cheese and olives and fruit and biscuits, and sometimes one of them if they were in the mood cooked soup or risotto. Mainly they lived on black coffee which Simon always bought at one particular deli-catessen; he oversaw the details of its making with fastidious care. They were both very thin (the nurses at antenatal had been worried about Zoe); they certainly never avowed thinness as anything they were aiming for (that was for idiots, demeaning), but they had had a disdain for the greedy corporeality which betrayed itself in sweet puddings, second helpings, thickened flesh. The only chore which had ever presented itself as any kind of a burden of obligation was cleaning the toilet, and it was true that they had sometimes neglected this; only

Zoe had cleaned it scrupulously before her parents came to stay (that was somehow why she had forgotten to provide them with sheets). Simon and Zoe had never talked together about any of these arrangements or choices; that would have been banal.

Now that she had Pearl, this order of life – in which the material arrangements floated lightly on the periphery and knowledge and books and music were the real dense substance at the centre – was completely overturned. Zoe looked back upon the ruins of the old life with astonishment at her innocence then; that she had really believed you could exempt yourself so easily from the grown-up burdens, as if you were children playing house. To begin with, she knew now that she needed to eat. She was hungry, starving hungry, all the time; but anyway, she knew that she must eat to make milk. One weekend when she had neglected to feed herself her milk had started to fail. Pearl had screamed without stopping all one night, Simon walked out, and the Health Visitor made her go to bed for a couple of days. She had phoned Carol, who came over and cooked her fish pie and rice pudding and sausages and mash and sponge cake.

After that Zoe knew she had to shop and cook food properly (although she didn't really have much idea of how to cook). And of course she could not pop out and do her shopping casually anytime, it was a whole expedition: she had to feed and change and bath and dress Pearl first, and somehow wash and dress herself (she looked up in the booklet to try and find out what you were supposed to do with the baby at those moments when you needed both your hands). Usually the rocking of the pram in motion put Pearl to sleep while they were out, and this would be the best sleep she had all day. Sometimes after shopping when they got back Zoe would be able to leave her asleep in the pram in the yard while she flew inside to tidy up from the morning's routine, rinse nappies and put them to soak, put a wash on, make the bed, wash dishes. Then the hard little cry would come again.

Very early on, lying on her front, Pearl could half raise herself up on her arms when she woke, lifting her head with its gingery crest of hair to peer around for Zoe. If she was in the pram, Zoe could watch for a few moments that veering seeking head that couldn't support its own weight for long, before Pearl discovered where she was, or began to cry. These were moments of eerie quiet, both of them awake but separate, Zoe allowed to see Pearl as she was when she was alone: an instant's premonition of her daughter's capacity for life without her, liberating and lacerating at once. Sometimes Zoe hurried to pick her up and restore their tight-wound connection. Then if it was time for a feed (following the booklet, Zoe worked hard to establish these four-hourly), they settled down together in the chair with no arms that was best for nursing, and into a day that was mostly an inchoate mess there would bloom a session of healing calm while the baby sucked.

Zoe wore an old copper bracelet which she changed from wrist to wrist to remind herself which side they had started with last time. After her first urgent hunger was satisfied, Pearl's hand would begin to wander exploringly across the surface of the breast and her eye would meet Zoe's gazing down at her. Pearl's look would heat up warmly, and grinning up at Zoe she would sometimes fall off the nipple, the bluish milk trickling out of her open mouth down Zoe's front.

Simon didn't watch the feeding, even when he was in the house. Mostly, he was out; on the market (he had taken over Zoe's old job on the greengrocer's stall), or at the library, or with friends, or supervising students (he did some at home, and some in a room in college). It was as if after the birth the house split into separate domains; his space in the front room where he often didn't bother to make a fire but sat in the cold reading or typing or playing records; her space in the mess of the kitchen and living room with the gas fire on and the clothes horse laden with wet clothes or nappies steaming. If she had cooked he ate at the table with her and they exchanged polite information about their respective days, but he didn't finish what she put on his plate: she tried putting less and less, but he never finished it. If he had a bath in the kitchen he pulled the curtain across.

In the middle of the night when Pearl was about a month old, Simon had reached out for Zoe in the dark. She had just climbed back into their bed after feeding Pearl and putting her down to sleep again. She lay huddled away from him; he put a hand on her shoulder and rubbed up and down her back. It was the first time he'd touched her deliberately since she'd come back from the hospital. He had taken Pearl from her a few times when she asked him to, always when she was sleeping or peaceful; he had carried her into his part of the house and sat studying her tiny face framed among the shawls with an intent concentration which for those minutes would make Zoe hope that he was coming to care for her. But as soon as she stirred or grizzled he handed her back to Zoe as if she was no further business of his.

Because he had only ever touched Zoe when he wanted to make love to her, it didn't occur to her that he meant anything different by it now. Her body ached with ugliness; even in her tired fog she was conscious of unwashed hair, sweaty heat, a baggy stomach, swollen breasts. Her sexual self seemed buried several miles deep (probably buried, it had seemed to her then, for ever). Also, she had just come from dropping tears on to the baby where she had been suckling her in the spare bed, dwelling angrily on Simon's derelictions. How could he be so cold towards his own daughter? How could he keep up his punishment of Zoe, even if she had done wrong in tricking him into fathering the child? Could it be fair that the whole impossible labour of managing this baby fell upon her, even if that labour was precisely the reason he hadn't wanted a baby in the first place? (He had said: 'It will spoil everything. I've seen it happen. People drown in all that mucky stuff, clever people get stupid, they forget what they used to think, they only think about rusks and sleep and potty training, they actually start to think that these are interesting.') Zoe had wanted a baby; didn't that count for anything? Much of her waking thought circled in the treadmill of this unspoken argument with Simon.

—How can you? she said that night when he touched her. —How can you even think I would want to? I'm exhausted. You haven't given me a kind look all day. And the doctor said anyway to wait six weeks.

As soon as the words had been said aloud and were floating in the chilly air above the bed, she was sure that sex wasn't actually what Simon had meant at all. Really, he'd only been proffering friendliness, and consolation. Perhaps he had even been intimating a willingness to hold her poor racked body in his arms while she went off to sleep; at the very thought of that possibility all accusation melted in her (for the moment). He had been offering her his hand across the rift between them; it might have been the beginning of everything changing. Instead she felt him withdraw his kindness as vividly as if an electric current had cut off, and they lay jangled and motionless, apart. She knew she ought to speak, she could imagine the words of her apologetic explanation forming between them, but no sound came. She lay longing for him to touch her again. She wanted it so intensely that she was sure he must know; she couldn't believe that such a power of desire aimed at someone close by wasn't tangible. 'Oh, please, please,' she willed.

She was sure he did know; but he wouldn't touch her again because he couldn't forgive her capacity to so grossly misunderstand him. After a while, without a word, he got up out of the bed and took his bathrobe from the door and went downstairs. He must have worked down there, or slept in the armchair. In the morning when Pearl woke at half past six and Zoe came down and lit the gas fire and put on the kettle to boil, she heard him go up and shut the bedroom door behind him, and the accusatory voice inside her thoughts struck up groggily again.

Simon could see the end of his thesis coming closer. Sometimes if he'd been reading late he found he was actually visualising the coming end as a figure approaching from far off in flapping robes across a wasteland; one day it occurred to him that the image was from the scene in Pasolini's *The Gospel of St Matthew* where the devil comes to tempt Christ. He felt abashed that he had associated even in his subliminal awareness two such absurdly disproportionate testings – he didn't really confuse his own petty intellectual agonies with those real ones – and he tried to suppress the picture.

Simon's supervisor, Kevin Fry, had said already that Simon would be able to publish the thesis when it was finished. Kevin had joined the faculty while Simon was an undergraduate (amid some controversy because of open hostility in the establishment then towards critics influenced by the ideas coming out of France). Simon had been one of a select few students who met in Kevin's rooms and drank with him; they adopted styles in imitation of his (French cigarettes, old suit waistcoats from the second-hand stall in the market worn over collarless shirts), and submitted to certain implacable judgements as to what one could and could not talk about (eighteenth century was good, Lawrence was beyond bad, T. S. Eliot was boring). When Simon had read more, he understood that some of what he had taken to be Kevin's original thought derived in fact from the Yale Deconstructionists and Foucault; and he was puzzled that Kevin's written work seemed dogged, never as fresh or as dangerous as his speech.

At a certain point in the course of the PhD supervisions, while Simon was working on Stendhal (the thesis hinged on a comparison of the representations of incarceration in *La Chartreuse de Parme* and *Little Dorrit*), he had felt Kevin relinquish his role at the prow of their relationship: he listened to Simon with a new relaxed assent, he marked the work more cursorily, and there was a distinct cooling of their friendship. His French wasn't as good as Simon's, but that wasn't all; Kevin couldn't keep up with him any longer, Simon had overtaken his mentor, he was better. It had been an almost weightless transaction, that exchange of authority. He had shut the doors to Kevin's college room behind him one day (double doors made with a six-inch gap between, to insulate the concentrating one from all the noise of the world), and walked out to find spring sunshine after rain in the quad. Everything was altered as if there had taken place a silent shift under the earth, and he had felt an elated triumphant lightness and a diminishment both at once (where would he put his marker now, to aspire toward?). He even began to have one or two undergraduate followers of his own, who listened to him to find out what to think. He knew you could live a lifetime dedicated to contesting such near-imperceptible shifts of intellectual power; and he was confident of his capacity to come out well in those contests. He did however ask himself whether this was the most serious use to which he could put his intelligence.

He was pursuing his thesis in all seriousness. It seemed to him that the only possible justification for academic work was to do something that was bigger than the mere turning around of familiar compost that the system required. One had to be able to work the system, of course; the ideal was, to do that – persuasively, authoritatively – with one's left hand, and reach outside it with one's right, away out of the small world of university into the big worlds of history and art (here, of course, was where one put one's marker for aspiration). One should always have a little bit of contempt in one's manner, for academic work. He thought seriously about other careers, when the thesis was finished; he thought about the diplomatic service, or news reporting from some war zone; he thought about getting a teaching certificate and going to work in the worst kind of schools in the state system. He thought he would be strong enough for any of these. On the other hand, he feared the constraints that would leave him without the space to be free to think largely.

The one ambition he didn't allow himself (not yet, not yet, not for a long time yet), was to write 'creatively' (the very word was absurd, evoking so precisely the dismal queue of hopefuls clutching yellowed carbon-copy typescripts). It was true, there were a few poems

(Beckett-like, if anything); but no one had ever seen them, and they didn't exist, God forbid, anywhere on paper, he only kept them in his mind. He had too vivid an imagination of disaster: a car smash or a fall from a high place, the poems discovered by Zoe or his mother going through his things, misguidedly shown round, the dissimulated smugness of those who had admired him at finding out their imperfections.

He was working, around the time that the baby was born, on his chapter on 'Tyranny'. The idea of his work, and what was good in it, was his strongest happiness; when he wasn't actually engaged in reading or writing for the thesis he was nonetheless constantly aware of the shape of it, hidden and precious like a smooth stone fitted to his hand inside a pocket, or a secret matrix glowing in his chest. The paper he had given at Manchester was on Byron's 'Sonnet on Chillon' and the aristocratic ideal of individual freedom; his basic argument in the whole thesis was that there had been an absolute shift in literature, between the end of the eighteenth and the middle of the nineteenth century, from representations of punishment as an issue between individuals, the tyrant and the oppressed one, to modern representations of it as the one-sided outcome of an implacable impersonal system, grinding individuality small in the name of normalisation and regulation. The logic of these modern representations ended in Kafka, as he would suggest in his conclusion. His title – which had, in the context, an irony he enjoyed – was 'The Chainless Mind', from Byron.

He was succeeding in keeping all this work on schedule, despite the extra day at the market he had taken on, and the broken nights that came with the baby. He had never slept well. Now, if Zoe couldn't stop the baby crying, Simon got up and went out and walked the streets as he had done years before in the time of his worst insomnia, a solitary prowling in a world turned inside out in the dark. He had not wanted this baby. He had always had a horror of a certain kind of semi-academic domesticity; PhD students turned whey-faced and sour-tempered over their grubby-mouthed and badly behaved offspring; rented flats filled up with a detritus of toys; typewriter and books pushed resentfully aside to make room for plates of baby pap. It seemed to him self-evident that intelligent women with minds of their own would not make the best mothers: how could they bear, if they liked room to think and breathe and read, to be constrained as the mothers of small children must be to the sticky and endlessly repetitive routines of domestic life? He was sympathetic to the conundrum for feminism posed by this tension between motherhood and intelligent life (Kristeva's fundamentalism was one kind of answer, though it didn't convince him as the right one). He had reasoned with himself that he had no right to oppose Zoe if she was convinced that a baby was what she wanted (no doubt there were imperatives of female biology he was not equipped to understand); after that first week of hostilities, he had never brought up his reservations again.

He had a distinct impression, however, that Zoe was

not managing the baby very well. It cried surely more than they were supposed to; and the mess and smell and chaos in the house were worse than he had feared. Zoe herself was so changed. Her pregnancy had disconcerted him; the distended belly grotesque in its sheer improbability, forcing on whoever saw it naked the unpalatable truth that the oneness of the body is not indivisible. That transformation however hadn't been unexciting. But he was sad that since the birth Zoe was so physically diminished from the proud girl careless of female fuss that she had been. She had always been scornful of women who made a bother about their menstrual cycle; now she was so jangled with hormones that she wept at the news on the radio (at what was happening in Beirut, for example), even if she thought he didn't see it. Her skin was lustreless; she didn't seem to find time to wash her hair, and wore it pulled back in an elastic band; her stomach was still slack, and her breasts were heavy. She moved him not to desire but at best to a kind of sympathetic pity, which he could perfectly well perceive was the last thing she needed from him or could make any use of. He guessed that she smouldered with resentment against him, and this was exactly the kind of deterioration of their life together – which had been spacious and generous and free – that he had feared would follow the arrival of a child.

Sometimes she gave him the baby to hold, no doubt in hope that the physical proximity would bring on the tenderness he was supposed to feel. It wasn't very pretty, although he was amused by its fierce frowning look. He asked himself what bond he felt with this creature made from his own body; and in truth he felt nothing that he might not have felt for anybody else's baby (some resentment, perhaps, at how its peremptory needs impinged upon him). If it moved him, it was to a blur of dismay at its feeble vulnerability contrasted with the more-than-hopefulness with which it attached itself to its life source, sucking and screaming and shitting, wanting everything. It made him fearful to think how much it didn't know.

Simon announced to Zoe one day when Pearl was about twelve weeks that he was going to take them to visit an old friend of his.

—What old friend? Do I know him?

—Her. She's got children, that's why I thought you'd get on. I've borrowed a car.

It was absolutely characteristic of Simon that Zoe had had no idea that he had learned to drive or passed his test; he frowned now when she interrogated him. —It seemed a kind of idiocy not to know. But it's a process of no intrinsic interest. First you can't do it, and then you practise, and then you can.

Actually, she thought he was more anxious about the driving than he would ever confess, and so she was anxious too, and the journey passed in a tense silence, with Zoe clutching the sleeping Pearl tightly and watching the road as if their lives depended upon her concentration. She had thought they would be driving somewhere in Cambridge, but he headed south out of the city, into Suffolk. After forty minutes or so, just outside Haverhill, and as if he had been here before and knew exactly where he was going, Simon pulled off the road into a stony puddled driveway and stopped in front of what looked as if it had once been a farmhouse, patched and extended with a straggle of outbuildings, screened by trees from the road, with open fields behind. The house was neither neglected nor done up but in a middle position between the two, with heaps of builder's sand and bricks and a cement mixer in the yard, all pooled with rainwater. The sun as they stopped was just struggling out from between lowering dark clouds; a blonde woman in high-heeled boots and jeans and a white polo neck came round the side of the house as if she'd been listening out for them.

—The front door doesn't open, we have to go in at the back, nothing works here, my heating was off all last week. Never marry a man who promises he's going to do everything himself. Hugh has been doing up this place for four years. But he's also running his own business selling these trough things for planting made out of old tyres. So of course meantime we live on a building site.

She explained all this ruefully to Zoe while she took them round the back – more mud, more heaps of sand and breeze blocks, also a brave showing of daffodils and narcissi – and into a big warm downstairs room with a low-beamed ceiling, Laura Ashley wallpaper, an old stripped pine dresser and a huge sagging sofa piled with patchwork cushions. Insulating material was visible around the edges of the windows, and the wiring hung in loops along the beams. Big logs smouldered in an open stone fireplace heaped with several days' worth of ash; a little fair-haired girl was drawing at a table.

—Everything's dirty. The woman wiped her finger along the dresser and showed the dust disgustedly to Zoe. She was pretty and brisk, with a long straight nose, eyes slightly too close together, and natural pink in her cheeks (although the blonde was dyed). —I've surrendered in the battle with dirt here. If you knew how I longed sometimes to live in a little new semi with central heating and constant hot water ... I'm Dina by the way. It's nice to meet you. Simon's told me all about you. And this is Simon's baby. I can't quite believe it. I must say, I didn't think old Simon would get caught so soon. But it doesn't look anything like you, Si. Oh, aren't they just delicious at this age? Couldn't you just eat them? Can I have a cuddle with her? No, wait, I'll put some coffee on first, I don't know about you two but I'm gasping. And I'm not allowed my first ciggy till I have a coffee. Which sometimes means I have it very early.

Simon was crouched poking at the fire. —Do you make decent coffee? I can't remember.

—So how do you two know each other? Zoe asked. She couldn't imagine how this woman came to be a friend of Simon's; she belonged to one of those types of person whose existence he usually managed to seem entirely unaware of, countryish and probably Tory-voting and definitely not bothered about things intellectual. There were some shelves of books but they looked like nature books and stately-home books and perhaps even Jilly Cooper.

—Oh! Dina looked quickly at Simon, as if he might want to answer first. —We grew up together. We lived practically next door. Our parents were friends. Of course I'm more Ricky's age than Simon's; horribly ancient as I'm sure you can tell. Simon, why don't you leave that fire alone before you kill it?

—Zoe doesn't know enough people with children, Simon said. —That's why I brought her.

—Well, children we do have here, if not much else. This is Bryony (the little girl had climbed down from her drawing and was tugging at her mother to ask if she could hold Pearl). Megan's upstairs having her nap, thank God. A moment's peace. You wait till you meet Megan. Hell on tottering legs, isn't she Bryony? And Charlie my son is at our local school, which is a sweet place. I'll have to go in the car and pick him up at three fifteen. My husband is away of course, as usual.

—I'll be back before then, Simon said.

—Be back? Zoe was astonished; she had had no idea he was going to leave her here.

—Won't it be nice? said Dina. —The girls will love to play with the baby. I've made some soup for lunch. And we could go for a walk if it brightens up. You can borrow wellies. We've got every size.

Zoe could hardly protest. And in fact she found herself not wanting to; it was better to be here with company than passing another long day in the mess of home. She might have been shy, but Dina seemed surprisingly eager to entertain her. Without Simon there, Zoe could study Dina uninhibitedly, trying to find out how one became a convincing mother of children. A certain flat manner seemed to work, without excesses of adoration or temper, wry in the face of catastrophe. Megan spilled orange squash at lunch, then scraped her knee jumping off the end of the sofa ('Mummy'll put magic cream on'). The trick was to manage tortoise-pace and business-like both at once. They all professed to adore Pearl, who didn't cry but watched the little girls with absorbed interest, and then peacefully fed, only twisting her head away to check on her audience from time to time. Dina said she was so envious of breastfeeding – 'that lovely time before the mucky eating starts'.

After lunch Dina found wellington boots for Zoe and put Pearl in a sort of backpack; Zoe had not known about these. ('Keep it. Megan's much too big for it. It's just clutter. See how she loves to look around her? You can get Si to carry her about in it. She's just not the dopey sort of baby. Dopey's much easier of course. I'll swear that Charlie just slept for the first six months. I had to wake him up to feed him.') They walked up the side of a steep ploughed field in fresh wet air under a ragged sky, and then into some woods full of bluebells; the little girls in their bright waterproofs and boots went stumping in the puddles. When they got back Dina made dropscones on a griddle and Zoe fed Pearl again at the kitchen table.

—I'll tell you the strictest rule of motherhood, said Dina. —Don't eat what they leave. Look at this tummy of mine. That's all fish fingers and bread and butter soldiers, truly.

—So what was Ricky like? Zoe asked.

A shock interrupted for an instant as rapid as a camera shutter the batter flowing from the spoon on to the smoking griddle. Dina turned an open and smiling face round to Zoe from the stove.

—Ricky? Oh, he was just a nice boy. A really happy, nice boy. Everyone loved Ricky.

—Simon worshipped him.

—It made a bloody mess of that family, the whole thing.

—Who's Ricky? asked Bryony.

—Just someone Mummy used to know, who sadly died.

—What from? She put on a grown-up commiserating voice.

—He just got poorly.

—That's sad. Was this long, long ago?

—It was, yes. In olden days.

Zoe didn't know where Simon went, while she was with Dina all day. He came late to collect her ('Oh, that's so typical,' Dina said. 'He never remembers'). Zoe had stayed with the little girls when Dina drove to school, and then they drank tea, waiting for him, running out of conversation, while the children watched television and it began to rain outside.

On the way home Zoe shook out a thought she hadn't known she'd had. —I suppose, she said to Simon, —that she was the girlfriend you once told me about. I mean your brother's girlfriend, who you were angry with when he died.

Simon concentrated past the pounding windscreen wipers. —You invented angry.

—But she was that girl?

—She was a friend. They wrote to one another when they were both away at school.

The baby slept. Simon leaned forward to peer through the windscreen because the rain was heavy, flickering in a confusing low light coming through a row of tall poplars beside the road.

—And I suppose you've had some sort of a thing going on with her at some point?

He was silent for long minutes, which she knew didn't mean denial or assent, only a disavowal of her right to know, a disgust at the slack words she'd chosen.

—Do you think that you possess me? he asked her.

Zoe got better at managing her new life. Her stomach shrank back to flatness, she could get into her jeans, she washed her hair in the kitchen sink and then had it cut off as short as a boy's; she grew less afraid of Pearl and manhandled her more boldly, kissing her with gobbling noises all over her head, blowing raspberries on her stomach while she was changing her until she laughed her throaty laugh. Pearl slept better at night and in the day, and then when Zoe heard her waking in her cot she hurried up the stairs to her with happy anticipation, eager to set eyes on her and hold her close again, as if even an hour's separation awoke a yearning lack in her. Zoe discovered there could be a strenuous kind of pleasure in managing her house and her days. She set herself a routine, she moved determinedly around inside it; at the end of the evening the dishes were washed and the kitchen floor was swept and the haricot beans were put on to soak. Then she sat up in bed giving Pearl her midnight feed, running over in her head a list of tasks to be accomplished for the next day. This wasn't the highest form of intelligent life, but it had its satisfactions.

This isn't to say that there weren't still bad days, of mess and mistakes and tedium. Four months after the birth she still hadn't finished a book, or been out in the evening. When she tried to have a coffee with Carol in Rose Crescent Pearl cried and wouldn't feed discreetly and she had to take her outside and leave Carol to finish. She longed for adult company, and then when occasionally friends came round she feared that she wouldn't have enough to talk about: she couldn't expect them to be interested for more than a few moments that she was trying Pearl on solid foods, or that she had taken her to the Botanical Gardens to show her the ducks. She longed for Simon to come home, and when he came he didn't talk to her, he sat in the cold front room to read.

She was thinking about Simon all the time, but not in the old way. There was a disorienting disproportion between their minimal actual contact and her passionate interior indictment of him that ran its dull marathon day after day inside her head. In the flesh they exchanged a few transactional words, friendly enough; they made their mutually considerate movements around the shared functional spaces of the little cottage – the bath, the kettle, the toilet in the yard; and in bed at night sometimes their feet touched accidentally or she woke to find that in her sleep she had bundled herself against his warm back and was breathing in his smell. And yet her argument with him was so clamorous when he wasn't there; in her imagination she appealed as if in some public forum and to witnesses, presenting all the evidence of his unnatural behaviour. If they could see my life, she thought, burning with its injustice. He's wrong, he's wrong! He believes he's so unassailably right but he's wrong. At the same time she was calculating how she could disguise this very madness of their private life from her parents when they came to stay.

Simon had taken over her job on the market, and she had had to give up any idea of going back to the bag shop; Carol had gallantly offered to have Pearl for a couple of afternoons (perhaps picturing a sleeping mouse-like creature in its shawls as Zoe once had), but Pearl screamed and wouldn't take milk from a bottle, Carol was helpless, and they gave it up after the second time. Then the landlord telephoned from the Portland Arms to ask if Zoe could do a couple of evenings, and because they needed the money they tried it. Simon stayed at home to babysit; it was usually in the evenings that Pearl slept best and longest, so he ought to be able to work without being interrupted. Zoe didn't admit to him that she quite enjoyed the synthetic companionableness of the pub; she adopted his own air of uncomplaining stoicism.

One night when she came home at eleven thirty Simon and Pearl were gone. She stood in bewilderment looking into Pearl's empty cot, breathing in the cigarette smoke soaked into her clothes; her long skirt was wet with beer at the hem where it had dragged in the mess behind the bar. Downstairs she saw that the pram was also gone from its place in the yard. She ran out into the lane at the back and up to the street that crossed it at one end, then ran back in case they came the other way and she missed them. It was a still summer's night, as cold as stone; the moon stood in a chilly ring of light. Staring along the empty lane her arms goosefleshed; she went back inside and tidied up, expecting any minute to hear them come in. Pearl must have cried, he must have taken her out to calm her. His books were left open on his desk, his pen laid down on his page presumably when he went to pick her up. Zoe went outside again, looked up and down. It would have been so easy for Simon to leave her a note, explaining where he was taking her. She changed into her pyjamas, to be ready for bed when they arrived; then she changed again into her jeans, thinking suddenly that if there were an emergency she needed to be ready to go at once.

After an hour she tried to phone the hospital, in case Pearl had been taken ill and Simon had rushed her in; but she could only find one number for the hospital in the phone book and when she dialled it she got the tone that meant it was discontinued. On an impulse, her heart hollow and her mind dazzling with panic, she dialled her parents' number; she thought she would ask them what she ought to do. Some pent-up anguish welled in her like a billowing-behind silk; she didn't know what confession might rip out of her if she heard her mother's voice. The phone rang but they didn't answer. Probably they were asleep. She pictured the nook where their phone sat on a blackened old antique chest beside a lamp made out of a stoneware bottle and a plateful of painted eggs; she pictured their bed, with its old throw of Irish white crocheted lace over the humps of their shapes in the dark. She let the phone ring for as long as it took her to pace out in her mind the distance between the two. That sleeping other house seemed an unattainable happiness in her present distress.

Retreating upstairs to sit on the bed with her arms hugged round her knees, she was seized by one terrible imagining. She seemed to see Simon pushing the pram down by the river in the dark to where there was a gap between thickly clumped trees, and the moon shone on the water; she heard Pearl's frantic bleating cry, knowing how it could wind crushingly tight around your sane awareness; she imagined she saw Simon lift a squalling bundle out of the pram and douse its noise in the dark water like putting out a light, holding it under for a long time. She knew there was no rational foundation for imagining this, but once she had glimpsed it so vividly the scene acquired a persuasive reality all its own; when she tried to suppress it, the moment of the dipping of the bundle in the black river flickered over and over compulsively in her mind like a stuck film.

What other reason, she half convinced herself, could

he have for being out so long? For two hours, with a baby, in the middle of the night?

Somehow from sitting up on the bed she keeled over so that her face was against the pillows; and then even in the midst of frantic anxiety she lost herself in her exhaustion, and tumbled into obliviousness (a voice came: 'if it's all over, then at least I can sleep'). Sometime later she woke to the sound of the back door latch and the well-known nudging of the pram wheels through the narrow entrance to the yard. By the time she got downstairs Simon was parking the pram carefully in its space under the kitchen window, reaching with his foot for the brake.

—What have you done with her? cried Zoe wildly.

He even sounded pleased with himself. —She wouldn't take the bottle, and I couldn't calm her down. So I thought if I pushed her in the pram it would probably be the most soothing thing.

—And where is she now?

An instant's hesitation while he took in her tone, and then a different coldness in his voice. —She's here, of course. It did work. She's asleep.

—But you've been hours! You can't have been pushing her around for all this time!

—On the contrary. That's exactly what I've been doing. It was an extraordinary night. There was a moon: I could see everything clearly. We went a long way down the cycle path beside the river.

—Good God! It's freezing cold out there: what were you thinking of?

Now they were frankly enemies: there was a terrible liberation in it.

—Actually, I think that she was cold in her cot and that's why she woke up: she'd kicked the blankets off. I put her outdoor suit on, I wrapped her up well. I felt her every so often, to make sure she was warm enough. Whatever have you been imagining?

—What did you think I'd think? Why didn't you leave a note?

He shrugged. —I didn't think we'd be out long. And then it was good, walking. I thought you'd be glad of the chance to get some sleep when you came back from work.

—Which just shows how much you've taken in of our routine. She has a feed at midnight, when I get home.

—Oh, obviously I didn't quite appreciate how tight a timetable you run on. My apologies if I've thrown the whole system out of sync by taking the baby for a walk. I have to say, she hardly seems to be desperate from starvation. One wonders if the baby isn't being managed to suit the system, rather than the other way around.

—Don't think I don't know what you think about my life. But you're wrong, you have no idea of how this has to be done. Why can't you just for once take it from me?

—This is intolerable, Simon said. They weren't shouting but hissing in whispers, so as not to wake Pearl. —We shouldn't let this go any further, in decency.

—Oh, absolutely. I absolutely agree, we shouldn't.

—Just what exactly were you imagining had happened?

—How was I to know? I thought you might have had to rush her to hospital, I thought you might have done something to her . . .

—Done something to her? Simon let those words settle around them where they stood squeezed between the bulk of the washing machine and the bikes and the pram in the ghostly grey yard: they could see because Zoe had left all the lights on inside the house. In the shadows the deep-set eyes and lean hollows of Simon's face were exaggerated.

—I think you're slightly unbalanced. Motherhood has made you sick. He found the brake under the pram and put it on. —Perhaps you should talk to somebody.

—But not to you?

—I don't think we have anything left to say.

When Simon had gone (he took a couple of books down from his shelves and then went out by the front door, which they never used), Zoe left Pearl sleeping in the pram. She moved around the house in a high bright humming lightness, as if something had been resolved; she took down her rucksack from the top of the wardrobe and began efficiently to pack clothes and necessities for her and for Pearl. She did wonder whether Simon would wake up his friend and borrow the car again and drive to Dina's; Dina's husband would no doubt conveniently be away, and she would move over for him in the big marital bed, glad to be relieved by this adventure from the boredom of life in the middle of nowhere with only small children for company. Zoe thought through all this without any

341

feeling about it whatsoever, simply as if a clear light glanced upon possibilities; in her mind's eye she saw the pair of them coupling busily, tiny and far off. She was only disgusted by her own prurience in imagining it.

She put together a travel kit in a separate bag for managing Pearl, with jars of home-made puréed vegetables and made-up baby rice and a spoon and a wet flannel in a plastic bag for wiping her face; and clean nappies and cotton wool and baby oil and a towel to change her on and more plastic bags for wrapping up the dirty nappies. 'He just doesn't realise how complicated it has to be,' she said to herself once, but that didn't seem to start up the old lumbering train of accusation and counter-accusation inside her thoughts; the wrangling with Simon's way of seeing things had blessedly subsided. Simon was right: something horrible had happened to them and in all decency they must end it. Making her plans – she would have to wait in the morning until the banks were open, then ask her taxi to stop on the way to the station so she could cash a cheque – she was light-headed as if she was escaping on holiday.

When she eventually fell asleep it was curled up on the side of the bed expecting to be roused at any moment; she dreamed a succession of rapid anxious dreams including one about trying to get ready for a party with a kind of tickertape machine strapped to her belly, trailing yards of read-out (there had really been one of these at the antenatal clinic, to measure the baby's heartbeat). In the pram Pearl slept all through the night without a feed for the first time, and only woke at seven the next morning.

Joyce had been reading Andrea Dworkin's *Pornography*. She was arguing about it with Ray while she cooked him fillets of chicken in wine and cream for his supper; he sat listening at the kitchen table in a posture of suitable abjection, enjoying his preprandial whisky and smoke. Joyce had her hair pulled up high on her head in an assertive ponytail; under her apron she was wearing some sort of black cheesecloth dungarees, cinched in at the waist with a wide elastic belt.

—What she's saying is that there isn't one special thing called pornography, which is separate from the other ways that men see women. She's saying that because of the whole system we exist inside, every time a man looks at a woman the way he sees her is a part of this whole exploitative sex thing.

—But you can't seriously believe that's true, Ray said coaxingly; he knew from experience that when Joyce was fired up in one of her rare but periodic ideological indignations, conciliation was a better tactic than outright contempt. —It's just such a reductive travesty. I mean, what about all those wonderful complex portraits of women in books and paintings? *Anna Karenina*, for example; you love that, don't you? But it's written by a man.

—Oh don't make it too easy for me! exclaimed Joyce, using her spatula to flip over the fillets in a noisy spatter of hot butter; she poured in a carton of cream and salted and peppered it, then turned the heat down. —*Anna Karenina*! Don't try to tell me Tolstoy hasn't got some sex thing twisted up in there. Why can't he let it work out between her and Vronsky? Every time Tolstoy describes how desirable she is he says how shamed and disgusted she ought to feel at herself.

—Anyway, how can you take seriously anyone with a name like Andrea Dworkin? I suppose she's got to be American. I'd love to see if there's an author photo. I can just imagine . . .

—You see there! You're doing it! Exactly what she says!

It was at this point that the doorbell rang.

—Who on earth can that be? We're going to eat in twenty minutes. You'll have to send them away.

Ray loped downstairs to the front door; he had a hunch it was going to be a particular ex-student of his – male, luckily – who seemed to have developed a bit of a fixation on Ray's work. He didn't mind the bloke, and quite enjoyed their late-night holdings-forth on art and philosophy, but Joyce couldn't stand him, she said he was creepy and his feet smelled. If it was Morris he'd have to send him away; possibly he could suggest a meeting later in the Buffy (the Beaufort Arms). He mentally gauged the temperature of the marital waters. It would have to be quite a bit later, leaving time enough for him to help with the washing-up, make coffee, be charming, bring Joyce round on this absurd pornography–Dworkin issue.

It wasn't Morris.

—Your mother told me, Ray said when he brought

Zoe and Pearl upstairs into the kitchen after his own exclamations and greetings on the doorstep, —that I had to send whoever it was away. It's lucky for her that although I almost unvaryingly obey her every command I made an exception this time.

He put down Zoe's rucksack and bag with an impresario air.

Joyce let the lid of the potato pan fall with a loud clatter.

—Zoe! What are you doing here?

They were so startling: this young woman their daughter, so tall and thin and changed, with new adult marks of tiredness and strain on her face, and her short boy's hair, and round breasts for the first time; and her astonishing baby who stared at them with unsmiling penetration from where she sat at home on Zoe's hip.

—How wonderful! Zoe, darling, this is marvellous!

—I know you won't have a cot or anything, said Zoe. —But we could make her up a bed in a drawer.

—Oh my God! She's so beautiful! Ray: do you see her hair? We can borrow something. The Chanders have got grandchildren. We can phone them, Ray. Oh, I don't believe her. Pearl? Hello, Pearl! Will she come to me? She won't come to me, she doesn't know me.

Pearl hid her face decidedly against Zoe.

—She just needs to get used to things. She's so tired, said Zoe, kissing her scalp. —She's never been on trains before. She was so interested in everything that she's hardly slept. And she's got a stinking nappy. I didn't know where to change her. Luckily she only pooed in

345

the last hour. People who were sitting by us moved away. I ought to change her now.

—Upstairs in the bedroom. I'll get out towels, I'll find a bowl for warm water. Poor little thing, poor darling, poor little sore botty. And you had to hump all this stuff right across London to Paddington on your own, with the baby? Where's Simon?

—I've left him, said Zoe. —I've run away. I don't know what I'm going to do but I'm not going back. I don't care.

—Zoe, what's happened?

—What about this chicken, Joyce? Should I give it a stir?

—Turn it off, said Joyce impatiently. —I'll see to it later. It doesn't matter.

—I just thought that Zoe might be hungry.

—I am very hungry.

—Then we can eat straight away, she can have mine. Ray, get on the phone to the Chanders: can we borrow everything they've got? Are you still feeding her yourself? What's going on with you and Simon?

Joyce watched over the changing of the nappy incredulously as if she was present at some miracle, pained at the soreness of the baby's bottom, distressed at the crying Zoe took no notice of. Then Zoe fed Pearl at the table while she ate, shovelling in chicken and creamed potatoes greedily, dropping peas on the baby's head.

In a great torrent, all Zoe's grievance poured out. She had never spoken about Simon to anyone for all the six years she had known him, except neutrally and trans-

346

actionally, or to speak for him, describing his work or his opinions. The relief of explaining now made her dizzy, mixed up with her hunger and exhaustion and the adrenalin that still flooded her from their rupture and her headlong escape.

—He sort of decides what the right position is for him to take, then scrupulously sticks to it. I mean, he didn't want the baby, and it wasn't even truly an accident, so that was my fault. Only, how come the fact I wanted it didn't count for anything? And you know he never touched me – I mean, literally, even with his hand – except when he wanted to make love to me. This isn't since the baby was born: I mean, ever, in all this time. Then there was this old girlfriend of his, he took me to see her, I think he wanted to show me how to manage to be a better mother, but of course I worked out that there was something between them. For all I know he's probably with her right now. He hates stupidity, so that you're always afraid of saying something false: only you wonder whether it isn't more false to think about everything you say. He wasn't with me when Pearl was born, he didn't really come in the next day like I told you, he had to give his paper at the conference because of course that was more important, and then when he came in to the hospital eventually on the last day you could see he was disgusted, physically disgusted by the whole place, even the smell of it. I've come to see how he uses intellectual ideas and books like a sort of stronghold to separate himself off from ordinary people, so that he doesn't have to stumble around in the mess like they

347

do. He was furious that I'd given her his surname, he said it was a conspiracy to try to implicate him.

Now she had her public and her jury in the palm of her hand. After the first tug, all this long-meditated treachery came away so fluently from inside her, rich and slick. So apt and so already-persuaded were her audience that she could even seem to bend over backwards to do Simon justice – to reiterate that he was only consistent with himself, that he had never actually physically hurt her – knowing that Ray and Joyce would supply the condemnation she withheld.

—And to be fair of course, last night, I had made a fuss about nothing and she was fine. He'd just taken her out for a perfectly innocent walk. So to him it must seem that I'm this sort of harridan, dementedly policing her routine, because he can't imagine what it feels like, trying to cope with a new baby without support. Although that's what I said to him, originally. I said he wouldn't have to do anything. I promised him I'd manage it all by myself.

—But how could you have known what you were promising, then? protested Joyce. —What kind of man could see the woman he loved struggling with looking after his own child, and not want to be with her, helping her?

—He's a pretty bloody mixed-up kid, said Ray.

—I wish you'd told us earlier.

—I could see he was very bright. But too careful. Afraid to give anything away.

—And how could he not think she's the most beautiful

baby in the world? Do you think she'll come to me, now? I can't believe she's got my hair. This was my dad's hair, you know. I wish Mum was here to see her.

—I wish it too.

—We always found him hard work, to be honest, to spend time with.

—Ssh, Ray.

Ray's sister Fran had gone to live with the protesters against cruise missiles at Greenham Common. Her husband had died suddenly of heart failure, and after subsiding into disappointed widowhood for a couple of years Fran joined a woman's group and CND, changing her sensible school-secretary clothes for dungarees and a reefer jacket pinned with political badges. When she moved up to live under polythene at Green Gate she left three indignant teenage children to fend for themselves. Her house had always been immaculate; in her absence it descended headlong into a dismayingly filthy chaos. Sometimes Fran came home at weekends to clean the toilet and disinfect the sink and run the washing machine non-stop, but she didn't seem to seriously care. Joyce had thought she was worried for Fran as well as for the children left behind to run wild. Fran was so trusting; who knew what kind of people she was getting involved with up there? She had lost her grip since Laurence died, she was making rash decisions which would affect her future. Ray reassured her. Fran had loved Girl Guide camp when she was a teenager and this was probably much the same sort of thing (privations and rivalries, high ideals and passionate crushes).

Now Joyce found herself telling Fran's stories to Zoe enthusiastically; how the women danced in toy police helmets in mockery in front of the lines of policemen; how they lay across the entrances to the base and had to be dragged away; how wire-cutting parties forayed inside the compound and sprayed the missile silos with red paint. She couldn't stop talking and being busy, as if Zoe's arrival had gone to her head; she emptied cupboards to find baby blankets, ripped up perfectly good sheets for the cot, poured big gin and tonics at a time of the evening when she and Ray didn't usually drink.

—You did the right thing, walking out of there. Starting off a completely new life. It wasn't possible for the women of my generation, we didn't know you could get away with it. I'm going to learn to drive. I don't want to have to depend on your father for everything. Wouldn't it be wonderful just to take off in the car whenever you felt like it and go anywhere you wanted? I so admire what Fran has done. Ray takes it for granted that I haven't got it in me, but you never know.

—But you're not unhappy? I mean, Dad isn't unkind?

Joyce looked at her unfocusedly, as if across wastelands of complications.

—It's not that. It's nothing he does particularly. It's just the whole house, the whole thing, keeping everything looking nice, worrying about everybody else. It's my own fault. I ought to have the courage to walk away from it all.

Zoe was cautious. —I think the driving lessons are a good idea.

Zoe had forgotten her pyjamas. She had to borrow one of Joyce's nightdresses: skimpy coffee-coloured satin and lace, nothing she would ever normally have worn. She seemed to fall into sleep through layer upon layer of delicious awareness: the silky gown, clean sheets, Pearl in the Chanders' cot which Ray had put together with some exasperated difficulty, the bright luxurious comfort of the house, the promise of days and days of respite to come when she needn't be perpetually on duty and vigilant. Joyce was only busy two mornings a week (she taught dressmaking classes); they could spend long hours talking and shopping and looking after Pearl together. They could talk on and on about Zoe's leaving Simon; Joyce would be bottomlessly sympathetic. Of course Zoe would have to decide what she was going to do with her life: but not yet. (She might perhaps pick up her PhD again, transfer it down here. Anything might happen.)

And then as she fell down and down, radiant with relief and vindication, Zoe came all of a sudden to some deep sad place, and knew she hadn't quite told her parents the truth about Simon. What she had said looked just like the truth, so that no one else but her would ever know the difference; but it wasn't the whole truth, she would need to start out all over again if she wanted to describe what he was actually like, in justice. Only it was too late to start now, she was asleep, she was so nearly asleep that all she could muster to represent her nagging worry to herself was a picture of Simon filling his fountain pen from a bottle of black ink at his desk – absorbed and careful, wiping off the surplus ink with a tissue – which didn't mean anything at all, and was extinguished anyway the next moment in the oblivion that crashed upon her like an overwhelming sea.

Eight

Daniel had gone into business with Uncle Cliff; then he married an Italian girl and they set up their own company importing delicatessen foods. After the first few difficult years they had done very well. They had moved to London and bought a loft apartment in Butler's Wharf. He and Zoe weren't exactly close. He read some of her articles in academic journals; although he hadn't been to university, he was good at quickly picking up an argument and testing it. He didn't positively disagree with anything she wrote. The world of arms trading and nuclear build-up seemed very remote from his innocent trafficking in olive oils and salamis, but he suspected nonetheless that Zoe judged him as if he was contaminated by it (even when he and Flavia made the decision to source all their products with organic suppliers). Perhaps she thought that making money was in itself intrinsically compromising. In return Daniel teased Zoe about the unworldliness of academics.

They got on all right. Sometimes when Zoe had to be in London she stayed with them; whenever Daniel went home to see his parents he called in on Zoe (especially if Ray was working up for one of his artist moods, feeling unappreciated and misunderstood). Daniel was privately amused that in spite of Zoe's expertise in conflict resolution she didn't seem to be able to control her own daughter. Pearl was disobedient and difficult; a non-sleeper, a scene-maker. She howled in her pushchair, she threw her toys. When she was older she called her mother a bitch, played her music loud, had her ears and then her nose pierced without permission, came home late and drunk from escapades in town. Even Joyce who adored Pearl (more, Daniel suspected, than she adored his own two much more charming and much better behaved little boys) had to concede that she could be hard work.

After Zoe published her second book (on the history of the relationship between arms manufacturers and defence establishments in Western Europe during the Cold War), he saw her name around even more often. She sometimes wrote for the broadsheet newspapers now. She was invited to be one of the keynote speakers at a big conference on civilians in conflict which was held (coincidentally) only a few weeks after the attack on the World Trade Center. She turned up at his place on the Saturday evening when the conference was over; Maryse their Romanian girl was putting the kids to bed, Flavia was out at the restaurant which was their pet sideline. Zoe was still frantic with adrenalin; when she'd been to kiss the boys goodnight she started telling Daniel some involved story about Palestinian students on their way to the conference being interrogated at Heathrow by immigration officials. He mixed martinis, but he couldn't make her sit down until she had drunk off the first one standing watching out of the windows as the sun went down over the Thames, behind Tower Bridge.

—I'm mad about your view, she said. —I'd like to stay looking at it all night. I could even be tempted to be rich, in return for this.

He was impressed with his sister in her public clothes: a narrow dark-green wool skirt and jacket with bone buttons, a little cream blouse with a square-cut collar, dangling chunky silver and green earrings. (At home she looked as if she didn't bother to notice what she was putting on in the mornings.) She used no make-up, her hair was cropped short, she didn't have any figure, she wore flat shoes and strode about like a man; but he could see that all this might appeal to a certain type. He put out bread and cheeses and cold meats on the glass-topped dining table and left the lights off so that they seemed to float in the pink and orange sunset. She tucked in hungrily.

—Look at you stuffing your face. But you're such a beanpole. How come you never put on weight? I wish I could get away with it.

—Eat with me, she said with her mouth full, pushing bread and cheese across to him. —Danny, it's all delicious. What's this one called?

—I'm not supposed to, I've already eaten. It's raviggi-olo. Sheep's milk cheese, from a new little place we've

355

found in Umbria. You should eat it with the pear. Perhaps I'll just cut myself a corner.

—It's fantastic. The food was probably all right at the conference but I'm always too busy talking, I forget to have any. And today I was too nervous about my paper.

—Go well?

—Mmm. She took a swallow of drink to clear her mouth so she could elaborate. —Do you know how many deaths from small arms are estimated annually? Four million. Knocks road accidents at thirty thousand into a cocked hat. Ninety per cent civilians. Eighty per cent women and children. Most of them aren't even war casualties. Revenge killings, murders, tribal conflict.

She sounded almost gloating. It was an occupational hazard, he supposed, that you would end up exulting over the excesses that proved your case. Her readiness to name horrors in ordinary conversation always embarrassed him as if it was an error of taste.

—Flavia and I are starting to think it might not be a bad idea to move out of London. Wondering if this is really how we want to bring up our children and all that. I'd like them to know something about green fields. And, being realistic, if anything happens we're right in the middle of it. I stood at these windows a few weeks ago expecting God knows what to fall out of the sky.

—You mustn't think like that, said Zoe earnestly, wiping a smear of grease off her cheek with the napkin he gave her. —If you start to think like that, they've really won.

—Well. Easily said.

—No, truly; if once we start to abdicate from these city spaces we hand imagination of them over to the rhetoricians of apocalypse on both sides. And that brings their horrible endgame one step nearer. We have to go on asserting by sheer persistence that it's possible to live here, live our ordinary hopeful life.

She was emphatic; he could imagine her waxing passionate like this in front of her audience, gesturing at them with those hands that seemed big in proportion to her narrow thinness. (Perhaps she had used the very words she used to him, at the conference today.) She was drunk on power, probably, as well as the martini. He could guess how it could go to your head, all those faces turned your way, all that deferential assent and stimulating contest.

—Any male talent at your conference, Zo? Aren't you academics supposed to get up to all sorts of wickedness when the papers are over and the bar is open?

He wondered if he'd got it right from the way she laughed, tearing off more bread, the usual tension in her posture unlocked and slack.

—Dear little brother. Concerned as ever for my happiness.

—I just worry that you pick them so deep. I wish you'd find one with a sense of humour.

—You sound just like our mother.

Zoe had a window seat in the train home on Sunday morning. She had some work from one of her graduate students to mark but she let it lie on the table in front of her, she couldn't read more than a sentence before her mind was possessed again by images and snatches of remembered exchanges from the weekend. The aftermath of these high points for her was always a kind of excruciated awakening, as if she had been drunk or dreaming and must now sort over the rash things she had done in cold judgement. Even the talks she gave seemed to her afterwards full of risk; she worried that she had stressed the wrong thing, or that in her fixation on certain interpretations of the facts she had allowed herself to be oblivious to others.

Now she had added to that usual exposure the foolishness of a flirtation. She wondered scaldingly how conspicuous it had been. Had she shown in her face how she glowed in response to his persistence, when he made everyone move up so he could sit beside her in the bar and introduce himself? It was that moment of his choosing her that snatched away her peace now, rather than the shy and fumbled kiss they had exchanged before they retired to their respective single rooms. He had been young. Not impossibly young, but quite a bit younger than her, in a skinny jumper with a little string of amber beads round his throat. (Perhaps he had only been trying to further his academic career.) She had danced, she never usually danced. It had not seemed stupid to her at the time. She had lain awake after they kissed goodnight, burning with the idea of him, fantasising over and over that she got out of bed and went padding along the corridors in her pyjamas to find his room (they were both in the same conference accommodation block), or that he came knocking softly at her door. But now in the train she wrapped her arms tightly around herself and thought it was stupid. It was humiliating. It was particularly humiliating that they hadn't even had sex together. What was she doing at her age burning up at the idea of a look, and half a kiss? Thank God at least that probably nobody would believe it had only been that. No one need know she was susceptible as a virgin girl.

She stared out of the windows at autumnal England. All the debate of the conference – retaliation, escalation, war – was a receding tide in her ears. Nothing happened here. Her irritation at it steadied her, the deep secretive fertility of this countryside, its dense thickets, the fur of its woods snuggled around the hills; it was all shelter for the sentimentalities of those who thought this was the 'real' England, whatever else went on (even foot-and-mouth, even the burning pyres of stiff-limbed dead cattle). In the dells nestled mock-Tudor mansions and real Georgian ones, weathering attractively together; the pleasure boats cosied up on the river; the once farm-labourers' cottages had been made over expensively for the nostalgic consumption of a different class. The creamy-mauve long grasses soughed and flattened themselves seductively in the fields.

But nowhere is safe, she thought.

Amidst all the professional glooms and denunciations it was easy to forget to be afraid. An irrational panic flapped a disorienting black wing across her thoughts. She was anxious to see Pearl. She had not been vigilant, she had not phoned; anything could have happened to her daughter while she was distracted. Pearl had been left alone in the house for all this time. (She was seventeen, she had reacted to the idea of a babysitter with outrage.) Zoe had called home from Paddington but she hadn't answered. Probably she was still in bed. Often she didn't get back from clubbing in town until three or four in the morning, and then she would sleep until late afternoon the next day. (A twinge of painful adjustment as usual on returning home: how was it possible that in the same world there existed students like the serious hard-working ones she met at these international conferences, burdened with gratitude for the opportunity of an education, and seventeen-year-olds dedicated as unswervingly as Pearl to her own pleasures?)

Zoe rang the bell while she paid off the taxi; then she had to hunt in her bag for her key. The front door opened directly off the terraced street whose length was only punctuated by streetlamps (the tree that had been put in on the corner had died). Of course there was no reason to expect Pearl to be at home. She might be at a friend's; she might be at her grandmother's (Joyce was supposed to be keeping an eye on her). The front-room curtains were drawn across. They must have been drawn across all day; perhaps for the whole four days that Zoe had been away.

—Pearl? Sweetheart? I'm back! Zoe called, into the darkness of the narrow hall. The light didn't seem to work; the bulb must have gone.

She hardly thought about her house while she was away. It was her shell, her refuge to crawl into and be private; she loved it but took no interest in it beyond keeping it clean and tidy. Joyce itched for her to move the kitchen out of its little scullery space into the back room, or build a second ensuite bathroom upstairs. ('What for?' asked Zoe.)

—In here, came a muffled voice from the front room.

Pearl must be watching television with the curtains drawn, something Zoe's grandfather used to do on weekend afternoons. In the dark Zoe was taking in some surprises: a mess underfoot she couldn't quite see, as if she was treading on gritty cloths, and a pall of soured (forbidden) cigarette smoke. She pushed the front-room door open with some momentary difficulty (more cloth); the gas fire was on full and the room was stiff with heat. Pearl with bright pink cheeks was on the sofa in her pyjamas, wrapped up in Nana Deare's old green silk eiderdown, which was filthy and leaked feathers and ought to be thrown out. Zoe looked around and saw that the cloth she was trampling underfoot was, in fact, a tangle of clothes; mostly Pearl's clothes and unidentifiable others, but some of them Zoe's own (that cream cardigan with the roses; that denim jacket).

—Why didn't you answer the bell?

—I'm really ill, Pearl said.

—What kind of ill?

—My head hurts, I feel sick, and all kind of weird and shivery.

Zoe was filled with apprehension; her heart contracted

361

to stone in her chest. —Does the light hurt your head? Is that why you've got the curtains closed?

Pearl glanced at them in surprise. —Not really. I think they were just like that.

Zoe put a hand on her forehead; it was hot, but then the room was very hot. Pearl's cheeks were wet. —My love. My precious girl, are you crying? Is it that bad? Tell me exactly where it hurts. She sat down beside her on the sofa, holding her tightly in her arms, drinking in her smell (unwashed, with notes of last night's perfume and the stale grey of fags, but behind them the incorruptible sweetness of her youth). She kissed her hair (that horrible dyed colour, instead of her own rare strawberry!), her cheeks, her forehead. She became aware of Pearl ducking the kisses and rearranging herself inside the embrace so as not to miss a moment of what passed on the television screen. She was watching her video of *Truly, Madly, Deeply.*

—Mum, get it in perspective. I'm not crying because I'm ill. I'm just crying at the film.

—I don't know how you can. Haven't you seen it a hundred times already?

—You've got no imagination.

—It strikes me that there are some rather more serious things worth crying about just at the moment.

—You would say that.

—There seems to be quite a mess in here.

—I was going to clear it up but then I got ill.

—And there's been smoking. I thought we were agreed that you'd confine it to your room?

362

—Mum! (Real indignation.) —Get off my case! You've only been back two seconds and you've started nagging me.

—All right, I'm sorry. But you did promise. Remember that this was supposed to be a test, of whether I could trust you to be left while I'm away? After last time.

—We've been really, really good. We've watered all your plants. And we made flapjacks, only they've all gone, because everyone thought they were so brilliant.

Zoe wanted to ask: 'We? Who's we? Who's everyone? Who's been here?'

But she went instead into the kitchen to make a pot of tea, and find the paracetamol and the thermometer. Pearl's illness probably wasn't anything alarming. You wouldn't cry at *Truly, Madly, Deeply* if you were that bad. She stared around her. The house was in a foul mess. Dishes were piled high in the sink and all over the surfaces, including the bowls and baking tins from the flapjack-making, not dealt with yet even though it looked as though the only flapjack left uneaten was the one trodden into the Portuguese rag rug in the kitchen. There were clothes in here too, all over the back-room floor, including a pair of tights half balled up and inside out, one foot snagged on the end of the bookshelf and the leg stretched around the cane chair as if they were scrambling to get away. There was a heap of blankets tangled with a sleeping bag in one corner. Everywhere there were ashtrays overflowing with cigarette butts and roaches and bits of torn-up Rizla. Actually Zoe didn't own any ashtrays; they had used jam jar lids and plastic bottle tops and her pretty little Moroccan bowls and the blue glass flower vase she had from Grandma Lil, and then in other places they had stubbed the cigarettes out directly on the end of the bookshelf and on to the tiled floor and into the arms of the cane chair. Her CD of Purcell Fantasias was opened and lying in a spill of something on the table; its booklet was pulled out and had little telltale oblongs torn off from one corner. Someone had indeed watered her houseplants but it looked as though they had done it with the big watering can from the garden, so that earth had splashed out of the pots and up the wall. The door to one of the kitchen units was pulled off its hinges.

—Oh, called Pearl from the front room, —the reason for all the washing up is there's something wrong with the dishwasher. We think a fork's stuck in it or something.

Zoe went upstairs. Her bed had been slept in, no effort made even to straighten the duvet and cover their traces. Her scarves and jewellery were pulled out and strewn across the top of her chest of drawers, and there were beer cans and Bacardi Breezer bottles and fag ends in here too. In the bathroom a cold and scummy bath hadn't been emptied, and it looked as though someone had been sick in the toilet; it had been flushed but was still filthy round the rim. She didn't even venture into Pearl's room. From the doorway it appeared a dark and roiling sea of bedding with a flotsam and jetsam of bottles, fag ends, discarded food, magazines, make-up, and miscellaneous items (the peacock feathers from the vase on the piano, for example). She went back downstairs and into the front room where she planted herself in front of the television screen.

—How can you? she said. —How could you sit there, knowing I was coming home, while the house is in this state?

Pearl tried to see the picture round her, turned up the sound with the remote. —Like I told you, I was going to clear up, only then I was ill. Anyway, I thought I could just put it in the dishwasher, but there's this fork or something, it's making an awful noise.

—No. That just won't do. I'm afraid I don't buy that. This isn't just a matter of not having cleared up yet. Quite apart from the fact that there are hours, hours, of serious cleaning work to do to get this house back to the way it was when I left. I'm talking about what happened here in the first place. This is an abuse of my home, and my trust. We said, no parties.

—Mum, like get it in proportion? It's not like anyone's died or anything.

—And as for you being ill, I should think the only thing that's wrong with you is a serious hangover, judging by the bottles left lying around the place.

—It's nice to know that my own mother is so sympathetic.

—And it makes me sick the way you watch this film over and over. I mean when, in real life, have you ever shown any interest in anyone's suffering outside the immediate orbit of your own tiny circle? What do you care about real disaster? You'd rather sit playing at soap opera sorrow over and over in an overheated room, calling your friends on your mobile and crying phoney tears about it to them.

—It isn't soap opera. That just goes to show how much you understand about it.

—You and your friends know nothing, you take no interest in the world outside.

—What do you know about what I feel about anything? When do you ever ask me?

Zoe was stony. —It's too pat, I've heard it all before. You're young and therefore it goes without saying that you're hard done by and misunderstood. But wait a minute: what we're talking about here is, you trashed my house! You do that and then you whine that I don't respect you, that I don't ask you about your feelings! Did you ask me about mine?

—You should listen to yourself one day, hear how you hate me. I've had enough of living in this prison house.

—Prison house? What would you know about prison? How can you be so innocent? Don't you have any shame? Anyway, that's fine by me, because I've had enough of you living here too.

—I'm going to go to Dad's.

—To Dad's? Zoe gave a hard hoot of laughter. —Oh yes, wonderful, go to Dad's. I love it. Let's see how you two get along.

—He said I could come and stay any time.

—Then pack your bags. Put your clothes on and pack

366

your bags. Do it now, right now. I'll give you a lift to the station. I don't see why he shouldn't have to put up with you for a while.

—But I'm really ill.

—I don't believe you.

Zoe stopped the video, threw open the window, and turned off the fire. Pearl stormed resentfully out of the room to run herself a fresh bath. From downstairs Zoe heard a sequence of indignant conversations on her mobile. Presumably one of them was to Simon. (Whatever had Pearl been telling him, that had made him offer to have her to stay?) Zoe would be figuring in all these calls as an unfeeling villain. But until she dropped Pearl off at the station she was adamant, she didn't falter. Then when she fixed her eyes on the retreating back as Pearl pushed through the doors to buy her ticket for Oxford – rucksack slung jauntily on one shoulder, dressed up so bravely and deliberately to meet the world with her painted eyes and her costume of bright colours, ripped jeans, embroidered patchwork cap – Zoe had a vision of things from a different angle, and the mess in the house seemed only a temporary problem. But there were taxis queued to stop behind her, she couldn't wait, she had to pull out and drive on, she couldn't jump out of the car and run after Pearl, and tell her that after all she loved her more than anything on earth.

—What if she was really ill? Zoe asked Joyce. She had called in at her mother's house on the way back from the station. —What if I've turned her out of her own home and there's something seriously wrong with her?

Joyce was ironing Ray's shirts. —You can phone Simon and ask him how she is when she gets there.

—I'm horrible. I'm so horrible.

Zoe nursed her coffee cup in her hands as if she was cold; her face was haggard with bruise-coloured swellings under her eyes. Joyce worried about her; she gave too much of herself to her work. Joyce was proud when she saw her daughter's name in the national papers, but she saw how Zoe was eaten up with nervous energy if she had to do one of these big lectures.

—Of course you're not horrible. Pearl's impossible. I feel badly myself because I said I'd keep an eye on things. But when I popped in yesterday morning it didn't look too awful, and she promised me she was going to tidy up. They must have had a party there last night.

—You wouldn't ever have turned me or Daniel out on the street.

—In Daniel's case it would probably have been very good for him. How was he?

—Really fine. We had a nice time. You know they've got some new girl working for them? From Romania.

—Oh dear. I wonder what happened to the last one. Those poor little boys.

—I suppose working for Flavia is better than being trafficked here as a sex slave.

—Marginally, perhaps.

—All the way home I was planning on a hot bath. That's why I went so mad. A long and mindless soak.

368

—Darling, have a bath here. Eat with us. We'll go round together this evening and tackle the mess when you've rested.

—I've got to face up to it. I won't be able to rest until it's sorted. I'll be all right once I get going.

—I'd come with you now, but I've got Vera for tea.

—Only, really, Mum, if you could see it! I truly don't understand her. How can she be so utterly absorbed in herself? It's not just the mess. It's the complacency of her. It's her unshakeable certainty that she's at the centre of everything.

Joyce folded a shirt carefully.

—You've always had to be so busy, she said. —I suppose if you'd been able to be at home more, she might have felt more secure, and not needed to behave badly to get your attention. Of course it's wonderful the way you manage things. But I do feel sorry for anyone having to juggle family and career. I was grateful, when I was your age, that I didn't have to work.

—Oh don't start that again, said Zoe. —Mum, we've been over that argument so many times.

—And then, she hasn't ever had a father at home. Which wasn't your fault.

—She didn't need one. We've managed fine without.

—You should listen to *Woman's Hour*. Everyone thinks differently about that now.

At home alone Zoe burned up with energy. She ran buckets of hot water with Flash, she filled black bags with rubbish and fag ends and beer cans and bottles, she

369

put on rubber gloves and wiped and scoured every surface, even the backs and seats of chairs, that they might have touched with their sticky hands. She grew to feel she was in intimate communion with 'them', down in their dirt and their discards: Pearl's gang, who congregated at weekends around the standing stones on the Heath in further pursuit of their ever more incestuously entangled intimacies, probably thinking it was an ancient sacred site although in fact it was a nineteenth-century folly. Their uniform of droopy tops and baggy ripped trousers and dangling scarves and strings and laces was a more mannered rerun of the fashions of Zoe's own teenage years. Some of 'them' she could picture; the inner circle of familiar friends, a few sweet ones she was fond of, a couple of losers and no-goods. Some of them she fantasised: louche and sinister strangers, men mostly, taking advantage of Zoe's absence and her good-will, peddling drugs perhaps, hunting after sex. She snooped through the ashtrays and the debris in search of evidence of anything worse than the dope and the pills she knew about (though she wasn't clear what the evidence might be). She scrubbed the toilet, and the bath and the sink and the bathroom floor, she put all the towels in the washbasket. She washed down the wall behind the plants, she scraped the kitchen rug free of flapjack and put it into the washing machine together with the sodden bathmat. After she had tried the dishwasher and heard the horrible noise it made, she stood washing and drying up for what seemed like hours, soaking the pans that were too far gone.

She phoned Simon, to tell him what time Pearl was arriving, warn him she might be ill.

—I've given her money for a taxi, she said. —I don't know how she'll get on with Martha.

—Martha's in the States.

—Oh right.

There was no point in holding on for more information. Martha was successor to Eve, successor to Ros, successor to Melanie. Zoe only knew about any of them because Pearl had told her. They didn't live in with Simon (at least, they kept their own places). They didn't bear his children (he only had Pearl). In Zoe's imagination they were a procession: stately, independent, striking.

—Does Pearl have a bedtime or anything? he asked. —Or a time she has to be in at night?

Zoe laughed hollowly. —You have to be joking! Just give her a key and hope she doesn't bring back all her friends at four in the morning.

—Oh, I think we'll have to have some pretty clear rules laid down.

—At least at first she won't have any friends.

—I don't know yet if this is going to work out, or for how long. It's a provisional arrangement. And we'll have to think hard about her education.

—Her education! I don't know if you remember me telling you, but she didn't even show up for half her AS exams.

—Precisely. I'm interested as to why.

—Oh.

—Insofar as one's allowed to be interested in anything

371

else, in the midst of the end of the world.

—You mean what's happening at the moment?

—We seem to be gathering ourselves ready for a just war. Isn't that right? It's very much your specialism, isn't it? Against the forces of evil.

She heard in his voice a grim exulting pessimism. Simon never wanted to be caught out feeling shocked and appalled. He always wanted to have thought of the worst in advance; then whatever happened he would be proved right, he would be ready with his irony.

—Actually, Simon, I don't really want to talk about this with you. I don't mean Pearl, I mean the rest of it. I've spent the whole weekend talking about nothing else. I need to shut it out for a few hours.

An instant retraction of intimacy was distinct as cold air in her ear. —Who wants to talk about it? Isn't there already too much talk?

There was a note from Pearl on Zoe's dressing table. 'No wonder you can't get a boyfriend, only sad Dyl. No wonder Dad didn't want to live with you.' Zoe had thought of phoning Dylan (who wasn't exactly a boyfriend, nor just a friend, but something awkward in between); after she found the note she decided not to. What did Pearl mean by 'no wonder'? 'No wonder' because Zoe was so shrill, so puritanical, so vindictive? Or because she was growing older and plainer, and had neglected herself? Perhaps this was why Pearl had left the note on the dressing table, where Zoe was supposed to work to make herself attractive: a warning from one female to another.

She studied her face with concentration in the mirror. She was forty-three. There must have been changes over the past couple of years, only she hadn't had time to take them in until today: a leaching of colour from her skin and hair, perhaps; a loss of resilience, so that the little lines didn't spring back when she stopped grimacing. She worried now, when it was presumably too late, that she had never used anti-wrinkle cream or taken vitamins. Joyce spent at least half an hour in front of her mirror every day, 'getting ready'. Zoe truly didn't know what you were supposed to do, in all that time; in the mornings she washed her face and pulled a comb through her hair. She had thought she was too intelligent to worry over the usual women's trivia.

When she stripped her bed she found a used condom shrivelled and stuck to the sheet (certainly not hers; she and Dylan only slept together at his place, and not recently, and in any case she would never ever have forgotten such a thing and left it there). She picked it up in a tissue and buried it deep in the black bag on the landing with a shudder of distaste, thinking that at forty-three it was certain now she would never have another child, although she had always supposed that she probably would.

Zoe wasn't teaching again until Wednesday. When she woke she didn't know what time it was, but it didn't matter. There was no Pearl to hurry off to classes at the city sixth-form college (where her attendance in spite of Zoe's efforts was insultingly perfunctory). Her watch had stopped, the battery must have run down. She hadn't been able to find her alarm clock; presumably it was drowned somewhere under the mess in Pearl's room, the one room Zoe hadn't tackled in her cleaning mania (she had shut the door on it instead, containing an inland sea). Downstairs Aunt Vera's clock said half past three, but this clock notoriously kept a time all of its own, and anyway it didn't feel like either kind of half past three, not like the middle of the night nor the middle of the afternoon. There was a grey muffled light outside the windows, and a fine rain swelled and ebbed against the panes; it could have been the beginning or the ending of a day. She didn't know whether she had been asleep for six hours or twenty or (surely not) thirty-six. If she put the radio or the television on she could have discovered which, but she didn't want the intrusion yet of the world and its urgent claims upon her attention into this eerie nowhere space she had happened upon.

She would wait to see whether the light came or went. Her sleep had been very deep and transforming, although she did not know where she had been, and had no memory of her dreams. In her pyjamas and a pair of thick socks and a jumper she boiled the kettle and made herself a cup of tea, then carried it steaming around the rooms of the house, turning the lights on and then off again, moving through the underwater texture of the deep quiet, sipping at the tea, lacing her fingers around it for warmth. Her rooms were restored to a chastened sobriety. She had thrown all the clothes she picked up through the door on to Pearl's bed. There were a few burns, a couple of breakages; the smell of cigarettes was still mingled perceptibly with the Flash and disinfectant. She would have to get Dyl to look at the dishwasher and fix the cupboard door. That was all. It was nothing.

And for this she had let her beloved daughter go off alone into the crowd where anything could happen, without Pearl's even turning her head to exchange last glances. Zoe was afraid for herself; that she could not keep anything safe. How absurd that she had quarrelled with Pearl over a bit of mess; didn't she profess not to care for material things? As soon as she knew what time it was, and if it was a time when Pearl was likely to be awake, Zoe would phone and ask her to come home (if you phoned when she was asleep, she snarled and cursed). Or perhaps she would go up to Oxford to see her, take her out to lunch, listen to her. How had she even for a moment wanted to catch her uniquely unknowable child in the net of her judgement?

Zoe wandered with her tea upstairs to the room she used as her study. The tide of the party had only just reached this far: she hadn't had to do anything in here when she was cleaning except straighten the cover on the bare mattress of the spare bed and take away one half-empty beer can. (And now she spotted a bitten-into piece of flapjack on a pile of papers). She had promised to write a piece for *New Internationalist* about the implications of the current crisis in relation to the arms industry. When she first sat down at the desk she hadn't made any conscious decision to begin it; in fact she hadn't thought she would be able to write anything again until she had Pearl back. Out of habit, however, she turned her computer on and opened a new document. Even when she started to type she threw down her first thoughts in easy freedom because she didn't seriously think that she had begun (usually she wrote effortfully, anticipating dissent). But she had happened upon one of those precious air pockets of clear work. Her line of argument bloomed, it leaped forward; her words embodied her thought without contortion. She forgot herself; all the mess of her personal life was absorbed for the moment into a larger responsibility. She must be scrupulous to get this right.

She hadn't switched on the lamps; the study if she lifted her head to glance blindly around at it was eerie in the blue light from the screen. Then the blue was swelled by the grey light of the day which grew outside the window (so it was morning, not night). The rain persisted; the blowing mist became an earnest earthwards downpour, soaking and steady. Zoe wrote concentratedly for three hours, only dragging her attention away from the screen when she needed figures and information from the journals and papers on her shelves. Once, she went downstairs to put the heating on and make more tea. When she was finally and suddenly too tired to do any more, she saved her work on a disk and crawled back to bed, still in her socks and jumper. Only instead of choosing her own bed she went on an impulse into Pearl's room and ploughed across the chaos of bedding heaped on the floor to climb under her daughter's duvet and fall asleep, curled up with her back to the warm radiator, cocooned among all the crumpled dirty clothes, pressing her face into a consoling inside-out T-shirt ripe with Pearl's young animal smell.

When Pearl rang him and said she was leaving home and cried and called him Daddy (mostly she called him Simon, and he had never given her the least sign of wanting anything else), he had thought that this might be what he needed, to have a child in the house. He had said she could come for at least a week or two, to see how it went, but in his heart he had for a moment imagined foolish things; how their lives might slip around one another weightlessly in his flat (there would be none of the searing, if none of the excitement, that came with sexual cohabitation); how he might choose books for her and play her music; and how she might with her ingenuousness and chatter heal whatever it was that was soured and thwarted in him. He had even pictured her sitting at his kitchen table drawing as she used to do, and thought how he would put her pictures up on his fridge and on his kitchen walls, which were too austere. (He used to refuse to put them up, scornful of the smug sentimentality of estranged fathers parading their parenthood. He had kept them all instead in a folder in his desk.)

Only, Pearl wasn't a child any more. She was something else.

Of course, he remembered now, she had given up drawing years ago.

Usually she only came for a weekend, and usually

Martha was around to take her off his hands and make sure she was fed and watered and to talk to her about whatever it was girls talked about (Martha was not a girl but had at least been one, and fairly recently too). Now, Martha had gone home to the States for a month, and he and Pearl were painfully exposed to one another. The first morning, he was already convinced that he should never have let her come. When he got up at eight he put croissants in the oven and made coffee and squeezed fresh orange juice (he had shopped at the supermarket in honour of her arrival). He called her several times before he realised that in spite of bleary assurances from behind her bedroom door she wasn't going to join him. Then he sat absurdly amidst the unaccustomed splendour of his breakfast (he usually only drank black coffee), and ate both croissants.

Pearl didn't get out of bed until well after midday. This should have given Simon a perfect opportunity to get on with his work. However, her mere presence in the flat was somehow catastrophically disruptive (also, the croissants gave him indigestion and made him sleepy). He kept imagining he heard her stirring or calling for him. Somehow the idea of her with her pink hair and her nose stud and all her rucksack full of female apparatus spilling out into his space prevented him from concentrating (she had explained one surgical-looking item in all seriousness to him as 'eyelash curlers'). He gave up trying to push ahead with the chapter of his book and turned instead to reading through a PhD thesis for which he was the external examiner. That was much easier. Pearl could have been one of his students. It was easier to think about her in relation to them. He liked it when the students had pink hair and piercings; he admired their irreverence for what was natural. He didn't know why he found it disconcerting in his own daughter.

When Pearl did eventually get up, to Simon's dismay she turned the television on. He had a digital set – widescreen, with the sound wired up to come through his B & W speakers – but he didn't watch it often, and certainly never, ever, in the daytime. (Martha watched things on it that astonished him; he found her unapologetic assertion of a taste for *Ally McBeal* and *Sex and the City* provocative and intriguing, but it also made him glad she had kept her own place.) Pearl didn't have the television on particularly loud, but she didn't shut the door, and the sound inserted itself like a trip-wire between him and the furtive argument of this thesis which was escaping from him through a dense under-brush of language. (It wasn't very good: on Dickens and carnival, a stale theme. These enthusiasts for charivari were the same people, no doubt, who complained about joyriders and lager louts.) He found himself trying to determine from the patterns of speech and laughter what it was that Pearl was watching. It must be a chat show. You could recognise the rhythms of inanity without even hearing the words.

He went to ask her to turn the sound down and keep the door shut. She was still in her baggy stretch night-shirt, eating toast smothered in chocolate spread on his white-covered sofa. For a ghostly moment he heard his mother's words in the room. 'Don't make any marks, will you?' At least he didn't actually speak them.

—Grotesque, isn't it? he said instead, after stopping to watch for a moment. —'Forgive us for running our item on propagating bonsai in the home, which we know is overshadowed by September's tragic events, but after all life must go on.' I'll bet 'overshadowed' is doing overtime, isn't it? And 'spirit'? And 'inextinguishable'?

Pearl looked at him, pausing with her toast held ready for a bite. —But what happened was terrible. How else could they talk about it?

—It doesn't occur to you that if they meant it, if they really meant it, they could just cut the item? Cut the whole show. Turn their backs on the cameras and cover their faces with their hands. We could just contemplate darkness, for a few months. It might do us good.

She looked bemused, and then she shrugged. —But I suppose people expect there to be television. I mean, they might panic, if they turned it on and it wasn't there.

He contemplated continuing the argument with her, but decided that the abysses of her blankness might be too deep, he was not ready quite yet to navigate them with her, he was too afraid of what he might not find.

—No doubt, he said. —No doubt there would be panic.

And he went back to the thesis and worked on it for another twenty minutes, until he began to wonder guiltily whether she might need instructions on how to work the shower, or hot drinks. Or perhaps she had come to him because she wanted to confess to him, to consult him. Of course if that were the case she should really have got up to have breakfast with him, they might have talked then, she could not expect him to interrupt his work. On the other hand, he was only marking a student thesis. He had put aside his book, his 'real' work. He had made his preparations for the week's teaching. It could not matter if he broke with his routine for just one day. (Martha accused him of living like a monk, with his rigid routines. 'In some respects,' she said. 'Although a very licentious monk.')

He got up to suggest that they went out to tea. Wasn't that what fathers did? He would buy Pearl tea, he would take her somewhere done up to look old-fashioned, she would think Oxford was a charming place, he would ply her with cake, she would consume it with youth's insatiable appetite for sweet things, she would artlessly open up to him her life, her reasons for disenchantment with her education, her complaints against her mother. However, when he opened the door to his study he heard that she was talking: not to herself – as he imagined for one disorienting moment ('she's mad, she's actually talking to the television') – but on her mobile phone. Although she was loud with that particular autistic loudness of the mobile-phone user, he could not catch exactly what she was saying. The rhythms of her talk were stagey and exaggerated; she sounded like the television she had been watching. He took a few steps along the passage, treading softly on the thick carpet. He had a need to know how his daughter's mind worked when she was unguarded and apart from him. He could hear her when he stood close up to the closed door.

—My dad's bought all this amazing stuff at the super-market because he knew I was coming? she was saying in an excited, swollen voice that rose up as if into a question at the end of almost every sentence. —Like orange squash and chocolate spread and Dairylea cheese? They're all the things I used to like when I was eight, it's really funny! He's so weird.

He hardly recognised himself, transformed into that funny 'Dad'.

—I haven't got any clothes, she wouldn't give me any time to pack, I've only got a really weird selection of things and none of them go together so I won't be able to go out of the door at all. She was really rabid, she just kind of stood over me while I packed up, I was scared, I was just thinking, oh my God, put anything in, I just wanna get out of here. So I've brought, like, no socks and two bottles of black nail polish?

Was she flirting? Was she talking to a girlfriend, or a boy? She seemed to be making such efforts to please, to go through the hyperactive motions of this elaborated code, its language evacuated of apparent meaning. He could make no connection between this material of her life and what he remembered of himself when he was her age. Where had she learned to be so false? Dis-approval overwhelmed him, like something rising in his throat; he withdrew soundlessly, he went back to try and concentrate on the thesis in his study. She had left chocolate marks on his white sofa. He found himself scrubbing at them later with 1001 upholstery cleaner (the same stuff his mother used to use), when Pearl went out. He didn't know where she had gone. She hadn't called out any message before she banged the front door of the flat shut behind her.

When Simon thought back now to his first book (the one on prisons and fictions that had been adapted from his PhD thesis), and to those obsessive writings and rewritings of it that had detained him, he saw now, for far too long in proportion to their results, he understood that he had been trying to disguise himself progressively further and further inside a language working as a self-enclosed system, purged of the treachery of personality. He knew now that such a language wasn't possible: literary criticism wasn't physics. (He also thought that the book was too dependent on Foucauldian modellings of culture and power, of which he had since become more sceptical.) His new book on the representations of music in prose fiction, which he had been working on already for three years, was going to be so much riper and warmer, was going to make the books that preceded it (the prisons book, the one on Dickens's irony, the little one on the history of *Madame Bovary* in English) look like cautious apprenticeship pieces. He thought of it as a reclamation in a renewed language of some of the humanists' old ground; a demonstration of a recovered trust, finally, in the best of the culture he was heir to. He had felt able, as he experimented with first drafts of sections on

Tolstoy's 'The Kreuzer Sonata' and Joyce's 'The Dead', to use the words of value judgement he had once trained himself scrupulously to resist: he wrote about 'greatness', and 'mastery', and even used (carefully, and with explication) the term 'classic'.

It wasn't perfectly clear to him, given his deep confidence in it, why the writing of the book had stalled, just recently, in the few weeks since he and Martha came back from their visit with friends in Uppsala. It didn't even seem to be an intellectual problem, more of a physical one. When he sat for the prescribed hours at his desk it wasn't that the complexity of his argument defeated him, or that he was trying to do too much (as Martha somewhat bruisingly suggested); what he felt was a lassitude, a paralysing indifference to adding one word more to what was already on his screen. He felt as if the book was written already, somehow, the effort was expended, he was on the other side of it, and he didn't have it in him to toil back up to the top of the mountain of his argument. He found himself playing for ages with a couple of sentences, or scrolling up and down through what he'd finished, fiddling with the syntax, pouncing on awkward repetitions. In order to forge forwards, he knew that something in the mind must tense itself, reject peripheral stimuli, lunge into new words, persist in pursuit of the idea and not let go. And suddenly he felt bored with that virtuous conquest which was his life's story.

Pearl's arrival was the last straw; or she was his convenient pretext. The mess she left around the flat stunned him. He was incredulous at how much time she spent in empty chatter with her friends at home on her mobile phone. He found himself actually counting on his watch the hours she spent watching television. An outraged awareness of the dissipation, the indiscipline, the pointlessness of her life would float like a fog between his eyes and the screen he was supposed to be focused upon. She spent money like water – his money – then asked him for more in a tone that presupposed her right, and the bottomlessness of his responsibility to provide. Although he asked her not to smoke in the flat, he knew she sometimes did, he smelled it and found the fag ends carelessly half-buried in the wastebin. She went out 'shopping' every day (she claimed she was looking for a job, too); even Martha, who was quite capable of using that horrible verb 'to shop' without irony, didn't indulge in it very often. If he didn't quarrel with Pearl, not yet, not in their first week, it was because he saw any domestic bickering as the ultimate extension of the banality he couldn't bear.

He did once mildly reproach her for cutting food on the kitchen surfaces without a board, leaving knife marks.

—Oh God! You're just like Mum, always getting at me! she'd snapped; with such flagrant injustice (it really was the very first complaint he'd made) that he'd been deflected from persisting by her sheer illogic.

He became curious as to how Zoe had managed things at home; he wondered what Pearl's perceptions of her mother were. Zoe's restless conscientiousness made her perpetually strained; he could imagine how that was hard on a child. And when Pearl was small Zoe had surely been too passionately and unremittingly attached to her, too anxiously guilty about managing employment and motherhood together. Pearl hadn't responded well to that anxiety. He wondered if his daughter wasn't temperamentally more like himself. In truth, he had probably felt flattered, even vindicated, when Pearl called him and asked to take refuge with him. It was difficult to resist attributing some of what he deplored in Pearl's attitude to flaws in her mother's system of child-raising.

Zoe phoned Pearl at Simon's almost every day; Pearl was blithely offhand in response.

—No, I'm all right, she said. —No, don't come up, there's no need. No, it's OK, I'm chilling out, it's cool.

When he talked to Zoe himself she was very brisk. —I'm busy, she told him. —I've got a couple of articles to write, I'm teaching two new courses, and there's a lecture in the States to prepare for, as well as the book. As you can imagine, this all feels rather urgent at the moment, in the context of what's happening. So long as she's OK with you. I'm amazed how much I can get done with the house to myself. She's missing her classes at college, but to be perfectly honest, with the levels of attendance she was managing last year, I don't know why she was bothering with it at all.

Above all, Simon wanted to resist falling into Zoe's pattern of conflict with Pearl, a cycle of repudiation and reconciliation that she couldn't break. He never wanted to hear his own voice rising in Zoe's futility of indignant allegation: 'she did this, she said that, I told her, once and for all, I really thought we were getting somewhere this time, but then last night she . . .'. He tried to focus his mind instead on the phenomenon of Pearl's generation, so technologically well equipped, so well fed, so beset with innumerable trivial stimuli: the music that poured in at their ears, the flashing dancing pictures in front of their eyes, their swollen pay packets, the incitements to purchase and consume on every side, the exposed flesh promiscuously, blandly available everywhere (he couldn't bear to look at the expanse of tender pale belly that Pearl bared bravely, even going to town, even in the middle of the afternoon).

He speculated as to what drugs she took when she was with her friends. He probed to see what in the world she knew about. She didn't know the dates of the World Wars. She didn't have any second language. She didn't know who Stravinsky was or Metternich or Frantz Fanon; although she had vague ideas about Lenin and Germaine Greer ('isn't she some kind of feminist?'). She thought that the Black Sea was 'somewhere in Africa' and she had never heard of the World Bank. Except when she was engaged in dialogue with her friends she spoke moderately clear English, although it was tainted with the cultish slang of the American teens. She didn't seem to have read anything. Astonishingly, when he asked her for her favourite book, she said it was *To Kill a Mockingbird*. How had that dinosaur of stuffy hopeful decency somehow endured into the age of techno and

Ecstasy? Presumably it was something she had had to read at school.

As long as Simon didn't criticise and was compliant, Pearl played at being sweet with him. She made weak dripping mugs of tea and brought them in to where he was working (he didn't really drink tea: Zoe's house would be a tea-drinking house, it went with the vegetarianism and the good causes). Because he couldn't write what he ought to be writing, he was busying himself instead with reading and making notes he knew he didn't need; to Pearl it must look as if all was as usual with the scholar in his study.

—You ought to get out more, Simon, she said. —Apart from work and driving to the supermarket, you've been locked up in here with your books all week.

—I've been swimming, he replied defensively. (He went every day, and every day did twenty lengths.) She was right, the air amongst his heaps of papers was stale.

—Just because Martha isn't around, it doesn't mean you have to shut yourself away.

—She says I'm a monk. Do you think I'm a monk?

She caught her bottom lip in her teeth, considering.
—You are going just a teeny bit bald, on top here.

He anxiously felt. —No, no I'm not.

Then he had to go and inspect in the bathroom mirror; she held his shaving mirror up behind for him.

—It's only a very, very small patch, she reassured.

—Good God, you'd need a magnifying glass.

He didn't like it though, even the small patch. He wondered what Pearl saw when she looked at him.

Perhaps he seemed ancient to her. He hadn't seriously thought much about what it meant that he was growing older. Without children to hand he had not had any markers against which to test how he appeared, and whether he was showing the beginnings of absurdity.

He took her out to dinner at Le Petit Blanc. She spent hours dressing up for it in some of the new clothes she'd bought for herself with his money. She looked vivid and extravagant in a green top sewn with sequins cut low across her pushed-up breasts and some sort of short jacket with a fur trim. There were green combs in her pink hair. Her face was wide and slightly pasty (he could see a spot she had tried to cover up with make-up); her pouting mouth with its swollen lower lip was glossy with dark paint; her eyes, drawn all around with kohl, were the real beauty of her face, commanding and deep-lidded. Girls her age did themselves up like this to attract attention and then froze rigid in the glare of it. He wondered what her contemporaries thought of her, whether the boys found her attractive, or too overpowering. He knew there had been boyfriends, none of them 'serious'. He thought she might be the kind of girl who has to wait until she's older to generate passion in men.

If he was spotted by anyone he knew, would they guess Pearl was his daughter? They might decide disapprovingly that he was taking out one of his students. She grew talkative after several glasses of wine, although he still detected something guarded in her, a certain bright falsity of manner like a defence, clichés of expression behind which she eluded him. She never for one moment lost awareness of the crowd of others in the restaurant. When she smoked a cigarette she did it with studied nonchalance as if she'd been practising. She told him that she was thinking of finding a job and taking a year off before starting her A levels again.

—I need a break, she said.

(He didn't ask, a break from what exactly? What have you actually ever done?)

—I'd like to travel.

—Travel's OK, he said. —But education's better. If I were you, I wouldn't want to be foolish. Knowledge is power, you know. I would want to find out what was going on. I would want to learn to understand it.

She looked down into her dessert, poking it with her spoon, blushing. —I'm not so bad as you think. I did know where the Black Sea was, really. I just forgot. And I read a lot, honestly. I just said *To Kill a Mockingbird* because I thought it was something you'd approve of.

On their way home she slipped her arm into his and clung to him (perhaps it was the drink, perhaps he was walking too fast for her heels). She asked him to lend her one of his books.

—With all of those you've got, she said, —there must be something I would like.

He thought about it, and when they were home he pulled down for her his copy of Turgenev's *First Love*.

After a couple of weeks Pearl got a job working at a Virgin Megastore. She was taught to work the tills and the machine for the debit cards, then she stood behind a counter and took money for goods, over and over, all day long. She said it was boring but OK. A boy began to ring her at home, sometimes on the landline which Simon answered, hearing his own voice frigid with hostility.

—I'll just call her. Who did you say it was?

—Tell her it's Lozzy.

The voice was educated, slurred and complacent. In Oxford it was perfectly possible for people with those voices to work on the tills in chain stores. Simon couldn't bring himself to repeat this absurd name to Pearl; he only informed her that she was wanted on the phone. He was swelling in fact with a violent and no doubt irrational mistrust of anyone who came after his daughter; he couldn't believe that they could want her for herself, that she wasn't being duped.

Pearl went out in the evenings, perhaps to meet Lozzy, or perhaps other friends she had made at work. Simon told her to take care; he said he would be happy to come in the car to pick her up later, if she gave him a ring; he asked her what time she would be back. She threw him a fierce look as abrupt as a snap at his hand.

—Simon! Get off my back!

No one had spoken to him, ever, with such contempt. He lay awake, listening for her to come home. Sometimes he didn't hear her key in the door until two or three in the morning. One night he heard her and Lozzy come in together (presumably it was Lozzy? was it worse if it was someone else?), although they must have been tiptoeing scrupulously, taking much more elaborate care than she usually took, to be quiet and not wake him. What made him know they were there was not even really distinct sound at all, it was more like the liquid overflow of something warm and sweet; at one point a low bubble of laughter erupted in Pearl's voice, as if they were stumbling into one another in the dark in the passage, clinging to one another, stifling their mirth in one another's clothes. Thank God the spare room was at the other end of the flat, the carpets were thick, and the old doors were heavy: there was no chance that he would hear them once they were in there. He strained his ears to make sure he was not hearing them, nonetheless.

That was it.

That was enough. She would have to go, if he was reduced to the grotesquerie of listening out for creaking bedsprings, like some greasy landlady in a northern realist novel. In the morning he lurked in his room, monitoring the progress of their furtive bathroom visits and breakfasting, then bursting out at a moment calculated in order to confront Lozzy face to face before they left for their day behind the counter. They both started guiltily where they were drinking tea in the kitchen, looking wan and used up (too much bed and not enough sleep; hadn't that been the idiotic joke when he was a teenager?). He could see the beginnings of a sore beside Pearl's lip. Lozzy was worse even than Simon had imagined: he had one of those white cocky faces, with a turned-up nose, thin lips rather full with blood, and rings in his eyebrows. His hair was cropped to a tight fuzz over his skull, dyed yellow.

—Hi there. Lozzy got in first before Simon said anything.

—Lozzy missed his last bus home, lied Pearl lamely.

—I said you wouldn't mind if he slept on my floor.

He did mind. But as there were no words in which he could imagine conveying this without indignity, he silently tested the kettle (empty), filled it splashily at the tap, felt an awareness in his shoulder blades that behind his back they were exchanging conspiratorially amused looks.

Simon's own sleep patterns started to disintegrate. He had thought he had left his childhood insomnia behind him (gentle-handed Ros, whom he had been involved with for a while a few years ago, had been a hypnotherapist and had done wonders with him, for all his scepticism). Now it returned to sap his days and nights of goodness and reason. Because of the agonised absurdity of his lying awake at night waiting for Pearl, he once or twice even went out walking round the streets in the small hours as he had done when he was young. Then during the day, because he wasn't young any more, he found his mind was clogged with tiredness; he even laid his head down sometimes on his arms and slept in front of the humming screen of his computer. He was astonished at how far, far down the soul could drop out of such a makeshift and snatched repose; hauling it up to consciousness again, when guilt roused him after fifteen or twenty minutes, felt like pulling his resisting heart out of a deep well. His dreams in the instant he tore free seemed voluminous, significant, absorbing; he ached to drop back into them.

How was he supposed to act with Pearl? The first time they crossed paths after his encounter with Lozzy, she looked at him as if she expected him to say something, but he didn't know how to. Had he presided ingloriously over his daughter's deflowering? Surely not: he had a distinct memory of Zoe's telling him, although he hadn't in the least wanted to hear it, that she and Pearl had talked about which contraception Pearl was using. No doubt Zoe had also told him which this was, although he had chosen not to remember that (and certainly wasn't going to ask her about it now). When he put a wash in the machine, he found blood-stained knickers in the wash-basket, but then there were more straightforward explanations for that than the loss of anyone's virginity (and he wasn't going to ask Pearl about her periods, either, although he did notice that over a few days the contents of the box of Tampax Martha kept in his bathroom was depleted). He prowled around in the spare room when Pearl was out and he was meant to be working. He picked up a book with a flowery cloth cover that might have been a diary; he weighed it in his hands and held it for some long minutes but didn't open it, he was afraid of what he might read in there about himself, or about a whole kind of living he did not recognise and could not understand. He went away into the kitchen and made himself coffee and took up his collection of Adorno's essays on music, forcing himself to concentrate on these and not to wonder what Pearl might have written. He was grateful for the teaching and for the ordinary admini-strative busyness that got him out of the flat and into his office in college. He looked forward to Martha's return; this surely would fill up his days and steady him. There was something unseemly in his allowing his private angst to take up so much space in his thoughts at a time when the whole world was upside down.

—What did you make of the Turgenev? he asked Pearl tentatively.

—Yeah, I really liked it, it was so *sad*, she said. —I guessed what was going to happen though, right from the first time his father saw the princess in the garden.

—Interesting that of all the Russians it is the westernising believer in enlightenment and progress who writes the saddest stories.

—Are they Russian? I thought that they were French. Didn't they keep saying things in French?

He explained to her about the function of French-speaking in nineteenth-century aristocratic Russia. He also pointed out that the story was set in the country outside Moscow. Did she think that Moscow was in France?

—Oh, I never read the place names. My eye just sort of glances over them.

—I recommend you train yourself to glance back.

—The only bit I didn't like was the end, I didn't understand why she let herself be beaten. She kissed her arm where he hit her with his whip. That's gross.

Simon considered. —Perhaps your generation of women really won't ever know about that kind of power that Zinaida has at the beginning; on licence, for just as long as she's young and beautiful and hasn't given herself to anyone. The trouble is, it only makes fools out of the men; she can't wait to exchange it for submission to a man worthy of mastering her. I suppose that arrangement sounds fairly horrible to you?

—It doesn't make her very happy.

—It doesn't make him very happy either. I'm not sure that happiness is quite the point.

—Why can't they just be equals?

—Nowadays it would be possible to hope they could, of course. And you are quite right to wish for it. Everyone would be happier. Who would dare to put a name to what might be lost, now that we are inventing new patterns for men's and women's behaviour? Only one wonders sometimes whether women will really want these bland new men that they have engineered.

—I shouldn't worry about it, Pearl said. —There's probably a way to go yet, anyway, before we get to bland.

Another day when he was in her room he found English and history essays she must have done for her teachers at the sixth-form college, stuffed crumpled in the bottom of her rucksack. (Left there out of profound indifference to such a form of work, as if it was mere waste paper; or brought in case she dared to show them to him?) These he read greedily on the spot, frowning at the spelling, reliving the arguments he had had with Zoe when he had offered to pay for Pearl to go to private school. ('How can you?' Zoe had said. 'When I think of what you used to profess to believe, once.' He wondered sometimes how he had ever tolerated Zoe's righteousness, unambiguous as a ringing bell, even for the few years they had lived together.) If Pearl had gone to private school then she would have done better than this raw and unpolished work. There were gleams here and there, however, of something audacious and intelligent, unspoiled. Perhaps if she had gone to private school she would have been more knowing, and less true. He was surprised by her penetration of some godawful sentimental-feminist poem she'd been given to analyse; shaken, even, as if he'd stumbled on something she'd concealed from him.

Martha came back. Her summer of research work in the archives had gone well (this was for her book on women and politics in eighteenth-century America). She was surprised to find Pearl still around. Simon had told her on the phone that she was staying, but not for how long. Martha was less warm with her than she had been when Pearl had visited once or twice before for the weekend. She moved some clothes and bits and pieces out of his flat back into her own. When they made love it was at her place, and then Simon didn't want to sleep the night there, he said he didn't like to leave Pearl on her own.

Martha sat up in bed with the sheet over her breasts and smoothed her hair back behind her ears. Her hair was thick and very dark, as near as brown can come to black, with rich red lights in it. She wore it long, curling loose halfway down her back. She gave him a glance deep with accumulated questions; her eyes were brown too, almond-shaped and slanting (she had a Portuguese grandmother).

—It strikes me, she said, —that Pearl is perfectly capable of looking after herself.

Simon sat up too, so as not to be at a disadvantage. —I think I ought to be there.

She waited as if for more explanation, but none came. —What on earth does she do all day? What ever is she up to?

—She's working almost full-time, Simon protested.

—Yes, but what kind of work? I mean, what are her plans? Aren't you worried for her future?

He too had felt at first that Pearl's life, without books, music, study, goals, had nothing in it; and that vacancy had produced in him an anxious desire to fill it up. Now, when Martha complained, he found himself thinking differently. He had come to look on Pearl's idleness almost with envy. It would be possible to see his own zeal for improvement as a part of a whole history of cultural bullying, rooted in puritanical self-punishing; to see Pearl's resistance to it (her hours of telly-watching, her days of sleep, the indifference with which she sold herself to the chain store for those long pointless sessions) as an irrecoverable freedom.

—I don't think she has plans, he said.

Martha gave an impatient shrug of her naked shoulders. Her long tapering back with its hanging luxuriance of hair was poised and upright; she went to dance class twice a week. She was certainly not going to plead with him to stay at her place.

At home alone one night, he fell asleep waiting for Pearl

to come in. He dreamed fitfully. One horrible dream was of a miniature flamingo, tiny and pink as a finger, sprawled and damp, unconscious. He was cutting off its little wings, pressing with his fingernail as if with a knife feeling for a chicken joint. He had forgotten that the creature might not be dead: it lifted its head and its neck writhed, so he dropped it and stepped down hard on it with his shoe, to put it out of its misery, or out of its knowledge of what he was doing. He woke up covered in disgust.

He didn't know whether Pearl had come in while he slept or not; he got up and wrapped himself in his bathrobe to check. Her bedroom door was closed, but he couldn't remember whether it had been ajar before. He stood hesitating, not liking to open the door just in case she was in there with Lozzy. He heard a subdued moaning. He thought for a moment this could be sex, and gathered himself for retreat; then he was sure that Pearl was crying. He knocked and opened the door. In the light from the hallway he saw she was alone, and awake, pushed up on her elbows to see him; she reached over to switch on the bedside lamp. The room flooded in pink light (she had put a red bulb in). She was wearing her usual grubby nightshirt (surely it was time that went into the wash?). Her face was blotched and wet with tears; there was make-up smeared on her pillow.

She was not beautiful. Martha was beautiful: five foot ten, slender and muscular, her cheekbones and jawbone sharp as if carved from flint. Pearl was too indefinite, her face seemed to change shape and character according to her mood and efforts, and her figure when she was older would grow soft and shapeless like Zoe's mother's. Her looks touched him, though, as if they were part of himself.

—What is it? he whispered awkwardly. He had not had to comfort her since she was a small child; he did not know how to do it. —Should I go away?

She shook her head in her hands, sobbing. —It's nothing.

He sat down on the side of the bed, tried to pat her hair. —Well, evidently it's not nothing.

—Lozzy took me out in his car after work.

The words were broken up by the weeping erupting painfully from inside.

His heart clenched, his blood pulsed thickly. She was going to tell him the story he dreaded, that lurked in the under-levels of his imagination: of a violation, an abuse of her tender youth, some obscene thing done to her that she hadn't wanted.

—Well, it's not actually his car, it's his brother's. But he knew we were borrowing it, he was cool. And it was great to get out, you know, from the city? Lozzy's good like that, he really appreciates nature, he knows these fantastic places to go, woodland walks and country pubs and things.

So not a violation. An accident? An arrest? They'd been done for possession of drugs? He was all ready to mobilise his authority, as a middle-class parent, as a member of the university. He would be cleverer than the police, he would rescue her (and even Lozzy if need be).

—Then we saw this dead fox beside the road.

—And?

She renewed her sobbing. —You see, I knew you were going to say that. That's all. It was just this little fox. It was only a baby. You couldn't even see where it was damaged. It was just laid at the side of the road with its snout on its paws and a little frown wrinkling up its nose. It only looked as if it was asleep. Lozzy did get out to see if it was dead, though, and it was, it was cold, although it was still perfect. So we had to leave it there. And now I can't stop thinking about it.

Simon sat utterly perplexed. What reassurance was he supposed to produce, in response to this crisis? If she'd asked him about the gas chambers, or the massacres in Rwanda, or 9/11, he might have had some form of words ready.

He noted, at least, that Lozzy had not been able to console her.

—There are so many of them, he said, in what he hoped was a voice replete with adult confidence in ultimate meanings. —There will be plenty more baby foxes.

—But not that one. I just can't stop thinking: it was alive this morning! And now it's not. And what about its mother? She must be wondering where it is.

—Coincidentally, Simon said, remembering suddenly, —I had a dream just then, just before I got up to see if you were home, that was about hurting an animal.

She grew more quiet. —Did you? What kind of animal?

—A bizarre little dream creature. Like a tiny bird. I

was crushing it. When I woke up I felt disgusted with myself.

She put her hand on his, and squeezed it, and leaned her head against his chest so that he couldn't see her face. He put his arm round her.

In a different voice, muffled and reluctant, so that he knew that what was coming now was the true core of her confession, she said, —What I can't bear, Daddy, is what's going to happen to the fox now. That it's going to turn to rot.

—Someone will take it away. Crows will eat it. They'll pick it clean.

—They don't always. We saw others. Sometimes they just turn into a bag of brown rot.

Words of explanation ran in his head but they were nothing, he couldn't speak them. —It'll be all right, he could only say to her. —Everything will be all right.

—Don't be stupid, Pearl said crossly. —No it won't.

Ending

They have telephoned from the retirement home. Uncle Dick has died, aged ninety-six.

Joyce spoke to him only a few hours ago. He 'went peacefully, in his sleep', they tell her; although the last few weeks have been far from peaceful. Dick has tried to escape from the home several times; he has grappled with the cook in the kitchen, accusing her of hiding his tin of Epsom Salts, and rattling through her cupboards for it with his stick; one of his visitors found him sitting in his bed in soiled pyjamas; he has been phoning Joyce at three, four, five, in the morning, to beg and plead with her to help get him out from where he is being held prisoner. He seemed to think this was somewhere in South Africa, and that he could see the tall masts of the ships in the harbour from his window. If only he could get on board one of those ships, he confided urgently, then he could sail home to his wife and children. Joyce has taken to unplugging the phone before she goes to bed. She and Ann have been dreading that the niceish retirement home (at least there is someone playing the piano sometimes; at least the garden is lovely and the doors unlocked) will say they cannot look after him any longer, that he needs to move on to one of the other kinds of place, with nursing care. Ann, who is brave about this kind of thing, has looked into those other places.

—You don't want to know that they exist, she says. —Little wizened no-sex creatures batting backwards and forwards in their chairs screaming for Mummy. One crawling on the floor around my feet.

And now instead, thank goodness, release. (Though there's still Vera.)

Joyce phones Peter. This will mean extra sessions with his therapist. There have been reconciliations of sorts, Peter has visited his father once or twice a year for the last few years, he will have his share of the inheritance. Joyce and Ann get their share too: Dick has said often (he was prone to waxing sentimental in his declining years) that they have been better than daughters to him. ('Bloody right we have,' says Ann.) Even Martin gets something.

Joyce drives round to tell Vera the news. Vera has settled years ago for an air of triumphant righteousness at having outlived Dick's second and third wives (breast cancer and a car accident). She and Dick have often met at Joyce's, on Sundays and on all the festivals, where they have been as irritable and familiar with one another as any old married couple.

—I'd spoken to him only a few hours before they

rang me, Joyce says. —I'd arranged for him to come for lunch on Sunday.

She doesn't tell Vera that Dick had said he should be able to come, as long as he could clock off in time, and that he would be in plain clothes. This is not so much in order to spare Vera from the details of her once-husband's deterioration, but because Vera suffers herself from lapses of consequence, and if they set one another off a discussion can spiral quickly into dizzy realms of unmeaning. (At Christmas Joyce's grandchildren were both uncomfortable and giggly when Uncle Dick kept exclaiming 'Ah so!' as if he was imitating a Japanese soldier, and Vera loudly protested against his using the word 'arsehole'.)

Vera doesn't seem terribly affected by the news.

She is wearing a new pale pink cashmere cardigan Peter has sent her. Joyce did not think the colour was a good idea, because of spills (no doubt she will end up handwashing it); but it does look pretty with Vera's dark skin and iron-grey hair (Joyce and Ann are whiter now than Vera is). In extreme old age a new kind of pretti-ness is possible, nothing like the youthful one which Joyce still clings to, yearns after: it has to do with the beauty you can find in old twisted wood and patiently eroded stone.

—What about the gales? Vera says. —Did you hear them?

The gales are real. Joyce lay awake last night, unwill-ingly absorbed in listening to them while Ray snored beside her. She doesn't mind thunderstorms, and she loves to fall asleep to the sound of rain, but she hates the buffeting of strong wind, it agitates her strangely, makes her body ache, makes her want to cry. Also, she was worrying about the garden wall at the back, which was tottery and needed repointing. If the wind blew it down, they would be able to have it repaired on the insurance. On the other hand, if it fell down while someone was passing in the lane that ran behind, and anyone was hurt, it would be their fault; she would never be able to forgive herself. So she lay tensely, listening for footsteps in the lane. When she tried to wake Ray up to go down and see if the wall was in danger, see if he could push it over anyway (it would be better if it was just *down*, then she could sleep) he snapped at her crossly that she was being unreasonable.

—Some big branches have come down off the trees on the Heath, Vera says. —They've taped a lot of areas off from the public, for safety. You know that crooked Monterey pine that grows over the path, so that they've built that wooden support under it? Well, the tree's fine, but the support's down, it's broken in several pieces. Isn't that an irony? The tree stands, but the support is broken.

—How d'you know all this? Joyce asks suspiciously. Vera hasn't been up to the Heath for months. (Joyce really ought to take her, to see the daffodils.)

—One of the girls told me. Pammy, Polly, one of those. She cycles into work that way.

—Penny. The one with the short dark hair.

—Whichever. I don't know, I can't keep track, they come and go so often.

(Actually, Penny has been working there for at least eighteen months.)

—Ann and I will have to arrange the funeral. I suppose we'll have some sort of do afterwards, at our place. Peter can stay with us. I wonder if he'll want to bring any of the children?

—Typical of Dick to go like that, Vera chuckles.

—Like what? (Peacefully in his sleep: typical to have it easy at the end?)

—With all that banging about, says Vera. —All that wind and bother. Making such a to-do. Slamming on the windows, battering at the doors, howling away.

Joyce chooses to interpret this as a metaphorical association of ideas.

—Yes, isn't it typical? she laughs. —Never one to manage things quietly.

Probably, though, Aunt Vera has really got them muddled up, her husband's passing and last night's disturbance; as if what happens inside human lives is leaking out in her imagination into the texture of impersonal real things.

The funeral goes off all right if you approve of that sort of carry-on.

Ray doesn't.

Partly, he's thinking that it won't be long before it's him up there in the box while everyone snuffles over him (he is seventy-three: Frisch, the only friend whose work he was genuinely jealous of, died recently). Life is so familiar. You get so used to it, you can't easily be reconciled with the idea that it won't muddle on for ever.

Also, he didn't like Uncle Dick, and never understood why it was that such a significant proportion of his and Joyce's time was taken up with worrying over and tending to an old man who had after all acted all his life with abominable selfishness. Dick had never, in all the years since he sent Ray an extraordinary letter of so-called 'advice' when he and Joyce first got together, been able to resist an opportunity for telling him how he could manage everything in his life better. (That is, more like the way Dick managed it.) He once even tried to suggest to him, with what he probably imagined to be tactful persuasion, that he should take up painting water-colours of naval battles.

Also, on all these occasions (weddings included: weddings especially) Ray can't help a sense of outrage at finding himself under the roof of practising Christians, not only mingling in their company (he's a tolerant man) but actually participating, however passively, in their rituals. He thinks of religion as a left-over from the Middle Ages; when he was young he fully expected to see an end to all their mumbo-jumbo in his lifetime, and the churches turned into museums and art galleries. It was absolutely in character that Dick converted conveniently to a kind of turn-the-other-cheek Christianity as the end drew nigh (marginally worse, Ray thought, than the Masons, who at least don't sanctimoniously confess to all their sins on social occasions).

Dick had recently had a bitter falling out with the new vicar over a point of church tradition to do with the hymn for those in peril on the sea. Presumably however the vicar (a bleached and fastidious little man, with cold eyes) says today all the right appeasing things for the girls to have a weep over. Ray can't hear him anyway, he has been afflicted for several days now with a sudden deafness, which the doctor assures him unconvincingly is catarrh blocking his inner ear and will only be temporary. He discovered some sort of deaf-aid – a little amplifier – in Dick's drawer while they were going through his things at the home, and he has been using that, but he doesn't bother to turn it on for the vicar. It only works for a few minutes at a time and then produces shrill feedback, at which point he usually drops it. He doesn't care what the vicar has to say anyway. And Joyce doesn't like him using the amplifier, although she thinks he doesn't know it. She'd rather he were stone deaf than fumbling about with a hearing aid, giving himself away as an old man.

Visually, he admires the element of theatre in the proceedings. Especially the British Legion chap who follows the coffin up the aisle carrying the standard. And then there's his granddaughter Pearl who turns up unexpectedly from Oxford: to the delight of Joyce, of course, who's dotty about her, and in whose eyes she can't do any wrong. Pearl is dressed preposterously in black from head to foot, her hair is dyed black, even her nails are painted black (as far as he knows, she never actually had anything to do with Dick, beyond bestowing on him one or two of her withering glances on occasion, if something he said offended against the implacable received wisdom of the young).

Joyce whispers loudly in his better ear; probably about how marvellous Pearl looks and that he ought to paint her.

He mumbles something noncommital.

There are other young people here too (including two of Peter's sons from his second marriage); all of whom make Ray anxious. He suspects them, to begin with, of hypocrisy. They lean forward to pray when the vicar suggests it, they put their heads in their hands, they close their eyes. What can they know about praying? He doesn't believe in prayer, he doesn't do it, but at least he was brought up to know how to. None of these teenagers have surely ever been in a church, except at weddings and funerals. Are they engaged in a mocking parody of the mores of older folk? Or, more likely, is there such a moral vacancy in them, the product of an era of addiction to quick fixes and instant gratifications, that they will like unconsidering infants join in whatever new game offers itself?

In fact if he looks around him, they're all at it, all his family, all the generations, drooping their heads, closing their eyes: even Martin who only believes in the periodic table and his latest invention, even his niece Sophie's partner Joe, who was surely once in the Socialist Workers' Party. (Daniel isn't here, he is in Italy on business; which takes priority of course.) Some of them have even knelt down on those little stuffed square things: what are they, cassocks? hassocks? Joyce kneels. (He is filled with his customary mix of feelings in relation to her public behaviour; tender solicitude and exasperation at once. Her knees will hurt. What is she playing at?) Ray knows full well that none of them ever pray, from one year to the next, under ordinary circumstances. What words can possibly be going through all their minds at such a moment? Peter's droop is of course displayed more conspicuously than anyone else's; his forehead is pressed against the cuff of his Armani suit as though he struggles with ultimate reckonings.

At least Ray can count on his daughter Zoe. She sits bolt upright like him, with her eyes open. A warmth strikes up in Ray's chest at the thought of the painting he is doing of Zoe; he is filled with a sudden hopefulness and excitement, he forgets where he is. The parts of the painting which have already worked, and the parts which he does not yet know how to resolve, move him to equal enthusiasm. (It is only when he enters the studio and takes up his brushes that the dread of failing, and the burdensome labour involved in bringing the thing rightly to its completion, will begin to gnaw at him again.) He hasn't painted Zoe since she was a child. In the new painting she is sitting tensely forward, frowning as if she is seeking out something. He is using a lot of cobalt blue, unusual for him, not a colour he has felt much in sympathy with before: he is using it boldly, making marks that are deliberately effortful and dry, painted against the resistance of the canvas. He can't easily express it in words, but he knows what he means by this. The blue paints in the trace of an aura of effort and dedication that seems to him to surround Zoe. He has her wrapping one leg around the other, hugging

411

herself tightly with her shoulders hunched. She always looks as if she hasn't slept enough, as if she's feeling the cold.

While she sits for him she has been telling him (before he went deaf) about three of her students who are in Israel at the moment, operating as part of the International Solidarity Movement on the West Bank; riding in ambulances through the checkpoints to shame the soldiers into letting through the sick and women in labour; helping those Palestinians whose trees are out of bounds on the edge of Israeli settlements to harvest their olives; helping to coordinate a link-up one Saturday between Palestinian protesters from Bethlehem and Israeli protesters from Jerusalem. Others work in community conflict resolution in Kosovo and Aids clinics in Uganda. It seems to Ray extraordinary, beyond hoping for, that such people exist; that the British students and the Palestinian and Israeli demonstrators and all the others should be willing to sacrifice safety and comfort and private pleasure in the service of some cause that they believe in. The thought of it, a few days ago, filled his eyes unexpectedly with tears, which he had to wipe away with the dirty sleeve of the old jacket he wears to paint in. What Zoe does, he knows he is not capable of: sitting through meetings, marching, getting up petitions against war with Iraq, shaking collecting boxes in town. She puts up in her spare room all sorts of stray visitors and contacts from that other world of conflict and deprivation, come to campaign or raise money or give talks. The idea of these small sacrifices fills Ray with ennui even as it pricks at his bad conscience.

He helps Joyce to return to a sitting position; she shoots him an annoyed look, determined to manage by herself. Then the palaver is at an end and the undertakers carry the coffin out; the organ bleats and rambles, there is a shuffling of shoes and hymnbooks in the echoing space, a rumble of throat-clearing and subdued relieved voices as the congregation resume their everyday selves. (Not a bad turnout. And, judging by the things people stop to say to Joyce – Ray gets the amplifier out, twiddles with the knobs – a number of them are under the delusion that Dick was a charming old gentleman with a generous heart.) He and Joyce, Peter and Rose, Ann and Cliff, Martin and Ingrid, will all follow the coffin to the crematorium. Zoe will hurry over to the flat where Joyce has put food and drink out for whoever comes back to drown their sorrows. Sophie will go to pick up Vera who wouldn't come to the service (she didn't want to sit there under false pretences, she said: they weren't sure if she meant her relationship to Dick or her irreligion). Joyce always has these occasions so well organised.

Joyce and Ray have been in their new flat for eighteen months. They have the ground floor, the first floor and the garden of an elegant early Victorian terrace high up in Hilltop (the flats above have separate entrances). There are fine views over the sprawling city: the Georgian terraces strung like precious old necklaces round the hills, the tall glass office blocks, the disused city docks with their warehouses converted into art centres and café-bars and riverside apartments. Joyce has had major work to do: she made the kitchen into a studio for Ray and knocked a bedroom and a bathroom together to make a new kitchen on the first floor; then she took out a partition wall at the side of the staircase, restoring the entrance hall to its original proportions; she uncovered the old stone-flagged floor and hung the walls all round with paintings and drawings. Of course she and Ray don't actually do any of this work themselves these days; they have lived in an occasionally taxing intimacy for months with Dean and Alan the builders and Terry the carpenter.

Joyce snatches a moment while they leave their coats on the bed to show Ann the latest improvement: an ensuite third bathroom opening off the master bedroom. Ann (who is doing things to her house too) is almost as interested in all this as Joyce is. They talk about tilers, soil pipes, macerators, and a firm Ann knows of who will renovate old parquet floors. Joyce demonstrates the usefulness of the built-in wardrobes where their clothes hang in ordered spaces and their shoes are set out in pairs.

—Ray thinks it's grotesquely extravagant, she says, —but I want to replace the bedroom windows with new identical ones, because these rattle in the wind and keep me awake, and I can have them done in that new burglar-proof glass we've already got on the ground floor. He says I'm paranoid.

Ann attacks Ray's lack of imagination (she is always in favour of the spending of money). Joyce shows her the loose cover she is making for an armchair, matching the curtains. They would like to linger – there is always more to show and to discuss – but they feel themselves claimed by the murmur of their guests from the next room, their sociability dampened in respect for the occasion. There are some ancient old folk – friends from the church, Dick's sergeant from the Docks police – who must be put in the comfortable chairs, and must not be left without refreshments or without anyone to talk to. The vicar will need buttering up; they wondered why he wanted to come back at all, but it turns out he is an amateur watercolourist and means to bother Ray, which is bound to end badly.

—When are our children going to start looking after us, instead? Ann wails to Joyce. —Aren't we old and frail enough?

Ann these days still has her pretty fine-boned face and wrists and ankles, but in between her body has expanded extravagantly. She is using a stick to walk after a fall a few weeks ago (the pressure on those delicate ankles is too much). They visit the kitchen where Zoe has forgotten to take off the foil and cling film from the plates of food: no wonder no one has started eating. Ann made the cake; Joyce as well as sandwiches has made little patties with lemon and cream-cheese filling.

—I did Mum's proper pastry. The one where you roll it out and dab on bits of fat and then fold and roll twice. Zoe was supposed to put the oven on to warm these up.

—Life's too short for dabbing on bits of fat. I use frozen.

—Vera always notices. She always makes some remark about how you can hardly tell the difference, even when I haven't mentioned it.

Pearl is in the garden with her cousin Leo (Peter's son). They haven't seen one another for at least two years; this seems so long ago that they respond to one another almost like strangers. They were surely children in that past where they last met; now they both believe that they are grown up. He has grown skinny and tall, with dead-straight hair that falls over his eyes, a nervy eagerness that makes her wonder if he's speeding, and a slight lisp. They are not really cousins; they bicker amiably over just what their relationship is (his father is her grandmother's first cousin). They have escaped out here to share a roll-up; Leo has a little polythene packet of skunk in his pocket. (Granny's cool, Pearl explains, but Grampy's funny about that stuff.)

There is some evidence of last week's gales; crocuses and daffodils are flattened in the grass, and buds torn off an old blackened dwarf apple tree are silted up on the mossy path. It is cold, but the sun is shining and the sky is clear, pale blue flooding with pink as the afternoon grows late. Far below them they can see the streams of the city's traffic flow and part and join up again. Buildings are pastel-coloured in the light, like cake icing.

—D'you ever get this weird sensation? Pearl asks him.
—Where you don't believe that anything is real?

There is surprising delicate skill in Leo's big blunt finger-ends, crumbling tobacco, shredding the weed with his nail. He has to shake the hair back from his face before he runs his tongue along the edge of the Rizlas.

—Last night, she goes on, —in my old bedroom at my mum's, I lay there thinking, why was I me, instead of someone else. You know?

With the joint wagging unlit in his mouth he pinches the flesh at the top of her arm between his finger and thumb. —You're real, he says. —You're you. It hurts, doesn't it?

—Ow. But why is now real, and not a few minutes ago before you pinched me? Or before Uncle Dick was dead, say? What makes now the only moment that's real at one time?

—You're a philosopher.

—Sometimes, she says, —I do feel there's a whole world of real things out there, only I can't get through to them. I'm stuck in the pretend ones.

—It's funny to think, he says, —that in ten years' time we'll both be what we're going to be.

—I'll have been travelling, or I won't have been. I'll have gone to university, or I won't have gone.

—I'm shit at exams and stuff. Dyslexic. So I won't have done that.

—My dad's training me up to get into Cambridge like training a boxer for a fight. He follows me round the flat, feeding me bits of knowledge, sparring with me, trying to get me into discussing things. But I'm thinking all the time: I might, or I might not. When I split up with my boyfriend, I was in tears, desperate, all the usual stuff. And the other half of me was just watching, thinking, oh yes, this is what you're supposed to do, you're supposed to go through this.

Leo gets out his Zippo ('My dad's an arse, but he gives good presents'). They smoke and discuss money. Both of them will get a thousand pounds out of what Uncle Dick has left. This is good news for Leo. He has been doing temp work at some place that packages cheap jewellery, spending eight hours a day putting gold chains and earrings on to cards. Now he will be able to give that up and go out to stay with a mate whose brother is doing up a house in France. Pearl doesn't know what she will do with her money. For the moment she will stay on in Oxford. She certainly doesn't want to come back to live with her mother again. They aren't getting on any better.

Pearl is not working full-time at Virgin any longer; Simon has insisted on her studying with him for her A2 exams. He doesn't see much of Martha; he dedicates himself to Pearl in a way that half entrances and half frightens her. He will expect too much. She knew he was writing poems on his computer and once when he was out she looked for them and found them. She had expected poems to be confessions – she had hoped she would discover from reading them what her father really thought about her. But although she stared at them over and over, and although the words he used were easy ones (apart from 'incarnadine', which she couldn't be bothered to look up), they seemed to be written in a code she did not have the information to crack. She had no idea what they were supposed to be about. There were fossils in stones, there were the smoking freezer cabinets in a supermarket, there was a bird painted on a window (or was it meant to have flown into the glass?). Mostly there weren't even pictures. She printed the poems out anyway, and put them away inside her diary in a drawer, where he wouldn't look.

When Pearl and Leo retreat indoors – it's cold, as soon as the sun goes down – Pearl washes up accidentally against her mother.

—Isn't that my blouse you're wearing? Zoe can't help herself pointing out. —I thought I spotted something familiar.

She means to say this in a tone of fond amusement but knows as soon as the words are beyond recall that they make another link in the heavy chain of things misjudged between them.

—Jesus, Mum.

—Oh, we've all done that too, says her cousin Sophie quickly. —I'm wearing Ma's black cardigan because I didn't have one, and Joe had to borrow Dad's black tie. Anyway, I'm afraid that Pearl looks perfectly lovely in your blouse, Zo.

They overhear Aunt Vera from behind them.

—I lost my own little girl you know, she is saying to someone. —My nieces are very good, but it's not the same.

(She hardly talked about Kay for forty years. Recently

she mentions her often; she grows garrulous and confiding, squeezing hands and brimming easily with tears.)

Joyce has had two glasses of sherry. —I am always dreaming, she says, —that I have children in the house again.

—Auntie Joyce, says Sophie, —any time you want a loan of a houseful of children, please call me.

—You'd think you'd dream about little ones but actually my dreams aren't. They're adolescents: that phase when they're impossibly leggy and long and awkward. In the dream I feel so honoured, so lucky to have them there. They are so beautiful.

Later, Vera is holding forth to a circle of listeners on the subject of Uncle Dick. Sitting crooked but queenly in the tall winged chair Joyce keeps for her beside the fire, she is loud with her old schoolteacherly confident authority.

—He couldn't keep his hands to himself, she is saying. —He was all over me whenever he had the chance.

Joyce wonders whether this is indecorous, on the day of the old man's funeral. At least he is being remembered; at least there's only family left at the party. Ray luckily can't hear: he decided to lose the amplifier earlier in order to deter the artistic vicar and now he is listening to Coltrane through a Walkman turned up very high.

—Mother! Peter booms across the room in his big bass voice. —Are you being indiscreet?

—Am I dear?

—I fear it.

—Dick told me things I never knew about. When he was with his ship in Alexandria, the boys went to some club to see a woman dancing with a lighted cigarette in her wee-wee.

—In her *what*, Auntie?

—And there was me at the time still thinking babies came out of your tummy button.

—Did you marry him for love, Vera? Did you love him? Ann asks her.

Vera shrugs her high arthritic shoulders in the baby-pink cardigan. —Six menstruating women sharing one kitchen. Sometimes you couldn't move for all the rags hanging up to dry. I couldn't wait to get out.

—Good God, groans Peter comically. —Someone stop her.

—Why? asks Ann. —Isn't it fascinating?

Joyce stands up to collect the plates and cups; the intimacy of family is as thick as smoke in the air.

Pearl sits cross-legged at Aunt Vera's feet, texting somebody on her mobile.

Outside the long windows it is almost night; a few rosy clouds lit from below stand out in negative against the grey dark of the sky. Because it has come swiftly no one has drawn the curtains or switched on the lamps; they sit in the light from the coal-effect gas fire. For hours the children (Sophie's, and her brother's) have been playing some absorbing game of peril and escape and rescue around the flat, using as props one of Joyce's polished stone eggs and the mirror from Vera's handbag and a couple of plastic 007 guns. Under cover of the dusk they wriggle on their bellies along the skirtings of the sitting room into the bay, where they plan in whispers together behind a chair, thinking they are invisible to the adults.

Zoe is in the garden. She finds herself wanting a cigarette, even though it's almost twenty years since she gave up smoking: it would give her a pretext for escaping out here. A lozenge of yellow light from the kitchen window illuminates an array of Joyce's pots planted with spring bulbs. Joyce has a gift for making things grow: hopeless-looking bits of twig stuck in among the bulbs are swelling with new buds. Zoe sits in the near-dark on a stone bench to one side of the window. A numb cold seeps into her thighs, and into her shoulders resting against the back wall of the tall house: huge blocks of red stone, roughly finished. She hasn't brought her coat outside; she won't be able to stay out here for long. The garden is alive with animal rustlings, birdsong, a distant siren.

The family gathering was overwhelming; she had to get outside and be by herself. It isn't what her mother thinks; it isn't that Zoe disapproves of them. She only worries that it feels too safe inside. She prefers to sit out here for a while, with her back to them all, so that she can keep watch.

Tessa Hadley

ACCIDENTS IN THE HOME

'Fantastically subtle, absorbing and insightful...This is prose to die for'
Guardian

'Excellent...a novel that is as tight as a snare-drum and as bright as the moon'
Financial Times

An improbable coincidence brings Clare back into contact with someone she once had sex with at a teenage party; complicatedly, he is now going out with her best friend, Helly. The encounter needn't have meant anything – it could just have been funny, or embarrassing – but it seems to have the power to shake up everything in Clare's life. Clare is married with three small children, she bakes her own bread and buys her clothes from the charity shop. Helly is an actress and has her golden curves pasted up on billboards ten foot high. And each of them seems to want what the other has.

Clare's story is intertwined with other stories of her extended family. Her father has been married three times and left a trail of children. *Accidents in the Home* dips in and out of the lives of this complicated, close, fraught family, reaching out into the past for explanation and illumination as well as across the present. It is the debut of a quite formidable fictional talent.

VINTAGE